UNDER THE GUN

The two young FBI special agents slowly approached the truck from both sides of the cab, their revolvers drawn and pointed toward the driver.

The students slowly emerged. Hanna climbed off the bed of the pickup, shuddering, and lay facedown on the asphalt with the others.

Joshua ran toward his daughter.

The FBI agents ordered the five students off the ground, to lace their hands behind their heads, and to walk single file into the federal building. Hanna passed by her father, her mouth open, her eyes wide with terror.

"You'll be okay," Joshua said, trying to look and sound assured.

Her eyes twitched for an instant, and then she was gone. . . .

Also by Richard Parrish

Our Choice of Gods
The Dividing Line
Versions of the Truth
Nothing but the Truth
Abandoned Heart
Wind and Lies

Richard Parrish

◇

DEFENDING THE TRUTH

AN ONYX BOOK

ONYX
Published by the Penguin Group
Penguin Putnam Inc., 375 Hudson Street,
New York, New York 10014, U.S.A.
Penguin Books Ltd, 27 Wrights Lane,
London W8 5TZ, England
Penguin Books Australia Ltd,
Ringwood, Victoria, Australia
Penguin Books Canada Ltd, 10 Alcorn Avenue,
Toronto, Ontario, Canada M4V 3B2
Penguin Books (N.Z.) Ltd, 182–190 Wairau Road,
Auckland 10, New Zealand

Penguin Books Ltd, Registered Offices:
Harmondsworth, Middlesex, England

First published by Onyx,
an imprint of Dutton Signet,
a member of Penguin Putnam Inc.

First Printing, April, 1998
10 9 8 7 6 5 4 3 2 1

REGISTERED TRADEMARK—MARCA REGISTRADA

Printed in the United States of America

PUBLISHER'S NOTE
This is a work of fiction. Names, characters, places, and incidents either
are the product of the author's imagination or are used fictitiously,
and any resemblance to actual persons, living or dead, events, or locales
is entirely coincidental.

Dedicated to
Robert B. ("Buck") Buchanan
Judge of the Superior Court,
Pima County, Arizona (Retired)

Bernardo ("Bernie") Velasco
Judge of the Superior Court,
Pima County, Arizona

W. Randolph ("Randy") Stevens
Assistant United States Attorney (Tucson)

Michael Brink
my stepson

Joshua Parrish
my son

whose names I purloined for
five central characters
in the Joshua Rabb novels,

and, of course, to

Pat

ACKNOWLEDGMENTS

The words attributed to Senator Joseph McCarthy are either his actual words or close paraphrases as reported in Robert Griffith's *The Politics of Fear,* and Thomas C. Reeves's *The Life and Times of Joe McCarthy.*

Quotations from the Hebrew Scriptures are paraphrases of Psalms 94 and 119, an amalgam of the King James version and my own translation, essentially limited to modifying the archaisms.

In June 1950, Senator Margaret Chase Smith (R-Maine) and five other Republican senators published their "Declaration of Conscience" in which they said that they did not wish to see the Republican party ride to victory in the 1952 elections on "The Four Horsemen of Calumny— Fear, Ignorance, Bigotry, and Smear." They deplored the tactics of Joseph McCarthy, which had "debased [the Senate] to the level of a forum of hate and character assasination sheltered by the shield of congressional immunity."

The Lord is my defense, my God is the rock
  of my refuge.
And He shall bring upon my enemies their own
  iniquity
and shall cut them off in their wickedness.
—PSALM 94

Prologue

"Every man of decency here today should praise God that we have Joseph McCarthy in the United States Senate, our moral guardian, to protect us from the godless Kremlin puppets who are conspiring to corrupt and destroy our great nation from within."

Senator William "Big Bill" Maitland waited for the roar of approval to die down.

The Republican party leaders had gotten the rank and file out for McCarthy's stop on his way back to Washington, D.C., and "Big Bill" was milking a willing crowd gathered in the square in front of Arizona's State Capitol building in Phoenix.

"Tell 'em good, Bill, you tell 'em!" came a shout from the crowd.

The late May sun beat brutally down on the men on the dais, dressed in dark wool suits and white shirts, and the scent of starch and sweat hung in the burning air. Senator McCarthy mopped his face with an already soiled handkerchief. Senator Maitland was much more accustomed to the heat, but his two hundred thirty pounds brought beads of sweat rolling down the sides of his face.

"I give you one of the greatest patriots this country has produced since George Washington: Joseph McCarthy." Maitland clapped as the standing audience of at least five hundred men and a few women erupted in cheers. A small band played "The Star Spangled Banner," and McCarthy stood beaming out at the crowd from the lectern.

"With great men like Dick Nixon and Barry Goldwater and Big Bill Maitland out here in the West," McCarthy said, "I'm not needed here. It's time I get back to Washington and drive the Commiecrats out of the State Department."

The cheering of the crowd drowned his voice, and he basked silently in the adulation.

"The Communists, dupes, and fellow travelers who are prisoners of a bureaucratic Frankenstein must be ferreted out of the Truman administration and exposed before they turn this country over to Moscow. The parlor pinks and parlor punks must be destroyed before they rot our way of life."

More cheers and band playing. McCarthy waited patiently. Then he waved an inch-thick sheaf of papers in the air.

"I have here in my hand a list of two hundred and five names that were made known to the Secretary of State as being members of the Communist party and who nevertheless are still working and shaping policy in the State Department. That dilettante diplomat Dean Acheson whines and whimpers and cringes in the face of communism. And those egg-sucking Democrats in the Truman administration, with all their pitiful squealing, hold sacrosanct those Communists and queers who sold China into atheistic slavery. I pledge myself to the task of driving out the prancing mimics of the Moscow party line in the State Department."

Maitland was on his feet clapping. The crowd bellowed its approval.

Someone close to the dais called out, "Read us some names on that list, Senator."

The crowd grew quiet.

"These are dupes of the Kremlin who spew its malignant smear," McCarthy said, waving the sheaf of papers.

"Come on, Senator, let's hear the names." It was a newspaper reporter, pen in hand, in the front row of spectators. "You said the same thing in your speech in West Virginia, Senator, but you only came up with fifty-seven names in your Senate speech last February."

"You sound like one of those reporters who works for the Phoenix *Daily Worker* or the Los Angeles *Urinal.*"

The crowd exploded with laughter, and even the reporter joined in.

"Well, boys," McCarthy said, "I've got to be leaving you now. There's work to do back in Washington. I leave you in the able hands of my friend and colleague Big Bill Maitland."

Maitland joined him in front of the lectern, and the two men clasped hands and raised them high in the air like victorious presidential and vice-presidential candidates at a nominating convention. The band played "The Star Spangled Banner."

Chapter One

The setting sun broke under the curtain of billowy white clouds hovering over the Tucson Mountains, and a spoked wheel of yellow and orange fire ignited the canine-toothed crests. Joshua Rabb drove east on Speedway Boulevard for three or three and a half miles, and everything looked familiar in this town that had been his home for almost exactly five years; small two-story Victorian houses of desiccated wood under cracked and peeling paint, little stucco houses, boxy and painted tan or whitewashed, tiny Mexican-style adobes. Around the houses were drooping petunias, withered purple and yellow pansies, prickly pear and cholla and barrel cacti, eucalyptus trees sloughing off their gray-ish bark in strips, their leaves turning brown on the tips in the 105-degree heat, and an ornamental orange tree here and there, with parched forest-green leaves and limp limbs barren of fruit or blossoms or buds.

He turned south on Country Club Road, where there was no country club, but the houses began to get pricier. And a few blocks later he turned left on Fifth Street and entered a place that didn't look at all like the rest of Tucson. It looked like a desert oasis from one of those fanciful Hollywood *Arabian Nights* movies, lush and verdant, impervious to sun and wind, insulated by wealth and water sprinklers from the rest of the world.

He drove down Camino Español, and suddenly the dust and mold were gone and the smell was of roses and star jasmine and lilac, and he drove past luxuriant lawns of bright green grass in front of massive, two-story redbrick Georgian mansions surrounded by weeping junipers and Elderica pines that looked like huge Christmas trees. There were tall Santa Fe–style ranchitas with huge pine vigas extending through the tops of the white or tan or rust-colored stuccoed front walls, surrounded by carefully coiffured mesquites and palo verdes and red roses and blue and orange and white hibiscus. There were tennis courts behind or beside many homes and olympic-size swimming pools radiant and cerulean in the reflection of the pellucid sky.

In the center of this area on Tucson's far east side, called El Encanto, the Goldbergs lived in a two-story colonial mansion, like a Louisiana plantation house transplanted from the edge of a bayou to the middle of the Sonora Desert. It had a white-painted gleaming exterior with a second-story balcony supported by a colonnade of white marble columns. The acre of emerald green grass in front was being watered by a hundred sprinkler heads spaced equidistantly in the ground, and the droplets of water on the grass glistened in the sun like a carpet of diamonds.

There were a dozen shiny Cadillacs parked in the asphalt circle drive, two old, distinguished Packard touring cars, a royal blue Cord, a gull-wing Jaguar, and two MG-TDs.

And there was a conspicuous yellow 1946 Chevrolet convertible, snazzy and sharp when it was new five years ago, but now dulled by the inhospitable sun and rain, and rust had supplanted the paint in a few dented places. The once-white top was gray with age. The passenger seat had a burn hole where Edgar Hendly had once dropped his cigarette. The steering wheel was fitted with a special knob that could be latched on to by the stainless-steel prongs of a prosthetic hand.

There was no more room in the circle drive, and Joshua parked on the street. He opened the car door for his wife Barbara, and they walked into the house through a tall cherrywood double doorway. The entry-hall floor was squares of pale peach-colored Italian quarry tile. Off the entry hall was a spacious living room, cream wool carpeted and furnished in beige satin upholstered furniture; the den had polished knotty cherry-paneled walls, a floor of the same wood planks, a stone fireplace, and oak-tanned leather sofas and chairs. A Persian carpet covered much of the flag-stone floor of the dining room that seated twenty-four in mahogany Chippendale armchairs with ball and claw feet around a one-piece walnut burl table handmade in Minnesota. The last room off the hallway was a radio and television room with a dozen classic old cabinet radios lining the walls and a TV set in front of a long sofa.

A liveried butler carried around a silver tray with full flutes of champagne. Joshua took one, but Hannah didn't even notice the tray. She scowled at her father.

"How could you be so blasé?" Her voice was full of hurt.

"So what?"

"Come on, Daddy. You know what blasé means." She scowled at him.

"Please try to enjoy yourself, honey. Your lower lip is hanging so low, someone's going to step on it."

"That's real cute, Dad. Avoiding the subject as usual."

"Take it easy, honey. Enjoy the party. We'll talk later."

"I can't take it easy. And how can I enjoy Mark's graduation party when I'm going to lose him in two days? I want to talk now."

Joshua frowned and shook his head with frustration. "Okay, let's go into the TV room where everybody doesn't have to hear us."

They walked out of the bustling living room down the hallway to the TV room. Joshua closed the door behind him, switched on the overhead lights, and they sat down on the sofa in front of the television set. It was on, the sound turned down, but neither of them even noticed it.

"If this is the same thing about getting married, I haven't changed my mind," Joshua said, his eyes soft and his voice as gentle as he could make it. He took a sip of champagne, but suddenly it had no taste.

"But you're wrong, Daddy." Her eyes were filled with tears again, an ever ready spring that had begun flowing when Mark Goldberg had been commissioned a second lieutenant after four years of serving in the Reserve Officers' Training Corps at the University of Arizona. Just two days later, only a week ago, he had received orders to report to Camp Pendleton near San Diego.

The Korean War had been raging for almost a year, and there was hardly ever any good news about it.

Body bags were arriving back in the States by the tens, the hundreds, the thousands, and the letters from Chuy Leyva were devoid of the heroics and brave talk of a John Wayne war movie. Chuy had been a sergeant in the marines in World War Two and had been recalled to the marines ten months ago, in August 1950, a month after the United Nations "Police Action" began under United States command.

Chuy had been field-promoted to second lieutenant after his battalion had suffered huge losses when the North Koreans and the Red Chinese had captured Seoul, the capital of South Korea, in January. His letters to Magdalena and occasionally to Joshua and Edgar were chillingly filled with uncertainty and foreboding.

"I'm not wrong about this, Hanna," Joshua said as gently as he could. "I've been in a war, and I didn't know if I was going to come back. You and Adam could have been orphans."

"It's not the same, Daddy. All we want to do is get married so we can be together until Mark leaves."

"And what if you get pregnant, and then you get a telegram from the Defense Department that tells you how much they regret that you've just become a widow?"

She wept for a moment, sniffled, and blew her nose softly into the handkerchief that she was wringing in her hands. "At least I'll have a piece of him for the rest of my life."

Joshua swallowed and willed away the tears that pressed against his eyelids. "That's a wonderful, loving idea now," he said gently. "But you're only nineteen years old, and it wouldn't be so wonderful two years from now, three, ten, when you were raising your baby all by yourself."

She looked at him, her eyes tormented. "I pray to God every night that this is just a bad dream and to keep it from happening. And then I wake up and it's still real." She dabbed at her eyes with the handkerchief and sat a moment in silence.

"Why does there have to be a damn war, anyway?" she mumbled. "Everybody says it's just crazy. Truman replaces General MacArthur two months ago just because he wants to *win,* and now what do I do? Stay nice and calm while they send Mark over there to get killed for nothing?"

She began sobbing, and Joshua rubbed his eyes hard to force away the tears.

"We have to fight communism," he said, the words sounding just a bit hollow in his ears, like a politician running for office. But it was nonetheless what he believed, what virtually everyone believed. But still, fighting a war of "containment" that no one any longer expected to win, this was something new, something ominous.

"I know you're not happy about Mark being sent overseas, and neither are any of the rest of us. But it's his duty, and it's for our safety."

Hanna bit her lip and breathed deeply. "It should never be anyone's duty to die in a stupid war."

Joshua put his good arm around her shoulders and held her closely. His own tears fell on her auburn hair. They sat unmoving for minutes.

"He won't die, Hanna." But as he said the words

that were supposed to comfort her, they rang obscenely in his own ears. Had he magically been blessed with the gift of prophecy? Was he the elect of God who could guarantee good health and a rich life to whomever he chose? Or were the words just hollow bullshit?

"And what if he comes back like you, Daddy?" Hanna said. She looked fearfully at him, and her gray-hyacinth eyes moved to his left shoulder and down to the stainless-steel prongs where once his hand had been. Then they flickered back to his face, and tears came again in a gush. "I'm sorry I said that, Daddy, I'm so sorry," she said breathlessly.

"Go enjoy the graduation party," he said, his voice soft.

She sighed deeply to compose herself. Her eyes were bloodshot, and mascara had bled to the tops of her cheeks. She took a compact out of her small handbag, examined her face, and frowned.

"Better go to the bathroom and fix my face before anyone sees me." She left the room. Joshua sat on the overstuffed sofa and stared at a television show he had never seen before and didn't know the name of. Only a few wealthy Tucsonans had television sets, since Arizona's only TV stations were in Phoenix, and to access their broadcasts you had to have an expensive, fifty-foot-high antenna next to your house, which constantly needed expert repair because of wind damage.

Joshua felt nauseated. The chiaroscuro images on the twelve-inch screen of the Zenith television set were only the flickering background figures in his mind's eye. With his good hand, he touched the aluminum shaft that hung from the leather harness on his left shoulder. He winced and closed his eyes tightly and gritted his teeth, but he couldn't push away the nausea and despair. Ghosts danced in front of him.

The Battle of the Bulge, they will call it. But now it's just a nameless surreal montage of blood and explosions and bullets. It is two weeks until the annual celebration of the birth of the Prince of Peace, and I am lying in a foxhole in a foot of snow in a frozen field near a place prophetically named Diekirch, Luxembourg, and the 109th Infantry Regiment is pinned down by what appears to be every Tiger tank in the German Army. My company suddenly comes under a withering barrage of machine-gun fire from a battery set up at the edge of the winter-skeletalized forest. It rakes our exposed foxholes with bullets. I think that all of my men are going to be killed, and I find myself crawling through the frozen snow to within forty feet of the edge of the machine-gun emplacement and throwing a grenade into the hole and spraying the three German soldiers with the entire forty-round clip of my submachine gun. It is as though I am watching myself in a movie theater, and I have no control over my body.

Suddenly two of my men huddle with me on the ground, and I can vaguely hear one of them calling frantically through the field radio for a medic, but I can't focus on why. Then I allow myself to fall into an oddly warm sleep. I awake sometime later in an aid station, and it is the first time that I feel the pain. My left leg is no longer frozen, and the bullet wound in my thigh hurts like hell. My leg is in a slinglike contraption hanging from a metal rod over the bunk, and I can see that the four small toes of my left foot are a morbid purplish color, like shriveled plums hanging on a tree limb. I realize that I have frostbite, and then my foot really starts to hurt.

Some medics haul me into an evacuation ambulance and load my shoulder with something that stings a little and soon takes away most of the pain. I wake up on a cot in an army hospital in Antwerp, Belgium, in an officers ward with about thirty other men, and the doctor tells me that I have lost all of the toes on my left foot except the big toe, and that the thigh wound will heal without a trace other than the scar, but it will take time.

My father is Orthodox, as I was as a child and young man. But somewhere I fell away from orthodoxy, I stopped wearing a yarmulke, I started shaving every morning except Saturday, and I stopped putting on my t'fillin [phylacteries] and tallis [prayer shawl] each weekday morning. I didn't even take them with me when I moved from my parents' house in Crown Heights in Brooklyn to a tiny apartment on the edge of Harlem when I began law school at Columbia.

But now I feel differently. I need help. Seeing men die, seeing the gravely maimed soldiers in this hospital, has frightened me as I have never been before. I turn to the Psalms and read them, as millions of men do and have done for centuries in their moments of sorrow and misgiving: "It is good for me that I have been afflicted, that I might learn thy laws, O God. Teach me good judgment and knowledge, for I believe thy commandments. . . . How long shall the wicked tri-

umph? They break in pieces thy people. They slay the wicked and the stranger and murder the fatherless. He that created the ear, shall He not hear? He that created the eye, shall He not see? Who will rise up for me against the evildoers? Who will stand for me against the workers of iniquity? The Lord is my defense, my God is the rock of my refuge. And He shall bring upon my enemies their own iniquity and shall cut them off in their wickedness."

One day the colonel who is the hospital chief of staff comes to my cot and sits down in the field chair next to it and gives me a soulful look. "I was notified that your wife died in an automobile accident in Brooklyn," he tells me, "but I didn't think you were up to hearing about it till now. I'm very sorry, my boy," he says. "I'd have medicaled you back to the States, but we're on our last push through Germany, and we need every available man. I've got to send you back to light duty." He stands up, shakes my hand, and walks out, leaving me piercingly alone, staring into space, seeing nothing through tear-filled eyes.

What will happen to Hanna and Adam? Are they okay? I am sure that my parents have taken them to live in their apartment on Brighton Beach Avenue, and that they are well cared for. Just the distance from them, however, just the not knowing, makes me deeply fearful for them. And I had thought that my war was over and I'd made it through alive, and they would soon send me home in one of those huge hospital ships, and I'd be able to start living again, to be with my children. But now I lie on the cot in the midst of dozens of other men, and I have never felt so desolate.

I loved Rachel. I remember our last night together as though it were last night. We made love, and she cried. And I lay there with the scent of her on my lips, and I cried, too. Though I didn't let her see or hear me, because I didn't want to frighten her, for her to know that I was a coward, that I didn't want to go to war, that I just wanted to stay with her and Hanna and Adam. Rachel was just a girl, and she died. And I couldn't even be with her. And then the agony of not being able to take Hanna and Adam into my arms and cry with them. That is the worst thing that has ever happened to me, to know that my children were grieving and in terrible pain, but not to be able to touch them and hold them and kiss away their tears. How can the central elements of a man's life be taken from him just like that? Bang! Gone. And then a colonel says that he's sorry, but that's the way it is. Your wife is dead but you can't go home. And you pray and cry out to God to help you in your despondency. But God does not answer. God does not help. Does God ever help?

The day before I'm discharged from the army hospital to join my new unit, there is a little ceremony in the general's office. I'm promoted to major and awarded the silver star. The citation reads "for bravery above and beyond the call of duty," but I can hardly remember exactly what I did, and I have no idea why I did it. The only thing I know for certain is that I wasn't motivated by bravery but by abject fear.

I'm attached as JAG officer to a rear unit of Patton's Third Army. We rapidly cross Germany into Czechoslovakia. My company is sent around behind the heavy

*weapons company to guard their rear when they enter
a little town named Medzibiez. Intelligence reports that
there is a platoon or more of SS troops holed up there.
They had been in charge of a prison camp just south
of the town, and they had abandoned it when the
Americans were a day away. The prison camp is my
responsibility: secure it, disarm it, make sure there are
no Krauts around.*

*But it turns out not to be a run-of-the-mill prison
camp. There are four ramshackle wooden barracks in
which are huddled perhaps five hundred starved and
diseased human beings. They are covered with suppu-
rating sores and thriving lice and are but vacant-eyed
remnants of what had once been real people. Most of
them are obviously dying. And behind the barracks are
heaps of decaying, stinking cadavers, toothless protruding mouths gaping open, eyes rolled back white, sixty-
or seventy-pound skin bags of putrid flesh. They all
have filthy yellow Mogen Davids stitched on their
striped pants.*

That had been their crime.

*I and many of my men double over and vomit con-
vulsively, embarrassed to look at each other, frightened
to look at the still barely alive inmates. But they can't
simply be ignored. They need help, at least those few
who aren't obviously going to die.*

*My company remains at the concentration camp out-
side Medzibiez for several days waiting for orders to
continue our push to Vienna. Of the 511 inmates still
alive when we liberated the camp, 174 die despite all
of our medical efforts to save them. The survivors have
nowhere to go. They come mostly from the Ukraine,*

and if they try to go back there they will be hunted down and murdered by German soldiers or Polish and Russian partisan bands roaming the forests. So they have to continue to live in the same vermin-infested barracks in which the Nazis had imprisoned them.

Four of the survivors can't stand it any longer.

"But I can't protect you outside these gates,'" I tell them in yiddish. "There are reports of bands of SS troops from this camp in the forest between here and Medzibiez. Believe me, you're better off waiting here until the war is over. It won't be long now."

"It doesn't matter to us anymore. Don't you understand? We cannot stay another minute in this place where our families and friends were exterminated like cockroaches."

They stand there stolidly, these starved, head-shaved, walking cadavers with their jaws clenched resolutely shut. And I cannot and will not hold them against their will. So I go with them to the mess sergeant and draw them each a week's provisions, and then I take them to the armory and give them each a Luger, which have been left behind by the fleeing SS detachment. And then I stand dejectedly at the gate and watch them disappear into the forest, truly believing that they will be murdered within a few hours or days.

Three hours later a scouting patrol from the camp reports finding four bodies of emaciated, head-shaved men dressed in U.S. Army fatigues. They are on the north bank of the Kura River, about six miles from the camp.

I take a platoon of my men into the forest to flush out the killer or killers. We find the bodies by the river.

They have all been shot in the back, and their faces have been stabbed so many times that all that is left are small puddles of bloody, oozing mush. My men spread into the forest to round up the subhuman animals who have done this.

I am alone, walking slowly eastward. I see movement in the trees ahead of me, leaves rustling, a small sapling swaying, and I spray it with my Thompson submachine gun. There is a scream, and a voice hollers out something I can't understand in garbled German. A tall, thin soldier in an SS uniform, supporting another wounded soldier, comes out from behind a tree thirty feet in front of me. The wounded man's feet are dragging and his head lolls on his chest. The tall, thin one calls out in heavily accented English, "Enough, surrender, surrender, no shoot."' And I level my Thompson submachine gun at them and fire a long burst, from right to left and back, and the Germans slump to the ground. I do not even flinch, I do not even blink, as I stand over the bodies. I actually feel better than I have in many days. I pull my bayonet out of its scabbard and bend over and stab the dead Germans in the face, first one and then the other, again and again, until their faces are bloody pulp. I am gelid, emotionless.

Suddenly shots ring out. I feel the bullets rip into my chest and left arm. I don't know who has shot me or from where. All I can focus on is the ugly stain of blood spreading over the front of my field jacket. It is April, and an early spring thaw has melted the snow and ice in the forest, and it is too warm for the wound to be anesthetized by the weather alone, as my leg wound had been last December at the Battle of the Bulge. The pain is excruciating.

Two of my men carry me back to the camp. Medics deaden my pain as much as possible with morphine ampules in my thigh, but I remain semiconscious and feel cold and clammy. I am flown somewhere in a medical evacuation airplane. I lie on the stretcher and try to mesmerize myself by concentrating on the incessant whirring of the propellers. They sound to me like a long drawn out melancholy low string on a cello. A little grating, very mournful and distant, like a doleful dirge being played under my head.

They wheel me into an ambulance, and the cello dirge stops but the pain is still there. And they unload me like a side of beef onto a real bed, this time in a hospital, and still the pain does not relinquish its penetrating vibrato, but now it is a guttural oboe playing a whispery sound like hot wind rustling drapes by a window. They shoot my shoulder full of something and my hip full of something else, and then I drift on that reedy oboe whisper and float away from my pain, looking back at myself like someone I have just visited in the hospital and am damn glad to be away from at last.

When I finally wake up again and know that I am alive, my left arm is missing, part of my left shoulder is missing, and I drift in and out of dreamlike slow-motion ballet sequences in which Rachel dances on a cloud with only my arm and toes as her partner. And then she smiles down at me, and her face becomes a leering skull of death.

I remember, I see vividly the lugubrious faces of the inmates of that concentration camp, like hundreds of *haunted Ichabod Cranes, and they open their eyes wide to me in speechless pleas for mercy and help, but I am helpless. I must just watch them die, the gleam disappear from their eyes, their mouths fall open like the ricti of sparrows begging for food from their mothers.*

They put me on a hospital ship, and uncounted days later I'm in a little white room in the Brooklyn Veterans Hospital. My parents come to see me, and I see the shock and grief in my father's eyes, the tears pouring from my mother's. Hanna and Adam want to see me, they say, but I shake my head and tell them, "No, absolutely not, I don't want them to see me like this, I don't want to scare them to death."

The war is over for me, and I am still alive, but so much of my life has been shattered . . .

The door opened a few inches, then wider. Barbara came in and sat down next to her husband on the sofa. She put her hand lightly on his thigh. He looked up at her, startled, and then pushed away his memories.

"You all right?" she asked.

"Sure, honey."

"You look like hell."

"Hanna and I had another quarrel about Mark."

"I thought so. She came into the living room a few minutes ago, and I could see she'd been crying." She shook her head sadly. "It'll be an awful time for her with Mark gone."

He nodded. "Yeah, but the war won't last forever. The newspapers say that General Ridgway is trying to get truce talks going, and if that happens they'll start reducing our troop strength. Mark may never even have to go over there."

"Let's hope," Barbara said. "Come on back to the party. Everybody's missing you."

"I think I'm all partied out. I won't make very good company in there."

"Can't just sit here and watch TV. The Goldbergs may be insulted."

"They'll live." He shrugged apologetically. "I'm starving. How about going over to the Dixie Diner for some shrimp?"

"Okay. I'm hungry, too."

"You mean Mortimer's hungry." He patted her tummy softly.

"Esmeralda." She smiled.

Barbara's two-month pregnancy had just begun to show. But it was a bad time to be talking merrily about a new baby Rabb when Hanna was going through the worst misery that she had experienced since her mother died. So they hadn't mentioned it to her yet, and Barbara was wearing looser dresses and skirts. The low-cut yellow sundress she wore now was tied under her full breasts and fell loosely to just below her knees. Very stylish and very unrevealing.

"Let's round up Adam," Joshua said. "There's nobody here his age, and he's probably sitting in some corner waiting to be rescued.'"

In the forty-five minutes since Joshua had left the living room, dozens more guests had arrived. No one would notice him and Barbara and Adam leave. They found Adam sitting on the back porch on a small swing chair, drinking a Coke, looking terminally bored.

"I'm going nuts here, Dad."

"Yeah, I know. We're going over to the Dixie for some shrimp. Want to come?"

"God, yes," he mumbled. He stood up quickly and put the almost empty Coke bottle on the small side table. He was tall and muscular, but thin in a way that only fifteen-year-olds can be. His seal brown hair and deep blue eyes and the squareness of his chin were the same as his father's.

"Let's leave through the patio gate," Joshua said. "No need to traipse out the front door past everybody."

They followed the flagstone walk around the side of the house. Joshua unlatched the white-painted wooden gate, and they walked to their 1948 Dodge parked beside the purple plum tree hedge on the edge of the road.

"Can I drive, Dad?" Adam held out his hand for the key. He would be sixteen in two months, and he had his learner's permit. He loved to drive. Sometime after August 7, his birthday, Joshua planned to give him the Chevy convertible that Hanna was now driving, Hanna would get the 1948 Dodge, and Joshua and Barbara would buy a new car, an Oldsmobile maybe, or, if things really kept going well with Joshua's law practice, a Buick. Adam started the car and pulled carefully onto the asphalt road from the loose dirt shoulder.

"Why don't we go pick up Magdalena and Macario?" Joshua said.

"Good idea," said Barbara. "She got a letter from Chuy this morning, and she's been in her room crying most of the day."

Magdalena had been the Rabbs' "acculturation girl" for their first three years in Tucson, when they lived in the small adobe house across from the San Xavier Papago Reservation, six miles south of Tucson. Joshua and Barbara weren't married then, and Hanna and Adam were just kids. Joshua was the part-time legal affairs officer for the Bureau of Indian Affairs, and all white BIA employees were expected to take a Papago girl into their homes as a servant, to acculturate them to the ways of the white world and to make them capable of leaving the Reservation and living and working in the white cities.

When Magdalena had first come to the Rabbs, she was twenty yeas old, shy and delicate, and as exotically beautiful as the statue of the "Black Madonna" that Joshua had once seen in an art museum in New York. Her skin was nutmeg brown, her eyes anthracite. Both she and Hanna were tall and slender, and very soon Magdalena's meager wardrobe of two pairs of faded Levi's and a T-shirt and a threadbare blue chambray work shirt had been enriched by Hanna's own clothing, and they had become as close as sisters, and Magdalena had become a mother to Adam.

She was the granddaughter of Macario Antone, the former chief of the Papago tribe, and she had lived in a dormitory at the University of Arizona for two years while pursuing a degree in education, so she hardly needed acculturating. But she had had to leave the university to return to the Reservation and look after her aged grandparents. Macario had died a year later, and her grandmother Ernestina had gone back to Pisinimo on the Big Reservation, a hundred miles from Tucson, to live out her last years in her centuries-old ancestral home.

Magdalena had continued to live with the Rabbs. There had been no question about it. She was part of the family now. She had earned her education degree at the University of Arizona. And when she married Jesus ("Chuy") Leyva, the chief of the Indian police for the San Xavier Reservation, she and Chuy had gone to live in a small house, owned by the BIA and designated by BIA Superintendent Edgar Hendly as the official residence of the chief of police, across from San Xavier del Bac Mission. She had given birth to a son, whom they named Macario in honor of her grandfather, just a week before Chuy was recalled to the marines; and after Chuy had left, she had been too depressed to live alone on the Reservation. So she and Macario had come to live in the spare bedroom on the second floor of the Rabbs' house, separated by a small bathroom from Hanna's bedroom.

Adam parked in the driveway with the motor running, and Barbara went into the house to get Magdalena. They came out a moment later. Magdalena's shiny ebony hair was pulled back in a thick peasant's braid. She carried her baby in her arms. She got in the backseat with Barbara.

"What's new with Chuy?" Joshua asked.

She shook her head sadly. "He was up with MacArthur's spearhead across the thirty-eighth parallel. They were on the offensive, and he felt confident. Now that

MacArthur's been fired, Chuy's really worried." She paused and her voice got thicker. "I'm scared."

Joshua nodded. "When I was in Europe, the army censored all the mail and never let us write about what was really happening. Maybe that was better."

Magdalena shrugged. "There's nothing I can do or say to make anything change. I just feel helpless." Her voice trailed off, and she stared out the window of the car into the darkness.

Chapter Two

Bill Maitland sat on the black velvet upholstered armchair in the living room of his house on Camelback Mountain. He was a big, handsome man of forty-seven, blond hair and blue eyes. The expansive picture window and sliding glass doors to the patio gave him a panoramic view of the glimmering lights of Phoenix sprawling to the west.

"The guy is a fucking genius," Maitland said. He took a sip of the straight scotch in the old-fashioned glass he was holding.

"Yeah, he's got all the words," said Horton Landers, the senator's administrative aide. "The people love him. 'Commiecrats. Parlor pinks and parlor punks. Bureaucratic Frankenstein.' Where's he get that shit?"

The third man in the room was Herman Gruver, McCarthy's chief of staff in his home office in Milwaukee, Wisconsin. He had been McCarthy's assistant campaign manager and had helped orchestrate the intoxicating landslide victory of 1946.

"Some of that stuff he picks up from the reporters who follow him around," Gruver said. "Some of it just pops into his head, and he doesn't even know from where."

"Well, wherever it's coming from," Maitland said, "it's sure as hell working for him. I heard he got twenty grand in campaign contributions after that speech in Virginia."

"More like forty," Gruver said.

Landers let out a low whistle. "We oughta try to get in on some of that." He sipped at his scotch.

"That's why the senator asked me to come here," Gruver said. "You read the packet we sent you on those two professors in Tucson?"

Maitland nodded. "Sure did. Great stuff. But we have to have a good man down there working it for us. I don't want it biting me on the ass."

"We got one," Gruver said. "This Essert is on the team. I talked to him on the phone last week right after the senator called you about the Academics Against War. Essert said he'd put together a grand jury, no questions asked. He's a good boy. And the senator told me to go down there and stay as long as it takes to make sure it goes right.'"

"Fantastic!" Maitland said. "It's going to be just the ticket for me."

Gruver smiled and nodded. He was a thin man with a bony, narrow face, fifty-three years old, with thinning, short gray-brown hair and rheumy green eyes.

"This is my chance," Maitland said, his face sober. "I'm getting on Joe's bandwagon and riding it to the White House."

Landers's eyes got big. "McCarthy say something?"

"He said it's me or Dick Nixon. Nixon got a lot of distance out of the House Committee on Un-American Activities, but he doesn't have my kind of backing with the money boys. Joe wants a million bucks in private money."

Landers shrugged. "Hell, that shouldn't be any problem."

"That'll be music to the senator's ears," Gruver said.

"I already told Joe that," said Maitland. "He told me I better get this Academics thing boiling hot to get my name in the papers. If I make it hot enough and get national press on it, Joe will include it in his hearings. Then I'll get some real name recognition. Name recognition plus the million"—he snapped his fingers—"I'm Vice President Maitland in 1956, 1960 at the latest."

"I'll bring the packet down to Essert tomorrow," Herman Gruver said.

"I'll go with you," said Horton Landers.

Chapter Three

"Julio Moraga's on the phone," Frances Hendly said through the squawky intercom.

Joshua Rabb was sitting at his desk in his small office at the Bureau of Indian Affairs in Tucson. He pressed down on the intercom lever, said "Thanks," and picked up the telephone.

"Julio, how are you? What's up?"

"I've just been subpoenaed to a federal grand jury."

Joshua paused, thinking that he hadn't heard correctly. "What?"

"I'm in my office at the museum. The U.S. marshal just served a subpoena on me to testify about being a communist."

"A communist?"

"Yeah."

"You?"

"Yeah. But I'm not."

"I know that. But why?"

"I wrote an article with Mischa Livinsky for a scholarly journal."

"What?"

"Mischa Livinsky," Julio said articulately.

"What the hell is a Mischa Livinsky?"

Julio chuckled. "Sorry for laughing. Nerves. It isn't so funny. He's a professor of political science at the U."

Joshua thought for a moment. "Yeah, I think I read something about that a couple of days ago in the *Star*. He must be one of that Academics Against War group that the story said the attorney general declared to be a Communist front organization."

"Right. Me, too."

"Are you and—"

"Joshua, I've got to go. I'm already late for an appointment with the provost to talk about renewing my contract. I'll be at your office at one o'clock with Mischa."

He hung up the telephone, not waiting for a reply.

Edgar Hendly walked into Joshua's office and sat down on the straight-backed wooden chair. Edgar was the BIA superintendent for Arizona, almost sixty years old, nine inches shorter than Joshua and at least fifty pounds heavier. He wore a threadbare dark gray wool suit with sweat patches under the arms, a frayed white shirt, and a black silk tie anointed with tiny remnants of a variety of breakfast foods. He had a nervous habit of combing his few strands of gray hair over his bald spot with pudgy fingers. But despite his rumpled, unkempt appearance and rube demeanor, he was the best friend Joshua had ever had. He was one of the two reasons that Joshua had retained his fifteen-hour-a-week job as BIA legal officer and head of the Office of Land Management, although he no longer relied on the $129-a-month salary.

Joshua's private law practice had grown substantially since he had married Barbara and moved away from the San Xavier Papago Reservation into Tucson two years ago. The other reason that he had kept his job was that occasionally he had the opportunity to do something good for the Papagos. They were mostly gentle, poverty-stricken people, abandoned and ignored and repressed by the surrounding populace, and it gave Joshua a feeling of self-worth to be able to help them. *"Haud ignara mali, miseris succerere disco,"* Sister Martha Robinette, a Poor Claire nun, had said to him the first time he had come to this office in June 1946: "Not unaccustomed to misfortune, I have learned to succor the downtrodden." She had intended to insult him with that line from a poem by Virgil, not imagining at the time that this transplanted Jewish lawyer from Brooklyn might actually fit the description.

"Nice to see you, Edgar."

"What's new, Josh?" Edgar eyed him askance.

"Same old stuff."

"Aw now, don't be pissin' on my shoes and tellin' me it's a rainstorm. I hear ya got a call from Julio Moraga."

"You got antennas in your ears?"

"I got a wife who loves and reveres me and likes to keep me up on all the latest gossip. And she happens to answer the telephone 'round this joint."

Joshua smiled. "That would be Saint Frances the Fearless of BIA?"

"The very one. Now what did ol' Julio do this time?"

"Got subpoenaed to a grand jury."

"Punch out another voting registrar?" Edgar snorted.

"Nope. He's a member of the Academics Against War over at the university, and the attorney general declared it a subversive Communist front."

Edgar stared at him quizzically. "Julio, a *Communist?* Bullshit."

Joshua lifted the telephone. "Call the attorney general in Washington and tell him."

Edgar held up his hands in a halt gesture. "Shi-it no, man! That fuckin' Senator McCarthy'd have my ass in a sling in two seconds flat." He looked oddly at Joshua. "You ain't plannin' to take his case?"

Joshua shrugged. "I haven't been asked."

"Get outta town 'fore he can ask."

"What the hell do I have to be so afraid of?"

"Man, if you don't know, then yer a damn sight dumber 'n I think ya are. All them killers and thieves and gangsters ya represent gets folks round here a *little* pissed off. But this? They'll hang ya by yer dick from the flagpole in Armory Park. The gazebo'll be all decked out in red white 'n blue buntin' fer the occasion, and the Davis-Monthan Air Force band'll play patriotic music whilst all the little ol' ladies from the Daughters a the American Revolution admire how nice ya swing in the wind."

Joshua laughed. "And you'll probably set up a hot dog concession to make a few bucks off me."

"I don't think nobody'll be in the mood fer a hot dog when they see ya strung up by yer wiener. I think I'll do cotton candy and Cokes."

Both of them laughed. Then they sat quietly for a moment studying each other.

"Seriously. Don't do it."

Joshua screwed up his face and shrugged. "Seriously, I haven't been asked. If I am, I'll have to make a decision."

"Yeah, you 'n yer decisions. Yer gonna get into somethin' no smart person would touch with rubber gloves an' a pole."

"We'll see."

"This ain't only *you*, ya know. Ya get inta this som bitch, Harry Coyle gonna be callin' me from Washington wonderin' what kinda Commie I got on the BIA payroll."

"And you'll tell him I'm just a lawyer doing a job."

"I'll tell him," Edgar said wryly, "but there's no tellin' what he'll tell me."

Julio Moraga came into Joshua's office at a few minutes after one. He wore Levi's, a plain plaid cowboy shirt, and black cowboy boots. He was of average height and weight with straight black hair cut short and great bushy wild-haired eyebrows guarding deep-set angry black eyes in a fleshy, russet face. He was in his late thirties, one of the few Papagos who had ever earned a master's degree, and was the assistant curator of the Arizona State Museum at the University of Arizona.

As a native speaker of English, Spanish, and Papago, Julio was invaluable to the professor of anthropology who headed the museum and whose expertise was the history and prehistory of southern Arizona.

He and Julio, whose specialty was archaeology, had discovered and excavated the Ventana Cave about eighty miles west of Tucson on the Big Papago Reservation, which contained the earliest and best preserved artifacts ever found of the civilization from which the Papagos had descended.

Julio sat down on the edge of one of the straight-backed wooden chairs, perched and jittery like a Harris hawk searching for prey from a high limb of a mesquite tree. Joshua had brought a second chair into the office for Mischa Livinsky, who sat down heavily on it, a much older and meeker-looking man than Julio.

"This is my very good friend Mischa Livinsky, full professor of political science," Julio said.

Joshua stood up, as did Livinsky. They reached across the desk and shook hands firmly. They sat down, appraising each other. Livinsky was dressed dapperly in a light gray silk suit, white shirt, and royal blue silk tie. He was about six feet tall, thin and angular to the point of gauntness, with soft blue eyes, a drooping left eyelid, graying reddish blond hair, and a hatchet face that looked like it had been cut from a cracked and parched knotty pine log, yellowish skin striated with wrinkles. He may have been only fifty-five or sixty years old, but he could easily have passed for seventy.

"Professor Moraga has told me that you are the finest lawyer that he has ever met," Livinsky said, his voice deep and thick with the familiar Ukrainian accent of Joshua's parents.

"I think I'm the *only* lawyer he ever met," Joshua said, smiling.

Livinsky and Moraga both nodded and chuckled.

"Now that I know I come so well recommended, what can I do for you?"

"I should tell you first, Mr. Rabb, that I have been to see three other local attorneys in the last two days. They have refused to represent me. A fourth refused even to meet with me."

"Lawyers usually only refuse because the person can't pay."

Livinsky shook his head. "No, Mr. Rabb, that wasn't a problem and will not be with you. It was the nature of the matter."

"I think I have a pretty fair inkling of the nature of the matter. I saw the story in the newspaper a couple of days ago."

"The story was very inaccurate, Mr. Rabb."

"Anything written by J. T. Sellner is inaccurate, Mr. Livinsky. So why don't you tell me about it."

Livinsky took a thick packet of thermofax pages from his inside suit jacket pocket and pushed them across the desk to Joshua. Joshua unfolded them and scanned the first page.

"Have you ever read the McCarran Act, Mr. Rabb?"

"I've heard of it, but I thought that Tucson was a little bit out of the way for the attorney general of the United States to be hunting Communist front organizations, so I've never read it."

"Let me give you a short précis, Mr. Rabb. Otherwise it will take you an hour to read."

Joshua nodded.

"It's officially called the 'Internal Security Act of 1950,' enacted by Congress about a year ago, and it encompasses virtually all of the notions that have been adopted by Senator Joseph McCarthy as the essence of his quest to rid our government and our society of all Communists, which really boils down to harassing and persecuting or destroying the lives of anyone who doesn't go along with McCarthy. It is the most virulent hate campaign since Hitler, focusing on liberal thinkers in every sphere of governmental, academic, and entertainment life, and especially Jews."

Livinsky's nose blanched on the tip, his mouth tightened, and he breathed deeply to calm himself. His eyes were riveted on Joshua's. There was nothing meek about him now. He took another sheet from his pocket, unfolded it, and studied it.

"Julio and I have been notified that we are under investigation for the crime of failing to register as members of a Communist front organization called 'Academics Against War,' which consisted of nine professors at the University of Arizona. It is a crime carrying a penalty of ten years imprisonment and a ten-thousand-dollar fine per day of nonregistration." He looked up at Joshua and grimaced. "Ten thousand dollars per day," he repeated.

"Let me explain on exactly what evidence our organization was designated a Communist front. Our group opposes the war in Korea. We don't believe that the domino theory of world domination by monolithic communism is realistic, and we believe that there is a growing rift between Russia and Red China which will militate against such an eventuality. We believe that South Korea is too remote from the legitimate interests of the United States to support the sending of a half-million American soldiers there. And we think that the consequent threat of a nuclear holocaust is too real to be ignored."

"Well," Joshua said, "I happen to disagree with you. I think we do need to be there."

"That's perfectly fine, Mr. Rabb. But does your disagreement with my views arise to the level of wishing to silence me or to imprison me for them?"

Joshua shook his head slowly. "No, I think the First Amendment guarantees you the right to express your views, as long as you don't advocate the forceful overthrow of the United States government."

"I not only don't advocate it, Mr. Rabb, I would abhor such an action or even the very suggestion of it. And I stated that clearly in the article that Julio and I wrote."

"What article is that?"

"In January, it was published in the *American Journal of Governmental Studies*. That's what got the FBI investigation started. You'll see in section twelve of the McCarran Act that it created the Subversive Activities Control Board, which was appointed by President Truman and is charged with ferreting out all Communist front organizations and compelling all members of such organizations to register with the attorney general within sixty days. Failure to register is the felony with which Julio and I are about to be charged."

"Your organization was designated a Communist front, but you failed to register?"

"We *refused*. It was designated on March three of this year. We had until May three to register, and we refused. We are not Communists. We are now some seventy-five days late. That's three quarters of a million dollars in fines for each of us, just for starters." Livinsky and Moraga both stared gravely at Joshua.

Joshua rolled his eyes. "You think they'll attach your checking accounts?"

Livinsky said nothing. Moraga chuckled.

"So why did your article stir up such a furor?"

"Because the Soviet Union has denounced the U.N. entry into the Korean War, as has our group, and because section three of the McCarran Act defines subversive activity as including publications which 'advocate the economic, international, and governmental doctrines of world communism.' Since our article expressed the same view as the official Communist policy, we have been branded as Communists."

"That's all they have?" Joshua asked.

"That's all."

Joshua flipped through the pages and skimmed section three for a moment. He pursed his lips and shook his head. "Pretty scary stuff."

Livinsky nodded. "I'll tell you what is even scarier, Mr. Rabb. When the Subversive Activities Control Board designated our group as a Communist front, all of us simply sent written letters of resignation from the organization to the university president. Nothing has happened to the other seven. Only to Julio and me. We were notified just this morning by the provost that our contracts will not be honored for employment at the University of Arizona next year, even though both of us are tenured."

"How can they do that?"

"Because the McCarran Act says that a Communist front member may not hold employment with an agency of the United States government without disclosing such membership."

"I don't get it," Joshua said. "The U of A is a *state* institution, not federal. It's run by the State Board of Regents and supported by state funds."

"Except that the University of Arizona does accept federal funds for various of its research enterprises, and the university president considers *that* to fit within the definition of 'agency of the United States.' "

"That's plain nonsense," Joshua said. "He must be getting pressure from someone."

"Senator William Maitland," Livinsky said.

Joshua had read several times that Big Bill Maitland, the freshman Republican senator from Phoenix, had eagerly jumped aboard McCarthy's witch-hunting wagon. He had run for the seat that had been held for four terms by Jacob Lukis, whom Joshua had come to know quite well. Lukis was a native Tucsonan, very rich, powerful, and in his mid-seventies. A stroke had kept him from running for reelection in the midterm election of 1950. Maitland, in a vicious anti-Communist McCarthyite campaign, had soundly defeated the Democratic candidate.

"Okay, assuming it's Maitland, why would he single you two out?" Joshua looked from Livinsky to Moraga.

Julio answered first. "I'm a subversive because I assaulted the Pima County registrar when he refused to register me to vote back in 1948. And also because I helped Mischa write the article."

"I thought that punching the registrar made you a man of honor," Joshua said, "but that may not be the universally accepted opinion." He looked at Livinsky. "And you, sir?"

"I am from the Soviet Union, Mr. Rabb, and I am a Jew. The only way I could teach at the University of Moscow in the 1930s was by being a member of the Communist party. It was one of Stalin's rules, although for nonpolitical gentiles it was often overlooked. I fled Moscow in June 1941, when the Nazis invaded Russia. I had read *Mein Kampf* and heard enough of Hitler's speeches on the short wave radio to have a strong sense of what was coming. I fled to Sweden and finally to New York City. My undergraduate degree was from the University of Heidelberg in political economy and my doctorate from the Sorbonne, so I had sufficient credentials to get a teaching job at New York University. And in 1947 I accepted a tenured professorship at the University of Arizona."

"Did you ever renounce your membership in the Communist party?"

Livinsky shrugged. "I don't really know how I would do that. Would I write to party headquarters in Moscow and tell them that I'm not?"

Joshua pursed his lips and said nothing.

"At NYU I signed a loyalty oath. I avowed that I held no views inimical to the United States. And you must remember, Mr. Rabb, that communism wasn't illegal in the U.S. during the Second World War, and the Soviet Union was a vitally important ally. When I became a naturalized citizen here in Tucson two years ago, I again swore my loyalty. It was true, and it is true today."

Joshua looked pensive. Livinsky's case was not as clear-cut as Moraga's.

"All right," Joshua said, "aside from the article you wrote and your backgrounds, what specific evidence does the government have that you committed the crime? I can't imagine that Judge Buchanan, the federal judge here, is going to let the U.S. attorney go through with such a serious prosecution just on the basis of a pacifist article and your backgrounds. Certainly as to Julio, he knows the circumstances of his assault on the voting registrar, and he's not going to be persuaded by *that* that he's a Communist."

"Mr. Rabb," Livinsky said, "their entire additional evidence is that the McCarran Act lists as one of the elements of proof that an organization is subversive, that it keeps 'membership lists in code.' That's section thirteen e seven."

Joshua turned to it and read it. He nodded.

"When the FBI agents from Washington, D.C., came here—they have a special unit that witch-hunts Communists—they served a search warrant on my home. They found in my office a folder of papers in 'code,' which they sent to their expert code man back in Washington. They discovered that it was notes concerning the members of our group and several of our meetings, and that the notes were written in Yiddish. Not so odd, since my father was a Talmud teacher in a yeshiva in the Moldavanka ghetto in Odessa, and we spoke Yiddish at home, as did all the Jews in the Ukraine. But to the FBI, this clearly constituted a 'code.' "

Joshua breathed deeply. "Are you serious?"

"Yes, sir. I am serious."

"That's it? Nothing else?"

Both Livinsky and Moraga shook their heads.

"Jesus," Joshua muttered. "I never heard such bullshit in my life. Maybe I'd better stop writing letters to my parents in Yiddish. Except my mother doesn't understand English so well." He looked soberly at Livinsky and Moraga. "God save us from the patriots."

The men were silent.

"Did you bring a copy of your article?"

"Yes. It's the last six pages of those documents."

"Give me a few minutes." Joshua hunched over his desk and studied the article closely.

"Well," he said, sitting back in his creaky wooden swivel chair, "I can't see anything subversive about it. I don't agree with you, but it's still not subversive. But I can see what caused your problem." He turned a couple of pages and read the quote. " 'Senator Joseph McCarthy's tactics are those of a fascist demagogue, second in modern times only to Hitler. McCarthy's infamous crusade is a sick salacious search for whomever *he* defines as deviant and deleterious to society.' "

Livinsky nodded and shrugged. "It had a seductive poetic ring, Mr. Rabb. Wonderful alliteration. I simply couldn't bear to edit out those lines."

Joshua laughed. "Well, your poetry has landed you in the grand jury."

The laughter from Livinsky and Moraga was thin and nervous.

"When is your grand jury appearance?"

"Monday after next at eight."

"We'd better get started right now," Joshua said. "It doesn't give us much time to prepare."

A smile slowly broke up the vertical wrinkles of Livinsky's cheeks. "Thank you, sir," he said quietly. "Thank you."

The first thing that Joshua needed to do after Livinsky and Moraga left two hours later was to file a complaint in superior court to try to get their teaching positions reinstated. To do that he needed to have a copy of the personnel policy of the University of Arizona spelling out the rules of tenure.

He drove to the university administration building and went to the personnel department in the basement. A mousy woman in her sixties with a tight bun of white hair and an equally tight and colorless expression told him that employment policies could not be given out to members of the public.

Joshua cajoled her into letting him sit and read the policy manual at the small metal table next to her large mahogany desk. He copied the tenure provisions on a legal pad, thanked her profusely, and drove to the law library at the courthouse. It took him almost an hour to research the status of the Board of Regents and the right of a private citizen to maintain an action against it for breach of contract.

It would have to be an application for a writ of prohibition, which was simply a request for a hearing before a superior court judge in which Livinsky and Moraga would seek to prohibit state officials—the Board of Regents—from violating the professors' tenure contracts. One of the basic guarantees of tenure was that a professor was protected from the termination of his contract for any reason other than "conviction of a felony or a misdemeanor involving moral turpitude." Livinsky and Moraga hadn't even been charged with a crime yet. The writ of prohibition would hopefully result in a superior court order that would reinstate the two professors until they were actually *convicted* of a crime, if ever.

By the time that Joshua finished typing the writ application, it was after six o'clock and too late to file it with the clerk of the court.

The next morning at a few minutes after eight, he filed it and secured the appropriate subpoenas. The hearing was set for Tuesday, July 17, at nine o'clock, before Judge Bernardo Velasco, one of Tucson's three superior court judges.

Chapter Four

They drove in Mark's Cadillac convertible to the little town of Eloy, fifty-five miles north of Tucson. They couldn't go to a motel in Tucson, lest they be seen by someone they knew, or someone recognize the car, or the room clerk get suspicious that they weren't married and call the police.

It was dark, a little after nine—travelers didn't check into a motel in daylight—and they carried two empty valises into the room. The door was held open by the fawning clerk, a sixty-year-old fat Mexican with a wad of tobacco in his cheek and juice trickling down the furrowed grooves of flaccid skin by his mouth. They yawned at him and smiled tiredly, and he flipped the key on the double bed and left, closing the door behind him. Mark slid the dead bolt.

He turned around and smiled at Hanna, sitting on the edge of the bed. All of a sudden she felt shy. They had been going together for three years, and he had touched her and she him, but never like this. Good girls didn't go all the way. But this was different. Mark was going into the army tomorrow, and then almost certainly to Korea, and she might never see him again.

Her father and Mark's parents had forbidden them to marry, but they couldn't forbid her and Mark to love. Mark was gorgeous, big and tall, hazel eyes, brown hair. She had been in love with him since the first time he looked at her at Tucson High School five years ago.

He switched the light off. A sixty-watt bug bulb outside the door cast pallid illumination into the room, and the room brightened frequently with the lights of the trucks and cars whizzing by on Highway 87, just ten yards away.

He walked to her, leaned over, and they kissed. Her breath came hot and fast. He unbuttoned her cotton blouse and she held her arms up and he took it off. He fumbled with the hooks of her brassiere, and she helped him unhook it and slid it off her arms. Her nipples were puckered, and he took one softly in his mouth, and then the other. She lay back on the bed, and he unbuttoned and unzipped her shorts and pulled them off with her panties. He unbuttoned his Levi's, pushed them down along with his underwear, and stepped out of them. He pulled off his polo shirt.

She touched him timidly with tremulous fingers.

"Are you sure?" he whispered.

"Yes," she whispered.

He lay beside her and held her. She had no idea what to do, but she knew that he did. He had been to the whorehouses several times in Nogales, Mexico, just sixty-five miles south of Tucson. It was a rite of passage for high school and college boys in Tucson.

He spread her legs and touched her gently, and she forgot everything and everyone but him.

Mark, Mark, Mark, I love you. Why can't we be like this forever? Oh, God, I love you so.

She cried in the car all the way back to Tucson, and when Mark drove away from the house on Speedway Boulevard and Fourth Avenue, it took all the strength she had just to open the door and walk inside and up the stairs to her bedroom.

Joshua lay sleeping restlessly next to Barbara in the master bedroom. He and Hanna had had yet another argument earlier, late in the afternoon, and this time she had sworn that if Mark were killed in Korea, she would move away from Tucson and never see her family again. Her father had stolen from her the only happiness she would ever have.

He thought he had years ago conquered the nightmares about the war that used to recur regularly, ruining his sleep and wrenching him awake. But suddenly they were back, even cruelly invading his waking thoughts at the party a few days ago. And now, the dybbuks tore at his soul and choked him in his sleep as the familiar, frightful specters came alive again.

He jerked awake as he heard Hanna's bedroom door slam shut. Tears spilled out of his eyes onto the mattress. His body and the sheet under him were drenched with sweat, but he was trembling with chills.

Barbara rolled to him, wrapped her arms tightly around him, and rocked him softly like a baby.

Joshua and Adam stood at the end of the railway platform. Joshua's deep blue eyes were sunken and melancholy, his tanned, strong-boned face lined with pain. He combed his fingers through his thick brown hair, straight back from the widow's peak. It was graying at the temples, betraying his forty-one years.

At six feet three inches, he was taller than David Goldberg by four or five inches, but their weight was the same, about two hundred pounds. Unlike Joshua, David wore twenty-five pounds of it bulging from his belly.

Barbara stood next to her husband. She was almost his height in her high heels, and very shapely, even though she was wearing a full rust-colored silk skirt and a loose beige silk sleeveless blouse. Her face had the chiseled features of the photographic model she had once been, broad high cheekbones and wide-set brown eyes. Her light brown hair was pulled back in a simple, loose ponytail, glinting with red highlights in the early morning sun. She had worn no eye makeup so that the tears would not stream in colored rivulets down her cheeks.

Magdalena had come, too. She had asked the principal of Dunbar School, Morgan Maxwell, if she could have just an hour off in the mid-afternoon, and he had insisted that she take the entire afternoon. A big sister could not abandon her little sister at a time like this, he had said. His own son had left for Korea just a month ago, and he well knew the deep anguish of such a parting. Magdalena stood next to Barbara, holding her hand.

Although Judy Goldberg was dressed in the best that money could buy from her husband's department store, the biggest and finest in Tucson, she looked matronly next to Barbara, and even in her grief she edged slightly away from Barbara to avoid the comparison. Judy sniffled into a handkerchief and patted her eyes softly with it.

All of them were silent, absorbed in their own thoughts.

Hanna and Mark were sitting at a table by the window of the restaurant inside the terminal, fifteen feet from their families directly outside. The train had arrived a half hour ago, and a brakeman was walking down the track checking the air hoses. They could see his disembodied head and shoulders bob above the platform, and they watched him silently. Hanna had sworn to herself that she would not cry, that she would smile at Mark as he left so that her smile would be what he remembered last, and not her teary, swollen eyes.

There was nothing else she could say to Mark, nothing more she could do for him. Just watch him leave and pray every day and every night that he would come back to her the same man who had left.

"Let's go to the Dixie," Joshua said quietly to Barbara. "I don't want her just going home and lying in bed in her room, crying."

Barbara nodded.

The Dixie Diner was way out on Speedway Boulevard, almost to where the paving ended at Alvernon. It was about five miles from the Southern Pacific Railroad Station, but it was the only place in Tucson that served fried shrimp. Hanna and Adam loved the shrimp, and although Joshua didn't eat it, because it was unkosher, he had been reluctant to deny his children an occasional treat.

Tucson wasn't Brooklyn, where you could go to any of a hundred delicatessens and eat your fill of dozens of delicacies. Here there was only one delicatessen, and it only had lox and salami. Otherwise, when you went out to eat at the small cafés and diners, your choices were Mexican food everywhere, open-faced roast beef sandwiches at Suzette's, fried chicken at the Lucky Wishbone, hamburgers at Johnnies, or pizza at La Cucina.

Not that Joshua kept kosher any longer. The army had cured that. And the only thing that kosher meant in Tucson was something strange that some people did a long way from here. But he still didn't eat certain foods like pork and shellfish. Force of habit.

The Dixie was a small, white stuccoed box with ten chipped brown Formica tables surrounded by aluminum pipe dinette chairs with peeling plastic padded seats. Another big treat for Hanna and Adam was that on every table there was a little gizmo about the size of a toaster that you put a nickel into and pushed a selector, and the song you chose would come out of two wooden speakers hung high in the corners of the west wall.

Joshua put a nickel in the slot, and Adam said, "Rock Around the Clock."

"I don't care," Hanna mumbled.

Joshua pressed the button, and the song began to play.

"This table is too small for all of us," Joshua said.

He looked across the table at Barbara and asked her with his eyes to help Hanna.

"Come on," Barbara said. "Let's leave these guys and have some girl talk."

Magdalena and Hanna followed her to another table across the room and sat down. The waitress came and took their orders, and Hanna wanted only a Coke.

"A girl's got to eat," Barbara said. "Otherwise you'll be all bony, and nobody'll even look your way." She chuckled.

"Good," Hanna said. "I don't want anyone looking my way."

"He'll be all right," Magdalena said and held Hanna's hand across the tabletop. "Just keep believing that and praying for him."

"Is that what you do for Chuy?"

"Yes. That's all I can do."

Hanna's cheeks wrinkled, and she began to cry. She took a handkerchief out of her purse and buried her face in it. Magdalena and Barbara exchanged sad looks.

"I saw a letter from Chuy on the kitchen table," Barbara said quietly.

Magdalena nodded. She took a letter out of the pocket of her skirt and pushed it across the table to Barbara.

" 'Dear Magdalena,' " Barbara read silently.

"After MacArthur got bounced, my unit got sent to Seoul to keep the capital from being recaptured by the Chinese, and we go out on patrols in the city and get shot at by snipers every day. We can't even tell where the shots are coming from. I've lost seventeen men from my company just in the last two weeks. It's as bad as it was in the field, only here you can't even figure out where the enemy is. They're everywhere."

She glanced up at Magdalena, and their eyes met, and Barbara swallowed and returned to the letter.

"The only thing that keeps me alive and walking out of my tent every morning is you. I love you so much I can't die."

Barbara rubbed her eyes and breathed deeply.

"We got a new captain eight days ago. He's a redneck prick from Texas, thinks all Indians are subhuman. He demoted me (not in rank, just in duties) from company exec to platoon leader for third platoon. That's the unit that keeps getting point duty when we go on sniper-clearing patrol into the downtown. He got shot in the face yesterday, right in the middle of his nose. Took the whole back of his head off. I think the shot came from one of my own guys, black guy from Alabama named Washburn, everybody calls 'Stilts' because he's real skinny and must be six foot six, and the captain had been riding him for days, stuck him with every shit detail the marines have to offer. But it was a pretty big firefight with bullets coming from everywhere, so there won't be any formal inquiry, and nobody's going to miss the prick. I should have done it a week ago.

"Should I write you letters like this? No, I know I

shouldn't. I don't want to scare you. But what else should I write about? The sky is blue, the weather's a bit nippy, there's snow coming, they say, but I don't mind that. I never minded the snow. It always snowed up on the Baboquivaris, but our winter pastures were down at the ranch in San Miguel, so we'd just go up the mountain to throw snowballs at each other and then go right back to the ranch where it was warm. Solomon liked the snow better than I did. I remember once about eight or nine years ago, he was on Iwo Jima, they'd just taken it, he was the flamethrower in his company, and I got a letter from him saying he thought he'd like it a lot better living in one of the caves up on the mountain and throwing snowballs at hawks.

"So anyway, I guess I'd like about anything better than this. But I'll live. That I promise you. I just sit in my tent at night and think and talk about you. That's what we all do. Just talk about our wives and girlfriends. It's what keeps us going. I think about you, about the first time we went walking out behind the Mission and sat down on that smooth rock where Barbara and Joshua used to go and screw and thought nobody knew about it (don't let them read this letter!) . . ."

She looked up at Magdalena with a smile, and Magdalena bit her lower lip to keep from laughing, so that Hanna wouldn't think they were making fun of her.

". . . and I think about unbuttoning your blouse and your Levi's and you unbuttoning mine and then being inside each other so deep that the whole rest of the world disintegrates and nothing else even exists. And that's all that matters. Believe me, it's all that matters. You and my son, you and our sons and daughters. And so I will be back. Because God can't let anything happen to me. I even go to mass on Sunday mornings. I use the rosary you gave me when I left. I didn't even want it back then, but I kept it because it was what you gave me. Now it is around my neck, and it is keeping me alive.

"I love you. Don't worry about me."

There were tears in Barbara's eyes, and she glanced at Hanna to make sure she wasn't looking. She handed the letter back to Magdalena and wiped her eyes roughly with her hands.

The waitress brought the plastic baskets of shrimp and french fries and the three Cokes. Magdalena handed Hanna one of her shrimps.

Hanna nibbled on it absently.

"I want you to go to shul with your father and me this *shabbes*," Barbara said.

"Why?" Hanna had stopped crying. Her eyes were bloodshot and the rims were bright pink.

"Because it'll help."

"How's going to synagogue going to help?"

"It'll make you feel like you're helping Mark."

"Praying won't help him. It didn't help my dad."

"How do you know?"

"Because he came back real hurt." She glanced at her father, then lowered her voice, although he was too far away to hear. "Adam and me and Grandpa and Grandma used to pray every night for him. And then when he came back, he was still so hurt that we couldn't even go see him for six months."

"Maybe he wouldn't have even come back at all without your prayers."

Hanna shook her head, her face long and somber. "What if Mark comes back in a wheelchair, so that he can't walk or, or"—her voice became a hoarse whisper—"or have children? What will I do then?"

"I don't know," Barbara said.

"Or Chuy?" Hanna asked, tears coming again to her eyes, turning to Magdalena.

Magdalena's lips trembled. "We have a son," she murmured, "maybe that would make it better." She shook her head. "I don't know."

"That's all Mark and I wanted," Hanna said, "to make sure we'd always have each other." She began crying again, quietly, and she pressed the handkerchief to her eyes.

Barbara put her arm around Hanna's shoulders. "You put faith in God," she whispered, "and you pray for the safety of the people you love. And you hope that your prayers will be answered, because there's nothing else you can do, and at least it keeps you from feeling helpless and hopeless."

Magdalena nodded and crossed herself.

Chapter Five

Solomon Leyva didn't have his brother Chuy's good looks. He had acne scars common among the Papagos and a meaty, heavy-jowled face. He was two years older than Chuy and had also been in the marines in World War Two. But he had won no medals, achieved no heroism, and after the war he had drifted aimlessly in the white man's world for a couple of years until he finally returned to the Leyva family ranch in San Miguel on the Big Reservation, about seventy miles from Tucson. A year later he had helped the BIA rid the Reservation of a heroin smuggling ring, and Edgar Hendly had offered him a job working with Chuy as assistant BIA police chief. But Solomon had had his fill of the big city and the way most white people treated him, so he had gone back to the isolated ranch to run cattle, as he had done for ten years as a boy.

Now with Chuy in Korea, however, Edgar had talked him into coming to live at San Xavier and becoming acting police chief. There were actually three Papago Reservations in southern and central Arizona. The Big Res, as everyone called it, started about thirty miles west of Tucson and went for a hundred miles toward California and eighty miles all the way to the Mexican border. The second largest was the Gila River Reservation sixty miles north of Tucson. The smallest was San Xavier del Bac. It was only seventy-one thousand acres, six miles south of Tucson, but it was the best known. Its fame lay in the fact that in the middle of the village of Bac, which the Indians called *Wahk,* there was the best preserved of the two dozen Spanish colonial Catholic missions that (tradition had it) had been built by Father Francisco Kino and his Jesuit followers on their trek through Sonora and Arizona to convert the pagan Indians to the one true faith about two hundred fifty years ago.

Solomon's job was mostly boring and petty, arresting drunk drivers or stopping fistfights or domestic arguments. Sometimes he was called upon by FBI Special Agent Roy Collins, Tucson's only resident agent, to accompany him to Sells, the capital of the three Papago reservations, to deal with Henry Enos, the chief of police there. Henry always forgot his English and lapsed into Papago when Roy was around. The FBI had jurisdiction over all murders on the Indian reservations, and there had been two at San Xavier since Solomon had become acting chief. They had brought Solomon into close contact and cooperation with Collins, and the two men had become friends.

"You play a hell of a lot better than Chuy," Joshua said.

They were sitting in Solomon's office in the BIA, a cubbyhole adjoining Joshua's only slightly larger cubbyhole, and Joshua was pondering the checkerboard on the army surplus khaki metal desk between them. It was their usual Monday afternoon match.

"He only got the looks," Solomon said. "I got the brains."

"Damn. You got me one way or the other." Joshua sat back in his chair. "Best two out of three?"

"Don't be a sore loser, Joshua. You already owe me two hundred thousand dollars and a quart of Cuervo Gold from last week. You ain't got enough dough to—"

They were startled by the sound of running footsteps in the hall. A Papago woman rushed breathlessly into Solomon's office. She appeared to Joshua to be in her early twenties, very pretty, lissome, wearing a starched white nurse's uniform. Her large black eyes were frantic. She blurted something in Papago at Solomon. He appeared shocked. Her nose was running and her face was splotchy from weeping. He stood up quickly, came around the desk, and stood in front of her, speaking soothingly in Papago, trying to calm her.

Finally, he put both hands on her shoulders and shook her gently. She looked at him and gasped and slowly became composed. Her voice was low and weak now, and Solomon listened intently. After a minute he said something to her, she nodded, and he pointed to his chair behind the desk. She walked shakily to it and slumped down.

"This is Elena Moraga, Julio's wife," Solomon said. "She just got home from work a few minutes ago. She works from six in the morning 'til three in the afternoon as a nurse at Saint Mary's Hospital." He hesitated. "Julio is dead."

Joshua jerked up off the chair, staring incredulously at Solomon.

Solomon nodded. "She says that there's a woman with him, too. All covered with blood."

Joshua's mouth fell open. He shook his head slowly, still not fully comprehending. "With Julio? Does she know the woman?"

Solomon shook his head. "I've got to call Roy," he said.

He walked to his desk and dialed the FBI office downtown. He spoke for a moment and hung up.

"He'll meet us there. Let's go."

They went out to Solomon's BIA pickup, a battered five-year-old blue Ford with the word POLICE crudely painted in white on both doors. They drove up to Valencia, turned right to the Nogales Highway, right again to Mission Loop, and then bounced along the dusty, rutted dirt road south into the heart of the Reservation. There was almost nothing here for miles but scrub brush of creosote and desert broom and brittlebush.

Suddenly they were riding next to a mesquite wood-fenced pasture of lush, green alfalfa, with at least a hundred grazing guernsey cows. Beyond the pasture was a small pond surrounded by cottonwood trees, and among the trees were several adobe houses, little boxes with one-foot-square windows covered with cardboard and doorways with blankets for doors. Fifty yards from these small houses was a slightly larger one with real windows and a door. Five Indians stood stiffly outside it.

"That's Julio's place," Solomon said. He drove

toward it on the rutted path and parked beside Julio Moraga's black Chevy pickup truck.

The Indians remained stark still and silent, their arms folded on their chests. Solomon walked up to the old man and woman, and they spoke together quietly in Papago. Then he walked into the house followed by Joshua.

They were assailed by the cloying stink. It didn't take long in this heat for bodies to begin to decompose, and the stench was thick in the small house. Julio was sitting nude in an oak rocking chair in the middle of the living room. He had a bloated erection, a common by-product of rigor mortis. His eyes were open, staring sightlessly ahead. Blood had poured from his nose and mouth and dried on his chest and stomach and thighs. On the lamp table next to the rocker was a syringe and a thimble-sized pile of white powder on a piece of butcher paper. A candle had burned itself out in a tiny holder. Beside it was a teaspoon with congealed brown goo in the bowl.

The woman was on the small sofa opposite the rocking chair. Her eyes, too, were open and staring, and she had streams of dried, black blood from both nostrils and from the sides of her mouth. It had spilled down her neck and chest and soaked her lace brassiere, which was all that she was wearing. She might have been pretty once, soft brown hair and eyes, a voluptuous figure, perhaps twenty-eight or thirty years old. But her face was cruelly distorted in death.

Joshua stood between her and Julio, shaking his head. "I don't believe this," he murmured. "I just don't believe it.'

Solomon nodded. "Julio never used. We got some people around here who use, but not Julio."

"You know who she is?" Joshua asked.

Solomon shook his head. "White woman out here in the middle of the Res? And in Julio's house? I don't get it."

"Girlfriend?"

"No way. Julio was happily married. Just got married last year. You saw what his wife looks like."

Joshua nodded.

Solomon shook his head. "This is bullshit."

Roy Collins walked into the living room. "Touch anything?" he asked.

Both Solomon and Joshua shook their heads.

"Good," said Roy. He took a small jar of Mentholatum out of his baggy tan cotton suit coat and daubed a little of it under his nose. He offered the jar to Joshua. Joshua did the same. He handed the jar to Solomon, but Solomon shook his head.

"The smell of that stuff isn't any better than the bodies," he said.

"Looks like they had a little party that got out of hand," Roy said.

"I don't think so," Joshua said.

Roy studied him. "Why?"

"Julio was a decent guy, happily married. He wouldn't be here with her like that."

Roy wrinkled his brow and snorted. "Come on, it's the oldest story on earth. Happily married boy meets girl."

"It didn't happen that way," Solomon said angrily, his jaw set.

Roy shook his head in frustration. "So what is it?"

"Maybe when we find out who she is, we'll know," Joshua said.

Roy walked up to her, bent forward, and scrutinized her closely. "I think I know who she is," he said. "She looks like Anne Marie Hauser, an investigator from the Subversive Activities Control Board."

Joshua stared at him.

Roy straightened up and nodded. "Yeah, I'm pretty sure. She came to see me when she first came to town, about five or six months ago. She was the one who was sent out to investigate Academics Against War. She had been a staffer with the House Committee on Un-American Activities, and when that went out of business, she became an investigator for the Subversives Board. Word in the Bureau was she had a real close *friendship* with Senator McCarthy." He looked knowingly at Joshua. "Her report put Academics on the attorney general's list. She was going places."

"So what the hell is this Hauser woman doing here OD'd on heroin with the guy she tagged as a subversive?" Solomon looked around at Roy and Joshua.

Roy shrugged. "Maybe that's not how she died."

"Blood from the nose and mouth, a bruise and blood on the inside of her elbow." Solomon walked close to her and pointed.

"Let's get them over to Stan Wolfe and see," Roy said.

The Pima County coroner's office was in the county office building on the first floor of the north wing. The old building was shaped like a huge pink stuccoed two-story Mexican villa with a multicolor-tiled cupola in the middle. Solomon backed the truck up to the metal door. Joshua walked inside and came out a moment later with Dr. Stanley Wolfe. He was short and chubby with a pink baby face and brown hair. His brown eyes were magnified by round steel-rimmed glasses.

Roy Collins parked beside the pickup in his gray sedan. It had part of a decal of the great seal of the United States peeling off the driver's door.

"I guess this isn't a social call," Stan said.

"Who'd make a social call on a coroner?" said Joshua. "You could end up with your dick in a jar of formaldehyde."

They all laughed. A morgue attendant wheeled a gurney to the back of the pickup, and Solomon helped him put one of the bodies on it. It was in a military rubberized canvas body bag. The attendant wheeled it inside, and Solomon followed. They came out a moment later and took the second body bag inside.

The autopsy room had shiny white-painted walls and a sloping cement floor to a drain in the middle, over which a stainless-steel table was set. Various hoses on reels hung from the ceiling above the table, surrounding a hot white high-intensity lamp.

Stan Wolfe examined the body of Julio Moraga first. After peering at it closely for minutes with a magnifying glass, he took a scalpel off the small instrument table and made a long incision from the inside of the elbow to the inner wrist.

Roy watched impassively. Joshua swallowed and looked away. Solomon left the room.

The coroner extracted a syringe full of blood from the blood vessel. Then he took a larger scalpel, cut the abdomen wide open with a single sweep, and cut off a piece of the liver with a dissecting scissors.

"Get him off and bring the other one," he said to the attendant. The attendant zipped up the body bag, and he and Roy laid it on the stretcher. The attendant wheeled it out of the room. Stan Wolfe pulled off the rubber gloves, dropped them in a wastebasket, and washed his hands and forearms in the sink in the corner.

"My guess is he died of a heroin overdose," Stan said, still scrubbing. "I'll know for sure when I do the tox screen on the blood and get some slides of the liver. It'll take a couple of hours. The point of insertion was the radial artery just below the antecubital fossa." He pointed to the inside of his elbow. "Damn odd place for a hype to stick the needle. I've never seen that before."

"Solomon says he wasn't a user," Joshua said.

"Well, he may be right. I couldn't find any other pinprick sites or tracks. This might well have been his first time. And he sure as hell didn't know what he was doing. It would've had to hurt pretty bad sticking that needle into the radial artery. Anyone who knew what he was doing would use the ulnar."

"Maybe he didn't do it himself," Joshua said.

Roy shrugged. "That's also possible. There's ecchymosis on his anterior biceps and obvious extravasation under the skin on the left temple. Could have been someone punched him, held him by the arms. I can't be sure."

The attendant returned with the smaller body bag. He and Roy lifted it onto the table, and Stan unzipped it and laid the flaps back. He once again took the magnifying glass and examined her closely. He opened her blood-clogged nostrils with forceps and examined the insides. Then he took a vaginal smear with a long cotton swab and placed it in a test tube. He probed between her legs and examined her intently through the magnifying glass.

"Forced sexual intercourse, incomplete penetration. There's extensive bruising around the labia majora caused by inter vivos bleeding. The man raped her while she was alive, and he ejaculated, but most of the discharge is around the vulva and the outer lips."

He took a clean scalpel and incised the inside of her forearm from wrist to elbow. He dissected the ulnar artery, extracted an ampule of blood, and made scrapings for a slide.

"She didn't die from the heroin," he said, straightening up. He took off the rubber gloves and dropped them in the basket. "The heroin isn't broken down and didn't circulate farther from the injection site than the pressure of the injection itself would distribute it. This means that there was no blood pressure at the time of injection. In other words, she was already dead."

Joshua nodded. "They were both murdered."

Stan shrugged. "Well, gents, I'm not a soothsayer or a magician, and I can't make that determination for a certainty. But it sure as hell looks that way."

"Maybe she struggled with Moraga, bruised his

arms and the side of his head, and then he raped her," Roy said.

"Certainly a possibility," Stan said.

Joshua shook his head. "He didn't rape her."

"It could have happened," said Roy.

"Sure, it *could have,* but it didn't. I knew Julio pretty well."

The coroner shrugged. "Well, I'll try to type the semen in her against Moraga's semen. I'll have some more results for you later this afternoon."

Roy and Joshua left. Solomon was waiting in the pickup truck.

"They were both murdered," Joshua said to Roy, standing by his car door.

"Why the hell would anyone murder them? It makes no sense."

"Why would he murder her? She'd already done the worst she could to him. He knew that killing her wouldn't resolve that."

"It would keep her from testifying."

Joshua shook his head. "She's just an investigator. In this case, most of her testimony would have been inadmissible hearsay."

"Maybe, but did Julio know that?"

Joshua shrugged. "I think it's something else. I think some crazy people are trying to expand a little flap over a cowtown university group of pacifist professors into a bombshell national news story."

"Who the hell would do that?" Roy looked at him oddly.

Joshua shook his head. "I don't know."

"Don't start getting paranoid."

"Paranoid? Shit! Two bodies aren't paranoia."

Roy frowned and nodded. "Okay, hold your horses. Let's wait to hear what Stan says before you get carried away."

"I just heard from Dr. Wolfe," Roy Collins said.

It was almost nine o'clock. Joshua straightened up in his chair at his desk at home. He had been studying the McCarran Act for over two hours by the meager light of the banker's lamp. He rubbed his burning eyes. The translucent green shade of the lamp painted his face eerily.

"Yes?" he said into the telephone receiver.

"The rapist is a non-secretor. Moraga is a secretor."

Joshua nodded, relieved. "Then Moraga couldn't have raped her. Anything else?"

"Julio died from the heroin overdose, but the liver tests showed that he wasn't a regular user. The woman died of a brain hemorrhage. Someone shoved a long needle up her right nostril and pierced her brain."

"My God," Joshua breathed.

"She had a point two one blood alcohol, so she was pretty far drunk. It must have happened very fast, that's why there aren't any signs of defensive wounds around her head and neck. She didn't have time to fight back. He must have got her drunk, raped her, and put her lights out."

"Now what?" Joshua said.

"I went back to the Res and checked out Julio's truck. There's blood all over the right side of the seat. I don't think they were killed in the house. I think they were brought there in the truck after they were killed. There are blood spots all over the porch in front of the door."

"That means at least two people, one to drive Julio's truck, the second one in another vehicle."

"Right," Roy said.

"Did you talk to Julio's family? He's got about ten brothers and sisters who all live in those shacks by the watering pond."

"Solomon did. None of them saw or heard anything. It doesn't get light until about seven in the morning, and they don't get up until it's light. So it had to happen before seven."

"Well, what's next?"

"I'll check out where she was living," Roy said. "I think she had a room at the Cattlemen's Hotel. Maybe I'll get a lead there."

"Okay. Would you keep me informed?"

"Sure."

Chapter Six

The next morning Joshua parked in the small lot behind the Valley National Bank. The lot was next to the federal building and was almost empty at a quarter to eight in the morning. Mischa Livinsky hadn't arrived yet. Joshua settled back in the seat, turned the car radio on, and hoped that a few minutes of music wouldn't burn out the battery.

A moment later an old Model T Ford truck parked on Broadway Boulevard across from the entrance to the federal building. The bed of the pickup was filled with young men and women, late teens to early twenties. They jumped down from the bed, and several of them picked up signs from the floor of the bed, crudely painted squares of cardboard held up by long flat sticks. Joshua glimpsed a couple of them idly. One read, FREE LIVINSKY, FREE MORAGA, FREE SPEECH. The other had red letters on a white background, KEEP MCCARTHY OUT OF TUCSON.

Poor Julio, Joshua thought, too bad he can't see this.

Two cars parked along Broadway behind the pickup, and a dozen more young adults joined those from the Model T. A Dodge stake truck parked in the Valley National Bank lot thirty feet from Joshua's car. It looked as though it had just been recruited from a muddy vegetable field in the town of Marana, rotting lettuce leaves caught in the cross joints of its wooden staves. At least twenty more young men and women got out of the bed, and several placards were handed out to them. Hanna Rabb took a sign that read KOREA IS WRONG, BRING OUR BOYS HOME.

Joshua gasped and jerked straight up in the car seat. He shook his head slowly as he watched his daughter.

"Oh, my God," he whispered.

There were forty or more kids, some of whom he recognized, gathered on the sidewalk by the federal building. Hanna's roommate from Maricopa dormitory was with her. Some other girls were there whom Hanna had brought home from time to time. But most of them Joshua hadn't seen before, just average-looking, clean-cut kids probably from the University of Arizona.

Mischa Livinsky drove into the bank parking lot and parked next to Joshua. He got out of the car, looked toward the group of students, and waved. A chant now arose from the group: "Free Livinsky, free Moraga, free speech."

Joshua walked over to Livinsky. "Did you organize this?" he asked, trying to mask his shock and anger.

"No, but my students obviously did."

"Why did you let them? It's illegal to picket a courthouse."

"Illegal?"

"Yes, damn it! It's a provision of the McCarran Act. I thought you read it."

"I read it, Mr. Rabb." Livinsky was calm, almost

aloof. "That provision is as unconstitutional as the rest."

"It's very sage of you to make that pronouncement, Professor Livinsky," Joshua said hotly. "But this isn't a college classroom and you're not the judge or the U.S. marshal. They just may think this kind of demonstration injures the administration of the court and arrest these kids."

Livinsky swallowed, and his look of certainty melted. "I didn't ask them to do this, Mr. Rabb. But some of my students take the words of the United States Constitution to heart. They think that free speech is precisely that."

Joshua gritted his teeth and breathed deeply to suppress his anger. "This isn't the way I practice law. I practice it inside the courtroom with respect toward the judge and without any picketers chanting outside his chambers window. One of whom happens to be my daughter."

The professor suddenly appeared apologetic. He looked at the demonstrators, now milling noisily about in the street and halting traffic on Broadway.

"Hanna was in my Comparative Political Systems class last semester," he said. "A lovely and bright girl, Mr. Rabb. You must be very proud."

"Right now I'm not proud," Joshua muttered. He looked at his pocket watch. "It's eight o'clock. Better get up to the grand jury room. It's on the second floor. I'll be up in a minute. I'm going to try to get Hanna and her roommate to go back to the dorm."

"Where's Julio?" Livinsky asked.

Joshua looked hard at him. "You didn't hear?"

"Hear what?"

"It was on the radio this morning."

"What?"

Joshua swallowed. "He was murdered last night."

Livinsky's face screwed up in shock. "Murdered?"

Joshua nodded. "Somebody forced an overdose of heroin into his arm." He paused. "He was with a woman, also murdered. Anne Marie Hauser."

Livinsky's eyes narrowed and he looked oddly at Joshua. *"Du machts mi spass, neh?* [You're kidding me, right?]"

Joshua shook his head. There was no mirth in his face. *"Emmiss."*

A veil of total bewilderment clouded Livinsky's eyes. "Hauser?" he said weakly. "The investigator for the Subversives Board?"

Joshua nodded.

"Vay iz mir," the professor gasped. *"Vay iz mir."* He looked at Joshua with grave fear beginning to show in his face. *"Doss iz a catastrophe."*

He walked slowly down the sidewalk to the entrance of the federal building at the corner of Scott Street. The demonstrators cheered and hoisted high their placards, and the chant increased in volume. The noise was worsened by the blaring of horns by angry motorists caught unwittingly in the demonstration and being made late for work by the traffic impasse at one of Tucson's busiest morning intersections.

Joshua caught Hanna's eye and gestured for her to come over to him. She glared at him defiantly and looked sharply away. Her placard got higher, and he thought that he could hear her voice above all of the others. He saw Assistant United States Attorney Tim Essert come out of his office door on the corner of Broadway and Scott Street, directly across from the federal building. Four men were with him.

Three of them appeared to bear the stamp of the eastern FBI types: gray suits, starched white shirts, black or dark blue ties, "high and tight" crew cuts or butch haircuts, and black wing-tip shoes. They looked like military officers in civvies, one of them in his early fifties, gray and lean, the other two twenty years younger.

The fourth man was Roy Collins. He looked decidedly different from the other three. Almost five years being stationed in Tucson, ten years prior to that stationed in El Paso, Texas, had sanded off the regimented conformity of the FBI Academy in Virginia. He was a bit stout and shorter than the others, with graying, thinning blond hair worn slightly shaggy over his ears, a baggy off-white seersucker suit, a light yellow cotton shirt, and a bolo tie cinched up with a silver coyote with turquoise eyes, handmade by a Papago silversmith and given to him in gratitude by the chief of the Papago tribe, Francisco Romero, for the many favors he had done for the Indians.

Joshua watched Essert and his entourage enter the federal building. He walked down the sidewalk, glowered paternally at his daughter, who looked quickly away and steadfastly ignored him, and entered the federal building. He climbed the stairs to the second floor, and his footsteps echoed down the murkily lit hallway toward the grand jury room around the corner from Judge Buchanan's chambers.

Livinsky was sitting on the oak bench opposite the grand jury room. He appeared dazed. Roy Collins and the other three men stood silently down the hallway. Roy and Joshua nodded almost imperceptibly to each other. Joshua sat down on the bench next to his client.

Joshua was dressed in his usual "closing argument costume"—Hanna and Adam called it. Black wool suit and vest, white shirt and black wool tie, and a gold watch in his vest pocket linked by a long heavy gold chain to the top button of his vest. The watch had been his grandfather's, a jeweler in Kiev, given as a going-away present to Joshua's father when he left the Ukraine after the Cossack pogroms in 1905. Joshua's Hebrew name, *Jehoshua ben Aryeh-Lev,* was engraved in Hebrew script on the inside of the hunting case, along with the date in English, June 8, 1935, the day that Joshua had received his law degree from Columbia University.

Tim Essert came out of the grand jury room and closed the door behind him. He was about Joshua's age, thin and medium height, brown eyes and brown hair pomaded straight back on his head, and a deep tennis court tan. Usually Joshua would have described him as an attractive man, even handsome, but now his face was distorted and hateful.

"What the fuck are you doing here?"

"Representing my client," Joshua said blandly.

"The hell you are," Essert hissed. "You can't represent this Commie."

"Since when does the assistant U.S. attorney tell me who I can represent?"

"Since you're a goddamn government employee. The McCarran Act forbids a government employee from doing work for members of a Communist front organization."

"First of all it doesn't say that." Joshua stared acidly at him. "And second, your case against this man and his organization is total bullshit, and you know it. I don't have any respect for you because you're a dishonest scumbag, but stupid you're not."

The chant of the demonstrators became louder and more discernible. They must have come around the building to the rear, where the grand jury room was located. Two of the apparent FBI agents walked down the hallway and looked out the window.

"Assholes are right down there in the alley," one of them said.

Essert nodded and looked threateningly at Joshua. "You set up the demonstration?"

Joshua shook his head.

"They're all committing a felony. You know that."

Joshua tried to mask his face, to keep it unrevealing. He was suddenly fearful for Hanna and her friends. This vicious bastard could have them all arrested.

"They're simply exercising their freedom of speech," Professor Livinsky said in his thick Ukrainian accent.

Essert turned to him as though he had noticed him for the first time, and his lips curled into a sneer. His lips were twisted sourly, as though he had bitten into an unripe persimmon.

"Shut up!" Joshua snapped at Livinsky. "I'll do the talking with the U.S. attorney."

"Good advice from your lawyer," Essert said, fixing the professor with an accusatory stare. "Where were you last night, Commie?"

"Come on, knock off the crap!" said Roy Collins, stepping in front of the U.S. attorney. "If you're going ahead with the grand jury, get on with it. Otherwise, let's get the hell out of here."

Essert gaped at Collins and bristled with rage. "You stay here and keep an eye on your pinko pals," he said hoarsely. "Come on, you guys," he called out to the other three men. "Let's go back to my office for a few minutes." He walked abruptly down the hall, followed by the men.

Roy Collins stood in front of the oak bench and shook his head solemnly at Joshua. "Are you crazy, letting your daughter be in that demonstration?" His eyes were harsh. "If Essert knew who she was, he'd throw her into the marshal's holding cell and charge her with picketing and parading, just to fuck you."

Joshua nodded, very subdued. "I know. I didn't have anything to do with it. Neither of us did. It's just a bunch of university kids feeling their oats."

"Hell of a bad time for it," Collins said. "Why don't you both go down there and tell them to get the hell out of here. Go picket at the university or the dorms, but not in front of the federal courthouse."

"They have a constitutional right to picket here," Livinsky said.

"We're not talking *rights* here, Mr. Professor," Collins snarled. "We're talking a low-life U.S. attorney arresting a bunch of kids for a goddamn felony and throwing their asses in prison. Maybe in two or three years some appeals court says it was unconstitutional to arrest them, but the couple years they spend in the joint isn't going to be any less real or painful."

Livinsky swallowed and frowned and appeared chastened "Yes, yes, all right. There's no reason for them to be in jeopardy of that. I'll go down and ask them to continue their protest at the university, if they wish to do so at all."

Essert and the three men came out of the federal building, and there were no demonstrators on Broadway. One of the students at the mouth of the alley behind the courthouse noticed them and called out to the others.

All of the demonstrators ran around to the front of the courthouse brandishing their placards like chivalric banners and jeering at the government officers. The chant of "Free Livinsky, free Moraga, free speech" welled up even louder than before.

"Snot-nosed bastards," Essert muttered.

The four men entered the U.S. attorney's office and looked back at the federal building through the double glass doors. The demonstrators were on the Broadway Boulevard sidewalk again, milling around in small groups. Their placards were resting on their shoulders, and they appeared confused by the change in their expectations. The grand jury could not have convened and done anything substantial in the five minutes it took the prosecutor and the G-men to go in and out of the building.

Tim Essert and the men walked without explanation past the surprised secretary/receptionist into Essert's office.

"Let's go over it again," Essert said, sitting stiffly behind his desk, his hands so tightly gripped over the blotter that his knuckles were bloodless.

The three men looked around at each other. Holmes rolled his eyes at the other two agents.

"Come on, Holmes," Essert growled, "let's hear it again."

The crew-cut blond, blue-eyed FBI special agent pulled a spiral notebook out of his shirt pocket and flipped a few pages, then started reading: "The article was published in the *American Journal of Political Science* in September of last year. The *Journal* is known to cater to pinko professors."

"Known by whom?" Essert asked.

The agent looked up sharply, confused. "What?"

"I asked you who knows it caters to pinkos?"

Holmes looked around at the other two men, wrinkling his forehead quizzically, as though he were having to explain the obvious to a moron.

"The Bureau knows it. Senator McCarran knows it. Senator McCarthy knows it. We've had two other organizations listed as subversive with the attorney general by investigating supposedly scholarly articles written for the *Journal* by university professors who turned out to be the mouthpieces for Commie front groups."

Essert stared hard at him. "Tell me again what evidence you have that these two guys are subversives."

"Jesus H. Christ, Mr. Essert! We've been through this five times."

Essert leaned low over his desk and slammed his open hand down on it. "We'll go through it again. I don't just have to *indict* this guy, I've got to *convict* him. Shit, I can get the indictment like that." He snapped his fingers. "But it's not so easy to get him convicted. If I lose, my whole fucking career's down the shitter." He leaned back in his chair. "I figured this guy would never find a lawyer dumb enough to take his case. It's not exactly a career *maker*. But he comes up with this kike bastard Rabb. I should have known it."

Essert's nostrils flared and blanched. "Rabb's a piece of shit, but he's not dumb. I've had a lot of experience in court with him. Couple of murder cases, bunch of other crap with the fucking Papagos he works for." He glared at Holmes. "The guy hangs on like a bulldog with rabies. I want to hear hard evidence from you, not just a bunch of slogans."

The FBI agent bit his cheek. "We got Livinsky's membership list in code. We got the notes made by him on some of the meetings, also in code. We got his background, card-carrying member of the Communist party. What the fuck more do you need, a signed confession?"

Essert shook his head, annoyed. "The code you Bureau geniuses came up with is Yiddish. I don't think Judge Buchanan's going to let that one fly. Livinsky's from Russia, a Jew, and he probably had to be a Commie just to get a university-level teaching job, especially in Moscow. Millions of Jews have left Russia because of antisemitism. There isn't much love lost there."

"Yeah, how about Trotsky?" Holmes's voice was victorious.

"He ended up in Mexico ten years ago with a pickax hanging out of his brain."

The other young man walked to the desk. He squinted at Essert with vicious eyes. "So what're you telling us?"

"I'm telling you I'm not going to indict until I'm sure I can convict. I'm not putting my ass in a sling for this one case."

The middle-aged man, who had been standing by the side window watching Livinsky talk to the demonstrators across the street, looked hard at Essert. "That's final?"

Essert nodded. "I need some hard evidence." The side of his mouth ticked, and he bit his lower lip to keep it still.

The middle-aged man left Essert's office. Agent Holmes remained in the chair, staring blandly at the assistant U.S. attorney. The other young agent shook his head and walked back to the window. He stared out at the demonstrators.

"You're taking on a world of hurt," Holmes muttered.

Mischa Livinsky stood outside the Broadway entrance to the federal building. Small groups of demonstrators were in front of him strung down the sidewalk toward the Valley National Bank parking lot.

"I appreciate enormously what every one of you is doing," he said. "But unfortunately I must ask you for your own good to leave."

His voice was not loud enough to carry to all of the

protestors. The ones nearest the parking lot walked up the sidewalk to hear.

"I am asking all of you to continue this demonstration in front of the administration building at the university."

A few weak refusals came from the students, but most of them just listened quietly as Professor Livinsky explained to them the provision of the McCarran that outlawed protest demonstrations at courthouses.

A celery-green Studebaker passed by the throng of students on the sidewalk and turned into the bank parking lot. The students began walking slowly to the cars and trucks in which they had arrived.

The sound of an explosion was loud enough to jolt Joshua straight up from the oak bench on the second floor of the courthouse.

"What the hell is that?" Roy Collins said.

"Sounded like a grenade, maybe even a mortar," said Joshua. "The kids? You think they're shooting at the kids?"

Roy started running down the hallway to the west side stairway, the direction from which the sound had come. Joshua was close behind. They ran out of the building from a side door opening onto the Valley National Bank parking lot. A Studebaker's tires were in flames just a few feet away. Black smoke and licks of yellow flame billowed from them. Through the windshield they could see U.S. Marshal Ollie Friedkind slumped forward against the steering wheel. His face was twisted, his eyes rolled back lifeless and veiny white.

Gasoline spilled out of the car's ruptured gas tank and poured into the flames. The gas tank erupted with a roar, and the car was suddenly engulfed in an orange and red holocaust. There was nothing to do to help the marshal.

Two shots rang out from the direction of the corner of Broadway and Scott. Roy drew his .45 Colt automatic from his shoulder holster, and he and Joshua ran to the sidewalk. All of the demonstrators were gone, and Mischa Livinsky was the solitary figure in front of the main entrance to the building. He held his hands over his mouth, and his eyes were dilated in shock.

In front of him, in the middle of the intersection blocking traffic in all directions, was a Model T Ford pickup. Three of the demonstrators were crowded into the cab, and four more were huddled behind in the bed.

The two young FBI special agents who had been with Essert slowly approached the truck from both sides of the cab, their revolvers drawn and pointed toward the driver.

Holmes barked orders at the driver and the four demonstrators in the bed of the truck. "Out! Arms up! Get away from the truck! Lie facedown in the street!"

The students slowly emerged. Hanna climbed off the bed of the pickup, shuddering, her mouth and eyes gaping, and lay facedown on the asphalt with the others.

Joshua ran toward her. Holmes pulled an identification wallet from his inside coat pocket and held it toward Joshua like a stalwart Transylvanian peasant holding up a cross to halt Dracula.

"Stay back," he yelled at Joshua. "I'll arrest you for obstruction of justice!"

The other man, on the passenger side of the Model T, also pulled an ID wallet out of his shirt pocket, held it high overhead, and yelled, "Special Agent Herman Schlesinger, FBI, stay back!"

Joshua stopped fifteen feet away. He held up his hand in surrender.

Roy came up behind him, holstered his pistol, and put his hand on Joshua's shoulder to restrain him.

"All right, all right," Joshua murmured. He lowered his arms slowly. "What the hell happened?" he called out.

"One of these little sweethearts tossed a bomb at the marshal's car," Holmes said.

"Did you see who?" Roy asked.

Holmes shook his head. "Stand back, Mr. Rabb." He gestured with his gun hand for Joshua to go to the Broadway sidewalk.

"He's okay, he's okay," Roy called out. He pushed Joshua toward the sidewalk.

Joshua ran up to Mischa Livinsky. "You see it happen?" he asked urgently.

Livinsky shook his head. His face was waxen gray. "But I've seen it all happen before."

They could see Tim Essert looking out his office window across the street. They watched silently as the FBI agents, joined now by Roy Collins, ordered the five students off the ground, to lace their hands behind their heads, and to walk single file into the federal building. Hanna passed by her father, her mouth open, wheezing, her eyes wide with terror. She looked pleadingly at her father.

"You'll be okay," he said, trying to look and sound assured. His heart was flailing so hard against the inside of his chest wall that he felt sure it was audible.

Her eyes twitched for an instant, and then she was gone with the others into the building.

"Where are they taking them?" Livinsky asked, turning to Joshua.

"U.S. marshal's office, second floor at the west end. There's a holding cell up there."

"Then what?"

"If they're going to be charged with something, they'll have their initial appearance before the judge sometime today."

A bright red fire truck, its siren blaring, turned the corner of Stone Avenue and Broadway and swung into the parking lot. Several men in bulky black uniforms, wearing red helmets, pulled a hose off a winding wheel. One of them screwed the six-inch brass coupler into a hydrant at the street corner and turned the nut on top of it with a two-foot-long wrench. The gray hose wriggled like an uncoiling rattlesnake and became a rigid tube, held by firemen out of sight around the corner of the building by the Studebaker. Flames lapped up from the trail of gasoline that had streamed out to the sidewalk. The flames guttered and dipped in the breeze and quickly burned themselves out on the cement. A shroud of acrid black smoke drifted on the air. Joshua coughed violently, covered his mouth and nose with his hand, and walked into the federal building, followed by Livinsky.

Postal employees, who occupied most of the first floor, stood by the windows talking excitedly. Several of them warily studied the two men who had just entered the lobby through the main doors. One of them ushered the others back into the post office and turned the dead bolt on the inside of the single glass door. He stared out at Joshua and Mischa.

"I'd better go over to the marshal's office and find out what they've been arrested on," Joshua said.

"Is there still a grand jury?" Livinsky asked.

Joshua shrugged. "After I find out about these kids, I'll go across the street and talk to Essert. Better wait here."

Joshua climbed the stairs to the second floor. The marshal's holding cell was in the west end of the courthouse in a small room past the stairwell. He opened the door and walked in. U.S. Marshal Dominick Fratangeli was filling out some forms at a small metal desk. The five demonstrators were standing in a group behind the bars of the holding cell, holding a hushed conversation.

"You gotta get outta here, Mr. Rabb." The U.S. marshal said, standing up from his desk. He was shorter than Joshua but very stocky, and his green uniform shirt was pulled taut over his barrel chest and stomach, none of which was fat. He had been Ollie Friedkind's number-two man for the last three years, and Joshua had gotten to know him well. His black eyes were bloodshot from crying, and the wrinkled skin around his eyes was still wet with tears.

"I'm sorry about Ollie," Joshua said lamely.

Dom Fratangeli nodded. "Bad way to go. Burned

to death." He shook his head. "I just hadda call his wife Marian. She's goin' over to Tucson High to get the kids outta school." Tears began flowing again, and he rubbed his eyes roughly.

"Can we talk to you, Dad?" Hanna's voice was timid. She stood behind the bars like a hundred prisoners Joshua had seen in cells over the years, tortured, terrified.

"She's your daughter, Mr. Rabb?"

Joshua nodded.

"Shame on ya."

"Can I talk to them for a few minutes?"

Fratangeli shook his head. His face became hard.

"Can't do it. Tim Essert just called me. He's goin' over to the grand jury right now, gettin' an indictment for murder, conspiracy, and picketing. The arraignment is at ten-thirty. Ya wait till then."

Joshua nodded. He had no voice to speak, and this was no time to argue with the U.S. marshal.

"I'll see you all in court in an hour and a half," he called out.

He left the marshal's holding area and rejoined Mischa Livinsky in the first-floor lobby. The look on his face must have betrayed his shock and fear.

"Are you okay, Mr. Rabb?"

"They're holding them all for murder," he mumbled. "They're holding my daughter for murder."

"Come on over here, sit down," Livinsky said. He led him to a wooden bench next to the post office door. The man standing behind the door peering out at them backed away, as though some virus or palpable evil might penetrate the glass.

Joshua sat down heavily, his mind turbid with the events that had just occurred. He was unable to focus, suddenly overwhelmed by all of it, the dead, staring eyes of Ollie Friedkind, the terrified eyes of his daughter. For nineteen years—except the ones he had spent in war—he had wiped away her tears, pushed away her pain, succored her suffering, shielded her from the onslaughts of the world outside. But now, in the space of just one week, he could no longer shelter her in his wings, he could no longer take her pain upon himself and suffer it for her. He squinted his eyes tightly shut to press back the tears and began to shudder.

Livinsky left the bench and stood uneasily nearby. He turned away from Joshua Rabb, not wanting to embarrass him or to get too close inside his own pain and torment. Moments passed. Still he didn't turn around to see him, speak to him. He would wait until Rabb was ready.

Joshua got up from the bench and walked into the men's room. He washed his hand and wiped his face with cold water. The paper roller was empty. He walked into a stall and took some toilet paper, dried his hand, and patted dry his face.

He emerged from the men's room and strode through the lobby seeing nothing and no one. He swept through the swinging glass doors and waited impatiently at the street corner for the light to change. The secretary/receptionist in the U.S. attorney's office was new—Essert had never been able to keep anyone for more than five or six months—and she had the frigid demeanor and flat blue eyes of someone who might actually last with Essert. Her dirty blond hair was pulled back in a severe bun. She couldn't have been more than twenty-five, but she was succeeding admirably at appearing to be forty-five.

"Mr. Essert is in conference and cannot be disturbed."

"My daughter is under arrest in the marshal's cell, and she didn't do anything wrong. None of those kids did. I've got to see Essert."

"He is in conference, sir. If you'd care to wait." She pointed to the shiny blue Naugahyde sofa against the wall.

Joshua left the office, angry and frustrated. Suddenly his anger brought him a feeling of strength. The anger was good, mobilizing. He saw Mischa standing just inside the glass doors of the federal building.

Joshua walked quickly across the street and into the building.

"I've got to get over to the Pima County law library and look up some statutes," he said. "You better wait here. Essert's going to indict the demonstrators for murder, then there'll be an arraignment at ten-thirty. I don't know what he intends to do about you."

Livinsky nodded, grim-faced and silent.

The glass doors squeaked open behind them. They turned. Essert and the two young FBI agents, Holmes and Schlesinger, walked past them toward the stairway to the second floor.

"What are you planning to do with this man?" Joshua called out.

Essert and the agents stopped at the stairwell. "He can go for the time being," the assistant United States attorney said. His look was jaunty, even merry, his voice eager. "I've got a better use for the grand jury right now." He turned on his heels and ascended the stairs two at a time, followed closely by the agents.

Joshua left the building with Livinsky. They walked to the parking lot, past the smoldering wreck of the marshal's car, surrounded by firemen.

"Do you own a gun?" Joshua asked quietly.

Livinsky shook his head.

"Buy a gun," Joshua said.

The law library on the second floor of the Pima County Courthouse was empty as usual. Joshua took Title Eighteen of the United States Code off the shelf and sat down on a leather padded armchair at the nearest table. He thumbed the federal criminal code to the murder statute and studied it closely. He pulled a small leather three-ring binder out of his suit coat inner pocket, where he always carried it, and the Shaeffer snorkel pen, which had been a birthday gift from his father-in-law last year and had a habit of leaking now and then. But at least today the black ink wouldn't show on his black wool suit.

He studied the applicable language of the statute: "Murder is the unlawful killing of a human being with malice aforethought. Every murder . . . committed in the perpetration of . . . any arson, escape, murder, kidnapping, treason, espionage, sabotage . . . is murder in the first degree." The death penalty was automatic.

Joshua turned to the statues defining espionage and sabotage, and neither of them applied to the events of the morning. The treason statute made him gulp:

"Whoever, owing allegiance to the United States, adheres to their enemies, giving them aid and comfort within the United States, is guilty of treason and shall suffer death."

He turned to the statute prohibiting picketing and parading. It was defined in a manner that would precisely cover the acts of the demonstrators this morning: "Whoever, with the intent of interfering with, obstructing, or impeding the administration of justice, or with the intent of influencing any judge or court officer in the discharge of his duty, pickets or parades near a building housing a court of the United States, or resorts to any other demonstration in or near any such building, shall be fined not more than five thousand dollars or imprisoned not more than one year, or both."

The statute was almost certainly "overly broad," as constitutional lawyers would label it, meaning that it was an infringement on the First Amendment's guarantees of free speech and freedom of assembly. But that would most likely have to be decided by the court of appeals or the Supreme Court, long after Hanna and the others had spent their year in jail. Joshua shuddered at the thought. Again he forced away his fear and concentrated on the sentencing provision, which he hadn't fully thought through: ". . . imprisoned not more than one year."

He flipped quickly to the first statute in the criminal code, which classified offenses: "Notwithstanding any Act of Congress to the contrary: (1) Any offense punishable by death or imprisonment for a term exceeding one year is a felony. (2) Any other offense is a misdemeanor."

He started writing feverishly in his little notebook, flipping pages of the code.

He glanced at his watch. Ten-twenty. Got to get back over to federal court.

Judge Robert Buchanan's courtroom on the second floor of the federal building had an austere appearance that made it resemble an English courtroom from an Agatha Christie movie: black walnut paneling richly varnished, heavy walnut tables with four large mahogany and brown leather armchairs at each one, a carved walnut railing behind which the jurors sat in mahogany armchairs bolted to the floor, with padded seats of the same brown leather, a high bench of black walnut carved in a floral pattern behind which the judge sat in a tall oak-tanned leather wing chair that reclined and swiveled. The floor was squares of pale pink Mexican onyx veined in rust and brown, worn and dulled by the twenty years of lawyers and litigants and spectators and reporters who had trod upon it.

Now the courtroom was full. At least three hundred people had crowded, standing room only, into the spectator section. News of the Commie demonstration and the murder of the United States marshal had ricocheted through Tucson by radio and word of mouth and drawn the curious, the bored, the interested, and the angry. Reporters from radio, the morning and afternoon newspapers, as well as the television stations in Phoenix were sitting in the front row, their steno pads on the low black walnut railing before them. In the jury box sat four somber young women and one young man, little older than children, looking about furtively, mortified by their sudden fame, petrified by the grisly turn that their demonstration had taken. They were confused, amazed to be constricted in the handcuffs and belly chains and ankle chains that linked them together. They would awaken from this nightmare, they knew, and be back in their dorms or at home with their parents. Safe. Secure.

Joshua squeezed through the jostling spectators and entered the well of the courtroom through the latched wooden gate in the railing. The prosecutor hadn't arrived yet.

Joshua walked to the railing and addressed the five students, his daughter, three of her friends whom he had seen often, including her roommate Jan Diedrichs, and one young man he had never seen.

"I know you're all frightened," he said to them gently and low enough that the throng of spectators couldn't hear. "I'm going to represent all of you for the time being, at least for today's hearing."

Hanna appeared dazed, as though she didn't understand a word. Jan, next to her, stared at Joshua with tear-wet doe eyes.

"No matter what happens here, I don't want any of you to make any outburst." He paused. "I think that all of you will be charged with first-degree murder."

Two of the girls began to weep loudly. The young man appeared catatonic. Jan started gasping for breath like an asthmatic, and Hanna just stared in shock at her father, tears rolling down her cheeks.

"Being charged with a crime doesn't mean you're

guilty of it," Joshua continued. "I know that none of you had a part in the bombing of the marshal's car. But it's going to take some time to sort it all out. Just have faith in me for today. I'll do my best for you."

The rustling among the spectators grew louder and drew Joshua's attention. The ones blocking the aisle squeezed open a narrow corridor. Tim Essert and the two young FBI agents walked through the gate and sat down at the prosecution table.

Not more than a minute later, Mrs. Hawkes, Judge Buchanan's secretary and the official court reporter, came into the courtroom through the chambers door. She was followed by U.S. Marshal Fratangeli and Judge Buchanan. Fratangeli walked to a small table by the window and banged a gavel on a round block of wood. The courtroom became silent as Judge Buchanan sat down in his wing chair behind the elevated bench.

"United States versus Mergen, Rabb, Diedrichs, Rustin, and Rustin," the judge said, opening the manila folder he had carried into the courtroom.

Essert stood at his table. "Tim Essert for the United States, Your Honor."

Joshua stood up. "Joshua Rabb for the defendants, Your Honor. May the record reflect their presence in the jury box."

"Have you seen the indictment, Mr. Rabb?"

"No, Your Honor."

"Give him a copy, Mr. Essert."

Essert walked over to Joshua and handed him two sheets of paper.

"It's just been returned to me in the grand jury

room," Buchanan said. His face was drawn, and his soft blue eyes appeared world weary.

Joshua scanned the two pages. "Since none of the defendants have seen it, Your Honor, I can't waive the reading."

"Very well," Buchanan said. He put on a pair of glasses and began reading.

"Omitting the formal heading. The United States of America charges the defendants as follows:

"Count one. On June 19, 1951, the defendants did willfully picket and parade near a building housing a court of the United States, with the intent of obstructing the administration of justice and with the intent of influencing the judge, witnesses, jurors, or court officers, in violation of Title Eighteen United States Code.

"Count two. On June 19, 1951, the defendants, while owing allegiance to the United States, did knowingly conspire together to commit treason by adhering to their enemy, Mischa Livinsky, by giving him aid and comfort within the United States, in violation of Title Eighteen United States Code.

"Count three. On June 19, 1951, as a natural and foreseeable consequence of their crimes of picketing and parading and treason, the defendants did engage as co-conspirators and aiders and abettors in the crime of murder in the first degree of one Oliver Friedkind, United States marshal, by means of a firebomb, in violation of the felony-murder rule, Title Eighteen United States Code section four fifty-two, which reads in pertinent part: 'every murder committed in the perpetration of treason is murder in the first degree.'

"The punishment statutes provide that punishment for conviction of count one, picketing and parading, shall be not more than a five-thousand-dollar fine, not more than one year in prison, or both. The punishment for conviction of counts two and three is the death penalty.

"How do you plead to these charges?" The judge pursed his lips and fixed Joshua with a stern look.

"My clients plead not guilty, Your Honor."

"The record may reflect their pleas of not guilty. This is a capital offense and there is no bail as a matter of law. I will set—"

Joshua interrupted the judge. "May I be heard on a vitally important issue, Your Honor?"

Buck Buchanan took off his glasses slowly, frowned at Joshua, and sat back in his chair. "Is it relevant to *this* proceeding, Mr. Rabb?"

"It is, Your Honor."

"Very well."

"May it please the court, the defendants move to dismiss counts two and three of the indictment. Count two, treason, is predicated on giving aid and comfort to the enemies of the United States, namely demonstrating in support of Professor Livinsky. He is designated as the 'enemy.' However, he has not been proven by anyone to be the enemy of the United States. The same grand jurors who returned the true bill against these students in the jury box were actually here this morning for the purpose of taking testimony toward the indictment of Professors Livinsky and Moraga based on their failure to register as members of a Communist front organization. Moraga was murdered last night, and the grand jury never heard any evidence concerning Livinsky, and they returned no indictment against him. Even if they had, it would not be proof that the professor was an enemy of the United States until he had actually been *convicted* of the crimes of failing to register."

Essert jumped up at his table. "This is an improper time for the bringing of a motion directed toward the sufficiency of the indictment, Your Honor."

Judge Buchanan looked blandly at the assistant U.S. attorney. "That may technically be true, Timmy, but I'm about to hold these five young people in the Mount Lemmon Detention Center on nonbailable offenses, perhaps for several months. I think we ought to entertain Mr. Rabb's objections at this time. What is your response?"

"It's just pure nonsense, Your Honor," Essert sputtered. "The enemies of the U.S. are of course the Soviet Union and Red China. They oppose the United Nations police action in support of South Korea. Livinsky belonged to an organization at the University of Arizona called 'Academics Against War,' which has been designated a Communist front by the Subversive Control Board, and he helped to write an article published in a national magazine last September in which he opposed the participation of the U.S. in the police action, and he called the President and the administration dupes of Senator Joseph McCarthy, whom he describes as a 'fascistic Communist baiting demagogue.' The support of Livinsky by these five defendants, and the other thirty-five whom we didn't apprehend but soon will, is evidence of giving aid and comfort to the enemy of the United States."

Judge Buchanan looked slowly at the young man and four young women in the jury box. He turned back to Essert. "That is your evidence in support of *treason,* sir?"

Essert flicked his tongue at the dry corners of his mouth. "The government need not answer such an inquiry at this stage of the prosecution, Your Honor."

Judge Buchanan rubbed his chin and scratched his ear. "Count two is dismissed without prejudice. If you come up with some *real* evidence, Tim, bring it to the grand jury and we'll do this again."

An audible gasp broke out among the spectators. Marshal Fratangeli rapped his gavel several times. Quiet descended.

Joshua had remained standing. "The defendants move to dismiss count three, murder in the first degree. Since the charge of treason has been dismissed by the court, the felony-murder rule cannot apply to render the killing of Marshal Friedkind an act for which these defendants can be tried. Unless the United States attorney has any justiciable evidence that these defendants actually conspired together to kill the marshal, they cannot be charged with murder."

Essert's face was fire-engine red. "Judge, Ollie Friedkind's car was firebombed during the demonstration by these defendants and their compatriots. The murder occurred during the commission of the crime of picketing and parading and was a direct and foreseeable consequence of that crime. They have been properly charged."

"Mr. Rabb?" The judge turned to Joshua and raised his eyebrows.

Joshua took the notebook out of his pocket and studied the notes he had made earlier. "Your Honor, section four fifty-two says that first-degree felony murder is a murder during the perpetration of an arson, burglary, robbery, treason, sabotage, rape, kidnapping, or espionage. None of those crimes were committed by these demonstrators. That being the case, the murder of Ollie Friedkind can only be classified under the statute as *second-degree* murder, and then only if the government has evidence that the demonstrators actually committed some *other* felony. That's not the case here."

"Picketing and parading," Essert blurted out. "They committed the felony of picketing and parading," he said again, nodding his head vigorously at the judge.

"Picketing and parading is a misdemeanor, Your Honor," Joshua said. "It cannot support a felony-murder accusation."

Judge Buchanan reached for a book on the shelf behind the bench. He picked up the indictment, studied it for a moment, then flipped the pages of the book and read closely.

"Section fifteen oh seven is not designated a misdemeanor or felony, Mr. Essert. What's your position?"

"The McCarran National Security Act of 1950, of which Title Eighteen section fifteen oh seven is a part, designates all of the violations set forth in it as serious felonies endangering the security of the United States."

The judge looked at Joshua. "Mr. Rabb, is that so?"

"As Your Honor had indicated in the reading of the indictment, the possible imprisonment of the defendants for violation of the picketing and parading statute is not more than one year. If the court will turn to section one of Title Eighteen, the court will find the following classification of offenses." Joshua held his notebook in front of him and read from it. " '*Notwithstanding any Act of Congress to the contrary:* (one) Any offense punishable by death or imprisonment for a term *exceeding* one year is a felony. (two) Any other offense is a misdemeanor.' " He closed his notebook and laid it on the table.

Judge Buchanan flipped the pages of the book before him on the bench, studied a moment, and frowned. He looked up searchingly at Tim Essert, waiting for a response. There was none.

"The gravity of what happened here this morning cannot blithely be overlooked," Judge Buchanan said slowly. He turned pained eyes toward Joshua. "The murder of the United States marshal cannot go unpunished, Mr. Rabb. Perhaps Mr. Essert is correct that the government is entitled to more time before it must respond to your motion that the murder charge be dismissed."

Joshua had only one more card to play. "The murder of Ollie Friedkind is a vile act, and it is incumbent upon all of us to see that the perpetrator is punished. But the forum for that punishment must be in the state court. The murder occurred in the Valley National Bank Parking lot, which is on state land and over which this federal court simply has no jurisdiction." He sat down slowly, feeling his knees weakening and not wanting to start trembling.

A minute passed in silence. Two minutes. Judge Buchanan took the pocket watch out of his vest pocket, opened and closed the hunting case several times, stared at the watch face, and pressed his eyes closed in concentration. Essert sat down at his table, looking malignantly at Joshua.

The judge spoke softly. "This is a court of law and derives its only authority and power from the proper administration of the law. As repugnant as it is to me to dismiss the charge of murder against these defendants, I am constrained to do so in the interest of justice. I agree that the murder, which occurred on state land, must be prosecuted in state court. Count three of the indictment is dismissed. Bail is set for each of the defendants on count one in the sum of five thousand dollars, the maximum possible fine under the statute." He stood up, avoided looking into the startled eyes of most of the spectators, and left the bench through his chambers door.

Marshal Fratangeli smacked his gavel hard on the round block of wood and the crack reverberated among the shocked spectators. Tim Essert and the two FBI agents pressed through them quickly and left the courtroom.

"Clear the courtroom, please," Marshal Fratangeli called out. "Clear the courtroom now."

The hundreds of spectators began filing in silence out of the courtroom. Joshua stood up and walked to the jury railing. All of the defendants appeared stunned, lost.

"You are only charged with the crime of picketing and parading," Joshua said, looking at each of the defendants in turn, to be sure that they understood. Hanna stared at the floor. "I need to have each of your telephone numbers so that I can notify your parents and see about raising bail money. But it's a bit premature to post it right at the moment, since the United States attorney is going over to the county attorney's office—"

"That's all! Let's go!" barked Marshal Fratangeli, walking up to the jury box.

"Give me just a minute to get their phone numbers," Joshua said.

"Get outta here," Fratangeli muttered.

"You said I could talk to them after the arraignment."

"That's before you pulled that bullshit," Fratangeli growled.

"Do I have to go into Judge Buchanan's chambers and get a court order to talk to them?"

"Ya have to do whatever ya have to do!" Fratangeli unfastened the end of the chain from a steel ring attached to the jury railing. He yanked on it, and all of the defendants stood up and shuffled out of the courtroom in single file in front of him.

Joshua watched them go through the door, then walked behind the defense table and sank into the chair. He put his hand over his eyes, exhausted, frightened. It would only be a half hour or an hour at most before Pima County Sheriff Pat Dunphy would drive up to the marshal's office with two or three sheriff's cars and deputies with him to arrest the four young women and young man for murder. Joshua straightened in the chair and tried to think through what he would do next.

No lawyer should take a case in which he was personally involved, Joshua knew. It destroyed his objectivity, his ability to make choices that might be wrong, that might result in tragic consequences, but that must be taken if there is to be any hope of winning. It was okay to take chances on behalf of some stranger, to risk *his* life or *his* liberty. But it was virtually impossible to take those chances when your own daughter could suffer for your mistake or bad judgment.

Manipulate the statutes, twist and turn the case law to the advantage of his clients, that was what a lawyer did, that was what Joshua did. The law was not an eternally fixed, perfect creation of God, but an imperfect and time bound and necessarily changing tool created by human beings to enable them to live in an ordered society, as they themselves shaped and defined that society day by day. Men and women wrote it, and they either abided by it or ignored it. For sixteen years now, defending the innocent, mostly defending the guilty, Joshua had been arguing perfervidly to judges and juries that black was really gray and x was really y, that the law really meant *this* and not *that,* that it really only applied to *this* person and not *that* person. But this was different: Hanna Rabb was accused of murder. He could not maintain detachment. He was so totally and mercilessly drowning in this case that his thinking was blurred, and he tried to force himself to concentrate and not let his mind drift. But it was impossible. This was his daughter, not some stranger.

Will the law protect her? Will she be treated with justice?

But what the hell is justice? Who defines what is right and what is wrong? Is there some universal standard, "God's law," or is it the standard imposed by the religion in vogue, the government in power, the victor in a war? Or is it each of them at one time or other? He had no facile answer. He felt sick, so fearful that his breath began to come with difficulty through his constricted throat. He felt as though he were under water, gasping for air.

"Hey, Rabb. Get yer ass outta here. I gotta lock up the courtroom." Fratangeli had returned from the holding cell.

Joshua stood up, braced himself against the table, and breathed deeply. He stiffened resolutely and walked out of the courtroom.

"But I can't charge them with first-degree murder on those facts," Randy Stevens said. He had light blue eyes and thinning blond hair. He was shorter than Tim Essert but stockier, an ex-marine aide-de-camp to a fleet admiral on an aircraft carrier for three years during World War Two. He had been a deputy Pima County attorney for his entire law career since graduating from the University of Arizona Law School in 1935. In late 1945, when he returned from the South Pacific, he had been made the chief deputy county attorney. He had been a close friend of Joshua Rabb's since their first meeting five years ago.

"Jesus, Randy! The *Shockley* case says you can charge them all as co-conspirators," Essert said.

"*Shockley* is federal law, not state. I can't charge them with first-degree murder unless you have evidence that they actually had some role in planning or carrying out the murder of the marshal."

Essert shook his head and frowned. "How about *felony* murder?"

"What's your felony?"

Essert thought for a moment. "Obstructing justice, something like that?"

Randy opened the Arizona Code of 1939, flipped through it, and read: " 'Section thirty-nine ten, obstructing public officer. Every person who willfully resists, delays, or obstructs a public officer in the discharge or attempt to discharge any duty of his office . . .' It's a five-year, five-thousand-dollar felony. Does it fit?"

"You bet! They danced around me and Holmes and Schlesinger with those placards, held us up for a couple of minutes going into the courthouse, did the same thing when we came out to go to my office."

"Pretty thin stuff."

"Come on, Randy. Ollie Friedkind was murdered during their Commie demonstration. We can't just let them off without even a try at charging them."

Randy nodded. "Okay, but obstructing isn't an enumerated offense under first-degree felony murder, so I can only charge them with *second* degree. It's ten years to life and bailable."

Essert shrugged. "If it's the best we can do, then let's go with it."

"Okay," Randy said. He pushed a lever on his intercom. "Anne, come in here with your book please."

His secretary came into the office and sat down in the round-backed oak chair next to Essert. His eyes roamed her tall, voluptuous body. She had just graduated from the University of Arizona Law School a week ago, one of its first women graduates, and was studying to take the bar examination. County Attorney Morris Udall had promised her a job as a deputy county attorney if she passed.

Randy started to dictate the arrest warrant to her, then paused. "You got the list of defendants?" he said to Essert.

Essert handed him a sheet of paper. Randy read it quickly and looked up puzzled. "This is ridiculous. Hanna Rabb and Jan Diedrichs? Fred Mergen? They didn't commit murder. I've known Hanna since she was fourteen. I've known Jan Diedrichs since she was born. Hell, Paul Diedrichs's been my barber and my friend for twenty years. And Fred Mergen's dad works out at Davis Monthan Air Force Base. He's a civilian aeronautical engineer for the Strategic Air Command."

"So maybe Mergen knows something he shouldn't about our defense secrets." Essert fixed Stevens with a truculent stare. "They were in the demonstration. The murder occurred during the demonstration while they were obstructing justice. It's not your call, Randy, you're not the jury. It's your job to charge them, and if they're not guilty, the jury will cut them loose."

Randy shook his head. "This is bullshit and we both know it."

"It happens to be our jobs. We don't decide who

did it, we just gather the evidence to let the jury decide. There's evidence enough here to charge them."

Randy sighed morosely. "Okay, Anne, here's the names of the defendants." He handed her the sheet of paper. "Count one obstructing, to support count two, second-degree felony murder, section forty-three, twenty-nine oh two."

Anne left the room, and Essert followed her behind with greedy eyes. "Great-looking piece of ass."

"Her husband died at Guadalcanal, she's got a nine-year-old son, and I don't think your wife would approve."

Essert laughed maliciously. "Yeah, she puts a definite damper on my love life."

Randy picked up the telephone receiver and dialed Sheriff Patrick Dunphy. "Pat. I got an arrest warrant that'll be ready in about ten minutes. I've just got to get Judge Velasco's signature." Pause. "They're five U of A students, caught in a demonstration over at the federal courthouse this morning when Ollie Friedkind got killed." Pause. "Yeah, really terrible." Pause. "They're over at the marshal's holding cell. They've been charged federally with a misdemeanor. The murder happened in the VNB parking lot. We're charging them with felony murder two." Pause. "Yeah, as soon as you get them, bring them up to Velasco's courtroom for the initial appearance." He hung up.

He stared wanly out of the window of his office at "A" Mountain a few miles away, where U of A students whitewashed an "A" on rocks preceding football season each year. "Shitty thing to do to Joshua

Rabb and Paul Diedrichs and Fred Mergen," he mumbled.

"They ought to keep their little bastards on shorter leashes," Essert said.

"Is this a kick in the ass, or what!" Pat Dunphy said, loud enough for Joshua to hear twenty feet away at the defense table. "Arrestin' ol' Joshua Rabb's little girl for bein' a Commie murderer. What's this world comin' to anyway?" He slapped his knee and belched out laughter. The raucous noise rebounded off the walls of Judge Bernardo Velasco's courtroom on the second floor of the county office building.

Velasco came out of his chambers and sat down in the big swivel chair at the bench. "This is the time for the initial appearance in the matter of State of Arizona versus Mergen and others." He looked around the courtroom and then studied the faces of the five students. His eyes were deep brown under thick black eyebrows. He had a bushy black mustache and a graying fringe of hair around an almost completely bald crown.

"Mr. Rabb, you're representing all of the defendants?"

"Yes, Your Honor," Joshua said, standing.

"Have you had the opportunity to read the charges?"

"I have, Your Honor."

"How do your clients plead?"

"Not guilty."

"Very well," Velasco said. He put on a pair of "readers" and studied the calendar on the bench before him. "The preliminary hearing is set for Friday, June 29, at nine in the morning. Bail is set at ten thousand dollars each." He glanced apologetically at Joshua and left the courtroom.

Pat Dunphy magnanimously afforded Joshua five minutes to talk to the defendants and get the names and telephone numbers of their parents. It was almost noon when Dunphy led them out of the courtroom to the holding cells on the first floor of the county building.

Joshua drove home, just five minutes away. Barbara was typing at the reception desk on the first floor of the small Victorian house.

Hi, honey," she said, looking up and smiling at Joshua. Her smile quickly faded. "What's wrong?"

"Hanna's been arrested for murder."

Barbara's mouth gaped open. "What?"

"The firebombing of the U.S. marshal's car. She was one of the demonstrators."

"Oh, my God!" she gasped. "But she couldn't have had anything to do with *murder*."

"Of course not. But she was there. It was an illegal demonstration." He shook his head and swallowed.

"What are you going to do?"

"First thing, I have to call the parents of the other kids. They'll have to pay a bondsman a fifteen-hundred-dollar premium so their kid can post bond and get out of jail. They'll probably have to put up their homes as security."

Barbara shook her head. "We don't have fifteen hundred. Maybe eight or nine." She rummaged in the center drawer of the desk and pulled out a bank deposit book. "Yes, seven hundred and ninety-two dollars." She looked at him in alarm. "I'll call my father. Then you can use the phone and call the others."

Carlos Moreno, the only bail bondsman Joshua knew, was ecstatic. But he had learned to hide his glee from the people whose money he was taking, and on whose houses he was securing a mortgage.

Moreno posted bail for Hanna and Jan Diedrichs at four o'clock that afternoon. Barbara picked Hanna up and drove her home. She went straight to her bedroom, avoided looking at her father as she passed his office.

The boy, Fred Mergen, made bail at five o'clock. The other two girls were sisters from Phoenix, and Joshua had been unable to reach their parents until after six o'clock. They were unable to withdraw money from their bank and get the mortgage papers on their house prepared at that hour. So the two girls would not be released until the next morning.

Barbara set the kitchen table with an elegant Irish linen tablecloth, matching cloth napkins, Lenox stem water glasses with gilt-edged tops, Wedgewood Florentine Cobalt dinnerware, and Gorham silver in the Medici pattern. All of it had been wedding gifts from her mother, and they had only used it three times since the wedding. Tucson was not a place of fancy dinner parties.

When Adam got home from summer school, Barbara took him into his dormer bedroom and told him what had happened. He had heard about Marshal Friedkind's death earlier in the day, because Nancy and Tony Friedkind had been taken out of school by their mother. But he hadn't heard about Hanna, and he was shocked and frightened when Barbara told him about Hanna's role in the demonstration and being charged with murder.

"God. Murder?" he gasped.

"Your dad is going to get her off," Barbara said, trying to look resolute, but feeling uneasy. "She and her friends didn't do anything wrong."

Adam was hardly listening, still trying to digest the fact that his sister had been somehow involved in a killing. And Tony Friedkind's father. They played together on the football team.

"Please don't kid her about it at dinner," Barbara said.

He shook his head. "I won't. I promise."

"All right. Get washed up. It's time to eat."

She walked down the stairs from the dormer and knocked on Hanna's door.

"Yes?" Hanna's voice was muffled.

"Time for dinner."

"I'm not hungry."

Barbara opened the door a foot and looked in. Hanna was lying on her back on the bed, staring at the ceiling. The drapes were open on the window, flooding the room with light from the low, late-afternoon sun.

"Come on, honey," Barbara said, "you can't hide from your dad forever."

"He's going to kill me."

"Maybe. But I won't let him do it at the dinner table and get blood all over our lace tablecloth."

Hanna sniffled.

"I think right now he's too tired to kill you anyway."

"Okay," Hanna said.

"What's all of this?" Joshua said from the kitchen, surveying the resplendent kitchen table. "Is it a holiday or something?"

"Maybe it'll cheer us up a little," Barbara said, walking over to the oven and opening the door. "I made stuffed kishka and potato kugel."

Joshua smiled at her. "By God, it's Rosh Hashanah."

"Nope, just a special day."

"That's certainly true."

Barbara walked close to him. "Take it easy on her. She's miserable enough."

Joshua's face was haggard and drawn. "It could get a hell of a lot worse than this," he whispered.

Adam came to the table and sat down, looked around warily, and said, "Is it Christmas or something?"

"Rosh Hashanah," Joshua said. "We don't have Christmas."

Hanna came out of her bedroom staring at the floor. She sat down quickly at the table, placed the napkin in her lap, and folded her hands on it. Her eyes were glued to her hands.

"Where's Magdalena?" Joshua asked.

"It's parent-teacher day over at Dunbar," Barbara answered. "She won't be back until about eight." Magdalena was teaching history in summer school at the segregated Negro school near downtown Tucson. Negro students in grades one through eight were required to attend Dunbar. After that, in the unlikely event that they continued their education, they were permitted to attend Tucson High with the white students. Magdalena had tried to get a teaching position at Tucson High, but the Board of Trustees had refused to let a Papago Indian teach there. The only place they would permit her to teach was in the segregated school.

"Too bad she's going to miss *this*," Joshua said, pointing at the china and silver and crystal. He sat down at the head of the table in the only armchair. "So how's summer school?" Joshua asked.

"I hate it," Adam said. "Bad enough I have to go all year, but summer, too?"

"Only five weeks."

"It's hot in there. The cooler doesn't work."

"Next year don't get a four in any of your classes and you won't have to take them over again in the summer."

"Geometry teacher didn't like me," Adam grumbled.

"Sure, some vicious vendetta," Joshua said.

"What's a vendetta?"

Barbara spooned a square of potato kugel on Joshua's plate, then on her own, and passed the metal baking pan to Hanna. "Careful, hot."

Hanna took the pan with the hot pad and took a small piece of kugel. Adam took two large squares. Joshua took a long piece of kishka off the serving plate and passed it to Adam.

"Have some stuffed cow guts," Joshua said.

Adam wrinkled up his nose. "Ugh."

"I also made some chicken for you two goyim," Barbara said, smiling at Hanna and Adam.

"Thank God," Adam murmured.

"Yeah," said his sister.

Barbara got up and took the baked chicken breasts out of the oven. She put one on Hanna's plate and two on Adam's.

"I didn't know you two were so squeamish about good ol' Jewish food," Joshua said.

"It's a new world, Dad, you gotta face it," Adam said. "We ain't living in the ghetto in Brooklyn anymore."

Joshua smiled. *"Aren't."*

"Aren't." Adam smiled sarcastically.

"And he was such a nice kid when he was twelve," Joshua said to Barbara.

She laughed, a little too gaily.

Hanna picked at the chicken breast on her plate, cutting a tiny nibble out of it and chewing on it endlessly.

"You'll starve to death doing that," Joshua said softly.

"I've got to get used to bread and water," she mumbled.

Joshua smiled at her. "Well, at least you haven't lost your sense of humor."

She put down her knife and fork and laid her face in her hands. She wept with deep gasps, her shoulders shuddering.

Joshua got up and walked to her. He put his good arm around her shoulders and kissed her cheek. She threw her arms around his neck and wept against his chest. Tears spilled over his eyelids, and he looked away from Barbara and Adam so that they wouldn't see.

Barbara caught Adam's eye and gestured with her head to his bedroom.

"But I'm starving," he whispered.

"Take it with you," she whispered back.

He took his dinner plate and a fork, walked up the stairs into the dormer, and closed the door quietly behind him. He could hear his father trying to console Hanna. "Don't worry, I'll protect you," he was saying over and over. "I'm going to take care of everything." But Adam was no longer a child, and he knew that there were things that his father couldn't take care of. And maybe this was one.

Joshua spent all night in the county law library doing feverish research. He returned home at six o'clock in the morning and spent the next three hours typing a motion. He showered and shaved, changed into fresh clothing, and drove downtown at ten o'clock. He got Judge Velasco's signature on an "Order Shortening Time for Hearing," got the hearing set for three o'clock that afternoon, delivered a copy of the motion to Randy Stevens, and met all five of the defendants in the second-floor hallway of the federal building at a quarter to eleven. Their parents were with them, Barbara with Hanna.

Harry Chandler, one of Tucson's "old boys' club" lawyers—perhaps its very nucleus—was there with Fred Mergen and his parents. Joshua shook Harry's hand and they exchanged brief greetings.

"What I am planning to do on my daughter's behalf, as her attorney," Joshua said to the group, "is to plead her guilty in federal court to the misdemeanor crime of picketing and parading, which is all that they're charged with in federal court."

The mood of the listeners was funereal.

"What's up your sleeve, Joshua?" Harry Chandler asked.

"A long shot, Harry, a real risky move. But it's all I can think of. The essence of the crime of picketing and parading is the same in this case as the state court charge of obstructing justice. If we plead guilty to picketing and parading in federal court, I can go over to state court and argue that the continued prosecution of the defendants for obstructing justice would be double jeopardy in violation of both the state and federal constitutions. If Bernie Velasco buys it and dismisses the obstructing charge, the state has to drop the felony-murder charge because it no longer has an applicable felony."

A smile slowly crept over Harry Chandler's wrinkled face. "Damn good," he said, "damn, damn good." He turned to John Bergen. "It's a helluva gambit, John. Let's go for it."

John Mergen and his wife appeared traumatized by everything that had happened. "But then he's pleading guilty to a crime," John said, his chin twitching, "and what will this Judge Buchanan do? He could give him a year."

"Yeah, he could. But I doubt it. He isn't going to buy any crap that these kids conspired to commit murder, and he's got damn good sense about freedom of speech. He was my law partner for a long time, and I know him. But even if he does give them a few months' jail time, it's better than doing life on a murder rap."

"How about Fred trying to get a job with a criminal conviction?"

"Hell, it's only a misdemeanor, not amounting to a hill of beans. Once Joe McCarthy drops dead of a stroke, who's gonna give a shit?" Chandler chuckled, trying to lighten everyone's depression. "If necessary, your boy'll have to be careful to submit employment applications only to Democrats."

A few of the parents twittered nervously.

"You've got to make your decision on this by eleven o'clock," Joshua said. "I notified Judge Buchanan and the U.S. attorney's office that there'd be at least one change of plea at eleven o'clock. Then I've got the state court hearing set up for three this afternoon."

"Does Essert know what kind of motion you filed over in state court?" Chandler asked.

"Hell, no," Joshua answered.

"Better hope he doesn't find out."

Randy Stevens finished reading Rabb's motion to dismiss and sat staring pensively at "A" Mountain. The motion called for Velasco, a state superior court judge, to render a decision on constitutional law that was both a departure from traditional legal notions and a hugely bold act in the face of the public fear of Communists and fellow travelers and their danger to the integrity of the American way of life. To hold that double jeopardy applied to state and federal courts alike would be plowing new ground, although it had been tried before in many courts throughout the country. But Bernie Velasco was just the guy who might do it. He had balls the size of muskmelons and a sense of fairness and decency that seemed to gusher up from a wellspring deep inside him.

There was one *sure* way to stop Joshua Rabb in his tracks: call Tim Essert and tell him to dismiss the federal picketing and parading charges. Then there would be no double jeopardy argument left, and Rabb's' motion to dismiss would be moot.

Randy reached for the telephone, stopped in midair, and picked up the indictment instead. Jan Diedrichs. Hanna Rabb. Fred Mergen. Randy had played golf several times with John Mergen over at the El Rio golf course in West Tucson.

Communists, these kids? Bullshit. Killers? Hell no. Someone damn sure murdered Ollie Friedkind, but not these kids. But in the overheated anti-Communist swamp of these times, they could damn sure be convicted of it.

Randy frowned, tried to push away his aversion to what he was doing, reached for the telephone, and began to dial. He sighed resignedly, replaced the receiver, and glanced at the clock on his desk. Already ten-fifty.

He got up slowly from his desk. Well, just enough time to get an early lunch so he could get back and prepare for the double jeopardy hearing at three o'clock this afternoon.

*   *   *

All five of the defendants pled guilty to picketing and parading. Joshua requested that the sentencing be set at the end of the summer, and Judge Buchanan set it for Monday, September 3, at ten o'clock in the morning.

Joshua and Barbara drove home with Hanna. Joshua went directly to his office without a word to continue to prepare for the hearing this afternoon.

At a few minutes to noon, Judge Velasco's secretary called. The judge had read the motion and decided that since all of the defendants were out of custody, the hearing should be delayed until Friday, June 29, just before the preliminary hearing, to give the prosecution appropriate time to respond in writing.

It was a blow, but there was nothing Joshua could do about it. Another ten days of severe anxiety for himself and Hanna and the others. And the judge would probably hear the motion and take it under advisement and not rule on it until after he had heard the evidence presented during the mini-trial that characterized the preliminary hearing.

Well, can't blame him. With all the Communist scare going on and the Korean War looking like the first defeat the United States would ever suffer in battle, the judge had to play this thing safe. He was going to run for reelection again next year, and this case would be just the kind of stuff that would create a great campaign issue for some McCarthyite opponent.

Chapter Seven

The fevered activity that had kept Joshua going for thirty hours without even thinking of rest suddenly came to a halt. He settled into the armchair behind his desk and was debilitated by exhaustion, so penetrated with fatigue that he simply closed his eyes and dozed for almost an hour. When he awoke, he felt as though he had a hangover. He stood up and shook his shoulder and head and jogged in place until he felt the blood moving in him. His head began to clear.

He called Solomon Leyva at the BIA. "I need your help, Sol."

"What's up?"

"I have to prepare for a preliminary hearing for Hanna and four of her friends in ten days."

"Yeah, I heard on the radio."

"They didn't kill the marshal."

"You don't have to tell me that. I know it."

"You going to be there for a while?"

"Long as you want."

"I'll be right over."

Joshua walked upstairs to the living room. The

house was silent. From his bedroom window he could see that Hanna's car was gone from the driveway. Barbara must have gone with her, he thought. Probably went shopping over to Goldberg's Department Store. A new pair of shoes, a dress. That always makes them feel better.

He took a shower and dressed in Levi's, a blue chambray work shirt with long sleeves, and tan penny loafers. He drove to the BIA. He walked through the reception area, said "Hi" to Frances Hendly sitting at her typewriter behind the smeary window, and sat down on the slatted wooden folding chair in front of Solomon Leyva's small gray-metal navy surplus desk. "We've got to find at least one witness to what happened yesterday morning," Joshua said. "There must be somebody. The street would have been full of cars at that hour. And there were thirty-five other students or apparent students in the demonstration."

"Where do I start?"

"I had Hanna write down the names of every demonstrator she knows. There are thirty-one of them. They were all in Livinsky's Comparative Political Systems class last year, so she got to know them at least by name. She said that there were four or five demonstrators out there she didn't know."

"No addresses, no phone numbers on any of them?" Solomon said, looking over the sheet that Joshua handed him.

"Right, but they must all be local. Otherwise they wouldn't be here during the summer."

Solomon nodded. "What else?"

"Two elderly people parked near me in the lot before the ruckus started. It was a little before eight, and they walked across to the Westerner Hotel."

"You recognize them?"

Joshua shook his head. "No, but at that time of the morning they had to either be hotel guests or going to the dining room for breakfast. Someone must have seen them: desk clerk, bellhop, waiter."

"You want *me* to go into the Westerner Hotel looking for two white folks? They won't give me the time of day."

"Wear your uniform and that hog leg," Joshua said, pointing to the .45 Colt Single Action Army revolver in the basket weave "gunslinger" holster hanging from a long nail in the wall. "They'll talk to you."

The next morning Joshua got out of bed at five o'clock. He made coffee and went downstairs for the morning newspaper. He sat at the kitchen table reading the lead story and couldn't swallow his coffee:

COMMUNISTS MURDER MARSHAL
FIVE STUDENTS HELD IN MARSHAL'S MURDER

Five students at the University of Arizona were arrested Monday for the firebombing murder of Oliver Friedkind at the United States courthouse. The tragic death of the United States Marshal occurred during an antiwar demonstration staged by the students and at least thirty-five of their confederates during the Monday morning session of the federal grand jury. The grand jury had been assembled for the purpose of indicting University of Arizona professors Mischa Livinsky and Julio Moraga for failing to register with the attorney general's subversives list as members of a Communist front organization. (See the story concerning the deaths of Julio Moraga and Anne Marie Hauser, page 2.)

"The demonstrators so completely disrupted the grand jury's deliberations that they were impeded from bringing an indictment," Assistant United States Attorney Tim Essert told this reporter. "They were screaming 'Free Livinsky, Free Speech' so loud on the street under the grand jury room that it was impossible to present evidence to the grand jury," Essert added. "Obviously the only free speech they cared about was their own. When I left the grand jury room, I was shocked to find local attorney Joshua Rabb in the hallway, sitting with Livinsky, ready to defend him. But I understood why a few minutes later, when his daughter was arrested by FBI agents for being one of Ollie Friedkind's murderers."

Joshua shook his head and rubbed his chin hard. He didn't understand the last sentence, but that was not unusual for him when he read one of J. T. Sellner's sensationalist newspaper stories. Logical reasoning wasn't her forte, nor obviously Tim Essert's. In Joshua's six years in Tucson, she had written several scurrilous stories about him. The story continued:

Due to some jurisdictional technicalities raised by Rabb, who is representing all of the students arrested for murder, murder charges were dropped in federal court. Mr. Essert then immediately went to the Pima County attorney's office and saw to it that state murder charges were filed. The students were then brought to the courtroom of Judge Bernardo Velasco where they were held to answer for murder. The accused murderers were released on bond yesterday afternoon.

In a stunning development, Mr. Essert announced yesterday that he was combining the investigation of the five students with the investigation of the murder of Anne Marie Hauser. "The two crimes have several elements in common," Essert said in his written statement. FBI resident agent, Roy Collins, refused comment to this reporter on the murders of Friedkind, Hauser, or Moraga. "The case is still under investigation," he said. "When we've fully completed the investigation, I'll have something to say."

Senator William Maitland's office in Phoenix issued a statement today deploring the lax moral attitude of the administration at the University of Arizona that has permitted these dangerous "Communists and fellow travelers to teach our unsuspecting sons and daughters at the university and to carry out the work of their puppet masters in Moscow by treacherously destroying our society from within. We must all join forces in total vigilance," the senator's statement continues, "to sweep the pinkos and Commiecrats out of the university, so that they cannot poison our children and our way of life with impunity."

Senator Maitland told this reporter that Julio Moraga was a perfect case in point. In 1948, he assaulted and severely injured the Pima County voting registrar when the registrar refused to register Moraga and ten other Papagos to vote. *It was the law.* Had the registrar done otherwise, he would have committed a criminal act. Moraga was arrested and convicted for this act of violence. But despite this, the University of Arizona administration neither saw fit to terminate his employment as assistant museum curator nor take any disciplinary action against him whatsoever.

Joshua shook his head grimly. What Sellner was leaving out of the story was that Moraga's case had been the vehicle that Joshua had used to take the voting rights issue to the Arizona Supreme Court and to win a decision by Justice Jesse Udall that Indians had wrongfully been deprived of their right to vote in all elections.

This reporter spoke to Senator Maitland yesterday in his Washington office, and the senator expressed deep grief over the murders of U.S. Marshal Friedkind and Investigator Hauser. "They were two of the finest examples of decent Americans whom I have ever had the privilege to know. Senator Joe McCarthy and I are filing a joint resolution in the Senate today demanding a federal probe into the festering pus boil at the University of Arizona where the deadly disease of communism has flourished with complete impunity.

Yesterday, in a surprise development, all five of the students charged with murder pled guilty in federal court to the crime of picketing and parading a federal courthouse. Their sentencing has been set by District Judge Robert Buchanan for September 3. The five will be in state court on June 29 for their preliminary hearing on the murder charge.

The door to Magdalena's bedroom squeaked open, and she came out on tiptoes. She looked back into the dark room for a moment, then closed the door softly.

"Macario's been collicky all night," she whispered. "He finally got to sleep."

She walked to the coffeepot on the stove and poured herself a cup, then sat down at the table across from Joshua.

"What's wrong?" she said, looking into his eyes.

He turned the newspaper around and pushed it toward her. She looked down at it and began to read. After a moment she knit her brow. She looked up at Joshua, shook her head, then continued reading silently.

Joshua watched her. She wore no makeup, dressed in the simplest of clothing, Levi's and T-shirts or work shirts, wore scuffed cowboy boots or sandals, and she was one of the most beautiful women he had ever seen. Her black eyes were wide-set and almond-shaped over high cheekbones and a small nose. She was as stunning and stately as an Indian princess from one of the legends, Pocahontas from the famous poem, Son Siaray, Cochise's daughter who had fallen in love with a white man and brought peace to the Chiricahua Apaches.

"What are you going to do?" Magdalena asked, pushing the newspaper away and putting her hands in her lap, as though she were afraid of being contaminated by its virulence.

"I guess I have to find out who murdered them," he said quietly. "Otherwise, Essert is going to try to pin everything on the students and Livinsky."

"Jesus," she murmured, "sweet Jesus." She crossed herself and kissed her thumbnail.

Macario's whimpering could be heard through the

bedroom door. "Better feed him," she said, standing up from the table. "See you tonight." She walked into her bedroom and closed the door.

Joshua stuffed the newspaper in the garbage can, hoping that Barbara wouldn't notice it was gone and look for it. With all that had happened in the last two days, she didn't need this added to it.

The L and L Restaurant, Larriva and Larriva, affectionately dubbed the "Lewd and Lascivious" by most people who frequented it, was south of Tucson just a mile from the San Xavier Reservation. The patio in front of it was ringed about the top by a wooden frame that carried water pipes. They emitted a fine spray around the small outside eating area, and the spray acted as a primitive but effective cooling system.

Joshua, Solomon Leyva, and Roy Collins sat around a small table against the adobe wall of the kitchen. Joshua had asked them to meet him for dinner. Roy didn't want to meet where he might be seen breaking bread with the father of a girl charged with murder. It wouldn't be very helpful to his career as an FBI special agent. The L and L was a perfect choice. It was deep in the Mexican neighborhoods south of Tucson, far from where anyone who was likely to recognize Roy would ever come for dinner.

"I spoke to fourteen of the students this afternoon," Solomon said. "Nobody saw anything. They were all listening to Professor Livinsky up near the entrance of the federal building when the bomb went off in the parking lot. Ten of the other students don't have phones. I'll have to visit them personally."

"Did the ones you spoke to know any names of demonstrators that Hanna didn't?" Joshua asked.

"Yes. Three names."

"Good," Joshua said. He turned to Roy. "We need your help with these visits to their homes. Solomon isn't going to get too far with them alone."

"They probably won't even open the door," Collins said. It wasn't meant as a joke. "Okay, but I can't start until tomorrow morning, after the FBI guys leave for Washington. A state court murder case isn't in my jurisdiction, and Holmes and Schlesinger will have me up before a Bureau review board if they get wind of me being involved. Anyway, they think they have the killers, at least five out of forty of them."

"Do they really?" Joshua asked.

Collins nodded.

Joshua was chagrined. "What's Essert think?"

"Who knows what's on that prick's mind?" Roy said. "I don't think he's ever concerned about whether somebody's guilty or innocent. To him it's just charges. If you have any evidence, you bring charges. Then let the judge and jury take a crack at the defendants."

"A real prince among prosecutors."

"Well, he's Big Bill Maitland's kind of guy," Roy said. "When Eisenhower wins the election, all the Democrat U.S. attorneys are out on their asses, including Dillan Hopkins up in Phoenix. Word is that Barry Goldwater's going to give Maitland the choice, kind of a bone from the senior senator to the junior one, and Essert's just his kind of guy."

"At least it'll get him out of Tucson," Joshua said.

Roy nodded.

Big Bill Maitland had run for the Senate in the mid-term elections of 1950 and had won by a landslide, campaigning against Commies and pinkos and all those shadowy subversives in American society whom nobody ever really saw, but who everybody knew were undermining the very soul of the greatest nation on earth. Pinkos were poisoning the Truman administration, compromising the State Department, destroying the army. And it seemed as though every Jew in Hollywood was accused of being a closet Communist. Arizona now had two of the most conservative and pro-McCarthy Republican senators in the country: Barry Goldwater, elected in 1948, and William Maitland, elected in 1950.

"So we start Thursday morning?" Solomon asked Roy.

"Yes. I'm taking the guys to the airport at seven-thirty. Come on over to my office at about nine o'clock."

Chapter Eight

"**Y**a gotta come over right away," Edgar said.

"What's going on?"

"Cain't talk on the phone." He hung up.

Joshua drove to the BIA. It was ten o'clock Wednesday morning, and the sun had already reached blast furnace proportions. Mid-June was always very hot in Tucson, and it was at least 105 degrees, promising an afternoon bake oven of at least 110. It hadn't rained for weeks, and every plant by the road was withering, even the weeds.

Edgar's face was colorless. He pushed a sheet of paper across his big walnut desk. Joshua picked it up and read it.

"I don't get it," he said slowly.

Edgar didn't seem to hear him. "Friday. The som bitch wants me there Friday."

"What does the Senate Select Committee on Communism in Government want with you?"

"Joe McCarthy's on that committee."

Joshua was suddenly somber. "Damn," he muttered.

"It's that fuckin' Essert. He called me yesterday

morning, told me I had to fire you for representin' Livinsky 'n Moraga, that you was violatin' the McCarran Act, 'n that if I kept ya on, I'd be violatin' it, too."

Joshua studied Edgar's mottled pink face.

"I tol' 'im to eat shit 'n die," Edgar said. "An' now I'm the sucklin' pig for McCarthy's next barbecue." His voice displayed none of its usual humor.

"How in hell did we get so important out here?" Joshua asked. "I figured nobody in Washington would even give a damn what happened in this pissant little town."

"Well, nobody *there* does. But Bill Maitland does." Edgar breathed deeply and frowned. "I just called Harry Coyle in D.C. He says Maitland called 'im 'n said he wants to clean out all the pinkos in the BIA, specifically us down here in Tucson. Harry already knows all about Hanna bein' arrested for that protest at the courthouse and how her daddy is defendin' her and that Commie professor."

Joshua shook his head gravely. "How did the committee get you subpoenaed so fast."

"Harry says Maitland called 'Tail Gunner Joe,' and America's greatest patriot authorized a subpoena to be issued out of Maitland's office in Phoenix. Maitland sent it down here yesterday afternoon, and a coupla FBI agents I never seen before handed it to me an hour ago."

"Tail Gunner Joe" had been McCarthy's nickname since he first ran for the Senate in Wisconsin. He claimed to have spent the war years in the marines as a B-24 tail gunner in the South Pacific and to have shot down a dozen Japanese fighters. No one seemed to know the truth, since his military records had some-how disappeared.

"You going to testify?"

"I ain't got no choice. I'm a gov'ment employee. Harry says I gotta get my ass on a plane tomorra mornin' and show up bright-eyed and bushy-tailed in front a the committee on Friday."

"Too bad Jake Lukis isn't still senator."

Edgar nodded. "Yeah, this Maitland is some piece a work. Harry says Maitland tol' 'im he wants to put his own kind a people in the BIA."

"What'd Harry say?"

"Shit! Harry ain't far enough up the totem pole to say nothin' to a senator. All's he does is call me up 'n ream my ass." He grimaced. "I kinda feel like that senator from Texas, what's his name, big guy?" He paused a moment and pondered, squinting his eyes closed. "Lyndon Johnson, that's it. He says that servin' in public office is just about like bein' a dog out in the country. When ya run, they're always a snappin' at yer ass. When ya stop, they fuck ya to death."

Joshua erupted with laughter. Edgar didn't smile, and Joshua quickly sobered.

"Well, I'm sorry," Joshua said, realizing how inade-quate his words were. "I wish I could help."

"Ya can." Edgar stared hard at him. "Drop Livinsky."

"Even if I do, what about Hanna and the four other students. Do I just walk away?"

Edgar shrugged. "Guess ya don't."

"I can't. Anyway, Livinsky isn't a subversive, and he doesn't deserve what's happening to him."

"What's *deserve* have to do with it? This character

Maitland wants to be the biggest Commie baiter in the country next to his idol, the tail gunner. He don't need to have real Commies, and he don't need to have real evidence. Alls he needs is some Roosian Jew jackass teachin' at the University a Arizona who opens his fat mouth when he should oughta keep it shut tight, and a idealistic moron Jew lawyer who thinks the guy got the right to say any damn thing he pleases, long as he don't advocate the overthrow."

"I plead guilty to that."

"Yer prob'bly gonna be pleadin' guilty to a whole lot more 'n that 'fore this mess is over. This Maitland's got a lot a juice."

"We got juice, too, Edgar."

"Oh, yeah? What?"

"The truth. We didn't do anything wrong."

"Look what happened to me three years ago, and I didn't do a damn thing wrong neither."

Joshua frowned.

"Best thing that could happen to us is that Livinsky ends up in a chair starin' out the window with a needle in his arm."

"Come on, Edgar, quit being an asshole."

"*I'm* the asshole? You need an anatomy lesson, Josh boy."

"Okay, okay. Enough of Edgar Hendly, boy philosopher. So what are you going to tell the committee?"

"Reckon it depends on what they ask me."

"You shouldn't have any trouble. Just throw some of your famous poetry at them, maybe a few quotes from the Bible that aren't really there."

"Ya mean like 'Thou shalt not spread malicious rumors and injure the innocent and the righteous, for the Lord thy God shall not justify the wicked.' "

"Well, I think that one *is* in there."

"So why don't God keep his word and strike down those wicked bastards, Maitland 'n McCarthy, 'n leave us alone?"

"I think the trick in all this is that you have to strike down the bastards yourself, because if you wait for God to do it, you might just turn into a puff of smoke like about six and a half million Jews."

Edgar's voice was humorless. "The Pentecostal minister Frances drags me to ever' Sunday mornin' says that God takes care a folks like me 'n you, ya know, the poor and the oppressed. But I ain't seen much evidence of it."

"God helps him who helps himself."

"Zat in the Bible?"

"No, it's from one of Aesop's fables."

Edgar rolled his eyes. "Well, I hope it ain't just a fable, 'cause I'm a gonna take a helluva crack at helpin' myself."

Edgar had been to Washington, D.C., twice before, but both times had been for pleasure. The first was nineteen years ago, when Jacob Lukis had been elected senator in Franklin Roosevelt's Democratic tidal wave. Lukis had then pushed Edgar's appointment as BIA superintendent for Arizona through the Department of the Interior. Edgar had left the Southern Pacific depot in Tucson with the senator's entourage in Lukis's personal railway car, and he ate steaks and drank privately bottled Tennessee sour mash

whiskey for four days, despite the Depression, despite
Prohibition. It was 1932, Roosevelt had just promised
a "new deal" for "the forgotten man," and it snowed
so hard in Washington the day Edgar arrived that he
had been forced to take a cab directly to a haberdash-
ery and buy the only overcoat he had ever owned in
his life, before or since.

His second trip to Washington had been just four
months later, to be present at Roosevelt's inauguration. Again the private railway car, but no bonded
sour mash, because Frances was along on this trip,
and she didn't cotton to her husband getting himself
plastered on John Barleycorn and snoring away his
drunk collapsed into a plush red velvet recliner. But
the trip had been wonderfully memorable to Edgar
anyway, despite his enforced sobriety, and he could
still remember much of the magnificent oratory of the
new president. It had infused new life into a mori-
bund nation.

Nineteen years had passed, and the face of the
world had vastly changed. Instead of unemployment
and hunger, Americans now confronted the "red men-
ace." Instead of a visionary president with a bold icon-
oclastic economic miracle up his sleeve, the current
administration seemed to be wallowing in a mud puddle of uncertainty, whether to win the war in Korea
or lose it, whether to buy into the malicious dema-
goguery of those who would once again blame all the
world's ills on some transcendently malignant group
of traitors, the Jews, or Communists, or "fellow travelers," whoever the hell *they* were supposed to be.

"Give 'em hell Harry" was chin deep in quicksand and didn't seem to have a clue how to get out.

If an inauguration were to be held today, Edgar thought, the platform would have to be draped in black.

Edgar checked into the Adams Hotel, the only hotel where government employees on business in Washington could charge the room directly to their agencies. He ate stolidly at a little diner a few blocks away, trying to shake off his throbbing headache, born of fourteen hours of sitting behind the vibrating propeller engine of an airliner. Travel was quicker these days, but ol' Jake's railway car was a damn sight better.

You couldn't walk into a Senate hearing room for the first time and not be overwhelmed by its aura of solemnity and consequence. *Things* happened here, things that changed the history of the world. Not just the kind of things that happened in Edgar's little office in the old adobe building three thousand miles from here, a place most people never even heard of and where nothing of historic moment ever had occurred or ever would. No, no, no. Here was a place of such vast importance that dozens of men with steno pads and bright lights and cameras followed you down the aisle and shoved microphones in your face and asked questions about matters that you knew nothing about and had never even contemplated.

For those who asked germane questions like, "When did you join the Communist party?" and "Do you employ Commies and sex perverts in your agency?" Edgar had no response save for a clenched jaw and balled fists and an act of will to refrain from busting a nose or two or smashing a chin.

He sat at a twenty-foot-long table covered in dark green felt in front of a high mahogany bench with a huge seal of the United States carved into the middle. A half-dozen senators milled about behind oak-tanned leather swivel chairs, chatting idly with each other or mumbling behind their hands to fawning aides. The ceiling was high, perhaps fifty feet, and the hum of voices from the hundreds of people resonated hollowly in the poor acoustics. Edgar sat alone in the middle of the witness table and squinted uneasily at the array of microphones and cables that looked like a cluster of poised cobras.

Most of the men on the platform were elegantly attired, silk being the fabric of choice, shades of gray and blue the predominant colors, crisp white shirts with French cuffs and gold links. Edgar had bought a new white shirt for this event, although it had button cuffs since he owned no cuff links. He had worn his best suit, medium gray wool herringbone only slightly shiny at the elbows, which looked appropriately somber with the black silk tie that Frances had carefully washed to remove the food stains.

The senators slowly took their seats at the raised bench, their names displayed on small wooden plaques in front of their microphones. They were important men, men of substance and honor, protectors of the faith, avengers of treachery, men who brooked no insolence and gave no quarter to the defilers who sat before them in this righteous inquisition.

Despite the fact that Joseph McCarthy was not even

an official member of the committee, he had become
its most visible and powerful participant. It had provided him a forum from which to promote his message
that American politics and society were perforated by
Communists seeking the overthrow of their own government, and that he was his country's savior.

A small, thin man in back of him bent forward,
whispered something in his ear, walked behind the
senators, down the steps, and handed Edgar a sheet
of paper. It had the title: Tydings Committee Witness Protocol:

Senate Resolution 231 authorized the creation of a
select committee to investigate charges by Senator Joseph McCarthy, which he made in a speech on the
floor of the Senate on February 20, 1950, that there
are "57 card-carrying communists" in the Department
of State. The chairman of the select committee is Mil-
lard Tydings (D-Md). A witness may not speak except
in direct response to questions from any committee
member. Failure to respond to the satisfaction of the
majority of the select committee may result in the ini-
tiation of proceedings for contempt of the Senate. Senator Joseph McCarthy has previously testified before
this select committee and has asked to be made a
nonvoting member, and his appointment has been ap-
proved. At the formal request of Senator Henry Cabot
Lodge, the scope of inquiry of this select committee
has been broadened to include an investigation to determine the State Department officer or officers responsible for hiring sexual perverts.

Edgar Hendly was jarred by the rapping of a gavel.

He looked up, and Senator Tydings was speaking into his microphone. His voice echoed in the now quiet hearing room.

"Good morning, ladies and gentlemen. The Senate Select Committee on Communism in Government is called to order." He smiled pleasantly at Edgar. "Please state your name and address."

"Edgar Hendly." His throat was tight and his voice squeaked. He heard several snickers behind him and cleared his throat loudly. "Edgar Hendly," he said again, distinctly, "Bureau of Indian Affairs, Indian Agency Road, Tucson, Arizona."

"I recognize the distinguished senator from Wisconsin," Tydings said.

There was nothing distinguished about McCarthy, as far as Edgar could see. He was hardly a man whose demeanor or appearance presaged a vast and sweeping intellect or charisma. He was balding and overweight and wore a baggy charcoal-gray wool suit. Small blue eyes peered at Edgar from under curved black eyebrows, in a phlegmatic, flabby face. He had a long, meaty nose and a slightly cleft chin. His voice was of medium pitch and monotonal. He shuffled papers in the file before him.

"This select committee has issued its subpoena to you to receive your testimony concerning your association with known Communists," McCarthy said.

"I have no such associations." Edgar's voice was strong, and his usual Southwestern twang was reduced almost to nonexistence. Here, in this Senate hearing room, before these people of substance, he would try not to sound like Gabby Hayes. He took a pack of

Camels out of his shirt pocket, shook one out, and lit it with a match. He inhaled deeply and held the cigarette in his right hand between his forefinger and middle finger. His hand was shaking just enough to send the stream of smoke zigzagging upward. He realized that it was betraying his nervousness and snuffed it out in the ashtray.

McCarthy shuffled papers in his file. "You employ for the BIA a legal adviser by the name of Rabb, Joshua Rabb. He's also the head of the Office of Land Management for southern Arizona."

"That's correct."

"How long have you employed him?"

"He's been part-time, fifteen hours a week—though he most always works longer than that, but he only gets paid for fifteen hours—since the summer of 1946."

"How long have you known that he is a Communist fellow traveler?"

"I don't know that, and he isn't." Edgar stared steadily at McCarthy.

"I have a report here from the distinguished junior senator from Arizona, William Maitland, that says he is." He held up several sheets of paper and rattled them at Edgar.

It wasn't a question, and Edgar didn't respond.

"Well?" McCarthy said.

"I ain't got an idea in the world what report ya have, Senator."

A few laughs from the audience. McCarthy's face became choleric. He clasped his hands together on the table and appeared to Edgar to be a white-knuckled alcoholic suffering from the unwanted abstinence enforced by the Senate hearing. He cast a threatening look around the room. There was immediate silence.

"It appears that you're not taking this matter seriously, Mr. Hendly," he rumbled.

"That is certainly not true, Senator. I take my appearance here most seriously. It is just that I cannot take as serious any report from anyone who describes Joshua Rabb as a Communist sympathizer."

"Let's look at the evidence, Mr. Hendly." The senator shuffled papers and again held up several. "He's representing a University of Arizona professor who violated the McCarran Internal Security Act of 1950 by failure to register as a member of a Communist front organization. The attorney general determined that the group, Academics Against War, is just such an organization. Just days ago, a second University of Arizona professor, Julio Moraga, who violated the same provision of the McCarran Act, raped and murdered Anne Marie Hauser, a Justice Department investigator and a woman of the highest integrity and moral qualities, well known to this select committee and to the senator."

"We believe that Julio Moraga was most probably murdered and didn't have anything to do with the young woman's death."

McCarthy sneered at him. "Is that Joshua Rabb's theory?"

"It's the Pima County coroner's theory, Senator."

McCarthy was unhindered. "And your employee, this Joshua Rabb, was Moraga's lawyer and continues to be Livinsky's lawyer."

"I ain't a lawyer," Edgar said, lapsing once again into his Western drawl. "But Mr. Rabb assures me that all that stuff we hear about ever' person being presumed innocent until proved guilty is part of our legal system. And he also tells me that someone accused of a crime is entitled to be represented by a lawyer."

"But not if the crime is being a Communist and the lawyer is a federal employee." McCarthy's voice was victorious. The small man behind him handed him a sheet of paper. McCarthy read it silently and brandished it at Edgar. "Section five, subsection two of the McCarran Act."

"I haven't seen that, Senator."

"You'll see it now, sir." McCarthy handed it back to his aide, who brought it to the witness table and placed it in front of Edgar.

Edgar put on a pair of readers and scrutinized the paper closely. "Well, Senator, the way I read this here statute is that an employee of the U.S. government cain't '*contribute services* to such an organization.' That's what it says here. And my understandin' is that Mr. Rabb ain't doing nothin' for the *organization,* alls he's doin' is representin' a man who may soon be accused of a crime. And I think I can guarantee ya that Joshua ain't contributin' none a his services. He charges pretty good."

A wave of laughter rolled through the room. Even several of the senators joined in, including the chairman. McCarthy's expression was acidulous. He leaned forward toward Edgar.

"You parlor pinks and parlor punks like to pick

apart the plain meaning of the laws of our country. But the McCarran Act wasn't written to protect you Commiecrats and fellow travelers who want to destroy the American way of life. It was written to ferret closet sympathizers with the Communist party out of government so you can't harm the decent, loyal folks of this great nation."

Edgar felt choked. This senator was a sick, malicious bastard. But this was his forum, his grandstand, and Edgar knew that he didn't have the experience or ability to face McCarthy down here. He breathed deeply several times to steady his voice and stared blandly at McCarthy as he spoke.

"Last time I peeked, Senator, I was a card-carryin' member a the *Democratic* party a the United States. That's about the only party I been near in the last forty years, 'ceptin' the inauguration of Mr. Franklin Roosevelt, an' that was one helluva party. Ya see, my wife's a Pentecostal, an' she don't cotton to no dancin' or singin'." Edgar waited for the soft laughter behind him to die down. "I ain't even got a clue what party these parlor pinks and parlor punks that yer talkin' 'bout belong to, Senator, 'cause I dunno zackly what them folks are. But I ain't a member, and Joshua Rabb ain't a member."

"And Rabb's daughter?" The question was a dog's growl. McCarthy read from the file in front of him. "She was arrested for the murder of a United States marshal while she was picketing the United States district courthouse in Tucson carrying a sign which read, 'Bring our boys home from this unjust war.' "

There was total silence in the hearing room. Even

the journalists sat rigidly, their pencils poised in mid-air, straining to hear the witness's answer.

Edgar visibly flinched and stiffened. "Hanna Rabb is a nineteen-year-old student at the University of Arizona. The boy she's goin' to marry is a United States marine officer at Camp Pendleton and will soon be in combat with the First Marine Division in Korea. We're all real proud a the boy. Hanna's just a nice young lady, wants him home in one piece. She also took a political science class from Professor Livinsky, one of the two men accused of being a Communist. The demonstration was at the courthouse on the day Livinksy and the other professor were supposed to be appearin' before the grand jury. There were thirty-five or forty demonstrators, and somebody threw a firebomb at the marshal's car.

"I've known Hanna Rabb since she was fourteen, and I know she didn't have anythin' to do with that. Now someone damn sure murdered the marshal, ain't no whys nor wherefores 'bout that. But it wasn't Hanna Rabb."

"She violated the McCarran Act by picketing a courthouse."

"I reckon she did, and her own father pled her guilty to that charge in federal court."

"Well, Mr. Hendly," McCarthy said, his voice now smug and confident, "I think we ought to defer to the judgment of the county prosecutor and the state court judge there. They charged her with murder. Maybe your own judgment is twisted by your relationship with this Rabb and Livinsky and the other one?"

"My judgment is that Joshua Rabb is a fine man,

as was Julio Moraga. I don't know Professor Livinsky personally, but it looks like he's done nothin' more than expressed the same opinion that a lot of other folks hold about the Korean War. And as for Hanna, she's just a kid who made a mistake, and she's prob'ly goin' to jail for it."

"That's all you have to say about this situation?" Senator McCarthy's voice was sarcastic, milking Edgar's discomfort. "You're not even going to fire this Rabb, as Senator Maitland has demanded, for defending a Commie while he's working as a federal employee, even though the McCarran Act says you have to?"

"I do not plan to do so, Senator."

"We shall see," McCarthy said, easing back into his deep armchair. "We'll certainly see about that, sir, and your own complicity in this treasonous conduct."

Edgar fixed him with an irate stare. "Exactly what conduct of mine is treasonous, Senator?"

McCarthy switched off the microphone in front of him. He laid his head back against the chair and stared out over Edgar and the audience.

"Do any other of my colleagues wish to question the witness?" Senator Tydings asked, looking around at the senators.

"I do have a question or two for this witness, Mr. Chairman," Senator Lodge said.

"The chair recognizes the distinguished senator from Massachusetts."

Henry Cabot Lodge was a New England patrician, handsome, his graying hair pomaded flat to his head, dressed in a navy blue silk suit with a pearl gray silk tie and a white shirt. He smiled benignly at Edgar.

"There is a part of this report from Senator Maitland that concerns me, Mr. Hendly."

Edgar nodded.

"It seems that this Mr. Rabb was living with an Indian girl in his own house in the very presence of his son and daughter."

Edgar felt nauseated. Power had corrupted these men of consequence and national importance and left them without common decency.

"All officials of the BIA had live-in Indian girls at the time, Senator, includin' me 'n my wife. It was part of the acculturation program mandated by the Department of the Interior. It was intended to give these Indian girls an introduction to life in the white world so they could make an easier transition from the Reservation to jobs in the cities. The granddaughter of the Papago tribe's former chief was the Rabb's acculturation girl for two or three years."

"Well, the report here from my distinguished colleague from Arizona indicates that there was widespread suspicion that Rabb and this girl were engaged in sexual perversion."

Edgar gaped at him in astonishment. "What?"

"Despite that little good ol' boy show you put on a few moments ago, Mr. Hendly, I trust that you do understand English?"

Edgar said nothing.

"Miscegenation and fornication are evils, Mr. Hendly. They undermine the very integrity of our way of life."

"Indins marryin' white men has been legal in Arizona since 1942, sir, and any allegation of fornication is a gott damn lie." Edgar's eyes were screwed up, his face pinked with anger.

"We don't use that dirty language in the Senate of the United States, sir," Lodge said, his voice mellifluous, the patrician senator to the plebeian rube.

"I see that, Senator," Edgar retorted, his throat tight again, his voice gravelly. "Polite gents like you just use nice language like treason and sex pervert to describe innocent people."

The hall was silent. Senator Lodge stared at Edgar, licked his lips, then switched off his mike and leaned back in his chair.

"Further questions, gentlemen?" Senator Tydings asked. He scanned the other senators. None of them made a move toward their microphones. "Witness is excused," he said, nodding to Edgar. Without pausing for more than a few seconds, he said, "The sergeant of arms will clear the room so that the committee can go into executive session."

Edgar left the hearing room followed by at least fifty reporters and cameramen. He felt dizzy for a moment and steadied himself against the wall. Then he walked as quickly as he could down the hallway, pushing away the microphones thrust toward him, not even hearing any of the shouted questions. This hearing was so thoroughly drenched in malice that he suddenly felt as though he were a traveler from a distant land, a tourist in an alien, ugly, unrecognizable America.

When he reached the Adams Hotel, the desk clerk handed him a telephone message: "Please see Harry

Coyle at BIA headquarters." Harry was Edgar's supervisor, and Edgar had met him many times on Coyle's travels around his assigned territory, the Southwest and California. This territory contained the largest Indian population in the country and the largest reservations of unassimilated Indians, the Navajos of the four corners of Arizona, Utah, New Mexico, and Colorado, the Zunis of New Mexico, the Hopis of northern Arizona, the Apaches of central Arizona, and the Papagos of southern Arizona.

The quarter of a million Navajos and Apaches were closely related and had settled in Arizona in the Athabascan migration of the sixteenth century. The ten or twelve thousand Papagos were almost certainly descendants of Arizona's earliest population, probably an Aztecan civilization that had migrated north from Central America and Mexico to settle in Sonora, Mexico, and southern Arizona, two thousand years ago or more.

America's Indians had been granted United States citizenship by Congress in 1926, at the same time that their earlier status as members of independent nations was largely abrogated. With their citizenship came the automatic right to vote, although the ultimate enfranchisement had been left to the states, and Arizona had not seen fit to permit them to vote until 1948. Giving the Indians the rights and obligations of all citizens had created a need for the Department of the Interior's Bureau of Indian Affairs to hire Indian agents who were no longer merely gunslinging brawlers and glorified policemen. The BIA needed men of understanding and knowledge of the Indians themselves.

Harry Coyle was such a man. He had been a professor of anthropology at the University of New Mexico and was fluent in Navajo and Zuni. Edgar Hendly had worked under him since 1932 as Bureau of Indian Affairs superintendent for Arizona. Edgar was a political appointee, but despite that he had worked out remarkably well. He had lived around the Papagos all of his life and had evolved from a bigoted redneck to the best superintendent Harry had. Part of that evolution, Harry knew, had been stimulated by this lawyer from Brooklyn, Joshua Rabb, who worked part-time as the BIA legal officer. Harry had met Rabb several times. His representation of the tribe against powerful opponents and threats had won the tribe's trust and affection. Edgar obviously had been infected by Rabb's compassion for this oppressed and impoverished people, and he had been changed by the close friendship that he had developed with Rabb.

Coyle looked the part of a college professor. He was short and thin, had a bleached, ascetic face, pale blue eyes behind thick spectacles, and a full head of unruly white hair. He sat stiffly in his chair behind a mahogany desk, wearing a heavily starched collar high on his neck, a carelessly tied blue and red polka dot bow tie, and a navy blue wool suit. He regarded Edgar with an apologetic look.

"I'm sorry, Edgar. It looks like that's how it is."

"I don't give a fuck what it looks like, Harry. It ain't gonna be thatta way."

Coyle shook his head and looked sourly at Edgar. "Look, I know how you feel. I feel the same way. But you two don't have any civil service protection. You're a political appointment, and your senator isn't even in Congress anymore. And Rabb is just part-time, no protection at all. You've got to do it or Secretary Kimmer is going to can your ass."

"Lemme talk to him."

"What are you, nuts? The Secretary told me twenty minutes ago he didn't need any potential crisis from some jackass from the sticks. McCarthy called him after your testimony and tongue-lashed him for five minutes about employing fellow travelers. The Secretary was so mad I thought he was going to fire me. And he damn well will if you don't get rid of Rabb."

Edgar gritted his teeth and stared balefully at Coyle.

"Come on, Edgar. Think straight about this. Michael Kimmer is a Democrat, and he doesn't take shit from Republican senators, especially that pile of fish guts McCarthy. But this is different. This Rabb is our employee and he's representing two members of an organization that the attorney general of the United States listed as a Communist front. And his daughter? Jesus Christ! She's facing murder charges, *murder,* Edgar, for killing a U.S. marshal during an illegal demonstration in front of the courthouse. Whether she's guilty or not, how the hell can we continue to employ this Rabb? It's crazy, just plain crazy. You go out on a limb for this guy, you'll end up out on your ass looking in the want ads for a job waiting tables. The Secretary will yank your pension, and then what? You're fifty-nine years old, you have a wife and a daughter—what is she now, four, five?—so what are you going to do?" He shook his head in frustration. "Don't buck the Secretary on this one, Edgar."

"I deserve a little more consideration than that, for the nineteen years I been doing this job."

"We haven't had a McCarthy before, Edgar. And now that Jake Lukis is gone, who's going to protect you, Maitland, Goldwater? Those two right-wing fucks would rather boil you in oil for the publicity."

Edgar grimaced. "I wanna see the Secretary."

"No, it's out of the question. He'll toss you right through his picture window."

"Then Undersecretary Anson."

Coyle sighed deeply. "You're making a mistake," he muttered, "but you're a big boy." He reached for the telephone on his desk and punched one of the buttons. "Mrs. Dainer, is the undersecretary available?" He listened for a moment. "All right, we'll be right there. We just need to see him for a couple of minutes."

They were ushered into Undersecretary Wallace Anson's office by his officious administrative aide. Anson sat behind a walnut burl desk so large that his desk chair of burgundy leather was twenty feet away from the two Chippendale chairs in front of the desk.

Here was a real politician, Edgar thought. Wavy light brown hair, a handsome tanned face, pleasant blue eyes, and a beige raw silk suit straight from the pages of *Esquire*. He looked up at Edgar and Harry and nodded toward the side chairs. There was no warmth in his eyes.

"I've a luncheon engagement with the Vice President, so I'll have to leave in a few minutes. Alben and I have some important matters to go over."

Edgar sat down uncomfortably. Whatever problem

he had couldn't measure up to the importance of Anson's meeting with Vice President Barkley, with whom Anson was obviously on a first-name basis. Suddenly Edgar was subdued, apprehensive. Harry was right. This was no place to be.

Anson stared from Hendly to Coyle, waiting impatiently.

"Mr. Hendly would like to discuss the Rabb matter with you, sir."

"There's nothing to discuss. You heard what the Secretary said after the call from McCarthy. He was fit to be tied." He turned imperious eyes to Edgar. "This is not a subject for discussion. This is an order from the Secretary of the Interior. We don't need to suffer a McCarthy witch-hunt in this department because of some nonsense going on in the sticks. And I'm not accustomed to rebellion from minor employees of the BIA."

He tapped a button on his desk and rose, towering over the much shorter Hendly and Coyle. Immediately the office door opened and the administrative aide swept in like Loretta Young. She waited as Coyle and Hendly left the office and closed the door behind them.

They walked down the hallway to the elevator. "Now maybe you'd like a visit with the Secretary?" Coyle said, his voice sardonic, his face even more ashen than usual.

Edgar got into the elevator, and the two doors shut between his supervisor and himself.

*   *   *

Edgar took the train back to Tucson. He needed time to think, and sitting in the Pullman car, staring out at the vast and varied countryside as the train sped by, began to restore his confidence that there was a whole lot of real America out there untainted by the malady of Commie hunting that was epidemic in Washington, D.C. But the three and a half days on the train did not lessen the despair he felt about what he had to do.

Frances picked him up at the Southern Pacific depot in downtown Tucson. She wore a shirtdress of pink cotton that covered her thin body almost to her ankles. Her graying hair was drawn back in a tight bun that lent severity to her already austere face. Her shoes were the same as four-year-old Jennifer's, strap sandals of white patent leather.

Edgar kissed Frances on the cheek and whisked Jennifer off her feet. She giggled as he kissed her again and again on her nose. Edgar had a sudden, fleeting sense that something was missing, that the picture had a hole in it. His son Jimmy had been murdered a few years ago, barely eleven years old, and he wanted to hug him now, to kiss him like he was kissing Jennifer.

He kissed Jennifer's tiny lips, put her down, and handed her the licorice rope he had bought at the station in El Paso just a few hours ago. She chewed on it, her face a bright smile, as they waited for Edgar's valise. A Negro porter carried it out to their Ford sedan and put it in the trunk. Edgar handed him a dime, and the lanky, thin man smiled broadly, revealing an entirely toothless upper gum, and limped back into the station.

"I got chicken fried steak all ready in the pan, Eddie, just waitin' for ya," Frances said.

"That's great. I need a little home cookin' to resuscitate me from what I been through."

"Was it real bad, honey?"

"It wasn't real good." He stared straight ahead at the road, still deep in thought over what to say, how to say it.

"We gotta have a little talk," he said.

Frances looked askance at him. "What's goin' on in that brain a yourn?"

He sighed and was silent for a moment. "A real tough thing I gotta do."

She kept staring at him, waiting for him to tell her. "Yeah?" she urged.

"I been ordered to fire Joshua."

The words hung in the air like a foul odor. Frances stared out the side window. "Well, it ain't like he needs the measly few bucks the BIA pays him anymore," she murmured, then sighed. "But ya ain't gonna do it?" She studied her husband's profile.

He shook his head slowly. "Doin' that to him would be 'bout like cuttin' out my own heart."

Frances nodded. "What's gonna happen to us?"

Edgar shrugged and looked at her with sad eyes. His voice was thin. "Get canned, I reckon, throwed outta our house."

It was almost dark. The sunset outlined Black Mountain two miles ahead of them on the Reservation, a shimmering orange and lavender glow.

"What'll we do?"

He shrugged again as he turned south on Indian Agency Road. "Guess I could go back workin' for Jake Lukis, manage the hotel or the sand 'n gravel plant, maybe even work up to bein' his chief honcho again, like twenty years ago."

"Yeah, but it'll be half the pay, and we ain't got a pot to piss in as it is."

"So what do I do? Fire Joshua Rabb?"

"No," she said.

He nodded. "That's what I'm a talkin' 'bout. We're just gonna suck in our gut and take what comes."

"We done it before," she said.

"Yip. It's just kinda tough to start all over again now. I ain't a spring chicken no more."

She looked at him and smiled. "I got a bit of news fer ya, Eddie honey. Ya wasn't never no spring chicken."

He laughed. "Yeah, reckon not."

"The Lord giveth and the Lord taketh away; blessed be the name of the Lord."

He looked over at his wife compassionately and nodded.

" 'Every terror that haunted me has finally caught up with me,' " she recited from the book of Job, which they both knew so well, " 'and all that I feared has come upon me. There is neither peace of mind nor quiet for me, and I chafe in restless torment.' "

He put his hand on hers folded in her lap. She slid close to him on the seat and rested her head on his shoulder. Tears rolled down her cheeks.

"A man ain't nothin' but what's in his own guts,"

Edgar said softly. "It took me fifty-five years to learn that, and it took a Jew lawyer from New York to teach me. It ain't the car or the house or the suit a clothes. It's just what's inside." He kissed the top of his wife's head. "Wipe away them tears, honey. We'll weather the storm, no matter what."

Chapter Nine

A monsoon season thunderstorm roared over Tucson the next day at about noon. It only lasted a half hour, but it left an inch of rain on the cracked earth. Most of the ground was baked so hard that it couldn't even absorb the water, and it ran off into the unpaved streets and gulleys, flooding them with mud.

A bright blue Cadillac convertible with a white top parked in the muddy street outside the BIA. The driver remained inside, and a tall, stocky man got out of the passenger door and walked carelessly through the mud puddles into the building. He stamped some of the mud off his cowboy boots inside the front door and walked up to Frances. She frowned at him from inside the reception window, open a foot at the bottom.

"Ya live in a barn, mister?" she asked.

"What do you call this?" he answered, looking around at the adobe walls, the terra-cotta tiled floor.

"I gotta clean that mess," she said.

"I'm here to see Edgar Hendly and Joshua Rabb."

"They expectin' ya?"

"Just tell them Senator Maitland is here."

Frances winced. She picked up the telephone, pushed a button, and spoke into it for a moment, then pushed another button and spoke low into the phone.

Edgar appeared at the door to his office. "Right down this way, Senator." He waved him down the hallway.

Maitland walked up to him, ignored his outstretched hand, and walked into the office. He sat down in one of the chairs in front of the desk.

Edgar sat down behind the desk. "Nice to see ya again, Senator."

"Is Rabb here?"

"Them's his footsteps yer hearin' right now."

Joshua walked into the office and sat down in the chair about five feet from Maitland. The senator stared at the stainless-steel hooks protruding from the left sleeve of Joshua's tan linen suit jacket. Joshua studied the senator: attractive, full head of slightly graying blond hair, a well-healed scar that went from his right eye down his cheek and ended at the side of his mouth. He wore a Western suit of cream cotton and brown ostrich cowboy boots covered with mud.

"How'd that happen?" he asked, pointing at Joshua's steel hand.

"Czechoslovakia."

"Which army were you with, the Russians?" He looked contemptuously at Joshua.

Joshua didn't react.

Maitland pointed at his cheek. "Corregidor."

"I heard it was South Phoenix," Joshua said, watching Maitland's eyes flash with anger.

The widespread rumor—admittedly mostly among

Democrats, but delicious nonetheless—was that the junior Republican senator from Arizona had been cut by a pimp in Phoenix years ago when he refused to pay for services rendered by a Mexican whore. But the Corregidor story, like the one about "Tail Gunner Joe," lent an aura of patriotism—even heroism—to these otherwise undistinguished and essentially indistinguishable politicians.

"What brings ya to our happy little home?" Edgar drawled.

"I didn't expect to find him still here," Maitland said, inclining his head toward Joshua.

"Can't account for what you expect, Senator."

Joshua looked puzzled. "What's this about?" he said to Edgar.

"Nothin' earth-shatterin'."

"You haven't even told him?" Maitland said.

"Nothin' to tell."

Maitland turned to Joshua. "You're fired."

"You don't have that authority," Edgar said.

"The Secretary of the Interior does."

"You ain't the Secretary," said Edgar.

Joshua looked at Edgar. "When did this happen?"

"Last Friday mornin'."

"How come you didn't say anything this morning, when you were telling me about the hearing?"

"Because I ain't firin' ya."

Joshua frowned. "Then what happens to you?"

Edgar shrugged. "Reckon I'll be bussin' tables over t' the L and L."

"You don't have civil service protection?"

Edgar shook his head. "Neither of us does."

"Yeah, but I can get along on the legal work I have. But what about you? They'll pull your pension."

Edgar nodded. "Me 'n Frances talked about it. I ain't firin' ya."

"Then I'll quit. I'm not letting this happen to you because of me and Hanna."

"What're ya all of a sudden, my daddy? I'm a growed man, nobody gonna call ya a Commie and order me to can ya."

"You two assholes ought to be in vaudeville," Maitland said. "You got a whole dog and pony show going here."

Joshua stared at him and gripped the arm of his chair with his good hand.

"I'm not going to stand still for having a couple of Commie sympathizers working for the BIA in my state." Maitland wagged his finger at Edgar. "I'm not going to fuck with you if you give this lowlife the boot. But if you buck me on this, I'm going to rip you a new asshole."

Edgar sat silently.

Maitland's voice was rising angrily. "You know all I have to do is go to my friends at the *Arizona Daily Star* and the *Arizona Republic* and both of you guys are finished. You'll have to move to Canada to find jobs. Haven't you read enough about that daughter of yours in the paper?" He turned malevolent red-rimmed eyes on Joshua.

Joshua stood up slowly and stepped toward Maitland. Maitland stood up as well, the taller and heavier of the two.

"What is it you were thinking of doing, you Commie cocksucker?"

Joshua clenched his steel-pronged hand, released it, and clenched it again. "You have immunity on the floor of the Senate, and nobody can do a thing to curb your malicious lies. But you don't have immunity when you're telling lies to a reporter. If I read anything defamatory you say about me or Edgar or my daughter, I'll sue you and the publisher, whoever it is."

"You're a bag of stinking wind, Mr. Commie," Maitland snarled. "You just cut your own nuts off." He turned abruptly and left the office.

Joshua was too angry to sit down. He began pacing in front of Edgar's desk.

"Take it easy, Josh. Ya'll have a damn stroke."

Joshua breathed deeply and sank into the chair. "You should have told me," he said. "I'm not going to get you fired."

"It ain't yer call, Mr. Rabb. And I ain't doin' it fer you, I'm doin' it fer me. It's high time I paid ya back a little fer what ya done fer me."

"Getting yourself fired isn't paying me back."

"If that's the result, then so be it. But I don't think I'm gonna be fired."

"But you said the Secretary himself ordered you to let me go."

"Well, not exactly. What really happened is that McCarthy called Secretary Kimmer and pissed all over him, and then Kimmer turned around and pissed all over ever'body down the line. But I'll tell ya somethin'. I think when push comes to shove, Kimmer is a

Democrat in the Truman cabinet, and he ain't about to let Republican Tail Gunner Joe tell him how to run the Department of the Interior."

"You're putting a lot of faith on a hunch. You've got a wife, you've got a four-year-old daughter."

"Yeah, and she's gonna be fourteen and twenty-four. And no matter what else happens, when someone says to her, 'What's yer ol' man like?' she's gonna be able to look 'em in the eye 'n say, 'He's a honest man, and he's a man a honor, just like his pal Joshua Rabb.' "

Joshua sat staring at his friend, and he had no retort. His eyes became moist, he couldn't help it. He suddenly felt humbled and overwhelmed by this unlikely martyr who had once been a bigoted "yes man."

It was almost as predictable as night following day that the Tuesday morning *Arizona Daily Star,* which the paperboy took great pride in bouncing off the screen door so that it landed almost exactly two feet in front of it, would carry the story on the front page covering the entire right-hand column under J. T. Sellner's byline:

SENATOR MAITLAND DECRIES COMMIES IN BIA

CALLS FOR FIRING SUPERINTENDENT AND LEGAL AFFAIRS OFFICER

Senator William ("Big Bill") Maitland of Phoenix has called upon the Secretary of the Interior, Michael Kimmer, to "clean the Commies and fellow travelers out of the Bureau of Indian Affairs."

Joshua sat at the kitchen table and blanched. He put down his coffee cup with a clatter, and Barbara turned around and stared at him. She put the spatula down on the stove, turned the light off under the frying pan with eight eggs in it, and wiped her hands on her apron.

"What is it?" she asked.

He read her the headlines and the first paragraph and continued reading aloud. When he got to the last few paragraphs, he sucked in his breath and read silently. Then he read them aloud. Barbara stood watching him, her eyes wide with shock.

"Senator Maitland has been assembling a dossier on Joshua Rabb and his family ever since Senator Joseph McCarthy began leading the much needed crusade against Communists in government. Just last Friday, Rabb's supervisor, Bureau of Indian Affairs Superintendent Edgar Hendly, responsible for the state of Arizona as well as those corners of New Mexico, Colorado, and Utah covered by the Navajo Reservation, was summoned to Washington, D.C., to testify before the Tydings committee. The testimony concerned Joshua Rabb's and his daughter Hanna's complicity in violations of the McCarran Act, permitting an employee of the federal government to defend two well-known Communists, and Hanna's role in the murder of United States Marshal Oliver Friedkind. (See related story at page 6.) The Tydings committee demanded the termination of Joshua Rabb as the legal affairs officer for the BIA. When Superintendent Hendly refused to do so, it formally requested Hendly's own resignation. Secretary Michael Kimmer has been given an ultimatum: Get your house in order or get sacked yourself!

"Hanna Rabb and four of her co-conspirators will be held to answer on murder charges this coming Friday at a preliminary hearing before Superior Court Judge Bernardo Valasco. Ordinarily, such a hearing would be conducted by one of Tucson's two justices of the peace, but both of them have recused themselves from hearing this infamous affair. In fact, this reporter has learned that Justice of the Peace Ken Chapman wrote to Velasco and decried the fact that there was no grand jury system in Arizona to save the taxpayers money in clear cases like this one, by simply indicting the criminals and bringing them all the more rapidly to justice, as is done in federal courts throughout the country. 'It is high time that the courts punish the pinkos who are a cancer eating at the very heart of our nation's greatness,' Chapman wrote to Velasco.

"Senator Maitland has called for a major crackdown on Communist sympathizers in our colleges and universities, of whom Professor Livinsky is merely 'the ten percent of the deadly iceberg which we can see above the surface.' As for Rabb and his daughter, he said, 'I'm sending my dossier to Senator McCarthy today. There's enough evidence in it to stop these traitors in their tracks and clean out a chancre sore that has been a blight on Tucson for several years.' "

Joshua looked up, and there were tears streaming down Barbara's cheeks. She held her hands over her bulging belly as though she were in pain.

"You okay, honey?" Joshua asked, standing up quickly from the table and going to her. He took her by the hand and led her to the table. She sat down carefully.

"How can they print trash like that?" she said, her voice barely above a whisper.

Joshua shook his head. "I don't know," he mumbled. "It's libel."

"But I read more and more of that kind of stuff every day," Barbara said. "It's like it's almost become a fad to call anyone you disagree with a Communist. I read where some senator called Secretary of Defense George Marshall 'a living lie' and accused him of 'conspiring with the most treasonable array of political cutthroats ever turned loose in the executive branch.' Can you believe they'd say filth like that?"

Joshua nodded. "Yeah, that was Senator Jenner from Indiana. He's been making headlines with that garbage for months."

"And some senator from Nevada, Molly Malone, I think his name is, even accused President Truman of 'echoing the thoughts of Communists who want to set up a welfare state.' Don't these people have any limits? Can they say those kinds of terrible things about *anybody*?"

"No," Joshua said, "there are limits. But not when you're dealing with senators or congressmen making speeches on the floor of Congress. They have what we call absolute immunity to say anything they want."

"Even if it's a lie."

"Yes. But they don't have immunity when they're not in Congress making a formal speech. They can't say those things to newspaper reporters who try to ruin people's lives with it. Some of what's in that article is true, but a lot of it is lies."

The telephone rang. Joshua glanced at his watch. Just ten minutes after seven, too early for social calls. He answered the telephone warily.

"You read J.T.'s article in the paper?" Edgar Hendly asked.

"Yeah. Barbara and I have just been talking about it."

"Can you do somethin' 'bout it?"

"I'm not sure. I've never had any experience with defamation law."

"Well, I'm gonna help ya out. That stuff she wrote about the Tydings committee demandin' that I fire ya and givin' Secretary Kimmer a ultimatum is all pure crap. I just got off the phone with Harry Coyle. He says that it was only McCarthy who talked to the Secretary, and there was no decision or resolution or anythin' else by the committee. And Harry says that Kimmer's cooled down and ain't after either of our asses. I tol' ya that would happen. The whole Truman administration's gettin' its back up about McCarthy's bullshit, and they're finally startin' to be willin' to lock horns with the son of a bitch. And he ain't even an official member a the committee, ya know." He didn't wait for a response. "So anyways, Harry's sending me out by plane a copy of the Congressional Record for last Friday, hot off the press. We can prove that stuff about the committee is a pack a lies."

"When's it coming?"

"This evenin', the only flight that comes from Washington. It arrives at nine."

"I'll pick you up at quarter to."

"I'll be ready."

Joshua hung up and told her what Edgar had said.

"Can you sue the newspaper for libel?"

"I don't know. I have to research it. I'll have some time to do it this afternoon."

"I hope so," she said. Her face contorted with pain for a few seconds.

"You sure you're okay?" Joshua walked to her and kissed her cheek.

"Yeah, I'm all right."

"Why don't you go back to bed, stay off your feet."

"I'm fine, really." She smiled brightly at him to dispel his misgivings.

He studied her face and kissed her. She wrapped her arms around his neck and he pulled her up. They hugged for a moment, then pulled back from each other, holding hands. His mechanical arm hung loosely at his side.

"You're gorgeous," he said.

"I look like a cow."

"I feel like a bull."

"You better get out of here while you can."

They smiled at each other and chuckled.

Joshua drove to Maricopa dormitory to see Hanna. He wanted to tell her what was in the newspaper so that she could gird herself for the inevitable wisecracks and kidding from other students. The dorm mother told him that she and her roommate, Jan Diedrichs, had left ten minutes earlier to have breakfast at the restaurant just off campus on Park Avenue.

Joshua walked to the restaurant on the next block.

There were at least a hundred students and faculty having breakfast. Joshua sat down next to Hanna.

"Hi, Daddy. You don't look so happy."

"I just wanted to warn you that there's an article in the newspaper about us this morning."

"Bad?"

He nodded.

"Thank God nobody we know ever reads the paper," Jan said.

"I see a lot of the faculty in here reading it," Joshua said.

"Yeah, but they're all behind Professor Livinsky," Hanna said.

Jan nodded in agreement.

"Well, anyway, I thought I'd better warn you."

"Thanks, Daddy."

"You hear from Mark lately?"

"Got a letter yesterday. He's sure they're sending the Seventh Regiment to Korea real soon. I guess they need more cannon fodder."

Joshua didn't react to the remark. "Let's hope the war ends before he goes."

Hanna nodded. She held up crossed fingers.

Joshua left the restaurant and walked by several piles of newspapers in front of a news kiosk on the sidewalk outside the restaurant. His eyes fell on the morning Phoenix newspaper, the *Arizona Republic,* and he reached down, pulled a copy off the top, and dropped a nickel on the stack. His eyes were riveted on the same headlines and same story he had read this morning. Sellner had apparently submitted the story to wire service, and it had been picked up at least for

Phoenix publication. He felt sickened and weak-kneed standing there reading the story again.

Then he became furious. The shock of it had worn off. The pain of it had passed. But a fury arose in him that made his heart beat quickly and his breath became labored. He had a contract to review for the Big Reservation, but that could wait a few hours. First he had to get to the law library at the Pima County courthouse and research the law of defamation.

Joshua drove to the Pima County law library and spent over two hours reading every case he could find on the subject, from the Supreme Court of the United States down to the federal courts of appeals and the supreme court of Arizona.

It was "black letter" law that you could not call somebody a criminal or accuse them of a crime unless you could prove the truth of the allegation. Such defamatory *speech* was slander per se. If it was published in writing, it was libel per se. Some of what Senator Maitland said fit the definition of slander, calling him and Hanna Communists and traitors. And Sellner had libeled them per se by publishing it in the newspaper and had specifically libeled Hanna and the other students by writing that she and "four of her coconspirators *will* be held to answer" for murder at the preliminary hearing. But the critical question was whether the newspapers who published these calumnies would be answerable and required to pay damages for the libel committed by a reporter. If they weren't liable, then they'd just fire the reporters to make everything look good and hire new reporters to commit the same defamation to sell newspapers. Joshua spent another hour researching that issue.

He drove home to his office, took pleading paper and five carbons and five onionskins, and began rapping out one-handed a lawsuit on his Remington typewriter. By the time he finished, he had sued Maitland for slander per se, and Sellner, the *Arizona Daily Star,* and the *Arizona Republic* for libel per se. He drove to the clerk's office and filed the complaint at noon. He brought four copies of the complaint for service on the defendants to the Sheriff's Department Civil Division, just down the hall from the clerk's office.

Chapter Ten

Tim Essert was excited, the kind of excited that didn't happen to him very much anymore. He was forty years old and had been the assistant United States attorney in charge of the Tucson office since the end of the war. He had actually been the acting office chief since the middle of 1943, when Norman Ridder had joined the army and was sent to England. Norm had gone over to France the day after D day, and his jeep had hit a land mine near a French town with a long name that nobody could even spell. Pity. Norm wasn't a bad guy. And it wasn't that Essert was a coward or a 4-F'er, avoiding the draft. He would have been happy to serve, but like the good Catholic he was, he had seven children and was exempt from service.

The position of chief assistant U.S. attorney for southern Arizona was about as important as being an egg candler over at the big chicken farm on Highway 89. There were always crimes to prosecute, of course, mostly Indians from the Papago Reservation getting drunk and fucking with each other, and there were legal problems and contracts to work out for the government. It was just local crap, though, didn't affect a single hair on the head of anyone who lived beyond shouting distance of Tucson's city limits. Which meant that out of a hundred fifty million Americans, 149,960,000 of them would never hear the name Tim Essert. But now, finally, a real case had come along: Communists, traitors, murder, McCarthy kind of stuff. A first-rate career maker.

Essert hummed the tune to "This Could Be the Start of Something Big" and drummed his fingers rhythmically on the steering wheel. Horton Landers, Senator Maitland's administrative aide, had called him yesterday evening and asked him to come up to Phoenix to the senator's home for a meeting. Big Bill had just been served with a defamation lawsuit brought by Joshua Rabb, and something had to be done. Tim had dressed carefully for the meeting: a cream silk suit, brown and white wing tips, a pale yellow shirt, and a subtle beige silk tie: elegant, tasteful, a man on the move.

He turned right on Lincoln Road and ascended Camelback Mountain, a small dromedary hump of sandstone in East Phoenix where only the very rich lived. Senator Maitland had made a fortune in construction during the Second World War, building military camps in Arizona and southern California's Imperial Valley. The most obvious fruit of his success, besides the senatorial seat that he had just spent several hundred thousand dollars to win, was this fabulous house. It perched like an imperial palace over the desert kingdom below, pink marble columns and an immense, peaked copper roof turned to glaucous verdigris by the constant sun and occasional rain.

Senator Maitland himself came to the door to answer the bell. Tim had met him three times before, twice very recently in Tucson having to do with Livinsky and Moraga, and he was used to the senator's back-slapping, gregarious manner.

"Timmy, good of you to come, good of you to come."

Maitland stood a head taller than Tim and fifty pounds beefier. He was dressed in a white cotton Acapulco shirt and peach-colored raw silk trousers. He put his arm around Tim's shoulders and walked him into a spacious living room with a floor of checkerboard black and white marble tiles. Large overstuffed furniture was upholstered in solid black or solid white crushed velvet. Scattered about the room were several glistening wood tables with inlaid leather tops and gilded corners and Queen Anne legs, and in the corner of the room next to the black onyx-topped wet bar was an eight-foot-tall white marble elephant with tusks of oriental carved ivory. The thirty-foot-long glass sliding doors and picture window looked west over all of Phoenix, directly into the setting sun.

The heat through the glass was brutal, as Maitland took Essert to it to gaze properly awestruck at the senator's domain. They backed away from the burning glass, and Tim sat down on a huge black overstuffed armchair. Maitland sat across from him on the white velvet sofa and rang a bell on a corner of the Louis Quatorze cocktail table.

The affable look on Maitland's face remained, as

though etched in tin, until the maid had served them tall glasses of planter's punch and closed the double doors behind her.

"That fucker's got to go," Maitland growled.

The abrupt change of demeanor startled Tim. "Who?"

"Rabb."

Tim nodded.

"You know what the motto of my Scottish ancestors is?"

Tim shook his head.

"Nemo me impuni lacessit." He stared knowingly at Essert.

"Sorry, sir. I don't know it."

"Nobody injures me with impunity," the senator said.

"A good saying, sir."

"I'm looking to you to right the terrible wrong that's been done to me, Timmy." He smiled at Essert and winked. His blue eyes twinkled with warmth and camaraderie.

"What do you have in mind, Senator?"

"I have in mind what I know you've had in mind, Timmy. I've been following your career for almost two years now. And I've told you before and I tell you again, you've got what it takes to go places. Big places. I've got plans for you."

Tim smiled engagingly. "You know I'll do anything I can to help, Senator."

"I know that, Timmy. I know you're one man I can count on to do the right thing. It's time to clean those

Commies out of the university down there and put an end to this Rabb."

Tim nodded. "I've been thinking a lot on just how to do that, sir. I think it's high time we moved decisively, but Dillan Hopkins has been reluctant to stick his neck out."

"Listen, Timmy, Hopkins is dead meat, an elk just waiting to be skinned and mounted. He's a Democrat, and as soon as Ike wins the election, Hopkins is history, and I appoint the next U.S. attorney for Arizona. You got the picture?"

"Of course, Senator, but Hopkins still has a year and a half to go, and he can fire me like that." He snapped his fingers.

"Barry had a talk with him last night. They're old friends, even if they are in different parties. Nobody's real pleased about that lawsuit Rabb filed. Today it's me he's trying to screw. Tomorrow, one of the others. You can't let a guy like that think he can get away with this kind of shit. Hopkins told Barry he'll stay out of whatever you do in Tucson on this Communist matter."

Tim assumed that the Barry that Maitland was talking about was Goldwater, but he wasn't sure. Just as long as he had protection, however, he didn't care who was doing the protecting. He straightened in his chair and nodded soberly at Maitland.

"So let's see how you can help our party and do some good for me and you at the same time."

"Anything, Senator."

There was a knock on the double doors, and a tall, slender man, perhaps fifty years old, dressed in a brightly colored Hawaiian shirt and white linen trousers, came into the living room. He had a receding hairline of graying brown hair in a military haircut, a thin face, and dark brown lusterless eyes.

"You know my administrative aide, Horton Landers, don't you Timmy?"

"Sure do, Senator," Tim said, standing. He shook hands with Landers. The aide's hand was moist and flaccid. "Nice to see you again, sir. That was some mess down there that day, huh?"

Landers smiled mechanically and made no reply. He sat down on the opposite end of the sofa from the senator.

"Horton just got back from Washington. He delivered some important information to Joe McCarthy for me." Saying the name brought a look of great importance to Maitland's face. "Horton's been putting together a few ideas on this Commie shit that's been going on in Tucson."

Tim nodded avidly, showing how amenable he was to any suggestions.

"First thing, this Livinsky gotta be indicted for failing to register," Landers said.

"I absolutely agree," Tim said.

"And we gotta indict him for treason and Rabb for giving aid and comfort by representing him and Moraga."

Tim swallowed. "Well, Mr. Landers, I've done a lot of thinking on that. I can charge the professor with treason, but I don't think I can put Rabb in the indictment."

"Why not?" Maitland asked. His face had lost the pleasantness of a moment ago.

"Rabb is a lawyer. If I indict the Commie, he's entitled to be represented by a lawyer. And that statute in the McCarran Act just doesn't apply to Rabb."

"Joe McCarthy thinks it does," Maitland said.

Essert squirmed uncomfortably. "With all due respect, Senator, it's a lot easier to think it applies when you're in a Senate hearing room in Washington than to convince Judge Buchanan in Tucson that it applies. Buchanan can read statutes as well as anybody, and I'm telling you he isn't going to go for this. It's just like a lawyer representing a murderer. It doesn't mean that he believes in murder or is an aider and abettor of the crime. But the murderer is entitled to a lawyer under the Constitution. This is no different. Buchanan would throw out Rabb's indictment and probably recommend me to the State Bar for disbarment."

Maitland frowned. "This isn't what I'm looking to hear from you, Tim." He turned to Landers. "Can we handle this Buchanan?"

Landers shrugged. "Probably not. I've asked around. He's a tough-minded guy, marine officer in the First World War, sixty-three years old, acts pretty damn independent. He's not politically ambitious, and he's happy being a district court judge. If we go near him, it's liable to backfire real bad."

"Well, goddammit!" Maitland exploded. Essert flinched. "We gotta do *something* about that Jew bastard. He's got his hands on my throat."

"I have an idea on that, Senator," Essert said.

Maitland gritted his teeth and looked sourly at him. "Okay, let's hear it."

"Well, there's two things. Rabb's got a writ of prohibition hearing coming up in front of Judge Velasco, to try to get Livinsky reinstated at the U of A because of his tenure contract. Velasco's probably going to grant the writ. He's a fuckin' Mex, should never have been appointed judge in the first place back in '46 or '47, but his greaser pals love him, and there are a shitload of them in Tucson, so he got reelected in '48. But if the case gets removed up to superior court in Phoenix, and you get the right judge, Livinsky won't get reinstated. And the statute on suing state agencies—which the Board of Regents is—says that any lawsuit brought against them in a venue outside of Phoenix can be removed by the state attorney general to Phoenix."

Maitland's face softened. A hint of a smile crossed his lips. "Well, I guess we can get that done easily enough. I'll call the attorney general in the morning. He's a good man, wants to be governor. We understand each other. What's your second angle?"

"The defamation case. It's also in Velasco's court. It's a tougher thing to deal with, because Rabb's got the right to bring the lawsuit wherever the publication of the defamation occurred, and that includes Tucson. But filing a lawsuit isn't worth a damn unless you can get it to trial. So screwing it up procedurally is almost as good as winning it. Do you have a good lawyer up here, sir?"

"Sure, Frank Snell. The best."

"How about the federal judges up here? Is there one you can count on?"

"You bet."

"Get your lawyer to file a federal court lawsuit against Rabb based on abuse of process and malicious prosecution. Then file a state court motion up here asking for a change of venue on the writ of prohibition."

Maitland appeared bewildered. "I don't have a clue what you're talking about, Tim."

"Well, I'm sure your lawyer will. A local judge up here, who you have some influence with, will order Velasco to transfer the case up to federal court in Phoenix. Rabb will go bananas and appeal or take a writ to the state supreme court or the Ninth Circuit Court of Appeals. No matter what either of the courts do, it can be appealed or writted up to the Supreme Court of the United States. In the meantime, for the next two, three, or even four years, everything is up in the air. Rabb's suing you, you're suing him, the reinstatement hearing for Livinsky is all snafued up. By the time the legal issues get decided, if ever, anything might happen."

Maitland began to smile broadly. "Yeah, maybe Rabb'll get run over by a truck. Huh, Horton?" He turned to Landers. "Why don't you break out that good bottle of scotch I bought last week. I think Timmy'll like it." He looked back at Essert. "I had a feeling about you, Timmy, a gut feeling that you were my kind of guy. You've got a big future with me, a big future."

Essert relaxed into the deep armchair, and he smiled graciously.

There hadn't been a story in Thursday morning's *Arizona Daily Star* about the lawsuit against it and one of its reporters. But that didn't surprise Joshua. The competing evening newspaper, the *Tucson Citizen*, would probably feature it prominently.

He went to the BIA for the morning, talked to Solomon about the progress that he and Roy Collins had with potential witnesses for the preliminary hearing, and then spent two hours with a group of Papago cattle ranchers from the Big Reservation who were concerned that a suspected anthrax outbreak on two white ranches adjoining the Reservation would infect their own cattle. They wanted Joshua to call the state veterinary inspector in Phoenix to quarantine the cattle and to put up a barbed-wire fence for about five miles to keep them from mingling with the Indians' cows.

The vet inspector said that he would be down in a day or two to check out the suspect cattle, but he didn't have the money in his budget for barbed wire and posts, and he didn't have the manpower to put up a fence. Maybe Transportation could help. Joshua called the chief engineer at the Department of Transportation and was told that only an order from the state legislature or the governor's office could authorize such an expenditure.

Joshua called the Corps of Engineers office in Phoenix. The head of the office was an army colonel, and he agreed to pull the wire and 5,250 steel posts from the surplus storage facility at the All American Canal near Yuma if the Indians would put up the fence themselves. They readily agreed. Since it was a federal OLM project, the fence would have to be on Reservation land.

Roy Collins telephoned Joshua late in the morning. "I got a tiny little lead," he said.

"What?"

"The evening desk clerk at the Cattlemen's Hotel says that the night before Anne Marie Hauser was murdered, she met a guy in the lobby of the hotel and went out with him. He was middle-aged, thin, graying short hair. They seemed to know each other pretty well. Real chummy, he says."

"Maybe she knew him from Washington?"

"She'd been in Tucson on and off for five or six months. Plenty of time to meet someone here."

"Any idea who the man is?"

"No. He matches the description of about ten million other guys."

"Anything else?"

"Nothing. That's all I got."

"Tiny little lead is right."

"Well, it's a start. I have to do some legwork, find out where they went. It's going to take a while."

"Hanna and those kids don't have a while."

"Don't lay that all on my head," Roy said.

"Sorry. Let me know."

Joshua returned home a little before noon. Magdalena was feeding Macario at the kitchen table and Barbara was preparing chicken salad and potato salad for lunch. As he sat down at the table, the phone on the kitchen wall rang. It was Mischa Livinsky.

"I'm at the United States marshal's office," he said.

"What happened?"

"I'm under arrest. Those two FBI agents came out to my house and picked me up a half hour ago."

"What are the charges?"

"I don't know. They wouldn't tell me."

"Okay, I'll be right there."

Barbara looked at Joshua, and her eyes were frightened. "The professor?" she murmured.

Joshua nodded. "I'll be back in a couple of hours."

Barbara sat down on a chair at the table. She breathed deeply several times and held her hands on her belly. "I wish you wouldn't be doing this."

He looked in her eyes and felt enormous guilt. "I can't abandon him. He hasn't done anything wrong."

"But we're going to be destroyed." Tears spilled over her lids.

"Honey, honey." He stepped to her and held her face tenderly in his hand. "He has no one else to help. I can't refuse."

She swallowed and sniffled, and he wiped the tears from her cheeks with the side of his hand. He kissed the tip of her nose.

"I'll be back in a couple of hours," he said softly.

How many times had he been to visit prisoners in the marshal's holding cell and bridled at the stink of the place, the filth of it. There was no toilet, so anything that anyone had to do resulted in a pile or a puddle on the floor. The cell was hosed down once a week—or so he had been told—but he had never seen it clean.

Mischa Livinsky was sitting silently in a corner. He stood up and walked to the bars when Joshua came into the room. Joshua stood in front of the holding cell, his hand grasping a vertical bar.

"What's going to happen?" Mischa asked.

"The U.S. attorney assembled a grand jury this morning. You've probably been indicted for violations of the McCarran Act."

"How do you know?"

"The two FBI agents. They're downstairs in the marshal's office bubbling over with joy."

"So what do I do?" Mischa's voice was high and squeaky.

"We go before Judge Buchanan at one o'clock for your initial appearance and arraignment. I'll try to get you out on your own recognizance without having to post bail."

"I thought Buchanan was one of the good guys."

"He is. But the grand jury is strictly under the control of the U.S. attorney, and when it brings an indictment, the judge has no function other than to accept it on face value and have the accused persons arrested. That doesn't mean he approves it."

"I hope not," Mischa murmured. "I guess this is related to the article in the newspaper yesterday morning."

"Actually it's related to the defamation lawsuit I filed yesterday at noon. I suppose that as soon as the senator and the newspapers got served, they were on the phone to Essert planning whatever strategy they had to discredit me and the case."

Mischa nodded. "Well, this ought to do it just fine," he said. "Getting me convicted will definitely take care of the lawsuit."

Joshua smiled, trying to appear confident. "Actually, I can't imagine that there's sufficient evidence to convict you."

"You sure?" Mischa asked.

Joshua shook his head. "Nothing is absolutely sure in the law. But I've been practicing for fifteen years and doing mostly criminal law for the last five, and I think I'm right."

Mischa frowned. "*Im yirtzeh hashem* [if God wills it]," he said in Yiddish, "*ayl molay rachamim vet uns helfen* [God full of mercy will help us]."

"*Ayl molay rachamin,*" Joshua said quietly, grimacing with the poignant flash of memory of all those whom God had helped at the concentration camp at Medzibiez.

"What are you Commies cooking up?" Marshal Fratangeli asked, walking up to the bars.

Under different circumstances it would have struck Joshua as funny, but not now.

"Let's go. Time for the arraignment," the marshal said, unlocking the barred cell.

He bound the prisoner with a belly chain locked to his handcuffed wrists. Joshua and Livinsky walked in front of Fratangeli down the hallway to the federal courtroom. Livinsky took a seat in the jury box. Joshua sat down at the defense table. The courtroom was empty except for Tim Essert, the two FBI special

agents, and J. T. Sellner, who appeared gleeful. She
smiled at Joshua. She was in her early sixties, thin and
short, with a furrowed face and brown eyes and dyed
dark brown hair coiffed in Mae West waves on her
small head. As unattractive as she usually was, the
happy smile brightened her face. Joshua looked away
in disgust. He couldn't stomach looking at her in her
moment of dubious exultation.

Mrs. Hawkes came through the chambers door followed by Judge Buchanan. She took her seat at the
court reporter's table, and he ascended the bench. He
sat down in his large chair and looked around the
courtroom. He was not wearing his black robe, just
his charcoal gray suit and black wool tie and heavily
starched shirt with an old-style detachable collar of
high, stiff cotton with folded-over tips, the kind of
shirt most men these days wore only with tuxedos or
tails.

"We'll consolidate the initial appearance with the
arraignment, if the defendant consents," Judge Buchanan said, looking at Joshua.

Joshua stood up. "Thank you, Your Honor. Yes,
we consent."

"The clerk will enter your appearance on behalf of
the defendant."

"Thank you, Your Honor."

"Mr. Essert," the judge said, turning his attention
to the assistant United States attorney, "you have a
true bill?"

"I do, Your Honor." He stood up at the prosecution table.

"Bring a copy to Mr. Rabb," Buchanan said.

Joshua took the indictment from Essert's hand and read it carefully. Livinsky was charged in count one with failing to register as a member of a Communist front organization. This violation of the McCarran Internal Security Act carried a penalty of five years in prison and a fine of $10,000 per day of nonregistration. Nothing surprising here. But he sucked in his breath and felt his stomach constricting as he read count two: treason. It carried the death penalty.

Despite his cavalier assurances to Livinsky, the charges against him were grave. The Subversive Activities Control Board *had* declared Academics Against War a Communist front organization and the attorney general *had* put it on his infamous list. And Livinsky hadn't taken the proper legal steps provided in the McCarran Act to contest and appeal these determinations. He was therefore by definition guilty of the crime of failure to register. Would a jury be persuaded that the journal article he wrote, coupled with his membership in a Commie front organization and Livinsky actually having been a Communist party member in Moscow, added up to treason?

"Sir?" Buchanan asked.

Joshua swallowed and nodded. "Waive reading," he said, his voice reedy. He cleared his throat. "Not guilty, Your Honor, on both counts."

Buchanan turned to Essert. "You looking for bail?"

"Your Honor, treason is a capital offense. The government asks that the defendant be held without bond at the Mount Lemmon Detention Center pending trial."

"Denied," Judge Buchanan said casually. "The defendant is released on his own recognizance." He looked at J. T. Sellner sitting in the first row of spectator seats behind the walnut railing. "Did you get that, Miss Sellner? The court holds that the defendant has substantial community ties, that he poses no danger to himself or others, and that the charges against him on the evidence stated in the indictment do not persuade the court that the presumption is great with respect to the capital offense."

Sellner wrote noisily on her steno pad, keeping her eyes glued to it. Only the flush of blood in her cheeks betrayed her anger.

"The government objects to the court's action with respect to bail," Essert expostulated loudly. "Federal law requires the court to hold the defendant in custody without bail in a capital case."

"Thank you for your learned dissertation on the law, Mr. Essert. Take it to the court of appeals."

"The question of bail is simply—"

"Be silent, sir!" Buchanan roared. He struck his gavel on the round wooden block so forcefully that the head of it flew off and clattered to the floor twenty feet in front of the bench, skipping another ten feet.

"Jury trial is set for Wednesday, October seventeen," Buchanan said quietly. "Marshal Fratangeli, you will release him now." He walked off the bench and through his chambers door.

"We're going to have to look into that motherfucking pinko judge," Special Agent Holmes muttered. He and Schlesinger and Essert stood at the prosecution table staring at the defendant and his lawyer leaving the courtroom.

Chapter Eleven

Joshua met Solomon at the Pima County Courthouse at eight o'clock the next morning to prepare for the preliminary hearing. They reviewed the evidence that had been discovered. Roy Collins had dropped out of the effort since the arrest of Mischa Livinsky. Whatever his personal opinion may have been of Joshua and Hanna and the professor, he still couldn't actively help the cause of a lawyer representing a man under federal indictment for treason.

Joshua's adrenaline made him bristle with energy and anticipation. He was dressed in his black vested suit with his shiny pocket watch chain hanging from the top buttonhole of the vest and dipping down to the pocket watch in the right vest pocket. He had buffed his stainless-steel prongs so that they would glisten in the light of the courtroom chandeliers. When he walked into the courtroom at almost exactly nine o'clock, the five students were sitting in the jury box, warily surveying the huge crowd of spectators.

The *Arizona Daily Star*'s lead front-page story had been a careful one, this time, but it had predicted fireworks and bold histrionics by attorney Joshua

Rabb in superior court this morning. The story was a detailed but unslanted report on the murder of Oliver Friedkind and the charges brought yesterday against the professor.

Joshua squeezed through the hostile crowd and took his seat at the defense table. Randy Stevens looked over at him and rolled his eyes. "Don't buy any green bananas," he said. "You won't live long enough for them to get ripe."

Joshua grinned and chuckled. "What am I laughing about?" he said, looking around at the spectators.

There were two other lawyers at the table with Joshua. He shook hands with Harry Chandler, representing Fred Mergen. Harry introduced him to Mel Craddick from Phoenix, representing the Rustin sisters.

"Ya got anything?" Harry whispered.

Joshua nodded his head.

"Enough?"

"God willing," Joshua said.

"I don't much like puttin' somethin' like this in God's hands," Harry said.

"A guy's gotta cover all possibilities," Joshua whispered and shrugged his shoulders.

"If the judge binds them over, will he impose additional bail?" Mel Craddick asked.

"I think that—" Joshua's answer was drowned out by a loud outburst from the spectators as the bailiff came through the rear door followed by the court stenographer and Judge Velasco. Velasco was tall and stocky. A walrus mustache covered his upper lip. He wore a black robe zipped up to the middle of the white, starched collar of his dress shirt.

The lawyers all stood up. The bailiff banged his gavel several times as the judge took his seat behind the high bench.

"Note your appearance," the judge said curtly. He tugged at the collar of his shirt as though it were too tight.

"W. Randolph Stevens for the state, Your Honor." He sat down.

"Joshua Rabb for the defendants Rabb and Diedricks, Your Honor."

"Harry Chandler for Mr. Mergen, Your Honor."

"Melvin Craddick for defendants Rustin."

"Very well," Velasco said. "I've read all of the double jeopardy pleadings submitted on behalf of all parties and I don't want to hear any further argument on any of the issues raised there. Is there additional argument any counsel wishes to make?"

"No, Your Honor," Randy said.

Joshua shook his head. "No, sir." Chandler and Craddick both shook their heads.

"I'm going to conduct the preliminary hearing before I rule on the defense motion," Judge Velasco said. "Call your first witness, Mr. Stevens."

The Judge was proceeding as Joshua had assumed he would: very cautiously.

Tim Essert was the first witness. He testified that he and the two FBI special agents from Washington, D.C., had been obstructed in the performance of their duties by the demonstrators. They had been impeded as they walked to and from the courthouse, even jostled by several of the protesters. He testified that "the howling of the mob was so loud and insistent" that it caused trouble to him in the grand jury room making himself heard.

Joshua and Harry declined cross-examination. Mel Craddick spent ten minutes trying to dissect the testimony.

Harry leaned toward Joshua and whispered, "We obviously got us a wet behind the ears co-counsel here."

"Tell him to shut up," Joshua whispered.

Chandler leaned toward Craddick and whispered something in his ear. Craddick blushed, shot an angry glance at Joshua, and continued with fifteen more minutes of pointless questioning.

Tim Essert was a witness merely reciting facts. It was unlikely that he was going to stumble and fall, but the repetition of the facts gave them more damaging emphasis to the judge than would otherwise have been the case had there been no cross-examination.

The next two witnesses were the FBI agents. Schlesinger testified that he had not been anywhere near the area of the firebomb when it went off, but that he had heard the explosion from Essert's office. He then detailed the arrest of the five fleeing demonstrators. Holmes testified almost identically.

This time, after a withering look from Harry Chandler, Craddick followed the lead of both of his co-counsel in declining to cross-examine.

The final witness for the state was Pima County Coroner Stanley Wolfe. His lachrymose blue eyes were accentuated by round-lensed, steel-rimmed spectacles. He verified that the cause of death of Oliver Friedkind was anoxia from asphyxiation caused by the heat-related destruction of the alveoli in both lungs.

This time Joshua did have some questions.

"Dr. Wolfe, was any testing done to determine the construction or composition of the explosive agent?"

"Yes. I examined the site after the car had been towed away. The point of detonation of the device had created a small blackened cavity in the cement. I took scrapings of the charred material and brought them to the chemistry laboratory at the University of Arizona for testing. It was cordite."

"Would you tell us what cordite is, sir?"

"It's a smokeless powder composed of nitroglycerin, guncotton, and petroleum gelatinized by the addition of acetone. It's pressed into cords resembling brown twine."

"Then the explosive device wasn't a Molotov cocktail or some other simple incediary that any layman could make."

"That's correct."

"Is cordite just a more technical term for a stick of dynamite, which can be purchased in any mining supplies store down around the copper mines south of Tucson?"

"No, sir. That would be a different composition of materials containing either ammonium nitrate or cellulose nitrate."

"Then the particular explosive device was a fairly sophisticated one?"

Randy Stevens stood up at his table. "Objection, Your Honor. Conjectural, no foundation."

"No, I'll let him answer," Judge Velasco said.

Dr. Wolfe shrugged. "Well, it's more sophisticated than a Molotov cocktail and less sophisticated than an atom bomb. Somewhere in between."

There were a few laughs from the spectators.

"Such a device would have to be created by someone who had experience with sophisticated explosive devices, such as a person who had military experience in the demolition corps?"

Randy was still standing. "Objection, there's no foundation for this testimony, Your Honor."

"Sustained."

Joshua sat down.

"No further witnesses, Your Honor," Stevens said, sitting down.

"Defense?" said the judge.

"Call Lawrence Joslin, Your Honor," Joshua said.

It took several minutes for the bailiff to squeeze through the spectators and out of the courtroom to the witness waiting room. He returned with an elderly, white-haired man in tow.

The man stood in front of the court clerk, put his hand on a Bible, and swore to tell the truth.

"Your name, sir?" Joshua asked.

"Lawrence Joslin."

"Do you live in Tucson?"

"Yes. Me and the wife came out here from Iowa after I retired ten years ago."

"How old are you, sir?"

"I'm seventy-seven."

"How is your eyesight?"

"With these here eyeglasses, it's just like normal."

"Were you in the Valley National Bank parking lot on the morning of Tuesday, June 19, 1951?"

"I was. Me and Marger both were."

"Marger?"

"Yeah, yeah, I'm sorry. That's my wife Margaret. I call her Marger."

"Why do you remember that morning so specifically?"

"Because there was a riot going on. And a man got burned up in a car right in front of our eyes. We won't forget *that* morning."

There was a shocked murmur among the spectators. Judge Velasco banged his gavel twice and waited sternly for quiet. He nodded at Joshua to continue.

"Were you wearing your glasses at the time?"

"Yes, I always do."

"Did you see any person whom you believe planted or threw the explosive device?"

"Yes, I did."

Another wave of murmurs from the spectators. Another bang of the judge's gavel. Silence.

"Describe what you saw, Mr. Joslin."

"I was watching the demonstrators with the placards. I remember that one young woman there"—he pointed at Hanna—"and the other one next to her, because they was both holding a sign that said KOREA IS WRONG, BRING OUR BOYS HOME, and I thought it was a damn unladylike thing for them to be doing, there being a president and a whole Congress to make that decision—"

"Where were they standing?" Joshua interrupted him.

"Oh, maybe sixty, seventy feet down the sidewalk in front of the courthouse."

"Okay, please continue, Mr. Joslin."

"So anyways, I seen this gray-haired guy, skinny, tall, maybe fifty years old, couple years more, dressed in a pretty snazzy gray suit. Looked to be silk. He come across Broadway Boulevard just as the car turned into the parking lot, and he threw something under it. Then he turned heel and began walking real fast away down toward Stone Avenue. As soon as the explosion happened a couple seconds later, I was shocked and distracted and I lost sight of him."

"Did he look like one of the demonstrators?"

"He sure didn't."

"Can you remember seeing where he had come from?"

"Nope."

"Did you get a good enough look at his face to be able to recognize him again if you saw him or a photograph of him?"

"I'm honestly not sure."

"Thank you, Mr. Joslin."

Randy Stevens cross-examined him for twenty minutes, but the man's story didn't change.

Mr. Joslin was excused from the witness stand, and his seventy-three-year-old wife Margaret took the stand and testified virtually identically to her husband, except that she also remembered that the gray-haired man was wearing a white dress shirt and somber black tie. But she wasn't sure that she had taken enough notice of his face to recognize him again.

Randy declined to cross-examine, and the woman was excused.

"Defense rests, Your Honor," Joshua said, standing.

"Rebuttal?"

"No, Your Honor," said Randy, also standing.

"Very well. Please be seated."

The judge opened the file before him. Then he glanced around the courtroom at the spectators and the reporters, his dark eyes intense under thick brows.

"If any one of you utters a peep in response to the decision I'm about to read, I'll have you arrested and jailed for contempt of court. Understand?"

There was absolute silence in the courtroom. Velasco perched a pair of half glasses on the bridge of his nose and began to read.

"The fundamental nature of the guarantee against double jeopardy can hardly be doubted. Its origins can be traced to Greek and Roman times, and it became established in the common law of England long before this nation's independence.

"It was written into Arizona's Constitution forty years ago in article two, section ten: 'No person shall be twice put in jeopardy for the same offense.' One hundred sixty-five years ago, the founding fathers of our nation incorporated it into the Bill of Rights in the United States Constitution as part of the Fifth Amendment: 'No person shall be subject for the same offense to be twice put in jeopardy of life or limb.' The validity of the protection against double jeopardy is fundamental to the American concept of justice and applies to the state and federal courts equally.

"Notwithstanding the fact that the state and federal

governments are distinct and separate sovereigns, it would disembowel the very meaning of protection against double jeopardy if I were to find that once the federal government had determined the guilt or innocence of a person under *its* law, named 'Picketing and Parading,' the state could subject that same person to yet another prosecution based on precisely the same facts under *its* particular law, named 'Obstruction of Justice.' Applying the concept of fundamental fairness to the instant case, I therefore hold that the plea of guilty by the defendants to the charge of picketing and parading, a violation of federal law, precludes the state from prosecuting the defendants a second time for the same conduct, even though it is under a law with a different name, obstruction of justice.

"Count one of the indictment, obstruction of justice, is dismissed." Judge Velasco looked up from reading, "Gentlemen, I'll entertain any further motions you may have at this time."

Joshua rose rapidly to his feet. "Move to dismiss the felony-murder charge, Your Honor, there being no predicate offense to support it. Moreover, the state has introduced insufficient evidence to hold the defendants to answer on any charge of murder, no matter how it might be alleged."

Randy Stevens sat silently at the prosecution table.

Judge Velasco looked at him, waited, and then said, "Count two, second-degree murder, is dismissed. The bonds are exonerated." He got up from this chair and left the courtroom through the rear door into his office.

Joshua felt as though a tight belt had been un-cinched from around his chest. Air flowed freely to his lungs for the first time in many days. He shook hands with Chandler and Craddick, both smiling hap-pily. The five students remained seated in the jury box, looking shell-shocked, as the bailiff directed the spectators to clear the courtroom.

Essert, followed by the two FBI agents, walked up to the railing.

"How the hell can this happen?" he snarled at Randy Stevens.

"In a world where a carpenter can get resurrected," Randy said quietly, "anything can happen."

"That's real cute, Randy." Essert bit off the words. "Ollie's dead, and the only damn thing we got to show for it is a misdemeanor in federal court." His voice was husky with emotion.

"Find the guy who did the killing and we'll have a murder charge," Randy said, his voice growing with anger. "And how come Rabb turns up two eyewit-nesses and you don't even go looking?"

Essert turned around, bumped into Special Agent Holmes, pushed him roughly aside, and strode out of the courtroom followed by the two agents. The court-room door slammed shut behind them.

Late in the afternoon, Roy Collins called. "Congrat-ulations on the preliminary hearing. You did a great job."

"Thanks. But I don't think your boss Mr. Essert would agree."

"Fuck him."

Joshua chuckled. "Now all we have to do is find the real killer."

"Well, I got some more on that. I found where the Hauser woman and her friend went after they left the hotel."

"Where?"

"Palomino Bar, downtown on the corner of South Sixth Avenue and Pennington."

"I know the place. Barbara and I have been there a couple of times. But it's real dark inside."

"Yeah, but the bartender is positive on the ID. He said the woman had been in there ten or twelve times over the last few months, but she'd always been alone and never got picked up. This was the first time she ever showed up with someone."

"Gray-haired, skinny, fifty to fifty-five, wearing a snazzy gray silk suit?"

"That's the guy."

"Bingo!"

"There's more. About nine o'clock or so, an Indian came in and sat down with them."

"In the Palomino? I thought they didn't let Indians in."

"They don't ordinarily. But this guy was average height, stocky, short hair neatly combed instead of the usual shoulder-length shag, white dress shirt and brown slacks and tan wing tips, and he joined the two white people. So the bartender left him alone."

"Sounds like Julio Moraga."

"Sure sounds like him to me."

"The bartender see or hear anything."

"No. He said they sat at a corner table talking quiet, businesslike for a half hour, forty-five minutes."

"Was anyone around them, nearby? A waitress?"

"No, there weren't any customers near them, and it was a real slow night anyway, so the waitress was off. Then they left together."

"Did he know any of the other customers' names?"

"Yeah, two. I got the names, I'll check them out tomorrow. Maybe we'll get lucky."

"Why would Julio Moraga be meeting in a bar with the woman who got him onto the subversives list in the first place?"

"I guess when we find the gray-haired guy, we'll ask him."

Joshua thought for a moment. "I bet the guy was planning to murder both of them from the start, make it look like Julio killed her. He set it up by having her call him to talk about something important, maybe rolling over on Livinsky in return for leniency or immunity."

"That's possible. But if so, he would have to be someone in a position to make Julio think that he actually had that power."

"Right. Maybe someone working for the government. Someone important. Had the bartender ever seen him before?"

"No."

"Damn," Joshua murmured. "He's our boy. No doubt about it. We have to find him."

"I'll try to contact these two other customers first thing in the morning. Maybe it'll lead somewhere."

Chapter Twelve

The application for a writ of prohibition, to reinstate Livinsky to his teaching position, was set to be heard on Monday. On the preceding Thursday, U.S. Marshal Dominic Fratangeli served Joshua with a civil lawsuit that had been filed in Phoenix and assigned to Federal District Judge Coxon. The lawsuit alleged that "Joshua Rabb had acted in concert with a known member of a Communist front organization to *abuse the process* of the state superior court by filing a lawsuit against United States Senator William Maitland and a reporter and two newspapers in a coercive attempt to infringe their First Amendment rights under the United States Constitution, all of which constituted *willful and malicious prosecution* by Joshua Rabb in violation of the ethics of the American Bar Association and the McCarran National Security Act of 1950."

They sought one million dollars in actual and punitive damages from Joshua. Inasmuch as he didn't have ten cents to his name, having posted all of his meager savings as part of Hanna's bail, the money threat wasn't very fearsome. They could take away his and

Barbara's house and car, but there wasn't anything else to get. In any case, the whole thing was pure legal hogwash, Joshua knew, and the allegation of the violation of the McCarran Act had been thrown in just to provide some appearance of legitimacy to the jurisdiction of the federal court. But worse was yet to come.

Not more than fifteen minutes after Joshua received the federal lawsuit, a sheriff's deputy came to his door and served him with more legal documents, this time a state superior court civil order to show cause, filed in Phoenix. The superior court judge in Phoenix to whom the matter had been assigned, Jason Wing, had held a hearing ex parte, with only the Phoenix lawyer present and with no notice to Joshua Rabb, ordering Joshua to appear in superior court in Phoenix for a hearing on Monday at precisely the time that had been set for the writ of prohibition hearing in Tucson before Judge Velasco. The OSC hearing in Phoenix was to determine if the writ of prohibition hearing in Tucson should be transferred to Judge Wing's court in Phoenix.

Joshua took the Arizona Code of 1939 off the bookshelf and researched the venue matter for a half hour. He satisfied himself that the OSC in Phoenix had been wrongly filed, and that the only proper way for the Board of Regents to change venue to Phoenix was to file a motion for change of venue in superior court in Tucson and to have Judge Velasco rule on it. To file an independent OSC in Phoenix was both unethical and legally unsound, but it demonstrated the power that Senator Maitland and the newspapers could wield when challenged.

Joshua sat back in his office chair in the BIA and shook his head in frustration. Fantastic what you can do to justice if you have a few bucks in your pocket and some influence to peddle. You can turn otherwise honorable lawyers into sleazy connivers and supposedly decent judges into whores. And you could create a procedural morass that took years to resolve, while the genuine issues of substance were totally ignored.

Well, one good turn deserves another.

He walked down the hallway to Edgar Hendly's office. Edgar was on the telephone and waved Joshua to a chair in front of his desk. He finished the conversation after a few minutes and replaced the receiver on the cradle.

"What's up, amigo? Looks like ya got a burr under yer saddle."

"More like an entire barrel cactus. I've just been sued by Maitland and the newspapers for malicious prosecution."

Edgar's easy grin faded. "Don't know what it is, but it sure sounds serious."

Joshua shrugged. "Legally it's total crap, but their lawyer concocted something in chambers with the judge and they have a hearing scheduled in Phoenix on Monday at the same time I'm supposed to be in court here on the Livinsky reinstatement hearing."

"Ya know what they say about a judge's chambers, doncha?"

Joshua shook his head.

"Difference 'tween a judge's chambers and a cactus is that with a cactus the pricks are on the outside."

Joshua smiled. "Old joke."

"I do my best fer ya." Edgar splayed his hands. "So whattaya gonna do?"

"I think I'm going to fight fire with fire. They back doored this Judge Wing up in Phoenix. I guess I'll take a shot at Judge Velasco down here."

"How's Velasco gonna react to that?"

"I don't know. He's a man of honor with a hell of a strong sense of justice. I can't do it in chambers, because he'd probably kick me out. Does he still eat lunch at the Mountain Oyster Club?"

"Yeah, I see him there reg'lar."

Joshua glanced at his watch. "Eleven-thirty."

"Ya think ya might like a mountain oyster omelette fer lunch?"

"Or maybe one of those open-faced roast beef sandwiches with all the gravy."

"Let's go."

They drove in Joshua's car downtown to the Santa Rita Hotel on Congress, a block from the federal building. The hotel looked like a tall Mexican villa. They walked on a flagstone path from the parking lot through a wrought-iron gate in an adobe arch, through a courtyard gaily flowered with lavender periwinkles and glossy blue lisianthus, through a heavy wooden door into the M. O. Club. The first room was a bar with a few men staring at their drinks. The next one was a spacious dining room with a high ceiling covered by a trellis interwoven with English ivy, either alive or excellent fakes. The small round tables were covered in fresh baby blue tablecloths and set with white china, apparently real silverware, and raspberry-colored cloth napkins.

Several waiters in tuxedos were serving the two dozen men in Tucson's only private lunch and dinner club for men. Business was often conducted here over tequila or Jack Daniel's shooters or omelettes with sliced bull's testicles, the namesake delicacy of the club. Membership in the private club was the single "perk" of Edgar's position as superintendent of the Bureau of Indian Affairs.

Bernie Velasco was sitting at a table in a small alcove off the main dining room. He was reading a small paperback book with a lurid picture on the cover, a knife dripping blood, a voluptuous woman in a negligee shrinking backward in fear. He had a small smile on his lips.

Edgar and Joshua walked up to the table.

"Nice t' see ya, Bernie," Edgar said.

The judge looked up, startled, and closed the book. The three men shook hands.

"Studying up on some criminal investigation techniques, Judge?" Joshua asked.

"I wish they were all so easy to solve," Velasco answered and laughed. "So what brings you boys all the way downtown on a boiling hot day like today?"

"Well, Josh here has a little matter that's gnawin' at him."

Velasco looked quizzically at Joshua.

"If you're uncomfortable, Judge, we'll have a seat in there." Joshua nodded toward the main dining room.

"Naw, hell no. This is lunch, not the courthouse. Have a seat."

Edgar and Joshua sat down, and Joshua handed Velasco the two lawsuits.

Velasco read them, quickly at first, then intently. He breathed deeply and wrinkled his brow. "Rough sons of bitches," he drawled. "Out to fuck you pretty good, and it looks like they got these low life scumbags Wing and Coxon on the payroll to hold you down while they do it."

Joshua said nothing.

"When's the writ of prohibition hearing set here?" Velasco asked.

"Monday at nine, same time as Judge Wing set the OSC up in Phoenix."

Velasco's face was drawn. "Figures," he mumbled.

The waiter came to the table, and they ordered.

"They don't have a whole lot of respect for me either, do they?" Velasco said.

Joshua didn't reply, letting his silence be assent.

"I guess they figure that I'll reinstate Livinsky at the same time Wing is transferring the hearing to Phoenix and divesting me of jurisdiction. That'll create a nasty little snafu, and everyone will be appealing on technical jurisdictional grounds. The whole mess will be in limbo for at least three or four years till the appeals courts sort it out." He shook his head disgustedly.

Again Joshua offered no comment. The waiter brought their lunches, and they ate quietly. Velasco was deeply absorbed in thought. His black eyes were squinted almost shut, his thick mustache working up and down methodically with each chew. He sat back after a few moments and wiped his mustache carefully with the cloth napkin.

"If the reinstatement hearing is Monday," he said, "their written objection to it had to be filed yesterday, right?"

Joshua nodded. "But they didn't file anything."

"To change venue, they can't file a separate OSC, can they? Don't they have to file a motion in my court?"

"That's what the statute says."

"They're just figuring that the OSC in Phoenix will cure everything. They don't even have to bother showing up in my court. I'm just a greaser piece of shit."

Joshua remained silent.

Bernie Velasco sat back in his chair and wiped his lips with the napkin. "Did I ever tell you what the good Judge Wing did?"

Both Joshua and Edgar shook their heads.

"Well, last year the annual judges' convention was held up in Phoenix. Wing was the guy chosen the year before to set it up and coordinate it all. The year before, it was held at the Safari in Scottsdale, real nice, took my wife and kids and we all had a good time. But Wing's a member of the Phoenix Country Club and decides it would be nice to have a little golf tournament among the judges as part of the convention, so he sets up the convention at the Phoenix Country Club." Velasco rubbed his chin and his left eyebrow twitched slightly.

"So I get up there with my wife and kids, and I go to register at the convention center in the clubhouse, and I can't get past the club manager. He stops me in the lobby and tells me no greasers, niggers, or kikes allowed. So I'm steamed, really fuming. My wife's got to hold my arm so I don't pop the bastard in the chops. I tell him to get Jason Wing over here, and about a half hour later—me and my family cooling our heels waiting—Wing comes in off the golf course. He's got Coxon and Harry Franklin and Tom Moore with him, I guess his whole foursome, and he asks me what's the problem, and I tell him this manager says I can't attend the convention because I'm a greaser. And Wing says to the manager, real innocent, gosh, I didn't know you had a restrictive policy, and the manager just shrugs. And Wing tells me that he can't do a thing about it, it's legal to have restrictions in private clubs, and all four of them just turn their asses to me and my wife and kids and walk back out of the clubhouse to the golf course."

He looked around at Joshua and Edgar. Both men had stopped eating and were watching him intently.

"Helluva group a guys," Edgar said.

Velasco nodded. "Well, why don't we just unfuck the situation the best we can," he said. "When I get back to my office, I'll issue an order moving the hearing up to tomorrow morning at eight o'clock. I guess if my secretary calls Maitland's lawyer in Phoenix at about three minutes to five this afternoon and notifies him of the change, it'll be too late for them to get Wing to do anything. Anyway, since they didn't file an opposition, I could rule ex parte without even holding a hearing. But I'm going to be a gent and give them every consideration."

*   *   *

At two minutes after eight the next morning, Judge Bernardo Velasco climbed the bench in his courtroom. The bailiff rapped the gavel and announced, "Come to order, please."

"This is the time set for the hearing on the application for a writ of prohibition," the judge said. "Make your appearances, gentlemen."

"Joshua Rabb for Professor Mischa Livinsky, Your Honor."

The other lawyer looked as though he had been bitten by a wasp on the tip of his thin nose. It was bright red, the rest of his hatchet face was squeezed white. He was tall and thin, had a full head of carefully slicked-back blond hair, and was dressed in an obviously expensive white linen suit.

"May it please the court," he said, standing stiffly at the defendant's table, "I am Harrison Dix from Snell and Wilmer in Phoenix, representing the Board of Regents of the University of Arizona on special appointment by the attorney general of Arizona. I respectfully object to the acceleration of this hearing. I received improper notice of the change and was unable to file a timely objection with the court."

"You didn't file a response to Mr. Rabb's application for a writ, did you, Mr. Dix?" Judge Velasco asked, looking blandly at him.

The Phoenix lawyer swallowed. He was unaccustomed to being upbraded by judges. His law firm was Arizona's largest, and one of its senior partners had been instrumental in guiding Barry Goldwater's campaign for the United States Senate. Mere judges did not fuck with lawyers from Snell and Wilmer.

"I have brought it with me, Your Honor," he said, pulling a sheaf of papers from his briefcase. He walked to the court clerk's desk and handed it to her. She handed it to Judge Velasco. Velasco put on a pair of half glasses and read it carefully.

He took off his glasses and spoke softly. "Let the record reflect that despite the fact that the memorandum in opposition by the defendant was untimely filed, the court has fully considered it. The court, having considered the application for writ as well as the opposing memorandum filed on behalf of the Board of Regents this morning, hereby orders that Professor Mischa Livinsky be reinstated to his position as tenured professor at the University of Arizona in accordance with the contractual provision of his employment contract. Anything further, gentlemen?"

"Your Honor," said Harrison Dix, standing quickly, "I most strenuously object to your decision under the circumstances. An OSC has been filed in Phoenix which divests you of jurisdiction in this matter."

Velasco opened a book on the bench in front of him. "I'm looking at section 21-102, Code of 1939, which says that even if venue for a lawsuit is improper, the original judge has preemptive jurisdiction to hear all matters unless the defendant files an affidavit with him requesting that the lawsuit be transferred. I did not find any such affidavit in the file, Mr. Dix. Am I in error? Did you file an affidavit before this hearing?"

Dix didn't answer the question. "Surely this court does not arrogate to itself the power to make any definitive ruling until there has been a formal determination by an appellate court to determine whether you have jurisdiction?"

"Do you have a case or a statute that requires me at this time to give up my jurisdiction over this case?"

Dix stood rigidly, making no response.

Judge Velasco closed the book in front of him. "I have just exercised my lawful jurisdiction pursuant to section 21-102 and rendered my decision in this matter. Mr. Rabb will prepare a formal order for the court's signature."

The bailiff rapped the gavel and the judge left the courtroom through his chambers door.

By the time he got off the telephone, Tim Essert's left ear actually hurt. He had pressed the receiver against it so hard that it was sore. He rubbed it gently.

"Two Commie Jew bastards," Horton Landers had said to him. "Scum like that making Senator Maitland look like an asshole, and all you can say is 'I'm sorry'?"

"But we've been through this, Mr. Landers," Tim had said. "If I get the grand jury to charge him with treason or conspiracy or something like that, I'm liable to get Judge Buchanan all over my ass."

"If you don't you're going to get Joe McCarthy and Big Bill Maitland on your ass, and you can kiss your future good-bye. And don't worry about Buchanan. Mike Brink will be calling you in a few minutes."

Tim stood in front of the window of his office, staring at the courthouse across the street. "Shit!" he screamed at the window.

His secretary came through the door. "Did you want me, sir?"

"Get out!" he hollered.

She quickly closed the door behind her.

He sat down in his swivel chair and rubbed his eyes with balled fists. Then he sat back and breathed deeply, trying to control his anger and frustration. The telephone rang, he answered it quickly, and he and Mike Brink spoke for about five minutes. Tim hung up, feeling quite relieved, and pushed down the lever on his intercom.

"Yes, sir?" Her voice was thin and frightened.

"Let's get the grand jury recalled for a special session on Wednesday morning."

"Yes, sir. What time?"

"Make it nine o'clock. And call the Bureau in Washington, tell them I need Special Agents Holmes and Schlesinger back here that day."

Tim again walked to the window and stared out. He began to smile, both pleasure and a sense of wonder scrubbing away his earlier gloom. McCarthy, Maitland, Gruver, Landers—these men really *were* the toughest bunch he'd ever seen. Real movers who knew how to get things done. One of them had just pulled off the best goddamn power move that Tim had ever seen.

Tim would manipulate his old cronies on the grand jury, and they would bring back an indictment against Joshua Rabb charging him with conspiracy to commit picketing and parading. Then, instead of having Rabb appear for arraignment and trial before his pinko pal Judge Buchanan down here, they'd arrest Rabb and take him up to Phoenix, arraign him, and have his trial in front of Judge Frederick Coxon.

It had never been done before, and maybe it would never be done again. But it was perfectly legal and brilliantly simple, an elegant fucking. You had to have real respect for men who had the power, influence, and courage to go to Coxon, the chief federal judge for all of Arizona, and pull off a coup like this one.

Chapter Thirteen

Joshua was at the kitchen table eating breakfast when the FBI agents came. It was a little after seven o'clock Thursday morning. He answered the knock at the front door, and they took him by both arms and walked him up the stairs without a word. He had expected some kind of serious retaliation after the reinstatement of Livinsky, and he was not surprised to see J. Edgar Hoover's hit squad at his front door.

"What are the charges?" he asked.

"Shut your mouth," Holmes muttered.

They told him to take off his left arm, since it could be used as a weapon. Barbara was standing at the stove making some more flapjacks, and she rushed toward Joshua. Schlesinger blocked her way, and she stood stiffly, tears falling from her eyes, one hand clasped over her gaping mouth, the other on her bulging belly. Magdalena started to come out of her bedroom and stopped abruptly, frozen in the doorway.

Joshua took off his coat and tie and shirt and unbuckled the two-strap leather harness on his shoulder. Holmes took the arm and dropped it to the floor.

Joshua struggled back into his shirt and didn't have time to button it before they handcuffed his right hand behind his back, by a three-foot chain, to his left ankle.

He had to shuffle with short steps and then hop carefully to keep from falling down the stairs. They placed him in the backseat of a gray Ford sedan, and he could see both Barbara and Magdalena standing close to the picture window, looking down at him. Barbara's hands were on her belly, and Magdalena had her arm around Barbara's shoulders.

Holmes drove to Stone Avenue and turned north. This was not the way to the federal building downtown.

"Where are we going?" Joshua asked.

"Shut up, asshole," growled Schlesinger.

They reached Phoenix two and a half hours later and pulled into the parking lot of the federal building. They pushed Joshua ahead of them through the rear door of the building and into the elevator. On the second floor, they got out and walked to the double wood-doored courtroom with a large rosewood plaque on the lintel with engraved, gilded letters: HON. FREDERICK COXON, CHIEF JUDGE, DISTRICT OF ARIZONA.

The agents sat him in the jury box and Schlesinger stood behind his chair. Holmes walked through the chambers door marked PRIVATE. A few moments later, Assistant United States Attorney Mike Brink came into the courtroom and sat down at the prosecution table.

"Long time no see, Counselor," he said, smiling

pleasantly. He was in his early thirties, good-looking, with brown hair and gray eyes and an impish smile.

Joshua had run into him once before, when he had represented Meyer Lansky during a grand jury probe being conducted by Brink into alleged Mafia ties to the Flamingo Hotel in Las Vegas, and Lansky's role in the ownership of it as well as his role in securing huge construction loans for it from the Valley National Bank in Phoenix. After fruitless hours in the grand jury room, Brink had learned nothing from Lansky, and he had shaken his finger at Joshua and said, "The worm turns, you bastard. The worm turns."

The worm had turned.

Judge Coxon came through his chambers door and took the bench. Behind him came Holmes, the court clerk, and the court reporter.

"This is the arraignment in United States versus Joshua Rabb," said the judge. "Please stand, Mr. Rabb."

Joshua stood up in the jury box.

Judge Coxon read the indictment: "The United States of America accuses Joshua Rabb of the crime of conspiracy in that on or about the eighteenth day of June, 1951, he did conspire with Hanna Rabb and others known and unknown to the grand jury to commit the crime of picketing and parading, all in violation of Title 18, United States Code sections 372 and 1507. The penalties upon conviction are a fine of not more than five thousand dollars and not more than six years imprisonment. How do you plead?"

"Why am I being arraigned in Phoenix?" Joshua asked. "If any such crime was committed, it occurred in Tucson, and under Title Rule 18 of the Federal Rules of Criminal Procedure, the Tucson Division is the proper venue for the prosecution."

"I'm afraid that's just not so, Mr. Rabb," the judge said mildly. "This isn't a great big place like New York. The District of Arizona has no divisions, and Title 18 permits the prosecution to be anywhere in the district. As the chief judge, I designate the place of trial. How do you plead, Mr. Rabb?"

Joshua suddenly felt wobbly. "Not guilty." His voice was weaker than he wanted it to be.

"The trial in this matter is set for Monday, October 22, 1951, at nine o'clock in the morning. Bail is set at five thousand dollars." The judge slammed his gavel on the round piece of wood before him and left the bench.

"All rise," intoned the bailiff.

By two o'clock, Hal Dubin had arrived in Phoenix with a certified check for five thousand dollars. He posted it with the federal clerk of court and waited for Joshua to be released from the holding cell in the basement. They drove back to Tucson in almost total silence, very uncharacteristic for Joshua's usually voluble father-in-law. Hal dropped him off in front of his house without a word and drove rapidly away.

Upstairs in the kitchen, Joshua found a note taped to the refrigerator in Adam's handwriting: "Taking Barbara to TMC. She's bleeding, very sick."

Joshua gasped and fought away a surge of nausea. He saw Barbara's face in his mind's eye, distorted with pain, standing at the picture window looking down at him.

He ran down the stairs and out of the house to his car. He sped down Speedway to Swan, turned left to Grant, and was at the emergency room of Tucson Medical Center Hospital in less than ten minutes. It only took him a moment to get her room number from the receptionist and run down the hallway to the obstetrics ward.

Adam was sitting stiffly in a straight-backed metal folding chair by the window of the three-bed room. All of the beds were unoccupied. He was staring vacantly at an orange tree whose branches were weighted down by hundreds of immature green oranges the size of golf balls. Magdalena was sitting beside the bed on a padded wooden chair holding her sleeping baby in her lap. She looked up at Joshua and smiled reassuringly.

"Barbara's okay," she said. "But we don't know about the baby yet."

"Where is she?"

"In the operating room."

Joshua sank into an overstuffed armchair covered in dull green Naugahyde. It was warm from the heat in the room and clammy from the moist air of the noisy cooler. He stood up and walked to Adam, still staring out the window.

"You all right?"

"Yes. It was just seeing her like that." He bit his lower lip and looked away.

"I couldn't stop the bleeding," Magdalena said. "I almost panicked. It's a good thing Adam came home when he did."

Joshua patted his son on the shoulder and gave him what he hoped was a reassuring smile.

"What was that about with those two men this morning?" Magdalena asked.

"They're FBI agents. I've been charged with conspiracy to set up the demonstration that Hanna was arrested for."

"That's ridiculous. They can't prove that."

"With McCarthy's red scare infecting the entire country, they don't need much proof. All they do is say Commie, pinko, fellow traveler, and people get frightened. Who knows what a jury will do?"

She shook her head in disbelief. "Well, anyway, it's not so terrible. It's only a misdemeanor, right?"

"No, a conspiracy to commit a misdemeanor is a felony."

"Madre de dios," she murmured and crossed herself. "Are they ever going to stop?"

He shrugged. "They've got a lot of political influence on their side. Some ambitious men are looking at all of this stuff with Livinsky and the demonstration and Friedkind's and Moraga's murders as their tickets to national prominence. It's like a dust devil whirling and whirling around and working itself up into a tornado."

He began pacing, found the small room too claustrophobic, and paced up and down the hundred-foot corridor. The squeaking wheels of a gurney from the other end of the hallway drew him toward it. The orderly turned it into Barbara's room. A man in a surgical gown followed.

She was pale and silent, drained of energy and animation. She looked up at Joshua and began to cry.

"We saved the baby," said the man in the surgical whites. "But she's got to be very careful or she'll lose it."

Joshua nodded. "Thank you, Doctor." The man left the room.

Joshua buried his head beside Barbara's in the pillow. His body shuddered.

Adam and Magdalena walked quietly out of the room.

Minutes passed, and Joshua wiped his eyes on the pillowcase.

"What happened with you?" she asked, her voice hoarse and small.

"I've been accused of conspiring with Hanna and her friends to incite the demonstration that resulted in the U.S. marshal's death. The trial is going to be in Phoenix in October."

She sighed deeply and squinted back tears. She clutched the bedsheet with both hands for a minute and finally let go.

"We'll be okay," she said, "we'll be okay."

Joshua left the hospital when the night nurse supervisor ushered him out at nine o'clock. Barbara had been given a shot of something in her arm, and she was sleeping deeply. He knew that he wouldn't be able to sleep with what had just happened to her, to himself.

He drove home and parked in the driveway. The house was dark. Magdalena and Macario must have gone back to the reservation for the night. He walked through the rickety redwood gate into the backyard. It was eerily lit by a quarter moon, distorting the huge mulberry tree and making it look spectral. He sat down on an old metal spring chair with thick pads on the seat and the back and stared vacantly ahead. He felt deeply guilty, as though he had hurt Barbara himself. Visions began to roil in his mind's eye, blinding him, and he couldn't fight them off.

He was brought out of his reverie by the sound of footsteps behind him.

"I heard you drive up," Hanna said softly. "Are you okay?"

He nodded. He was oddly fearful of opening his eyes, afraid that the army hospital at Antwerp or the concentration camp at Medzibiez would be there instead of a patio with honeysuckle bushes and a mulberry tree and a half-dozen crepe myrtles in full bloom.

"Barbara will be fine," she said. She kissed him on the cheek.

He opened his eyes slowly. "It's my fault," he whispered.

"No it isn't, Daddy," she said. "It just happened. It's nobody's fault."

He took a deep, shivering breath.

"Here, I brought you this," she said, handing him a full tumbler.

He took a sip. Jack Daniel's. It stung his tongue. Hanna walked back into the house. He took two long swallows and settled deeply in the chair, laying his head back on the cushion and staring at the dull stars

in the aubergine sky, waiting for the bourbon to anes-
thetize him.

Barbara came home from the hospital two days
later, still a little weak and pasty from loss of blood.
Magdalena and Macario remained in their house on
the reservation. She didn't want to intrude on the
Rabb's privacy during these first few days. Hanna returned to Maricopa dormitory.

Barbara and Joshua and Adam sat on the sofa in
the living room listening to Abbott and Costello. Barbara didn't stay for the end of the program. She
yawned and went into the bedroom.

When the show ended at nine-thirty, Adam went
upstairs to his dormer bedroom, and Joshua lazily listened to "Racket Smashers" and then "The Whistler."

There were a few commercials, and then "The Gor-
don MacRae Show" came on. But before he had even
finished singing the show's theme song, a monsoon
rainstorm began suddenly with several explosions of
thunder and two lightning strikes that lit up the windows, and the radio went to grating static. Lighting
must have hit the transmitter up in the Catalina
Mountains again, Joshua thought. No more radio till
tomorrow.

The telephone on the kitchen wall rang. Joshua
jumped up to answer it before it woke everyone. He
got it on the second ring.

"You fuckin' Commies get out of town or we'll burn
ya out," said a deep, husky voice, muffled by a handkerchief or a T-shirt or something.

"Who are you?" Joshua asked. This was the fifth

or sixth call that he had received. Different voices, some muffled, some not. But each time the same message.

"I'm the guy gonna rip you 'n yer cunt daughter new assholes, you don't stop spreadin' yer Commie shit around our home."

"Thanks for the kind thoughts," Joshua said and hung up. Better get a new private telephone number tomorrow, he thought. He took the receiver off the hook and let it hang free by its three-foot-long cord. He walked to the picture window and looked down at the rain-swept street below. A single automobile was moving on the street. It slowed as it passed the Rabb house. Joshua moved to the side of the window and peeked out. The car stopped, lingered a moment, and then drove slowly away. Stop it, Joshua chided himself. You're just being paranoid.

He tiptoed into the bedroom and closed the door as softly as he could. He stood in the darkness by his bedstand, took off his Levi's and polo shirt and underwear, and lay down on the bed.

"Who was it?" Barbara asked.

"Just a wrong number." He pressed his body against her. She was lying on her back, wearing a thin cotton nightgown.

"Like those other wrong numbers."

"What do you mean?"

"I've gotten a couple of those hate calls."

He kissed her cheek. "I'm sorry. I'm getting us a private line tomorrow. No more calls." His hand caressed her breasts. He needed her.

She rolled over, away from him. "No, I'm not ready yet," she whispered.

He touched her back, and she shook her shoulders and moved farther away from him. "Don't," she said.

He lay on his back, sleepless, staring at the periodic flashes of lightning setting the curtains aglow.

Chapter Fourteen

Edgar Hendly knocked on the doorjamb and walked into Joshua's office. Edgar had the look of a mournful hippopotamus.

Joshua looked up from the papers on his desk and sat back in his chair. "This can't be good news."

"It ain't," Edgar said, sitting down on the chair in front of the desk. "I just got a call from Wallace Anson."

"Wow," Joshua said. "The undersecretary himself. How exciting."

"Can ya guess the rest?"

Joshua studied Edgar's troubled face and nodded. "Reckon so."

"I'm sorry about this. But he says the Code of Federal Regulations requires that if an employee is charged with a felony, he's got to be suspended till the matter's decided."

Joshua nodded. "Yeah, I know. I've just been cleaning up a couple of things."

"Ya can take 'em home with ya."

"What do you mean?"

"I ain't firin' ya, and I need a legal adviser. So yer

suspended official-like, but ya can do the work at yer own office, and the BIA's gonna pay ya. I reckon your private law practice is gonna fall off considerable, and you'll be needin' the money. Just don't show up here no more."

"How's that going to work?"

"We both got telephones, and anything that's gotta be delivered to ya or picked up, Solomon can do."

"You're going to get your tit in a wringer."

"It's my tit."

"What happens if they find out in Washington?"

"They ain't gonna find out."

Joshua nodded. "Okay. I need the money. I appreciate what you're doing."

"So what're ya gonna do about this latest shit."

"Guess I better hire myself a lawyer."

"Who ya got in mind?"

Joshua shrugged. "Don't know. Haven't even met any Phoenix lawyers."

"I know a guy. I growed up with 'im. He 'n his people lived in an adobe and corrugated tin shack 'bout a mile from us. His old man got killed in the First War and the insurance money put 'im through law school at the U of A. He's gone a long way, but he ain't forgot where he come from."

"What's his name?"

"Charlie Clements."

Joshua wrote it on the corner of one of the sheets of paper on his desk.

"I called 'im 'bout twenty minutes ago," Edgar said. "He's expectin' yer call. And he thinks yer poor as a coyote, so don't be braggin' to him about yer rich father-in-law or the fee'll be six times what it oughta."

Joshua laughed. "Is he a criminal lawyer?"

"Shit, what kinda question's that? All lawyers are criminals."

Joshua laughed again. "No, I mean does he have experience in criminal law?"

"How in hell would I know? But we'll find out come late October, whether yer sittin' here in that chair or bustin' rocks at Alcatraz."

It wasn't so funny.

"You got friends in high places," Charlie Clements said with a sarcastic smile, reading the indictment. He was a gaunt, angular man in his mid fifties, almost completely bald except for a graying black fringe, thin eyebrows, piercing green eyes, and a hawk nose. His office was as small as Joshua's at the BIA, except that the floor was peeling gray linoleum and there was no window. It was at the end of a dingy corridor on the fourth floor of the Luhrs Tower, an old building across the street from the Maricopa County Courthouse and two blocks from the federal building. From the directory downstairs, the Luhrs Tower was full of lawyers, and Joshua had the sinking feeling that he had drawn the only one of them whose office had no window.

Joshua had dressed carefully in his gray sharkskin suit and vest and paisley silk tie to meet Clements, but Clements was wearing a baggy seersucker suit that had seen better days and a white shirt with a frayed collar open at the neck.

"You must have really pissed somebody off to get

indicted in Tucson and get your case assigned to Coxon up here. He's the biggest asshole judge in Arizona."

Joshua nodded. "I sued Senator Maitland, the *Republic,* and the *Arizona Daily Star.*"

"Yes, I remember reading something about you and your daughter. Bad situation."

Joshua was reluctant to ask the lawyer about his experience in criminal cases, but the looks of this office frightened him, and Clements appeared to have achieved no success in his thirty or more years of practice.

"Do you do federal criminal cases," Joshua asked.

"Sure. I've done maybe ten, a dozen. Mostly though, to be honest, I do divorces and collections now. I got a contract with Sears for the deadbeats who don't pay on their agreements."

Joshua swallowed. "Listen, Mr. Clements, this is a real rough case. maybe it's not something you want to get into."

"Truth is, Mr. Rabb, no lawyer with a brain bigger 'n a pea would be anxious to take this sucker on. Bad for business, but my business isn't so good in the first place."

Joshua began to rise. "Maybe I better—"

"No, no," Clements said, waving him back into the chair. "I'm not as bad as I look. I had a little trouble the last couple of years. My wife was running around, and I started taking it out on Four Roses and lost all my regular clients, except for Sears. Me and the area superintendent did some big-time drinking together. But anyway, I'm off the booze now. Kicked my wife out. I'm going to get back up that hill. And I'll take your case. I don't mind pissing off Big Bill Maitland. And this Coxon was a fucking sleazy crook of a lawyer, and he's even worse as a judge. This Commie binge he's on is straight out of horseshit."

"Look, Mr. Clements, we're both lawyers who've been around the block a few times. Let's talk straight. These guys got my balls in a vise, and I need some real help. Maybe I need somebody with more experience in federal court."

Charlie Clements shrugged. "Who do you think you can get for a case like this, Mr. Rabb? John Cleary is one of the best around. He belongs to the Phoenix Country Club and raised money for Maitland's campaign. You think he'll defend you? And Dick Hanshaw is good, too. But he's getting up in his late fifties and wants to be a federal judge. Is he going to toss that in the crapper to represent you?"

Joshua sat back in the chair, chastened. "So why are you willing?"

"First of all, because Edgar asked me to do him a favor. We go back a long ways, and I don't turn Edgar down. And second, I'll get my name in the newspapers. An old lawyer friend told me a long time ago that when folks read your name in the paper, they forget after a few days what the story was about, but they don't forget the name. Then if they need a lawyer someday, they look you up in the phone book." He shrugged. "Anyway, what have I got to lose. It don't get much worse than this." He looked around his office and back at Joshua.

The prospect of being represented by Charlie Clements was hardly uplifting, and Joshua had a panicky feeling for a moment. He gripped the arm of the chair and steadied himself, breathing deeply.

"Okay, Mr. Clements. What's this going to cost me?"

He raised his eyebrows and studied Joshua. "Five hundred?"

Joshua nodded. "That's fair. I'll have to pay you fifty a month."

"No problem," Clements said. "Now that we're done with the foreplay, let's talk about the evidence in this case."

Chapter Fifteen

Joshua's eyes were tired. His face was craggier and more lined than it had been just a few months ago. He was sitting on the sofa in the living room with Barbara. Hanna was in one of the armchairs. It had been a month since he had been arrested and Barbara had almost miscarried, and things were mostly back to normal. Magdalena was teaching eighth grade at Dunbar school. Hanna was living at the University of Arizona dorm preparing for the start of her junior year in a week, and Adam was going to be a junior at Tucson High.

Magdalena was heating something in a saucepan on the stove in the kitchen, and Macario was in his high chair at the kitchen table, banging a little toy cowboy figure in his right hand on the small round tabletop of the high chair. The Indian figure in his left hand fell to the floor, and he began crying. Magdalena picked it up and handed it to him, and he happily began banging them together.

"But you could drive me," Hanna said, looking at her father imploringly.

Joshua shook his head. "No, I can't. The conditions of my bail release restrict me from traveling outside the state of Arizona. Yours do, too."

"You mean I can't go?"

"Not unless I apply for permission for you to leave."

"Can you do that?"

"Yes. Ordinarily I'd just ask the prosecutor, and we'd agree you could leave for a few days. But Mr. Essert isn't going to agree."

"Is there another way?"

Joshua nodded. "I'd have to make a motion before Judge Buchanan. Essert would probably oppose it, and it would be strictly up to the judge."

"Would you do it for me, Daddy?"

"I can't drive you. There's no chance that Judge Coxon up in Phoenix is going to modify *my* conditions of release to let me go to California. And I won't let you drive alone."

"What if I go?" Barbara asked.

Hanna nodded energetically. "I'll help with the driving, and we can get a motel room together. Nothing will happen to us."

Joshua's sad look disappeared. "Well, that would make all the difference," he said. "But are you sure you're up to it?"

"Sure, I'm sure," Barbara said. "I feel fine." She couldn't let Hanna down, so it didn't matter how she herself was feeling at the moment. All that mattered was making sure that Hanna got to see Mark, perhaps for the last time. Though this was not said by anyone, it hung thickly in the air about them and was the primary thought in their minds.

"When is his pass?" Joshua asked.

"Well, his regiment finishes training on August twenty-fourth, and there's some kind of parade on the morning of the twenty-fifth. That's a Saturday. After the parade, he's off until Monday morning at six. Then on Tuesday or Wednesday, all of what's left of the First Marine Division is going to Korea."

"A whole day and a half off?" Joshua said. "That's real generous of the marines."

Hanna shrugged. "It's better than nothing."

"Okay, I'll try, but there's no guarantee that Judge Buchanan will let you go."

"Assuming the judge gives you permission, we'll leave early Friday morning," Barbara said to Hanna.

Hanna smiled gratefully.

"So what's doing with Chuy?" Joshua asked.

Magdalena was sitting at the table next to Macario, feeding him. "I don't know," she said. "Last letter I got was dated August fifteen. Usually he writes every day or two." She shrugged. "I don't know what's going on. He got promoted to first lieutenant and was made company executive officer. That's the last I heard."

"That's great," Joshua said.

"I don't know how great." Magdalena's voice was subdued. "Three other execs have been killed in his regiment."

"That won't happen to Chuy," Joshua said. "Most junior officers have no combat experience, and since they're out in front of their troops, they have short life spans. But Chuy had three years in combat during the last war. He knows when to duck."

His words were meant to be soothing, but they didn't alter the worry on Magdalena's face. She sighed and lifted a tiny spoon to Macario's mouth.

*   *   *

They left their little motel in San Diego at eight o'clock in the morning and drove north beside the Pacific Ocean for almost an hour before they reached the huge marine base. The southern part of Camp Pendleton was one of the most beautiful stretches of beach that Hanna and Barbara had ever seen. Broad yellow sand for several hundred yards from the lip of the ocean, then another hundred yards of red-blooming ice plants up to a chain-link fence bordering Highway 1. But as they reached the entrance to Pendleton, the beaches were crowded with amphibious landing craft and armored personnel carriers and rubber boats and mock assaults being conducted by hundreds of screaming marines.

At the guard shack, a marine corporal took the mimeographed card that Mark had sent Hanna and directed them to the parade field next to the Seventh Regiment's barracks at the north end of the "living area." Barbara parked in the asphalt lot filled with hundreds of vehicles. She and Hanna walked to the bleachers next to a grassy field as large as three football fields. In the bleachers were at least three thousand spectators, mostly women, sweethearts and wives and mothers in gay summer dresses, and a liberal sprinkling of fathers in tan and light gray suits and white straw hats to ward off the sun, although the sun here was mild and kind.

It was about seventy degrees, and flocks of wailing seagulls and squawking pelicans soared overhead in the cerulean sky. The ocean waves rolled gently ashore a few hundred yards away. A dozen cormorants pecked at piles of seaweed at the ocean's edge.

From the white clapboard barracks area adjoining the field came the unmistakable sound of a Sousa march, and a marine band came serpentining out of the living area onto the parade field. The three hundred band members were dressed in dull green uniforms, black-billed white hats, with oversized black and yellow patches of rank on their right arms. The band assembled at the end of the field in front of the bleachers and played another march.

Out of the living area marched the Seventh Regiment, almost two thousand men in battle fatigues with M-1 rifles at their shoulders. They marched onto the field behind the band and assembled in stiff ranks in front of which the officers stood facing the men.

"Can you see him?" Hanna asked.

"No," Barbara answered. "They all look the same to me."

"Oh, there, there." Hanna pointed to the far right of the field. She was peering through small binoculars. Mark was standing with three other men in front of about a hundred sixty or seventy marines lined up in four files. In front of the four officers was a single man and then another single man, and yet a third in front of him.

An order appeared to be given by the officer closest to the stands, wearing a yellow oak leaf on his collar. The next officer, wearing two silver bars on his collar, spun around and transmitted the order of the man in front of him, with one silver bar. He saluted smartly and about-faced and barked orders to the four officers, including Mark, whose single bars glinted golden in the sunshine. They in turn about-faced and barked something to the files of men facing them, and all of them did some fancy maneuver with their rifles and about-faced in unison and marched away from the bleachers toward the far end of the parade grounds, joined sequentially by other companies of marines.

The marching and close order drills went on for twenty minutes, from one end of the field to the other and back. Hanna watched Mark through the binoculars and felt genuine pride, seeing him give orders to his men and execute his own drill movements flawlessly. Somehow the impending tragedy of Mark's departure for Korea had magically been dispelled from her mind by this parade. She smiled and watched and felt proud.

The marching stopped, the regiment once again assembled stiffly before the bleachers, and a one-star general and a full colonel mounted a small platform standing directly in front of the spectators. The general gave a short speech about "duty, honor, and country," and talked about Iwo Jima and Saipan and Guadalcanal. Then he turned around, faced the regiment, congratulated them on their training record, and dismissed them until six o'clock Monday morning. The band played another rousing Sousa march as the men disbursed and the spectators left the bleachers and sought their husbands and brothers and sons.

They were all strapping young men, eager and bright-eyed and happy on this, their last day of training. They were going off to war in just a few days, and today they smiled and laughed and greeted their families with bravado and self-confidence. But this was a different war from the last one, and they knew it. The last one had been forced upon a sleeping United States by a man so malevolent and a country so insane that the entire world had been thrown into a battle for the survival of good over evil, democracy over vicious dictatorship. But this war, Korea? Some yellow guys had started a civil war with some other yellow guys, about a million miles away, and some white guys in the United Nations and the American government had decided that there was a "yellow peril" on the roll over all the peaceful nations of the world, and the yellows so outnumbered the whites that the yellows might soon wipe out all the whites and tumble the white governments one after the other like dominos.

These young marines had all heard the talk, seen the training movies about Communist Chinese hordes who flooded over the border, not caring if they lived, giving their lives gladly because they would thus have a better life in whatever reincarnation was to come. These marines were going to fight to save their country and the world from godless communism and the yellow peril. That is what they had been told, how they had been indoctrinated. But only the youngest and most naive and innocent among them believed it. Most of them knew—even if they didn't articulate it well—that this war was some kind of monumental bullshit, that the five and a half million American soldiers who would shoot at "slants" at one time or another and the fifty thousand who would never return from that faraway place and the hundred thousand who would return on stretchers and live their lives with scars and missing limbs and in wheelchairs, that none of them would be able to say what they had really accomplished there and why.

Mark and Hanna had embraced and kissed and held each other happily in the first moments of reunion; but an hour later, sitting in a little diner near the motel in San Diego where Mark also got a room, he was glum and distracted. He knew that he was supposed to be a "devil dog marine, ooo-rah, *semper fi,*" and that he should be gung ho and eager, but that brave facade had melted steadily away during the drive down the coast. He would have had to have been a congenital moron not to have been afflicted by the general malaise that had gradually swept the United States since the beginning of this war, the widespread feeling that it was a bottomless snake pit that no American should be near.

"I'm sorry, honey, making us all depressed," Mark said, putting his hand on Hanna's on the table.

"We're not depressed," Hanna said, smiling.

Barbara shook her head vigorously and forced a smile.

"So what do you want to do?" Hanna asked. "You have a whole day and a half left to get your fill of the good old U.S. of A."

"Maybe we ought to go to Chinatown so I can get used to the food and the surroundings."

Hanna laughed, strained and uneasy.

"How about the beach instead," Barbara said. "La Jolla is supposed to be really beautiful."

Mark nodded, braving away his depression and self-pity. "Good idea. Meet you at the car in five minutes."

They left the diner, walked across the street to the motel, and went to their rooms.

Hanna sat down on the edge of the bed. Her eyes became wet and her lips trembled. "I felt so good at the parade. Now I feel awful."

"Don't show it to Mark," Barbara said, sitting down next to her and embracing her shoulders. "Let the last look he has of you be happy."

Hanna nodded. She went to the bathroom, blew her nose, dabbed her eyes with a tissue, and applied lipstick and eyeliner and a little blusher to her cheeks.

Barbara wore a simple rust-colored cotton maternity beach outfit. Hanna put on the bra top and panties bottom of a bikini, vertically striped with wide bands of blues and reds. She swept her shoulder-length seal brown hair into a loose ponytail. They walked out of their room carrying white beach towels.

Mark complimented them with a low whistle. He was wearing the black briefs issued by the marines and a white T-shirt. He looked at Hanna and his eyes ignited, a smile replacing the glum look that had twisted his face for the last hour.

Barbara drove north on the Pacific Highway to the little village of La Jolla. The houses were close together, surrounded by thick cypress trees and blooming light purple wisteria and ruby red bougainvillea. Ranch-style redbrick houses were mingled randomly among clapboard bungalows and many much more opulent-looking homes with colonnades and marble entries and front yards full of ice plants and manicured English primrose and pansies. The beach was pristine white sand, miles long and hundreds of yards deep.

It was ten degrees warmer here than in San Diego, just fifteen miles south. Barbara and Hanna laid their beach towels on the ground. Mark threw his T-shirt on Hanna's towel, and Hanna ran into the water, splashing and laughing. Barbara sat down on the towel.

Thirty feet into the mild surf, up to their chests in the cool water, Mark took Hanna in his arms and hugged her closely. They kissed, and she felt the hardness of him, his arms, his chest and back, his legs. She slid her hand down to the front of his swimming suit and rubbed. It took just seconds, and he groaned and hugged her almost breathless for a moment, then slowly relaxed his hold on her. His hazel eyes were dreamy and soft.

Barbara looked away. Tears were in her eyes, and she wanted Joshua with her now, now, she needed him now. They had not made love since she came home from the hospital. She had rolled over each time he had touched her. Too soon, she would say, or it still hurts. But it had been a lie. She had felt alienated from him, as though he had betrayed her somehow, ignored and abandoned her, as though the near miscarriage had really been his fault. Her father and mother had nagged her relentlessly about her husband's penchant for getting wrapped up in losing legal causes, representing Indians and killers and drug addicts, none of them with a dime. As long as they ain't got two nickels to rub together, her father had said, your Joshua takes their case. No matter how many times she had told her father to quit *hocking* her, to quit *kvetching* [bitching] about Joshua, some of what he said had inevitably insinuated itself between her and her husband and embittered her.

He was a complex man, this Joshua Rabb, noble and innocent, cunning and relentless, tough, tender, a brawler who swore like a field worker and a gentle man who prayed with intensity. But was her father right, just a little, that some of the cases he undertook without thought of the consequences for himself and his family were actually evidence of selfishness and egotism rather than nobility?

Noble? her father had said. Noble, shmoble! It ain't noble a man should get in such a legal tzimmes that his wife almost has a miscarriage and him and his daughter are going to jail. And her father's words and feelings had affected her, subtly at first, making her a little colder and a bit more distant from Joshua than she had been in four years; and then not so subtly, actually shunning his advances and pushing him away.

Now she felt awful, guilty, as though she had helped put a nail through the hands and feet of someone good. She wanted Joshua now. She looked at Hanna and Mark, pressed together in love as though they were one body, one soul, and she felt a need for Joshua so great that her breasts began to tingle and her head ached.

She watched Hanna and Mark separate, swim around and splash each other playfully for a few minutes, then join together in an act of love so obvious and so attractive that she began to ache again with an intense need for Joshua. When I get back home Monday night, he won't know what hit him. Yes he will, yes he will. He will know that I love him, and that whatever has kept us apart for a month is over.

Hanna came running up to her beach towel and stood wringing her hair. Mark walked up behind her and cast a sheepish glance at Barbara. Barbara lay back on the towel, and Hanna and Mark lay close together beside her. They basked lazily for an hour under the eighty-five-degree sun.

Barbara dozed on her back and woke up feeling burned. She touched her shoulder, and her fingertips left a white impression for a few seconds in her reddened skin. She rolled over and sat up. Mark and Hanna were lying on their sides, facing each other, whispering solemnly.

"I'm cooked," Barbara said.

"Yeah, me, too," said Hanna.

"Want to go to the zoo?" Mark asked, sitting up. "I heard it's really a good one."

"Sure," Hanna said, sitting up.

"We'll have to go back to the motel and change," said Barbara.

They got up, Barbara and Hanna shook the sand out of the towels and wrapped them around their waists as skirts, and they walked to the car in the parking lot.

Barbara shook off going to dinner at Anthony's Fish Grotto. She just wasn't that hungry, she told them. You go, she said. I just feel like lying in bed and listening to the radio.

She ate a tuna sandwich at the little diner, and it was dark when she left to go back to the motel. The motel was on Harbor Drive, just a half mile or so from Nimitz Island Naval Center. Two sailors followed her out of the diner.

"Hey, honey," one of them called out, "how about five bucks, the both of us?"

She quickened her pace.

"Come on, sweetie," the sailor said. "Don't be playin' hard to get. Seven-fifty."

She spun around and faced them. The sailors stopped ten feet away.

"You come one step closer, I'll scream so loud every cop in San Diego will be here."

The sailors looked at each other and shrugged. "Okay, lady. We didn't see ya was in a family way. You go on ahead."

Barbara walked quickly to the motel and locked the door behind her. She felt relieved and oddly insulted. She looked at her reflection in the bathroom mirror and satisfied herself that she still had a model's face. She ran her hands down her breasts and hips, and although she was pregnant and no longer a kid, she was also no matron.

She took off her skirt and blouse and bra and patent leather flats and lay down in her panties on one of the twin beds. She switched the little bedstand radio on and settled back on the soft comforter and pillow.

"I've got the world on a string," crooned some big band singer, a swell of violins and muted horns behind her.

I will on Monday night, Barbara thought. I'm going to have the world on a string. She thought of Joshua and touched herself. It felt good.

*   *   *

Hanna and Mark ate lobster at Anthony's and stared out the huge picture window at the freighters anchored in the bay. Beyond them at a dock was an immense naval vessel. The lights from the ships glowed on the glassine water, brightening the night. A thick fog hung fifty feet above the water, and mournful foghorns sounded periodically from Harbor Island and Coronado.

It was a romantic setting, but they didn't need any setting to add to their romance. They walked slowly hand in hand along the dock for a half mile and then sat down on a bench. Mark was in his uniform, since civilian clothes were not permitted by the marines.

Down this far from Pendleton there were very few marines. But dozens of sailors were walking the docks and sitting on the benches. Many were alone and huddled in their double-breasted woolen pea coats. Some sat on benches, accompanied by girls of the evening, their pea coats over their laps to hide the purchased affections.

Hanna was wearing a thin cotton sweater, not having suspected fifty-degree nights. She hadn't brought any heavier clothing, and she was shivering. Mark hugged her to him and rubbed her back.

"Not here," Hanna whispered. "I'm not one of *those* girls."

"Where?" Mark whispered.

"Back at the motel."

"But Barbara."

"She won't say anything. Anyway, I'll go back to the room by midnight."

"Oh, yeah?" he whispered.

At four in the morning, the room door creaked open on salt air rusted hinges. Hanna crept in, holding her shoes, and closed the door as softly as she could. Barbara rolled her wrist slightly toward her face and studied the luminous dial. Dear God, just don't let her be pregnant, she thought.

Chapter Sixteen

Judge Buchanan was scowling. His usually tired blue eyes were wide awake and angry.

"You'd better not be backdooring me, Mr. Rabb."

"I wouldn't even try it, Judge. I called Essert yesterday afternoon and told him I'd made an appointment to see you this morning."

"So where is he?"

Joshua shrugged. "Maybe he doesn't see any need to show up. After all, I'm an accused felon."

The judge pushed down the lever on his intercom. "Mrs. Hawkes, please call the esteemed assistant United States attorney and tell him to get his sorry ass into my chambers now."

The judge sat back in his leather swivel chair and rocked slowly. Three minutes. Four minutes. There was a knock on the door, and Mrs. Hawkes opened it. Tim Essert walked in, and the door closed behind him. Judge Buchanan pointed silently to the desk chair next to Joshua.

"Nice of you to come, Timmy," Buchanan said. "You get notice of this yesterday?"

"Yes, sir. But I didn't think I had to jump just because Rabb wants to talk to you."

"Well, that's part of what judges are for, Timmy, to talk to lawyers when asked. So settle back, and let's hear what's on Mr. Rabb's mind." He nodded to Joshua.

"Your Honor, next Monday is presently set for the sentencing of my daughter and the other four students."

The judge nodded.

"I think that the interests of justice require that the sentencing be postponed. There are two witnesses to the bombing of Ollie Friedkind's car who say it was a gray-haired man in a gray silk suit, definitely not one of the student demonstrators."

"But you pled the five guilty," Essert said. "What's this, you want to withdraw the plea? I'll damn well let you. Then I'll dismiss and Stevens will file murder charges in state court."

Joshua shook his head. "No, they picketed and paraded, and they'll face whatever consequence Your Honor deems appropriate. But I think it's a very material element of Your Honor's decision on the appropriate sentence to know whether Ollie's murder had anything whatsoever to do with the demonstration. I think that justice would be properly served by giving us a few months time to find the real killer. The five students aren't going anywhere. There's no need for haste."

Judge Buchanan looked at Essert. "I understand you got a grand jury to indict Mr. Rabb, then bussed the whole bunch of them a hundred twenty miles up to Phoenix to return the indictment to Fred Coxon."

Essert nodded, the blood beginning to drain from his cheeks.

"Why'd you do that, Timmy?" The judge's voice was soft and ominous.

"Judge Coxon's the chief judge. Under Rule 18 he has jurisdiction."

"I'm not talking about jurisdiction, Timmy." Buchanan's voice was louder, more insistent. "I'm talking about you bringing a felony indictment against a fellow member of the bar and running up to Phoenix to get him prosecuted. Have you got one little piece of evidence that Mr. Rabb committed a felony."

Essert was indignant. "He's defending a Commie in court, and his own daughter is out in front of the courthouse carrying a placard which also defends the Commie."

"You got what, six, seven kids?" Buchanan asked.

Essert nodded.

"Oldest one is a senior over at Tucson High, seventeen, eighteen, as I remember."

"Seventeen."

"And he always does exactly what you tell him, and nothing he does ever surprises you?"

Essert swallowed. "Orders from Phoenix," he mumbled.

Buchanan nodded, his steel gray eyebrows bunched over glistening eyes. "You're a real man of honor, Timmy my boy." Turning to Joshua. "You've got a continuance, Mr. Rabb. How about December, during the winter recess over at the U of A?"

"Thank you, Your Honor," Joshua said.

"I'll issue the order," said the judge.

Chapter Seventeen

Chuy Leyva had never been this cold before. *Nobody* had ever been this cold before. Winter in southern Arizona started in late December, and the temperatures were generally in the fifties or sixties during the day and almost never below twenty-five at night. It snowed every five years or so in Tucson, and the fluffy white stuff would cling to the cacti and trees and ground for a few hours until the sun would melt it by mid-morning.

Korea, in the hills twenty miles north of the Hwachon Reservoir, was different. Winter began here in late August. The ground was frozen, the vegetation dead, and everyone and everything was buried in a foot of icy snow. Even when the sun shined, it was rarely over twenty degrees.

The oil on Chuy's and his company's M-1 rifles congealed, and it took hours with fingers burning and stiff from the cold to strip the weapons, remove the oil with solvent, and apply graphite lubricant. They were issued heavy woolen mittens with leather shells, but they couldn't operate their weapons with them, so most of the time they had to wear thin wool gloves.

They were issued white canvas bags to put over their boots, but frostbite was still a serious danger. All along the western edge of a several-square-mile circular plateau called the "Punchbowl," in the Taebaek Mountains of east central Korea, elements of the First Marine Division were dug in, the men burrowed into foxholes and crevices and caves and huddled over the small flames of C-ration heating candles.

Chuy's company commander, Captain DeFazio from Newark, New Jersey, had experience with a lot more cold weather than Chuy, but he didn't look any happier or more comfortable than the rest of his men.

"First Regiment takes the main thrust up Hill 983," he said to Chuy, pointing at the map tacked up on a two-foot-square corkboard on a rickety easel in the command post, a sagging canvas tent poorly lit by kerosene lanterns and pulsating klieg lights.

"Bloody Ridge?" Chuy murmured. "Second Division already lost a couple thousand guys up there."

The captain nodded. "Now it's our turn."

A small potbellied stove, stolen—"liberated" as they called it—from some farmhouse along the way, belched forth black smoke and little warmth in the corner of the tent.

"The other regiments will cover your flanks, second on your left, third and fifth on your right."

"What's on the hill?" Chuy asked.

"Fuck if I know." DeFazio shrugged.

"Why are we taking it?"

"Because some little bastard with eagles on his collar says so. And a skinny, tall shit with stars on his collar says so. And I guess some guy farther up the pole says so, too."

Chuy nodded, his face grim. "When?"

"Tomorrow, oh six hundred."

"Who we up against?"

"Chinks. At least a division, maybe a whole army."

Chuy grimaced. The North Korean People's Army hadn't proved to be particularly devoted to getting themselves killed, at least in the half-dozen skirmishes that his regiment had been in with them. But the Chinese forces were different. They were so reckless of life in battle that they seemed to the Americans virtually to be suicidal. They were poorly clothed and many wore rags for boots, but they didn't seem to be debilitated by the cold and the snow.

When the war had begun over a year ago, General MacArthur had chased the North Korean invaders back past the 38th parallel all the way to the Yalu River and Manchuria. But in November the Red Chinese had entered the war and counterattacked against the U.N. forces and pushed them down the South Korean mainland past Seoul, the capital. It took three harrowing, bloody months for the U.N. forces to free Seoul from the Communists, and the American soldiers had learned great respect for the Chinese.

Armistice negotiations had begun at Kaesong in North Korea in July, but is seemed to Chuy that the only fruit of these peace talks had been even more brutal battles with endless armies of Chinese and North Koreans. The negotiations had broken off completely by the end of August, and the marines had been ordered to capture the "strategic heights" north of the city of Yanggu, which Captain DeFazio called "*va fangu.*"

"Strategic?" Chuy had asked DeFazio. The captain had shrugged as he always did when he had no answer. "Fuck do I know," he had muttered. "When X Corps says it's strategic, I stop asking questions. That way maybe I get to be a major and get the hell out of this rathole."

Chuy's D Company had been in the fighting around the "Punchbowl" for almost two weeks now. Twenty-three of his men had been killed and thirty-nine wounded, reducing his company to a hundred two men. As far as he could tell, the other companies of the regiment had suffered equally. Not since the first wave of Allied forces came ashore in Normandy on D day, or the invasion of Salerno beach in Italy, had such a high percentage of casualties been suffered by any American forces.

Chuy walked back to his company area as Chinese 88-millimeter mortars began raining down near the foxholes. Two American "Long Tom" 155-millimeter cannons responded almost immediately, raising clouds of dirt on Bloody Ridge. But it was just a nightly exercise with exorbitant sound and fury and no efficacy. The mortars were too far away from the Americans to be reliable, and the Chinese were dug into bunkers so heavily fortified that day after day of bombing strikes by marine Corsairs hadn't made an observable dent in them. The only thing the Corsairs had accomplished was to obliterate a half-dozen Soviet built T-34 tanks in the shallow valley behind Bloody Ridge.

It was another sleepless night for Chuy. If the random mortar sounds and Long Tom cannon fire did nothing else, they kept everyone awake. The noise, first of all. But even if they had been silent explosions, the fear made your skin crawl and your scalp pucker and your throat go dry, so that by six o'clock in the morning, the entire First Regiment had but two choices to make: run like hell to the Punchbowl away from Bloody Ridge and beg to be taken to the aid station in shell shock, or run like hell up the hill toward the fortified ridge above. When Chuy gave the order "take the hill," some of the men chose the Punchbowl and most chose the ridge, but all of them were equally terrified.

A dozen M-26 Pershing tanks roared up to the edge of the hill to provide cover fire for the marines. The tanks' machine guns raked the rutted, frozen ground a hundred yards ahead of the assault troops, and their light cannons raised feathery puffs of dirt and snow just below the ridge. It was enough to give the marines time to climb into relative safety in the gulleys and crevices halfway up the hill.

Chuy huddled shivering in an icy crevice just wide enough for him to lie sideways in. He was sweating heavily, the droplets turning to tiny icicles on his chin. His breath was a thick shroud of steam.

I'll wait here until my men have rested and gotten back their wind, Chuy thought, trying to make himself reason sanely. Then we'll go up. I like it here, I'm safe and warm.

A mortal shell burst a few yards above him and covered him in frozen clods of dirt and ice. He struggled to free himself and not be buried alive. He started running up the hill, firing wildly in front of him with his rifle. An empty clip sprang out of the chamber, and he frantically took a loaded one out of his ammunition belt and pushed it home. He was followed now by a few of his men, then fifty, then the entire company. They fired indiscriminately ahead as they scrambled up the hill.

Machine-gun fire close ahead jarred Chuy to a halt. He stood straight up, confused, rigid with fright. But to his men he must have appeared to be a fearless commander, puffing out his chest at the enemy.

A bullet whizzed through the sleeve of his field jacket and terrified him into action. He could see the burp gunner about thirty yards ahead behind an outcropping of rocks that had been leveled by the bombing and shelling.

"Fireman!" Chuy called out.

The lance corporal carrying the flamethrower crawled toward him on hands and knees.

"There! Over there!" hollered Chuy, pointing at the rocks.

The fireman rose to his knees and pulled the flamethrower nozzle from its holster. He pointed the three-foot steel pipe toward the rocks and pulled the trigger. A swath of flame leaped toward the target but fell several feet short. The burp gunner stood up and fired a short burst, and the fireman crumpled to the ground.

Chuy ran to him and wrested the pipe from his hands. He turned and fired it toward the rocks. Again it fell short. Too damn far, he thought, got to get closer.

He lay beside the dead corporal and freed the steel tank from his back. He put his arms through the shoulder straps and struggled it onto his back. He rolled over, scrambled to his knees, then leaped up and began running up the hill screaming crazily, following the steady stream of fire from the flame-thrower.

There was not one burp gunner but three. The flames engulfed them and the rocks. Two of them came running out from cover, aflame. They ran down the hill past Chuy into a barrage of rifle fire. Chuy felt a bullet hit his thigh, and he tumbled to the ground. Must have been one of his own men, shooting wildly. But he was suddenly strangely calm. He felt the warm blood spilling on his leg, and it felt warm and good. Odd, no pain.

He stood up, erect and insane, and bellowed out, "Up the hill, men."

There was a sudden flash of John Wayne before his mind's eye, *The Sands of Iwo Jima,* storming Mount Suribachi. He smiled at the image and called out, "Follow me!" But John Wayne had died at the end of that charge, hadn't he?

He spewed a twenty-five-yard-long path of flame before him and climbed the hill. The gelatinized fuel ran out after a hundred yards, and he pulled off the tank and threw it on the ground. He held his rifle high and yelled, "Come on, men, we got 'em now!"

Every stupid cavalry charge from the cavalry and Indian movies he had seen kaleidoscoped in his mind: *Fort Apache, She Wore a Yellow Ribbon.* Goddamn,

I *am* John Wayne. I really am. I'm in charge of the cavalry. But that's crazy. Aren't I always the Indian?

Men were running, smallish men in padded cotton uniforms. Dozens of them, hundreds. Chuy was on the ridge of the hill now. He could see what looked like an entire battalion of soldiers in flight down the other side of the hill. He raised his M-1 and began firing at their backs. Suddenly he felt something thud against his back, and he sprawled forward in a heap.

He awoke in a rear area field hospital, a huge tent with rows of bunks. He didn't know how long he had been lying there, but it was warm, so who cared. He had a splitting headache, and a little gauze patch was taped over his right hip. He felt all over his body, and nothing was missing. He didn't remember anything about being wounded except the warm blood running down his thigh.

"Good afternoon, Lieutenant," came a deep voice somewhere near his head.

Chuy squinted and shook his head, trying to bring the owner of the voice into focus. It was a tall man dressed in a wrinkled white robe.

"You've suffered a concussion," the man said. "Nothing serious. You'll have a headache for a couple of days. I'm going to put you to sleep. When you wake up, you'll be in Pusan. You did one hell of a job up there, Marine."

The man's face almost became focused, but the pain of squinting and trying was too much. Chuy drifted off to sleep.

*   *   *

He saw Pusan from the tiny square tail door window of an ambulance, and it would always be for him a fleeting image of cement rubble and sagging thatched roofs and the superstructures of numerous naval vessels in the harbor. He was carried out of the ambulance and deposited, groggy and only half-conscious, in a small sick bay in the belly of a hospital ship. There was a porthole that looked out on the Straits of Korea, crowded with boats and ships of every shape and size.

Three other men were with him in the tiny room, and they appeared to be in much worse shape than he was. He lay back, his head splitting with pain, his vision bleary, and closed his eyes. A navy hospital corpsman came into the room, pulled up the sleeve of the hospital gown, gave him a shot, and he awoke again in an ambulance being unloaded next to a huge sign:

8TH ARMY GENERAL HOSPITAL TOKYO
UNITED STATES OCCUPATION FORCES

This was a white-walled, clean building with female nurses in army uniforms and real hospital gurneys instead of canvas stretchers. Chuy's headache had mostly abated, and his vision was clear. He was wheeled into a small room and left unattended. He felt himself again to make sure he had all of his parts.

"Throw on your class A's, Lieutenant. You got a public appearance." The corpsman shook Chuy's arm lightly.

The abruptness of waking up sent a pain shooting between Chuy's eyes. He squinted his eyes shut and waited for the pain to subside.

"What's up?" he asked. His voice sounded to him like someone else's.

"You're a hero, sir. You're getting the Congressional Medal of Honor."

"The what?" Chuy swung his legs slowly over the side of the bed. A needle-sharp pain in his hip made him grimace.

"The Congressional Medal of Honor, Lieutenant. You and two other guys from the First Marine Division."

Chuy looked at him quizzically. "What the hell did I do?"

"Took on the whole Chinese army, led your whole battalion up Bloody Ridge and secured it."

"Only thing I remember is something hitting me in the back, threw me ten feet."

"Yeah, one of our own artillery shells hit near you, killed a bunch of your men, gave you a pretty good concussion, and a piece of shrapnel tore a piece of skin off your hip. You'll be okay in a couple of days."

Chuy stood up and waited for the room to stop swaying. "Where do I have to go?"

"Auditorium, just down the corridor a ways."

"I don't know if I can walk that far."

"You got to, Lieutenant. Orders from General Van Fleet. They need to have you to hand the citation to. The two other guys are both posthumous."

"What's that?"

"Dead, sir. That's why the brass wants *you* on your feet looking like a hero."

Chuy took off the hospital gown and put on the wrinkled winter dress uniform from his overseas bag. It was thick wool, and he smoothed it over his chest and legs. The poplin shirt collar and the top of the linen necktie were all that showed above the lapels of the jacket.

"I got orders for something else, too," the corpsman said. He walked up to Chuy, took the single silver bars off the epaulets, and placed two double bars on them.

"Not bad, Captain," the corpsman said, standing back and looking Chuy over. "You ready?"

Chuy shrugged.

"Come on, I'll help you until the end of the hallway. Don't fall down on me. Anybody sees it, I'll end up in some fuckin' front line MASH unit up by Pyongyang getting my dick shot off."

They walked slowly down the corridor, and Chuy quickly got his legs and his balance. There was very little headache pain left.

"When did this all happen?" he asked.

"Three days ago. You got here yesterday afternoon."

The corpsman stopped in front of the double doors into the auditorium. Chuy took his arm off the sailor's shoulder and straightened up.

"You okay?"

Chuy nodded.

"You're on your own, sir." He opened the door and Chuy walked in.

On the stage were three men sitting behind a table. In the small auditorium were some thirty newspaper reporters and photographers. Chuy strode down the aisle as camera bulbs popped from both sides. He walked up four steps onto the stage, and the three men behind the table stood and saluted him. He stopped stiffly in front of them and returned the salute, awestruck. He had only seen these men in photographs in the *Stars and Stripes*: Major General Clovis Byers, Commander of X Corps; Lieutenant General James Van Fleet, Eighth Army commander; and General Matthew Ridgway, who had replaced MacArthur, commander-in-chief of U.S. forces for the entire Far East Command.

The four men dropped their salutes. The generals reached across the table and each shook Chuy's hand.

"Come around here, son," General Ridgway said.

Chuy had never been more surprised in his life. Generals didn't talk to junior officers. Whatever he did up on Bloody Ridge must have been good, damn good.

Chuy sat down on the chair that Ridgway pointed to. The other two generals sat down. General Ridgway walked to a microphone. Camera bulbs went off continually.

"Ladies and gentlemen, this is a proud moment for the United States of America," Ridgway said into the microphone. "One of our native sons has exhibited such stunning heroism under fire that from this day forward, every time he wears the Congressional Medal of Honor in uniform, every man in the armed forces of the United States will salute him, and every man, woman, and child who sees him wherever he may be will beam with pride that they have had the honor to see such an American hero in the flesh."

General Ridgway turned toward Chuy. "We salute you, Captain." He snapped a sharp salute, and Generals Byers and Van Fleet stood up and saluted as well.

Chuy didn't know what to do, but a junior officer did not stay seated while three generals were standing. He stood up, swaying with vertigo for just a few seconds, stiffened resolutely, and returned the salutes. A lightning storm of camera bulbs flashed from everywhere in the auditorium.

The generals dropped their salutes, and Chuy snapped his arm to his side and stood at attention. The crackling of the bulbs lessened noticeably. The two generals sat down. Chuy also sat down.

General Ridgway picked up a fancy-bordered piece of paper from the table.

"I shall read you all the citation for bravery," he said. "I can't hang the medal around Captain Leyva's neck, because President Truman will be doing that himself next week in Washington, D.C."

He held the sheet of paper before him, adjusted his eyeglasses, and read: "On September 5, 1951, First Lieutenant Jesus Leyva, executive officer of D Company, Fifth Battalion, First Regiment of the First Marine Division, displayed bravery under fire above and beyond the call of duty. Under orders to take Hill 983 North of Tanggu, Korea, known among the units involved as 'Bloody Ridge,' Lieutenant Leyva put aside all fear for his own safety and led his entire company toward the objective through a withering barrage of machine-gun and mortar fire. When his company commander was mortally wounded—"

Chuy flinched. He hadn't known that Captain De-Fazio had been killed.

"—he took command of the remaining men of Company D as well as three other companies of the First Regiment, which had all lost their commanding officers, and led the attack on Bloody Ridge. In the battle, over seven hundred men of the First Regiment lost their lives. The toll of enemy dead was at least five thousand."

Chuy only vaguely remembered making his deranged rush up the hill, calling out John Wayne's movie lines, firing the flamethrower.

The general began taking questions from reporters. Major General Byers leaned toward Chuy. "You able to take a few questions, boy?"

Chuy looked at the general's face, a waxen mask of a smile, and swallowed. "No, sir," he whispered. "I can't remember anything."

"Okay," Byers said. He caught Ridgway's eye and shook his head slightly.

"Thank you, ladies and gentlemen," Ridgway said. "We're going to let our Captain Leyva do a little more recuperating before he has to take you all on. The hospital public information officer will let you know when the press conference with the captain will take place."

The overhead lights in the auditorium went on, and the reporters and photographers filed slowly out.

General Ridgway extended his hand to Chuy. Chuy stood up and shook it, feeling slightly dizzy.

"Don't disappoint them, son," the general said. "They want to hear heroics, give them some. Our people back home need it." He winked at Chuy and smiled. He left the stage through a door behind the curtain, followed closely by the other two generals.

He had a private room in the hospital, and everyone who came into it or passed him in the corridor, when he was taking his walks, looked at him with awe and respect. Each morning when he awoke he was less dizzy and had less of a headache. Finally, after four days, he had practically no more pain or disorientation. The corpsman told him that he would be leaving the next day, and that cured all of the residue of the concussion.

Chuy dressed in his cleaned and pressed class A's. Someone had polished his shoes to a patent leather shine. The navy corpsman carried the overseas bag out to a jeep. Chuy ran the gauntlet of the saluting hospital commander, his staff, and a couple of dozen newspaper reporters and photographers. At the curb by the jeep was a microphone. The hospital public information officer, Major Hennessey, was standing behind it. He beckoned to Chuy. Chuy went to the microphone and turned around to face the reporters.

"How do you feel, Captain?" one of them called out.

"Good," Chuy said, "I feel real good. It's warm in there, and they don't serve K-rations."

There was some polite laughter. It was about thirty-five degrees, and the mid morning sky was slate-gray with a heavy overcast as though soot covered the entire sky. It had rained last night, and puddles were everywhere on the cement and asphalt.

"What's the first thing you're going to do when you get stateside?"

"Call my wife."

"What's the second thing?"

"Eat a hot dog."

More laughter.

"Any thoughts about what you did up on Bloody Ridge."

Chuy paused. "I wish that so many men didn't have to die. A lot of those guys were from my home outfit in Tucson, and I lost some very good friends." Tears misted his eyes.

The reporters scribbled furiously. Camera bulbs flashed noisily.

"What are you going to tell President Truman, Captain?"

Chuy thought for a moment. "I guess I'll tell him that I'm glad I made it back home in one piece. And this is my second war. If there's another one, I hope he'll call somebody else."

A great wave of laughter rolled through the receptive audience.

"That's all, gentlemen," Major Hennessey said into the microphone.

"Good luck, Captain," someone called out.

There were many other shouts of good luck. Chuy got into the front seat of the jeep next to the driver. He returned the salutes of the hospital commander and his staff, and the jeep pulled away from the curb.

Chapter Eighteen

A Marine Corps captain knocked on the door of the Rabb house. Barbara opened the door, immediately fearful that either Chuy or Mark had been killed. Mark had only left for Korea two weeks ago, she thought, panicked. It must be Chuy.

"Are you Mrs. Leyva?"

"No, she's upstairs. What's wrong?"

"Nothing's wrong, ma'am. Everything's fine. I'd like to talk to Mrs. Leyva. I'm Captain Nichols from Company C at the Tucson Armory."

Barbara led him up the stairway. It was ten o'clock Saturday morning, and Magdalena was on the floor in the living room playing with Macario. Building blocks. Joshua was reading the newspaper on the sofa.

"This is Captain Nichols from the Armory," Barbara said.

Magdalena looked up, terrified. Joshua lowered the newspaper slowly.

"You're Mrs. Leyva, ma'am?"

Magdalena nodded, voiceless. She couldn't remember being called "ma'am" before. Is that what they call you when they tell you that you'll never see your husband again.

"It's my honor to tell you that Captain Leyva has been awarded the Congressional Medal of Honor and will receive it from President Truman at the White House next Friday morning. He'll then be taken to the House of Representatives for a reception by members of the Senate and House. Then he'll go to New York City for a ticker tape parade."

Magdalena stood up slowly and covered her mouth with her hand. "Is he okay?" she whispered.

"Yes, ma'am. He was injured slightly in the Battle of Bloody Ridge a week ago, but he's fine now. He's in the Eighth Army General Hospital in Tokyo. It's just a concussion."

Joshua had gotten up off the couch and was holding Barbara around the shoulders. He beamed at Magdalena.

"The cadre of Company C have gotten together and raised a hundred thirty dollars. It should cover your expenses for hotels and meals in Washington and New York for a few days. Colonel Sylbert will arrange for you to get to Washington next Thursday on an Air Force MATS flight from Davis Monthan Air Force Base. Just drive up to the main gate on Craycroft and ask the guard for MATS. Then you can come back with your husband whenever he's released. We'll have a ceremony at the Armory and a parade downtown, and he'll be mustered out of the Corps here in Tucson."

Magdalena nodded, tears pouring down her cheeks, unable to say a word.

"We're very proud of him, ma'am." The captain saluted her.

LOCAL MAN AMONG HONOREES was the small head-line two days later at the bottom of page 13 of the *Arizona Daily Star:*

> On Thursday, the commandant of the Marine Corps announced that three men of the First Marine Division have been nominated to be awarded the Congressional Medal of Honor for service above and beyond the call of duty. Lance Corporal Lester Monger of Tuscaloosa, Alabama, lost his life on September 5 in the Battle of Bloody Ridge. He single-handedly assaulted an armored personnel carrier, rendered it inoperative with a bazooka hit to its underbelly, and killed seven Red Chinese soldiers before he himself was mortally wounded. His actions saved the lives of the ten other members of his squad who had been pinned down by deadly machine-gun fire from the APC. Gunnery Sergeant Mervyn Francks of Milwaukee, Wisconsin, was killed by a mortar blast after he led his platoon almost to the top of Bloody Ridge. His special weapons platoon was responsible for at least a hundred enemy casualties. In the same battle, Jesus Leyva, from the San Xavier Papago Indian Reservation, led four companies of the First Regiment on a frontal assault which was instrumental in securing Hill 983 for U.N. forces. The medals will be awarded in a Rose Garden ceremony by President Harry S. Truman on Friday, September 21.

"Sorry, no rooms available, miss," said the desk clerk at the Potomac Hotel near the Capitol.

It was almost ten o'clock at night, and the lobby was practically empty. A few elderly men sat in overstuffed armchairs smoking cigars and reading the newspaper.

Magdalena glared at the clerk. "Please call the manager."

"The manager can't help you, miss. We simply have no rooms."

The marine colonel who had met Magdalena at the airbase and accompanied her to the hotel came in carrying her cardboard valise.

"What's the problem?" he said to the bland-looking clerk.

"We have no room available for this woman."

The colonel put down the valise and narrowed his eyes at the clerk. "Call the manager."

The clerk turned around and disappeared into the room behind the lobby desk. He came out a moment later followed by a thin, gray-haired man dressed in a black suit.

"May I help you, sir?"

"I made a reservation for this lady. Leyva, L-E-Y-V-A. Now your man tells me that there are no rooms."

The manager made a busy show of turning around the register and thumbing several pages studiously.

"I'm very sorry, Colonel. There must have been some error. We have no notation of any reservation for Miss Leyva."

The colonel's face reddened, and his nostrils flared. His right eyebrow danced up and down.

The manager smiled politely. "I'm so sorry," he

said. "Perhaps we can speak for just a moment." He pointed to the end of the long desk.

The colonel walked to the spot, and the manager leaned over the desk, whispering confidentially.

"We just can't have nigras like her in this hotel, I'm sure you understand. Our guests would simply be appalled. But I'm sure I can find her a nice room at the Miramac or the River View."

"I'm the chief personnel officer for field-grade officers in transit," said the colonel quietly. "How many officers would you estimate that I've put up here over the last year? Two hundred twenty-five, two hundred fifty?"

The manager swallowed, and his lips worked in and out. Tiny red veins pulsed on his large nose.

"From this point on, the Potomac Hotel is off-limits to military personnel," the colonel said. He walked back to Magdalena and picked up her valise. She had heard the entire conversation.

"There's been some mistake, Colonel," the manager said. "I'm sure we can make a very nice room available."

The colonel put down the valise. "Make it a suite. Mrs. Leyva will be joined by her husband after President Truman awards him the Congressional Medal of Honor tomorrow."

Magdalena could read the images flashing in the manager's eyes: a couple of pickaninnies fornicating on his whites-only sheets in his whites-only hotel.

The manager wrung his hands. He bent forward toward her, chastened and obsequious. "So sorry for the mistake, miss," he said. "Hard to get good help."

He glared at the desk clerk. Then he slapped a bell on the counter. "Bellman!"

The room was wonderful, spacious and filled with what appeared to be a real nineteenth-century colonial-style furniture. A large window looked out over the Potomac. Sailboats and motor yachts were anchored everywhere, taking advantage of the lovely, warm weather. Their red and green running lights glinted off the flat water.

"Your husband lands at Washington National tomorrow morning at eight. I'll have a staff car here to pick you up at seven."

"Thank you, Colonel. I'm very grateful."

"No, ma'am, we're the ones who are grateful. Your husband deserves that medal." He saluted briskly and left.

Magdalena and Barbara had spent hours before the long mirror in Barbara's bedroom fretting over clothes. Magdalena's own wardrobe consisted of Levi's and cowboy shirts and a dozen modest skirts and blouses and dresses. But Barbara had been a model for seven years, and her closet held every kind of apparel.

The outfit that Barbara had pronounced perfect for the presentation ceremony and congressional reception was a beige silk pleated skirt, a cream-colored jersey blouse with pulled gold threads, and a pinch-waisted rust-colored raw silk jacket. The high heels were bone color with little gold bows. For the ticker tape parade, she would wear tight-fitting Levi's, a tailored white cowboy shirt, and a pair of new tan kidskin cowboy boots. Not only would Magdalena be stunning, but her outfits would blend beautifully with Chuy's dress white uniform and brown shoes.

Barbara cut Magdalena's hair so that the flipped-up ends were just above her shoulders. She gave her a little bottle of Chanel No. 5 perfume and a slightly larger bottle of eau de toilette.

When Joshua and Barbara drove her to Davis Monthan Air Force Base Thursday morning, they were all glowing with pride.

She had slept only two hours or three. She was just too nervous. She thought of Chuy being with her tomorrow night and became very stimulated and wet. She touched herself and rubbed gently and felt very guilty, then took her hand away. Save everything for Chuy, she thought. Just a few hours more. What would he look like? She hadn't seen him in fourteen months. Had he changed?

When the first glimmers of dawn began to lighten the window, she got out of bed and turned on the lamp on the nightstand. She didn't have a watch, and there was no clock in the room. She picked up the telephone receiver, and the hotel operator told her it was six-fifteen.

She wrapped a towel around her hair and took a shower and dried off briskly. She applied just a little of the perfume to her neck and breasts and under her belly button and was a bit more generous with the toilet water on her arms and legs. She smoothed silk stockings up her legs, making sure the seam was straight behind, clipping them to the lace pale pink garter belt over the pink silk panties. She looked at the effect in the mirror and couldn't help smiling. Wow. Chuy had never seen her in anything like this. They were all Barbara's. Magdalena had always worn white cotton panties, and she had never owned a pair of silk stockings or a garter belt.

When she finished dressing, she stepped before the window looking over the Potomac, but everything was fuzzy and gray from an early morning fog. She took her valise with the change of clothes for the ticker tape parade, and the small clutch purse, Barbara's, empty but for the $130, a lipstick, and Barbara's little sterling silver compact engraved *"To the most beautiful daughter in the world, May 8, 1943, Twenty-one."*

The bellhop watched Magdalena come down the stairs, his mouth open slightly. His eyes followed her into the restaurant but he made no move to carry her valise. She sat down at a table next to the wall in the rear of the spacious room. It had a high domed ceiling of sugar pine planks and a burgundy carpet with foot-long gold crowns. The tables had deep rose and gray veiny marble tops and the chairs were padded with a rich brocade fabric that replicated the carpet design in small scale.

A young girl in a soiled white scullery shirtdress came up to the table. "You can't sit heah, honey. You de new girl?"

"No, I'm staying in the hotel."

"Ya kiddin' wif me, honey. Dey don't lets none a us stay heah."

"I'm a Papago Indian from Arizona."

The waitress rolled her eyes. "Well, I dunno what dat is, but aroun' Washington youse just a niggah."

"May I have some orange juice, please?"

"Ya got's money? It's a dollah. Comes wif eggs 'n poke sausage and some fancy bread stuff."

"Just orange juice. I have enough." She took a crumpled dollar bill out of her purse.

The waitress shrugged. "Be jus' a minute. De waitah bring it. He just send me 'cause he thought you was the new girl." She walked through the swinging doors into the kitchen.

A moment later an elderly waiter in a tuxedo came to the table carrying a small glass of orange juice and a large glass of water on a round silver serving tray. He whisked the dollar bill off the table and walked away without looking at Magdalena. She drank the juice quickly and then took several sips of water. A seven-foot-tall grandfather clock near the restaurant entrance bonged seven times. Magdalena's heart began beating more rapidly. She got up, picked up the valise, and walked out of the hotel. The doorman stared at her, a small smile turning up the ends of his mouth, as she walked down the red carpet under the royal-blue canopy that stretched all the way to the curb.

A two-star marine general saluted her, took her valise, and opened the rear door of an olive green Ford sedan.

"Good morning, Mrs. Leyva," he said.

The doorman's uppers almost fell out of his mouth.

The general was an old man with a pronounced limp. His chest was so laden with little colored bars that it appeared to Magdalena that he must have distinguished himself at every battle since the Spanish American War. Around his neck was an inch-wide blue ribbon holding a medal that hung several inches below the knot of his tie.

"I'll be your official host for the presentation ceremonies," he said, his voice low and hoarse. He cleared his throat continually. "I'm General Trilling."

He was stout and short, and his uniform didn't look like Chuy's or the other officers' she had seen yesterday. He must have read the puzzlement in her eyes.

"I'm retired, 1945, took some shrapnel in the hip." He rubbed his right leg.

She nodded and smiled. "Is that the Medal of Honor?"

He nodded. "Got it a long time ago. Pearl Harbor."

"What did you do?"

He shrugged and chuckled. "Don't remember, really. They say I took a Browning automatic rifle and ran around the area in front of where some of our planes were parked and shot down three Zeros that were strafing. But I don't remember anything but the start of the attack and then waking up with a hole in my arm and my hip and wondering what the hell happened."

They rode awhile in silence, and Magdalena stared out the window, thinking about seeing Chuy.

"How'd they treat you at the hotel?" General Trilling asked.

She studied him for a moment, wondering why he had asked. Was it just polite drivel, or was he really expecting an answer?

"They treated me like I had tuberculosis."

The general laughed and slapped his leg. "Yeah, they used to do that to me. Then my hair turned all white and my cheeks got pink and now they treat me like a white man."

"Aren't you?"

"No, I'm a Cherokee Indian from Oklahoma."

She smiled.

"I read your husband's two oh one file. He's a Papago from southern Arizona?"

She nodded.

"You, too?"

She nodded.

"I guess that's why they called me, asked me to get my uniform out of mothballs. Two Indians with the Medal of Honor. Good ol' U.S. of A., where even a stinkin' redskin can get a medal."

Magdalena looked thoughtfully at him. "Well, I guess it's true."

He smiled and then burst into laughter. "Yeah, sure is. So what do you do in real life?"

"Teach school. Eighth grade."

"On the reservation?"

"No, in Tucson."

"White school?" He looked incredulous.

She shook her head.

"Well, maybe this'll do something for you. Even the rednecks know what a Medal of Honor is."

"But I didn't win it, Chuy did."

They entered Washington National Airport and drove to a broad asphalt apron in front of a long line of B-51 bombers. The driver parked the car close to the edge of the runway, and they sat quietly waiting. General Trilling looked nervously at his watch from time to time.

An olive drab hearse pulled up next to the car and parked. The marine corporal driving it got out and walked around to the driver's side of the Ford sedan. The sergeant got out of the Ford, and the two men walked several yards away and lit up cigarettes.

"What's that for?" Magdalena asked.

"Two other marines are getting the medals. The plane your husband is on is bringing back their bodies."

Magdalena swallowed. There, but for the grace of God, she thought and shuddered. She crossed herself and kissed her thumbnail.

A speck in the sky became larger and larger and landed far down the runway.

"There they are," the general said.

Her heart began beating so hard and fast that she was sure it was audible. She breathed deeply to try to calm herself, but it didn't work. The general got out of the car, walked around the back, and opened her door. Magdalena got out and stood next to the man, trembling. Tears came to her eyes, and she took a tissue out of her purse and dabbed them away.

The transport came to a halt directly in front of them a hundred feet away. Almost immediately the rear of the aircraft cracked open and the huge door lowered to become a ramp to the ground. Two marines wheeled a flag-draped casket down the ramp followed closely by another casket and its marine escort.

Chuy walked down the ramp, stood stiffly, saluted

the caskets, and walked away from the airplane. He stopped abruptly when he saw Magdalena, a smile grew on his face, he took off his hat and began running toward her. She began to run, too, but lost her balance on the high-heeled shoes and stopped. He slowed down twenty feet from her and stopped a foot away. Tears were running down his cheeks, and he swept her off the ground in his arms and they hugged silently for minutes.

He let her slowly down. She ran her hand tenderly over his cheeks and wiped away the tears. She stood on tiptoes and kissed him softly, then harder.

General Trilling walked up to them. "Sorry to move this along, but we don't want to be late for President Truman."

Chuy and Magdalena separated, and Chuy saluted the general. The general held up his hands in a halt gesture.

"None of that, Captain. Today everybody salutes *you.* The only people you salute are the commandant of the Corps and the President."

They walked to the Ford sedan. The general got in the front passenger seat. The sergeant driver ran around the rear of the car and opened the door. Magdalena and Chuy got in the backseat.

"Here's the drill for today, Captain," General Trilling said. "First we go to the White House. There's a ceremony in the Rose Garden where you'll be awarded the medal along with the wife of Gunnery Sergeant Francks and Lance Corporal Monger's parents. You salute the President after he puts the medal around your neck, and then you do an about-face and salute the commandant."

Chuy nodded.

"When that's over, we go to the House of Representatives for a short reception. There'll be a press conference. If you don't feel like talking or you're scared, just give short answers and smile a lot. Any of the senators or congressmen who want their pictures taken with a war hero will be there. I'm sure that Goldwater and Maitland will come. You're their local hero."

"I'm probably not their type," Chuy said.

"Fuck 'em," General Trilling said. He was turned around in the front seat, facing them. "Anyway, with that Medal around your neck, you're every politician's type. Don't worry about it. You two are a damn handsome couple. The photographers will be buzzing around you like fireflies. Then when that's over, probably around eleven-thirty, twelve, we'll go back to the airport and take a flight up to New York City. At three o'clock this afternoon you'll be the star of a ticker tape parade from the Plaza Hotel up Fifth Avenue to the Metropolitan Museum and then back down the other side of the park on Central Park West. You two will sit up on the back of a convertible with the mayor between you and Francis Cardinal Newman in the front seat."

"A cardinal?" Magdalena said, her voice reverential.

"Well, you're Catholic, at least your two oh one file says that your husband is."

"I was raised Catholic," Chuy said. "I never thought much about it back in Tucson. But before I went up on Bloody Ridge, I was praying like the fucking pope."

General Trilling and Magdalena both stared at him for a moment, then they all burst into laughter.

"Well, when the cardinal gives you a blessing in front of the Plaza Hotel, you're supposed to kneel and kiss his ring. That's the kind of press the Corps is after: America's native son hero, gorgeous wife, God."

Chuy shrugged. "Sure. As long as it keeps me out of Korea, I'll kiss his dick." They all laughed again.

He took Magdalena's hand and they looked at each other, smiling.

"After the parade, we'll fly back to Washington, and you'll be put up at the Potomac Hotel until Monday, compliments of the Corps. Monday morning at ten, you'll take a MATS flight back to Davis Monthan in Tucson, and on Tuesday you'll be discharged at the Tucson Armory. I don't know what kind of ceremony they'll have, but I'm sure there'll be something."

They went through a side entrance to the White House, and two marine sergeants in fancy formal dress white uniforms led the way down a long hall to two double French doors that looked out on a grassy garden surrounded by a ring of flowering roses. There were at least two hundred folding chairs set out on the lawn, and that many people were sitting in them. Many were pleasant-looking matrons wearing flowery dresses and big sun bonnets. Middle-aged men in white linen suits and Panama hats sat next to them. Sprinkled among them were dozens of military officers in full formal white dress uniform. The spectators made up a sea of white upon which drifted flowers of all colors and descriptions.

A moment later a young woman in a black dress and hat came to the French doors. She was escorted by an elderly three-star general in dress whites, wearing a Congressional Medal of Honor on its blue ribbon around his neck. Chuy saluted him out of habit and training, and the general smiled benignly and returned the salute. He shook hands with General Trilling, and they exchanged greetings like old friends. Then they all stood stiffly, waiting.

From the opposite end of the hall came two athletic-looking young men in gray suits. They gave the group a cursory glance, then stood in front of the French doors studying the crowd outside. One of them said a few words into a walkie-talkie.

President Truman appeared at the end of the hallway. He was followed by a dozen men and women. The entourage of America's most powerful individuals walked up to Chuy.

"Captain Leyva, I am honored, sir," the President of the United States said.

Chuy was terrified and didn't know what to say or do. The President extended his hand, and Chuy shook it. President Truman looked at Magdalena and then winked at Chuy.

"Mrs. Leyva?" the President asked, studying her face.

She nodded, her gleaming obsidian eyes wide with fright.

"You should be very proud of your man, Mrs.

Leyva. To do what he did requires the kind of bravery
few men in the world have ever possessed."

Magdalena couldn't speak. The President smiled,
then moved to the woman in black and exchanged a
few words with her.

Magdalena took a tissue out of her purse and wiped
away the tears. She hadn't worn any mascara or eyeliner, afraid that this would happen. She didn't want
a smeary black mess on her eyes and cheeks. Chuy
wrapped his arm protectively around her shoulders
and pulled her close to him.

The two young men in gray suits opened the
French doors.

"Mr. President," one of them said.

President Truman walked into the Rose Garden up
to a standing microphone. The crowd stood and ap-
plauded for fully five minutes. A four-star general,
who had been standing next to an elderly man in the
President's entourage, walked out and stood behind
the President as the applause died down.

"In every generation," Mr. Truman said into the
microphone, "young Americans are called upon to
give service for their nation in our country's military
forces. They are boys who come from every walk of
life and every corner of the land. Some of them do
not come back from serving their country, and to all
of them we pay homage, for their sacrifice enables us
to be here today."

He stopped speaking, and there was complete silence for a minute.

"Today, we honor two such soldiers whose families
have come here to receive the heartfelt gratitude of

our entire nation." He paused a moment. "And we also honor a third soldier who through the grace of God is with us today."

There was polite clapping.

Truman turned around, and the commandant of the Marine Corps, General James Galbin, handed him a narrow black leather case. The President opened it and took out a sheet of paper and unfolded it.

"Mr. and Mrs. Howard Monger," announced General Galbin.

The elderly couple walked out of the President's entourage into the Rose Garden. The man was short and thin, wearing a wrinkled, threadbare brown wool suit and dirty brown Wellington boots. His wife was all gray, her hair, her face, her long-sleeved Mother Hubbard reaching to her ankles, and the laced boots. They stood trembling next to the President. He read Lester Monger's citation for bravery and then handed the black case to the woman. She sniffled, and the President hugged her. He shook the man's hand, and they both stepped back from the President.

"May God go with you," President Truman said.

"Mrs. Winifred Francks," called out General Galbin.

The young woman in black walked up to the President. Her head was bowed, and she was weeping audibly into a handkerchief. The President read Gunnery Sergeant Mervyn Francks's citation, handed her the box, and kissed her lightly on the cheek. She stepped back.

"Your husband is looking down upon you now with great pride," Truman said. Her weeping and gasping silenced everyone. The President stood bowed before the microphone. After a few moments, she blew her nose quietly, and the President received the third case from the Marine Corps commandant.

"Captain Jesus Leyva." General Galbin pronounced it in the English manner, not *"Hay-sooce"* in the Papago pronunciation.

Chuy walked rubber-legged up to President Truman while the President read the citation.

"I think his wife should help me put this ribbon on him. What do you think?" Truman turned playful eyes toward the audience.

Happy for a release from the tragedy that had preceded this moment, the audience clapped heartily, and many of the men stood up.

"Mrs. Magdalena Leyva."

She was almost paralyzed with fear. General Trilling took her arm and urged her forward. She wanted to run out of the Rose Garden but couldn't. She walked up to the President, greeted by a torrent of applause and cheers.

Truman took the medal out of the box and handed the box to the general. He held the medal toward her and said, "Here, you take half."

She took one side of the blue ribbon in her right hand, and she and President Truman draped the Congressional Medal of Honor around Chuy's neck. She stood on tiptoes spontaneously and kissed him. Truman put his arm around them both and held his other arm up like a victorious politician on election day. Camera bulbs popped from every direction.

The Marine Corps commandant shepherded the sergeant's widow and the lance corporal's parents up beside the President. Their tears and glum visages disappeared slowly before the ingenuous adulation of the Rose Garden spectators, clapping and cheering, standing to show their respect. It lasted for minutes.

President Truman pecked Magdalena on the cheek and shook Chuy's hand vigorously. "If you ever need anything, son," the President said, "you call me."

Chuy couldn't think of anything more profound to say than "Thank you, sir."

The President turned to Mrs. Francks and spoke quietly with her for several minutes, then hugged her gently. He spoke with the parents of the corporal and held the woman's hands firmly in his.

"The Lord is my shepherd," the President said, and the Mongers joined in with thin voices, "I shall not want. He maketh me to lie down in green pastures. He leadeth me beside the still waters and restoreth my soul. . . ."

They ended the Twenty-third Psalm in stronger voice than they had begun. The President turned to the spectators, waved broadly with both hands, and walked quickly into the White House through the French doors. The crowd began to drift away, the military officers walking past Chuy and saluting, as military law required in the presence of a Medal of Honor recipient. Some of the other ladies and men filed past Chuy and Magdalena and the Mongers and Mrs. Francks and shook their hands. When all of the spectators had left, the commandant of the Marine Corps stepped out in front of them and saluted. He brought his hand down stiffly.

"The Corps is proud," he said to them. "The United States salutes you." He marched into the White House.

General Trilling limped in front of the group. "There are three Marine Corps staff cars at the side entrance where we came in," he said. "I'll go with the Leyvas, Lieutenant General Morgan with Mrs. Francks, and Major General Hood with the Mongers. We'll leave now for the joint congressional ceremonies at the House of Representatives. I've just been informed that it's pouring in New York City, and the wet weather is expected to continue throughout the afternoon. If it's still raining there at the end of the congressional ceremonies, we'll have to cancel the ticker tape parade."

None of them appeared to be upset. In fact, Mr. and Mrs. Monger appeared relieved. Chuy and Magdalena smiled at each other, holding hands, hoping that they would be spared the parade and be free to go to the hotel sooner.

They drove in close file to the House of Representatives. The cars pulled up to the curb, and the generals opened the doors for their charges. They all walked abreast up the expansive steps as hundred of waiting photographers danced around them taking pictures. At the entrance to the House, the Vice President of the United States, Alben Barkley, the President of the Senate, and Representative Sam Rayburn, the Speaker of the House, greeted them solemnly with concerned, compassionate faces fully available to the hundreds of cameras. They entered the chambers of the House of Representatives to a standing ovation and were led by General Trilling to a long table, draped with stars and stripes bunting, set up in the well of the House. They sat, and the generals stood behind them.

Speaker Rayburn and Vice President Barkley mounted the wooden dais. The senators and congressmen took their seats. Many wives and children and other spectators looked down from the balcony.

The Vice President rapped his gavel slowly three times. Conversation gradually died down.

"Mr. Speaker," he entoned, his voice stentorian, "it gives me great pleasure to present three brave soldiers of the United States Marine Corps who have been awarded the highest honor that we can afford them. Lance Corporal Monger gave his life in the service of his country, and his parents, Howard and Muriel Monger, are here today."

There was resounding applause.

"Sergeant Mervyn Francks also paid the highest price for his valor, and his wife Winifred is here today."

More applause.

"Captain Jesus Leyva led the charge up Bloody Ridge, a battle and an assault which will forevermore define the highest standard of heroism by which all men in arms are judged, and he is here today with his wife."

Explosive applause erupted in the House, and all of the spectators rose in a standing ovation.

When quiet was again restored, questions began coming from the reporters, men and a few women sitting in the ring of chairs that made a semicircle between the honorees' table and the House seats. Apparently out of deference to the obvious grief of the mourning parents and wife, very few questions were directed to them.

"How do you feel about all of this attention, Captain?"

"Scared," Chuy responded.

Twitters of laughter rolled through the House.

"Which is scarier, being up on Bloody Ridge or being here?"

"Here." Laughter rocked the spectators.

"What are you going to do when you get back home, Captain? Run for governor?"

Chuy smiled. "Back home they won't elect me governor. I'm a Bureau of Indian Affairs policeman, and I like my job."

"How about you, Mrs. Leyva?"

"I teach eighth grade." Magdalena managed to make her voice steady.

"Well you ought to be in pictures," one of the reporters called out.

Many of the spectators clapped in approval.

Magdalena blushed so deeply that her dark skin became deeply ruddy. Chuy leaned over and kissed her on the cheek. Huge applause and cheers broke out among the spectators.

"You're a lucky guy, Chief," called out someone. More deafening applause and cheering.

"You glad to be home?"

Chuy smiled and nodded.

"I'd sure like to be a fly on the wall tonight," someone yelled.

Thunderous applause and lascivious laughter.

"Now let's not get too personal, folks," Sam Rayburn said, a great smile on his face, always the master of ceremonies, his voice amplified by the microphone and echoing about the House chambers. The spectators roared with laughter.

"Mr. Monger," said a reporter in the middle of the ring, "what would you like the folks back home to know about your boy, Lester?"

The old man sniffled, and his voice was low and weak. "He was a good boy. He'd a come back 'n helped me on the farm like he always done, and someday soon it would a been his."

The humor left the spectators' faces.

"And you, Mrs. Francks. What do you want your neighbors to read about your husband?"

The widow blanched. Chuy felt deep sorrow for her. Mervyn Francks had been one of the toughest soldiers he had ever known. A big, meaty-faced German who was a career marine. When Chuy had been assigned to D Company over a year ago as fourth platoon sergeant, Francks was the senior company sergeant. They had become very close friends.

"I just want everyone to know that Mervyn died doing what he thought was right." She blew her nose into a handkerchief. "What with all this stuff going on these days about whether it's right we're in a war in Korea, Mervyn never questioned that the Marine Corps and the President knew what was best for our country."

The spectators rose to their feet and clapped, cheering their approval.

As the House quieted again, Vice President Barkley said, "Well, I guess that's enough questions for now. We'll ask our honorees to form a receiving line in front of the table."

General Trilling walked up behind Magdalena's chair and pulled it out for her as she stood up. The others also stood and walked around to the front of the table. Senator Barry Goldwater walked up to Chuy and Magdalena and shook their hands energetically.

"Everyone in Arizona is proud of you," he said.

"Thank you, sir," said Chuy.

"I'm going to stand here with you and introduce you to some of these folks," Goldwater said. He inserted himself between Chuy and Magdalena and wrapped his arms around them. A file of at least two hundred senators and representatives passed slowly by as uncountable camera bulbs flashed. Senator Goldwater introduced each of them, but neither Chuy nor Magdalena could remember any of their names. They were elderly men, dressed almost identically in light summer suits, showing their teeth for the cameras, posing with fixed smiles. They melded together like fungible corn cobs, virtually indistinguishable.

"This is Senator Margaret Chase Smith from Maine," Goldwater said.

She was a middle-aged woman, Magdalena's height, with short gray hair and bright brown eyes, a strong-boned face with sparse makeup, dressed in a staid cream cotton business suit. She shook Magdalena's hand, then held it in both of her's.

"You're straight out of that Nelson Eddy-Jeanette

McDonald movie," Senator Smith said, "you know, the one where she plays the Indian maiden. You should have had the part."

"I can't carry a tune," Magdalena murmured, feeling immediately attracted to the senator's guileless warmth, unlike most of the others.

The senator chuckled. "You're both genuine American treasures, Mrs. Leyva, you and your husband. Barry, you get out of there and let me have my picture taken with these two."

Goldwater stepped away several feet. Senator Smith stood between Chuy and Magdalena, her arm through Magdalena's. Flashbulbs popped.

"Charlie, you see I get a dozen of those," she said to a nearby photographer. Turning to Magdalena, "I'd be most honored if you and your husband would join me for luncheon at the Chez Crillon Restaurant after this is over."

"We're supposed to go to New York right after this," Magdalena said.

"Oh, I understand it's pouring cats and dogs there," the senator said. "I doubt that there can be a parade."

Magdalena looked at General Trilling for help. He came over to them.

"I understand the ticker tape parade has been canceled due to the weather," Senator Smith said.

"Yes, ma'am," said the general.

"Then the Marine Corps will have no objection to the Leyvas joining me for luncheon after this?"

"No, ma'am."

"The Chez Crillon Restaurant, then?" the senator said. "And you, too, General, of course."

"I'll get them there, Senator," General Trilling said.

"I'm delighted." She squeezed Magdalena's hand and smiled at her. "We'll have a lovely chat." She moved down the receiving line.

"She's one of the few politicians in Washington who has an ounce of honor," General Trilling said. They were driving in the staff car to the Chez Crillon Restaurant.

"Why is she making such a fuss over us?" Magdalena asked.

The general snorted. "You're today's news. Washington is starved for heroes right now, all of America is. Day after day of casualty figures from Korea and body bags at Andrews Air Force Base, and then Senator McCarthy and what's going on with this Communist thing." He grimaced and shook his head. "Take advantage of being heroes as long as you can. In three days, nobody will even remember your names."

Chuy nodded. He didn't care if anyone remembered his name. All he wanted to do was to go to the hotel and be with Magdalena. He held her hand.

"Why don't we go back to the hotel," she said quietly. "They're just passing us around like novelties in a gift shop."

"Well, Mrs. Leyva," the general said, his voice soothing, "if it were someone other than Senator Smith, I'd tell you to do that. But with her, I think you ought to go through with it. What the hell. One more hour and you'll be on your own for the rest of your lives. Might as well have a little caviar and champagne for once."

"Just don't develop a taste for it," Chuy mumbled.

They laughed. The car pulled up to the curb in front of a green canopy leading through wrought-iron gates to the Chez Crillon. A doorman in a fancy Revolutionary Army uniform and a white periwig opened the rear door of the car and Magdalena and Chuy got out. General Trilling got out of the front seat and preceded them into the restaurant.

Applause began to swell as the waiter led them through the tables to a long table set up in the middle of the restaurant. Many of the men stood up. Some twenty people sat around the center table, virtually all of them familiar faces from the House ceremony. They too stood and clapped. Senator Smith sat at one end of the table and gestured to the empty seats on either side of her. Chuy and Magdalena sat down, and the applause dwindled. General Trilling sat down on the last empty chair toward the center of the table.

"I imagine that it's been a dizzying day for you, my dear," Senator Smith said.

Magdalena smiled.

"It's hard to maintain one's balance in a situation like this," the senator said.

Magdalena studied her face and decided that she wasn't just a politician making small talk.

"I had no trouble keeping my balance, senator. All I had to do was look over at the Mongers or Mrs. Francks every few minutes. It kept me balanced."

The others at the table were busy with their menus as two waiters circled the table taking orders.

The senator nodded soberly at her. "I'm glad, my dear, because the cheering will die down, but at least you'll still have this magnificent husband of yours to be with."

"I know that." Magdalena looked across the table at Chuy and smiled. He sat staring at her with a small grin on his face.

"Where do you teach, my dear?" the senator asked.

"At a segregated school in Tucson. It's the only place that the school board would let me."

"There's certainly nothing wrong with teaching Negroes."

"Of course not. But it would be a lot better just to put all the students together in the same school and the teachers, too."

"Perhaps someday that will happen, Mrs. Leyva. The attitude of the country is changing. Ever since President Truman integrated the military, I've noticed a sea change in attitudes."

A waiter came up between them.

"May I order for you, Mrs. Leyva. I know the food here quite well."

"Certainly."

"The three of us will have the same thing, George," the senator said, looking from Magdalena to Chuy and back to the waiter. "Peasant potatoes and poached salmon."

She turned to Chuy. "I hope you do realize, Captain, that the show of honor and gratitude that you've seen today is genuine. Washington is a phony place full of ambitious people, but with respect to our soldiers who have demonstrated the rare courage that you and your comrades showed, the affection of all of us is real."

Chuy studied her face and found none of the professional mask that cloaked the features of so many others earlier in the day. He nodded.

"Thank you, Senator."

"Men like you, women like your lovely wife, will make a new world for your people." Her face was very intense, her brown eyes bore deeply into his. She took his right hand and Magdalena's left. She stood up and pulled them with her.

"Ladies and gentlemen," she said, looking about the long table. "Wonderful people like these bring a breath of sweet air to our country's capital. Too often we forget that it is not the political movers and shakers who really shape our country's destiny, but the simple people whom we call upon in our moments of desperation and who rise in spirit and courage to astonish us all with their accomplishments, which none of us could achieve. I am honored that Captain Leyva and Magdalena are with us today. The applause will die down for them, but never our respect and fondest wishes for their success in life."

"Here, here," called out several men at the table and clinked their water goblets with spoons, producing a light accolade of chimes.

The senator sat down. Chuy sat down, fidgeting nervously. Magdalena resumed her seat and felt hot blood rushing to her cheeks.

Waiters pushed up two serving tables. Everyone quieted as the plates of food were placed before them.

Magdalena ate sparingly of the caviar-filled baked potato. The little fish eggs were much too salty for her taste. She glanced up at Chuy, and he was working hard to keep a sickened look off his face as he chewed a mouthful of caviar and potato.

The poached salmon was much more palatable.

"What can I do for *you*, Magdalena?" the senator asked. "I feel like your fairy godmother today, and I'd like to grant you any wish I'm capable of."

Magdalena looked at Senator Smith, at a loss for an answer. "I'm not sure I have any special wishes, other than what I told you before."

"There must be something a stodgy old lady from Maine can do for a beautiful young woman from Arizona. And I'm serious."

Magdalena sat back in her chair and looked intently at the senator. "Maybe there is one thing," she said quietly.

Senator Smith appeared eager.

"It has to do with this red scare business."

The senator's face became solemn. "My dear colleague, Senator McCarthy?"

Magdalena nodded. "Indirectly, anyway."

"Has his venom trickled all the way to Tucson, Arizona?"

"It's not just a trickle."

"What can I do for you?" Senator Smith suddenly appeared doubtful.

"Chuy and I have a very dear friend who is the legal officer for the Bureau of Indian Affairs in Tucson. His name is Joshua Rabb, and he has a nineteen-year-old daughter named Hanna."

The senator leaned forward over the table, listening intently.

*   *   *

She stood in the bright afternoon light of the window overlooking the Potomac and the sailboats, but she did not see them. She was looking at her husband. He pulled off his boxer shorts and draped them on the chair, then sat down on the edge of the bed, very ready for his wife.

She unbuttoned her blouse and tossed it on the chair. The beige silk skirt crumpled around her ankles, and she stepped out of it.

Chuy caught his breath. He stared at her, grinning. She unhooked her brassiere and let it fall to the floor.

"Where did you get that outfit?" he asked hoarsely.

"Barbara."

"Jesus," he murmured. "No wonder Joshua always looks tired."

Magdalena laughed deep in her throat. She unhooked the stocking clips and dropped the garter belt on the floor. She stepped to him, and he buried his face between her breasts as she caressed his back. He pulled her panties down and drank in her delicious womanness.

Chapter Nineteen

The Davis Monthan Air Force Base Band filled almost half of Armory Park in the center of downtown Tucson. It began to play the Marine Corps Anthem as Colonel Sylbert's staff car pulled up in front of the Tucson Armory, directly to the east of the park. On the west side of the park was the Carnegie Library, and dozens of curious people pressed against its windows and sat on its dozen broad steps listening to the band and waiting to see who was so important. A few people had read the two-inch story on page eleven of the *Arizona Daily Star* this morning and had come to catch a glimpse of Arizona's only Congressional Medal of Honor winner in the Korean War.

Along the curb in front of the Armory was Senator William Maitland with the staff officers of Company C, Chuy Leyva's home unit. Next to them were Edgar Hendly, Solomon Leyva, Chief Francisco Romero, and seven of the Tribal Council members of the Papago tribe. Joshua, Hanna, Adam, and Barbara stood in front of the white-painted wood gazebo in the middle of the park. Maitland had given Colonel Sylbert orders to keep Joshua—an indicted felon—away from the dignitaries. Frances Hendly, holding her four-year-old daughter's hand, stood next to Barbara.

The Air Force Band played "Stars and Stripes Forever" as Chuy and Magdalena got out of the staff car. Big Bill Maitland bounded up to them, grabbed their hands, and hoisted them victoriously overhead for all the newspaper cameramen to see.

"A true American hero, our own native son," he bellowed for the cluster of standing microphones to broadcast and record.

"Who the hell's 'at?" said the fat man standing behind the small Coca-Cola ice wagon on the sidewalk in front of the Carnegie Library. He wore an old straw cowboy hat to keep the sun off his pink, bulbous face.

"Dunno," said the customer, fishing a Coke out of the melting ice. He was tall and good-looking, young, wearing grease-stained gray mechanic's overalls. "Some Indian, I reckon."

"Whud he do?"

"Beats the shit outta me. Maybe he drank more fire water 'n any other jarhead in C Company." He guffawed viciously, and the Coca-Cola seller joined in.

"Arizona is proud today," Senator Maitland said into the microphones. He had his arms around Chuy's and Magdalena's shoulders. His voice echoed across the park.

"Damn right," mumbled the Coke seller. "Best thing them Indians can do is drink like fuckin' horses guzzlin' from a trough. But we gotta give 'em a medal for *somethin'*, though, now that they can vote."

The customer chuckled. "Ain't that a fact."

The band was playing "America," and a small chorus of sixth- and seventh-grade Papago children from the San Xavier Mission School were singing on the dais in the middle of the park. A Poor Claire nun in full habit stood in front of them waving her arms rhythmically, a huge white wimple teetering precariously on her head.

"O beautiful for spacious skies, for amber waves of grain, for purple mountained majesty . . ." The fifteen little voices had difficulty rising above the band.

Maitland led Chuy and Magdalena to the gazebo where another battery of microphones was set up. Chief Romero and the council members stood behind them, ringing the rear of the raised round twenty-five-foot-wide platform with five tall wooden columns supporting a roof of loosely interwoven wood slats vined with bloodred bougainvillea. The Rabbs and Hendleys and Solomon Leyva stood in front of it.

"Who's the big son of a bitch in the perty white suit?" asked the Coca-Cola seller.

"Damned if I know," said the customer, lifting the bottle to his mouth, tipping his head back, and swallowing down half of it. He wiped his mouth with the back of his hand, smearing his lips and cheeks with grease. He rubbed at the grease with the sleeve of his overalls. "Must be some fat-assed politician. Them's the only ones got enough nose immunity to get close to a stinkin' Indian."

He and the Coke seller laughed with delight. Three teenage girls had just come out of the library and were standing near the ice wagon. They were close enough to hear the two men's banter, and they giggled.

Although it was the last week in September, the late-afternoon sun burned down belligerently from the bleached sky, flooding through the fenestrations of the gazebo's roof. It was almost a hundred degrees. Big Bill Maitland took a handkerchief out of his white linen suit jacket, wiped the inside hatband of his Panama hat, mopped his brow, then waved his hat at the band major for quiet. A few people walking by the park on their way home from work stopped and stared and listened curiously.

Maitland said something into the microphones, producing a harsh screech. He stood back from them, then stepped forward and spoke again. The same screech.

The Coke seller laughed. "I guess that says it all," he said. The others around him chuckled.

Horton Landers came around from behind the gazebo and quickly climbed the steps. He knelt by the large black amplifier and fiddled with the knobs. "Try it now, Senator."

Maitland returned to the mikes. "My fellow Americans." His voice carried clearly through the park. "No one could be prouder today to be from Arizona than I am."

Solomon Leyva wasn't listening. His attention was riveted on Horton Landers, kneeling beside the amplifier, waiting to squelch the next impudent screech. A gray silk suit, the Joslins had said. The guy who threw the bomb under Ollie Friedkind's car wore a gray silk suit. He was gray-haired, maybe fifty years old, thin, the witnesses had said.

Solomon edged up to Joshua. "Who's the guy by the amp?" he whispered.

Joshua looked at Landers, then at Soloman. "The senator's administrative aide," he answered, "Horton Landers."

Solomon nodded, his jaw set and tight.

"What's up?" Joshua asked, wrinkling his brow at Solomon.

"Remember the testimony of those witnesses, Lawrence and Margaret Joslin, at the preliminary hearing?"

Joshua nodded. He turned toward Landers and studied him.

"Go over to the morgue at the *Arizona Daily Star* tomorrow morning," Joshua whispered. "Get the most recent photos of him you can. There's bound to be one of him. He was a highly decorated marine or army colonel in the war. Bring it over to the Joslins, see if they can identify him."

Solomon nodded.

The senator was going through the presentation of the Medal of Honor. He asked Magdalena to help, and they solemnly draped it around Chuy's neck, as Maitland had seen President Truman and Magdalena do in the front-page photograph of the Saturday *New York Times*. If the President can do it, so can I, he had thought, sitting in his home on Camelback Mountain, staring out at the panorama of Phoenix, his personal fief. On one of the inner pages of the newspaper there had been a small picture of Goldwater lifting the Indian's arm victoriously. What a laugh! But if Goldwater can get some play out of this greaseball, so can I.

Maitland had called Landers and ordered him to make damn sure that the ceremony at the Tucson Armory would feature Senator Big Bill Maitland as its host and proud as punch enthusiast. The greaseballs had the vote now, at least Big Bill thought they did, and it wouldn't hurt to make them think that he gave a shit about them.

"All America salutes you, sir," he said, saluting Chuy dramatically, "and most of all, your fellow Arizonans. You will be recorded in the annals of this great state as a hero among heroes." Whatever the hell that means.

The band struck up the national anthem. Big Bill took off his broad-brimmed Panama and held it over his puffed-out chest as he bellowed the words. The microphones went haywire again, and Landers manipulated the amplifier knobs to no avail. Finally he switched it off in frustration. Big Bill shot him a vitriolic glance, then turned back to the patriotic business at hand, bellowing even more loudly.

"Fucker's got a pair of lungs on him, don't he," said the mechanic in front of the Coke wagon. "Must be runnin' fer somethin'." He looked over at the teenage girls. One of them was a real doll. She giggled coquettishly.

The seven men and one woman sat around the conference table in the glass-walled room at the west end of the hundred-foot-square floor of the *Arizona Daily Star*. This half of the floor was filled with reporters' and editors' desks. The east half was filled with idle printing presses.

Morgan Roth had been the managing editor of Tucson's morning newspaper for eleven years. He was of medium height and had a full head of dyed brown hair slicked with hair oil close to his scalp and combed straight back. He had soft green eyes and a ready smile. His tan was year round from the golf course and the tennis courts. He had come to Tucson from Chicago in 1937 for his health. Tucson's climate was good for asthma, his doctors had said. So he had left his city editor post at the *Chicago Herald* for a reporter's job on the *Star*. But his thirteen years with some of the best papers in the country, the *Detroit Free Press*, the *New York Times*, the *Herald*, and his skills as a newspaperman, had soon won him the job of city editor on the *Star*. And when Herman Dees had died of a stroke on New Year's Eve, 1940–1941, Morgan Roth had been his logical successor to manage the growing newspaper.

The fact that he was of German heritage had almost derailed him a year later. After Pearl Harbor, there was nothing but suspicion and incarceration for the Japanese Americans, even the many thousands who had been born in America. But the Germans had fared much better. They didn't have slant eyes and peculiar cultural peccadilloes. So the initial wave of hostility against them quickly passed, and the fact that Morgan's father had been a captain in the Wehrmacht in the First World War was never made an issue. His father had been killed in some anonymous battle in 1915, and Morgan's mother and two sisters had come to America in 1918 to live in Detroit with Uncle Werner, his mother's brother, who had immigrated to the

United States in 1906 and by then owned a highly successful and expanding factory that produced iceboxes.

Morgan had gone to high school in Detroit and college nearby at the University of Michigan, lost his accent, excelled in journalism, and gotten a coveted job with the *Detroit Free Press* after graduation. He possessed the typical stereotypes of the Germans of the time: the world's ills were the result of the wily machinations of Jew financiers who manipulated the entire world economy with the clandestine aid of godless Communists who were conspiring to undermine the legitimate governments of all Western European countries as well as the United States. The prejudices worked exceedingly well in the atmosphere of 1930s America, where fear and hatred of Communists and Jews in the major Eastern cities became the principal sociopolitical sentiments of the time. But in Tucson nobody seemed to have ever seen a Jew, and if there were any Communists, nobody could remember ever having come across one. By the time the Second World War ended, antisemitism as a quasi-official policy of the government and the universities and the school boards had become passé. It still flourished openly in the country clubs and the boardrooms of all major companies, and clandestinely in the principal old boy clubs of government—the State Department and the War Department, which had become the Defense Department in 1947—but the Nazis had rendered it disreputable as an official governmental policy.

Morgan Roth had bent to the trend, careful not to

endanger his position as managing editor. But the advent of Joseph McCarthy had opened wide the door to everyone's repressed hatreds, and Morgan had run many UP and AP stories, helping to build the careers of the senators and congressmen who were out to rid the country of Commies and fellow travelers, and, in the fabulously printable prose of Joe McCarthy, "parlor pinks and parlor punks" tearing insidiously at the heart of American democracy. Talk like that not only created skyrocketing political careers, it sold newspapers.

Now he sat looking sourly at the *New York Times* story of Jesus Leyva's award ceremony at the White House and the reception at the House of Representatives. He finished reading it and picked up the draft of the *Star* reporter's story about the awards ceremony at Armory Park yesterday afternoon. He shook his head grimly.

"He really said this?" Morgan Roth said, looking at Jim Hicklin, who had been a reporter for twenty-three years, in Los Angeles, Phoenix, and now here. Alcohol had worked him down the ladder, and on bad days he sometimes got the story wrong.

Hicklin nodded. He had a furrowed, emaciated face, watery gray eyes, and almost no hair. His scalp gleamed in the overhead fluorescent lights.

"I was with Jim, Mr. Roth," Eldon Hibbs said. He was a young reporter, eager, sycophantic. "It's word for word."

Roth read the quotes about Joshua Rabb from Leyva's press conference again. Roth had never met Rabb, although the lawyer had become newsworthy several times over the past few years by defending some scumbags in criminal cases none of the other attorneys in town were apparently willing to handle. But aside from those occasional bursts of notoriety, Rabb had remained unknown.

Roth picked up the AP teletype statement released just hours ago from the Washington, D.C., office of Maine's Republican Senator Margaret Chase Smith.

"I never knew this about Joshua Rabb," he said, looking around the table.

"It was in one of the first stories I wrote, five or six years ago, about him defending an Indian for murder," J. T. Sellner said, shifting uneasily in her chair.

"I remember some of those stories you did. It was the nun who got murdered out at San Xavier. The Indian they arrested was released by Buck Buchanan before he even had to stand trial."

Sellner nodded.

"The Indian was the son of the chief of the tribe, something like that. A drunken bum."

She nodded. "Grandson of the former chief."

"The real killer was never caught, and Antone got lynched, as I recall."

She nodded again. "A lot of people thought he was the killer, figured the Jew lawyer just pulled a fast one on the judge."

Roth stared hard at her. "I remember the copy you wrote, J. T., but I don't remember reading anything like this about Rabb."

"It's there." She shrunk deeper into the padded swivel chair.

"Charlie, get the Antone clippings from the morgue," Roth said.

The assistant managing editor got up from the table and left the glass-enclosed conference room. He walked toward the west staircase that led down to the basement. Emily Dolan, the elderly, schoolmarmish custodian of the morgue, came running breathlessly up the stairs.

"Mr. Hammond, there's an Indian policeman down there causing trouble."

"Take it easy, Miss Dolan. Is he from the police department?"

"I don't think so. He's wearing a gun and a ragged pair of Levi's and a cowboy shirt and a brass badge that says 'U.S. Police' that has a buffalo in the middle."

"What's he want?"

"He wants to take a picture out of Senator Maitland's file."

The assistant managing editor took the stairs down to the morgue two at a time. He walked up to the counter. The man wearing a .45 Colt Single Action Army revolver on his hip was a tall, powerfully built Papago with an acne-scarred face and shaggy black shoulder-length hair tied with a headband of faded red muslin.

"I'm Charles Hammond, the assistant managing editor. What do you want?"

"I'm a federal police officer with the Bureau of Indian Affairs. I'm here on official business."

"Yes?"

"I'd like to borrow this photograph just for a day or two." He held it up.

Charlie Hammond recognized Horton Landers immediately. Charlie had been the *Star* reporter assigned to Bill Maitland's senatorial campaign two years ago and had done a lot of drinking with Big Bill and his chief adviser, Colonel Landers. Maitland's victory had done well for Hammond. A few words in the right ears had won Hammond the promotion to assistant managing editor.

"What kind of business is it that you need his photograph?"

"Official business."

"Get out of here."

Solomon took the photograph and walked toward the stairway to the exit door into the parking lot.

"Leave that photograph!" Charlie Hammond hollered.

Solomon didn't hesitate. He walked up the stairs.

"Call Mr. Essert at the United States attorney's office, Miss Dolan."

"But, sir—"

"Just do it, Miss Dolan," Hammond growled. "I haven't got time right now."

"Yes, sir," she mumbled.

He went to a bank of filing cabinets, opened the drawer labeled "Aa–Ar," and thumbed through the manila files. He retrieved one and walked quickly up the stairs with it. The people inside the conference room were morbidly silent. Morgan Roth was reading the long, glazed paper copy in front of him. He was deadly when he was angry, a rattlesnake looking for someone to bite, and he appeared as angry now as Charlie Hammond had ever seen him. Charlie handed Morgan the file and returned to his chair at the opposite end of the table.

Roth opened the file and began reading. His lips were pressed closely together in a thin line and had lost their color.

"All right," he said, looking up. "National and city desks and J.T. stay with me. The rest of you can go."

Four men quickly left the room, grateful for the reprieve.

"Here's the first story you wrote, J.T. July 1946:

> "Mr. Rabb came to Tucson with his two children after his first wife died in an accident in Brooklyn. He apparently was injured in the same accident and lost his left arm."

He looked up from reading. "Where did you get that information?"

J. T. Sellner squirmed noticeably. "I don't remember exactly. I recall that Rabb wouldn't talk to me about his arm. I probably got it from Tim Essert or Ollie Friedkind."

"One of them told you he lost his arm in an accident in Brooklyn?"

She appeared thoughtful, less frightened. "Yes, I remember now. It was Ollie Friedkind." No problem there. A dead man can't tell anybody that you're lying.

Roth scowled at her. "And did you think to ask how he got *his* information?"

Sellner shrugged. "I assumed he knew."

Roth shook his head and pursed his lips. He swiveled around in his chair, opened the drawer of the credenza against the glass wall, and pulled out a file. He swiveled around again, laid it open on the table, and began reading silently.

Five minutes later. "This is the defamation lawsuit Rabb filed against us and the *Republic* and Senator Maitland. An hour ago, I still harbored the pleasant illusion that it was a crock of shit." Roth's face was ugly with anger. He closed the file and held up several sheets of paper.

"And this is the statement from Margaret Chase Smith on the AP teletype. I'm sure you'd like to hear it:

"The Four Horsemen of Calumny—Fear, Ignorance, Bigotry, and Smear—have invaded Tucson, Arizona. The once sleepy university town is the latest forum for the villainous crusade by Joe McCarthy and his power-corrupt henchmen to destroy men's and women's lives with lies. Now it is Arizona's junior senator, William Maitland, who jumps on the bandwagon and strikes up the theme song of the red scare. Through his self-professed laudable patriotic efforts, an innocuous group of professors at the University of Arizona were declared to belong to a Communist front organization by the attorney general of the United States, acting under his mandate from the National Security Act of 1950, a set of laws so evil and malicious as to challenge the British Stamp Act tax imposed on our colonies for first place in the list of injustices in our history. The Stamp Act tax precipitated the American Revolution. God willing, the National Security Act of 1950 will not be imposed with such malevolent fervor and wielded with such indiscriminate treachery to give rise to a second revolution.

"But Joe McCarthy and his willing Maitlands see their duty as ruining the lives and reputations of decent and honorable Americans. So here is what they did. A Tucson attorney named Joshua Rabb had the courage to sign on as the defense lawyer for two of the professors charged criminally with failing to register as members of the Communist front organization. So Maitland branded him a Commie and a fellow traveler and even accused him of being a traitor. Then he tarred the Tucson office of the Bureau of Indian Affairs with the same brush. Arizona's two major newspapers, the *Arizona Republic* in Phoenix and the *Arizona Daily Star* in Tucson, were only too eager to accommodate the senator and run the grotesque lies on their front pages."

Morgan Roth looked at J. T. Sellner. She was staring straight ahead, her hands gripped together on the table, her knuckles white.

"Joshua Rabb's nineteen-year-old daughter, Hanna, had by then been charged with attempting to subvert justice. And what was her crime? She had been in a class that one of the professors taught, and on the day that he was scheduled to be indicted in the federal courthouse in Tucson, she and several dozen of her classmates demonstrated their support of the professor on the sidewalk in front of the courthouse. In the course of the demonstration, someone threw a bomb

under the car of the United States marshal and he
was killed.

"The FBI immediately arrested Hanna Rabb and
four other students for murder. They were subse-
quently cleared of that charge when two eyewitnesses
testified that the bomb thrower was a middle-aged
gray-haired man in a gray silk suit. But the local U.S.
attorney decided, nonetheless, that such infamous
young criminals should not be set free, so he also
charged them with illegally picketing in front of a
courthouse. That statute they had indeed violated, and
they pled guilty to it and are awaiting sentencing. Undoubtedly some untainted judge at some time in the
near future will declare the antipicketing statute to be
an invidious infringement of the constitutional freedom of speech and assembly guarantees all of us are
supposed to enjoy. But for the moment, Hanna and
her fellow desperados stand convicted of that misdemeanor.

"Not satisfied with this perfidious persecution of
these young, well-intentioned students, and chafing at
the effrontery of Joshua Rabb continuing to represent
them and Professor Mischa Livinsky, a Jewish refugee
from Russia, our patriotic Senator Big Bill Maitland
contrived to have the federal grand jury in Tucson
bring a felony accusation against Rabb for conspiring
with his daughter to engage in picketing in front of
a courthouse.

"And who is this accused felon?"

"You'll especially want to hear this, J.T.," Morgan
Roth said.

Sellner folded her hands on the table and stared out
at the glass wall of the conference room.

"Joshua Rabb was a major in the United States Army in World War Two. He served with great distinction for over three years. He was wounded at the Battle of the Bulge in the act of destroying a machine-gun battery. His bravery saved the lives of the men in his company, as the citation reads for his award of the Silver Star. When he was released from the army hospital in Belgium, still partly crippled from leg wounds, he joined General Patton's Third Army in its victorious sweep across Germany into Czechoslovakia.

"Major Joshua Rabb was instrumental in liberating a concentration camp in Czechoslovakia. On a patrol for SS soldiers suspected of murdering several of the inmates who had left the camp to try to return to their homes, he killed four SS soldiers. In the firing, he was severely wounded in the chest and left arm, leaving him with a permanent injury to his lung and an amputated left arm."

J. T. Sellner was staring wide-eyed at Morgan Roth, her mouth open.

"This is the man whom Senator William Maitland brands a traitor. Big Bill sat out the war in his opulent home in Phoenix and propheteered as a cost-plus contractor for the government while the Joshua Rabbs of this nation risked their lives and lost them in an effort to free our country from the danger without.

"Now we are threatened by an equally virulent danger within. The Joe McCarthys-William Maitlands have debased the Senate to the level of a forum of hate and character assassination sheltered by the shield of congressional immunity.

"Just last Friday, A Papago Indian from Tucson,

Arizona, Marine Corps Captain Jesus 'Chuy' Leyva, was honored for his heroism in combat in Korea and awarded the Congressional Medal of Honor. I had the honor to meet with Chuy and his wife Magdalena for two hours, and I came away from that experience with a rejuvenated sense of the underlying greatness and goodness of the American people. Chuy works for the Bureau of Indian Affairs in Tucson as the police chief of the San Xavier Papago Indian Reservation. Joshua Rabb has been its legal affairs officer ever since his arrival in Tucson in June, 1946. Chuy and Magdalena have become close friends of Joshua and his family, and it was from Magdalena that I first learned the sordid details of Senator Maitland's witch-hunt against the Rabbs as well as the true facts concerning Major Rabb's background. I have verified his military record of heroism with the Defense Department."

Morgan Roth looked up from his reading and glared at Sellner. "There's a whole page more. Shall I continue?"

She shook her head slowly, gritting her teeth.

The intercom on the table buzzed. Roth pressed the speaker switch, annoyed by the interruption. "Yes?"

"Senator Maitland is on the phone, sir. He says it's urgent."

Roth picked up the telephone receiver and made an effort to sound pleasant. "It's good to hear from you, Bill. What can I do for you?"

"You can shit can that statement from the cunt from Maine, is what you can do."

The hissing was unusual from jovial Big Bill Maitland. "What statement?" Roth asked.

"Dick Phelps from the *Republic* just called and read it to me. Smith's statement over the Associated Press wire."

"Yes, I've seen it."

"You're not going to print it, are you?"

Roth paused, unsure what to say. "Every other paper in the country's going to print it, or at least part of it."

"Not you."

"Look, Bill, this has stuff in it that we haven't seen before. I don't know what I can promise. It may be out of my hands."

"Nothing's out of your hands on that paper."

"Well, I have to talk to Hank Pullam and Harry Chandler. The publisher has to know what he may be looking at with this libel suit that Rabb filed. And we're going to need some legal advice from Harry."

"Listen, goddamnit. The libel suit by that Jew cocksucker is going to evaporate when he's convicted of conspiracy. Just let it happen. All it's going to take is a little time."

"I have a newspaper down here, Bill, not just a daily pile of fish wrappers. I'll do what I can for you, but first I've got to protect Hank Pullam and the *Star.* J. T. Sellner took what you said on faith, and I printed it. Now I've got to make damn sure we're not in deep shit over it." His voice was rising with anger, and it carried through the glass walls. Several of the reporters looked up from their desks, staring quizzically into the conference room.

"That piece a shit Sellner prints any filth she can

dig up and some she can't, and you know it. As long as it sells papers, you don't give a rat's ass. Now all of a sudden you're getting self-righteous? I've heard you talk about kikes and Commies out on the golf course fifty times. Don't suddenly start getting religion." Maitland was screaming.

Roth maintained his composure with effort. "Okay, Bill, take it easy. I'll talk to Hank and Harry and try to bury it. I'll do what I can."

The receiver slammed in his ear, and he flinched away from the sound and hung up.

"Bill Maitland heard about the Smith statement from Dick Phelps." He grimaced.

"What's the *Republic* going to do with it?" asked Charlie Hammond.

Roth shrugged. "Don't know." His shoulders slumped, and he suddenly looked much older than his forty-eight years.

"What are we going to do?" asked the national desk editor.

"I have to call Hank in Indianapolis. Then I'll call Harry Chandler and Dick Phelps." He rubbed the twitch out of his left eye. "Damned if I know," he said. "Leave me alone."

Sellner and the two editors walked to their desks. Charlie Hammond went into his cubicle office on the south side of the floor and sat down at his desk. He could see the glass-walled conference room across the floor. Morgan Roth was on the telephone. Hammond got up and closed his office door. He sat down at his desk and telephoned Senator Maitland's home number. Loyal reporters had been given it during the campaign. Horton Landers had thought that it would make them feel privileged and indebted.

"Senator, this is Charlie Hammond at the *Star*."

"Do you know about Senator Smith's statement? I just talked to Morgan Roth about it. I can't understand his attitude."

"Yes, sir. I was there when your call came in. I don't understand it myself."

"You know, I've had some suspicions about Roth's loyalty, what with his background and all. Have you noticed anything peculiar?"

"I can't say I have, Senator. Although I do remember that he said that Stalin was a hell of a war leader."

"Well I'd be grateful if you'd keep a lookout for me down there. We can't let someone with dubious loyalty be running a newspaper in our state. Maybe it's time for an investigation."

"Yes, sir, I'll certainly keep my eyes and ears open. You know, just a half hour ago, some greaseball cop from the San Xavier Reservation was in the morgue downstairs looking at your file. He took a photograph of Horton Landers."

"Tim Essert told me," Maitland growled. "It's that fucking Rabb."

Charlie Hammond could now hear heavy breathing on the other end of the line.

"I owe you one for this, Charlie," said Maitland. "And I always pay my debts."

"I know that, Senator, and I certainly appreciate it.

I'll keep an eye out for what we were talking about. And I'll send you a few notes I've been making on Roth for the last year or so."

"Our country needs men like you, Charlie." The senator hung up.

Charlie Hammond replaced the telephone receiver on its cradle and smiled happily.

"Where'd you find it?" Joshua said, studying the grainy eight-by-ten photograph of Horton Landers in his army colonel's uniform.

"It was in the senator's file at the newspaper morgue," Solomon said.

Joshua sat in his desk at the BIA. Solomon was standing beside him, staring at the photo.

"They just let you take it?"

"Well not exactly."

"What happened?"

"The old lady who runs the morgue didn't want me to take it. But I told her it was official BIA business. She ran upstairs and got a guy, said he was the assistant managing editor of the *Star.*"

"So?"

"So he told me to get lost, and I walked out with the photograph anyway."

Edgar Hendly looked in the doorway of Joshua's office at the BIA. Joshua hadn't been back to the BIA in six weeks, since his arrest. Today he had come to the Reservation to visit Chuy and Magdalena, but their house was locked, and they were in Topowa, on Chuy's mother's ranch, the next-door neighbor said. Joshua had stopped at the BIA to talk to Solomon.

"What're you guys cookin' up?" Edgar asked.

"We're after Ollie Friedkind's killer," Joshua said. "The same guy who killed Julio and the woman."

"Yeah? Whatcha got?"

Joshua held up the photograph. Edgar walked over beside Solomon and looked at it, then shook his head and frowned.

"That's that Landers guy, works for Maitland."

Joshua nodded.

"Why the hell would he do somethin' like that?"

"Create a cause for Maitland to champion, ride it all the way to the White House, maybe."

Edgar looked at the photograph again. "Doesn't look exactly like him anymore."

"It's six years old," Solomon said, "taken when he left the army in 1945."

"Ya showed it to anybody?"

Solomon nodded. "The two old people who were witnesses at the preliminary hearing."

"And?"

"And they said they're pretty sure it's him. He's older now, less hair, more gray, they said. But they think it's him."

"Can we prove he was in Tucson on the day of the bombing?" Joshua asked.

Solomon nodded. "I called Roy Collins. He says that Landers came to Tucson that morning with the two FBI agents from Washington."

"Damn," Edgar muttered. "Why would he be so

dumb to pull some shit like that? People all around, he'd have to figger that somebody'd see 'im."

Joshua shook his head. "These guys are so cocksure and arrogant, they don't worry about anything. They have the U.S. attorney in their pocket, and Sheriff Dunphy sure as hell isn't going to do anything about it."

"You think Roy Collins will help?"

"I think he'll be willing to, but Essert isn't going let him."

"How's about our pal Randy Stevens over t' the Pima County attorney's office. They got his pecker in their pocket?"

Joshua shook his head. "Not Randy." He sat for a moment, rubbing his chin with his steel hand.

"Watch out for that weapon, Josh boy. Ya'll rip the dimples outta yer cheeks."

Joshua stood up quickly. "See you boys later."

"You out of your mind?" Roy Collins said, looking hard at him.

Joshua shook his head. "I don't think so."

"This guy'll unload on you like a ton of bricks."

"What more can he do? I'm getting prosecuted for conspiracy and sued for fraud. What else is there?"

"You can end up in an outhouse on the reservation with your head stuck two feet up your ass." Roy wasn't joking.

"I've got to run with it. I feel it in my gut. This guy staged all three murders so Maitland could climb on McCarthy's wagon as a national player. Vice president, secretary of state. Who knows how far it can take them?"

"I don't believe it," Roy said. "The guy's the administrative aide to a United States senator."

Joshua shrugged. "So what? Look at what Joseph McCarthy is doing, and he's a senator. Or maybe it's just Landers, off on his own, trying to insure his own future as chief adviser to a rising star."

"So what do you want?"

"A search warrant for Horton Landers's house, for starters."

"You nuts?"

"There's enough probable cause to ask Judge Buchanan for a search warrant on Landers's car and home, and I think we'd turn up stuff for making bombs."

"What makes you so damn sure it's Landers?"

"The description, the ID by the Joslins."

"But it's just a tentative ID of a thin, middle-aged man with gray hair in a gray suit. There was another guy here that day who fits the same description."

Joshua sat back in his chair, surprised. "What?"

Roy nodded. "Horton Landers came here with the two FBI agents and one of Senator McCarthy's staffers. I haven't found out his name yet or where he's from. But I know he spent some time with Essert and the agents. He was a thin guy, maybe fifty-two, fifty-five, balding, short gray-brown hair. I don't remember what kind of suit he was wearing, but all of these staffers wear the same thing, almost like a uniform. Their boss is supposed to be noticeable and stand out in the newspaper photos, but the staffers are supposed to just blend into the gray background of photographs like furniture."

"That's it," Joshua said. "That's it. Two men had to do the Moraga and Hauser murders. It's them!"

"We don't have anything. We don't go around accusing senators' aides of committing murder without a hell of a lot better evidence than what we've got so far."

"That's why we need the search warrant."

"First I've got to find out who the McCarthy staffer was."

"Why don't you ask Essert?"

"And what am I going to tell him the reason is, that I'm investigating Maitland and his aide and one of Senator McCarthy's aides for three murders?" Roy frowned. "I'd be around here about two more minutes before the Bureau yanked me and sent me to Coos Bay, Oregon, to monitor fishing violations."

Joshua shook his head. "These people have got to be stopped. They're literally a danger to democracy."

"I'm not going to disagree with that. But I'm not the one that's going to stop them. Nobody is, at least on this evidence. Anyway, I'd have to get Tim Essert to apply to Buchanan for a warrant, and that just isn't going to happen. Not even if I had a picture of Landers throwing the bomb. You'd better put your witnesses eyeball to eyeball with Landers and see if you can get a positive ID. Then maybe Randy Stevens can get a warrant from one of the state court judges."

Joshua sighed in frustration.

"Look, it's the only way."

"Okay," Joshua said. "Call him and tell him I'll be over in five minutes."

He picked up the photograph of Landers with the stainless-steel prongs of his mechanical arm.

"You're getting pretty good with that thing." Roy jutted his chin at Joshua's steel hand.

"I've been practicing picking up paper clips in my office. Since I got indicted, I haven't had any clients."

"Go use it on Landers and Maitland. That'll take care of everything."

Joshua rolled his eyes. "It's crossed my mind. Believe me, it's crossed my mind."

"Roy just called me and told me you were riding your broom over here," Randy Stevens said as Joshua walked into his office.

"All we need is a search warrant."

"From who?"

"Judge Velasco, I guess. The other two judges are Republicans."

"You think Velasco is going to flush his career down the toilet to issue a search warrant for a United States senator's home?"

"His aide's home."

"Same thing."

"If I get a positive ID from the Joslins, there's plenty of probable cause."

"Jesus, Joshua! We're not talking probable cause here. We're talking real life. If we found a mountain of nitroglycerin in his living room, who the hell's going to prosecute him?"

"How about you?"
Randy snorted. "You got brass balls, baby."
"So do you."
Randy frowned.

Chapter Twenty

"Who's that, Marger?" the voice said from inside the small house.

"Some of those people from the courthouse thing," she called back.

"Who?"

"The lawyer, Joshua Rabb, father of one of the girls. Got that Indian with him."

Lawrence Joslin came to the door, hitching his suspenders over his shoulders. "What is it?"

"Mr. Joslin, I'm Joshua Rabb. Remember me, from the preliminary hearing? And this is Officer Solomon Leyva with the San Xavier Reservation Police. I think you've met Solomon before."

"Yeah, sure did. He come out here to show us a picture."

"Right. Now I need a little more help. I'm defending my daughter and the other students."

"Yeah, I remember. I remember ya at that hearing. I also reckon I read about ya in the newspaper a while back."

Joshua's face colored. "Yes, it was a lot of lies, Mr. Joslin. I'm as much a traitor as you or your wife."

The elderly man studied him for a moment. "Okay. Come on in." He opened the door wide, and they walked into the living room, cramped by a long gold velveteen sofa and two large rocking chairs upholstered in celery green burlap.

"Marger, throw a kettle on the stove, rustle up a little java."

"Thank you, sir," Joshua said, "but that really isn't necessary."

"It's my house, and I decide what's necessary."

"Yes, sir."

"What's on your mind?"

"The identification you and your wife made of the photograph that Officer Leyva brought over here the other night."

"Well, now, we never said we was for sure on that. We *think* it's him, but we couldn't say it was for *sure.*"

"Okay, Mr. Joslin. I understand that and that's the problem. We need to have a more positive identification so we can investigate further."

"Who is the guy, anyway? He was wearing an army officer's uniform."

"He's the administrative aide to Senator William Maitland."

Lawrence Joslin tilted his head at Joshua. "You don't say. You think the senator had something to do with that bombing?"

Joshua shrugged. "I honestly don't know."

Joslin shook his head. "This Commie business is scary stuff, ain't no question about it, what with 'em fighting us in Korea and looking to take over all of Europe." He pursed his lips and studied Joshua. "But

I think it's going just a tad too far when the politicians start using that stuff against anyone who doesn't agree with 'em. When ya got this guy McCarthy screaming that Secretary of Defense General George C. Marshall hisself is a Commie sympathizer, ya done gone too damn far.''

Joshua nodded.

Mrs. Joslin brought in three cups of black coffee on a small wooden carving board. She set them on the table and handed a cup to each of the men.

"Ain't no sugar," she said. "What with Lawrence's diabetes, I don't even keep no sugar around."

"This is fine, ma'am," Joshua said. He dutifully took a drink from the cup and smiled his appreciation. Solomon took a shallow swallow and smiled politely.

"So what are ya after with us?" Lawrence Joslin asked.

"There's a Republican election rally over at the Congress Street Sports Arena tomorrow evening."

Joslin nodded. "I read about it in this morning's paper."

"Senator Goldwater is going to be there with Maitland and Senator Richard Nixon from California."

"So?"

"Where Maitland goes, Horton Landers goes. I'd like you to come with us and look him over up close. If you can make a positive ID, great. If not, well, then I was just barking up the wrong tree. But it's the only way to be sure."

"I don't think you should, Lawrence," his wife said. "Fooling around with United States senators is a little out of our bailiwick."

"I'm just an old retired packing plant inspector from Iowa, Mr. Rabb. Got bad lungs getting gassed in France in the First War. Got some shrapnel in my guts, still working out of me piece by piece. All I got is my social security. They take that away from me, we plum starve."

"They can't take away your social security, Mr. Joslin."

He nodded. "Yeah, I know. I was just being dramatic." He laughed and his wife smiled.

"What do ya think, Marger?"

"I think it's too dangerous. What happens to us if they find out we identified this Landers? Who protects us?"

"Well, Mrs. Joslin, they're certainly already aware that you both testified at the preliminary hearing. You haven't been threatened, have you?"

"No, but we didn't identify nobody, neither. This is a whole lot different. If their people murdered a marshal, what'll stop 'em from hurting us?"

Joshua sighed deeply. "Truth is, Mrs. Joslin, every time a witness testifies against somebody in a court of law, the witness is in danger. But I've been practicing law for sixteen years now, and I've never had a witness stalked or hurt."

"Well, we don't want to be your first ones, Mr. Rabb," she said.

"And I don't want you to be."

"I got a gun," Lawrence Joslin said. "Nobody's going to hurt us, Marger." He turned toward Joshua. "I'll help ya, Mr. Rabb. But Margaret, she'll stay here."

Joshua nodded. "Thank you, sir. I really appreciate it."

"Okay, Mr. Rabb. You pick me up and bring me back so's I don't have to waste my own gas. Twenty-one cents a gallon lately is pretty damn rough on the pension."

"I'll be happy to, sir. I'll pick you up at seven."

The Sports Arena was a couple of blocks west of downtown Tucson, past the Congress Street bridge over the Santa Cruz River. The river was dry now. It had run about two feet deep from the monsoon rains that had doused southern Arizona in August, but now the bottom was as parched and cracked as its desiccated banks. Sporadic clumps of bright yellow daisies and lavender Mexican primrose only slightly ameliorated the roughness of the land and the sandy riverbed.

They drove past the wood and tin and tarpaper shacks of the destitute Mexicans who lived on this side of the river. There was no use getting to the huge arena early, since the entourage of politicians would undoubtedly arrive late to make their heraldic entrance to the roars of the eagerly waiting crowd. So by the time that Joshua parked his car on the street a block away from the arena, they could already hear the tumult from the rally. He and Solomon and Lawrence Joslin walked on the rocky dirt path by the equally rocky dirt street and entered the open doors of the arena.

In the central area where the boxing ring was usually set up for the Monday night fights, there was a stage. The instantly recognizable Richard Nixon stood behind the podium, speaking closely into a tall microphone, trying to be heard over the roaring and cheering of the Republican faithful.

Joshua pushed his way through the men standing in the aisle. Solomon and Joslin followed. They worked themselves forward to the stage, over their heads, and Joshua didn't see Landers. They worked their way around to the back of the stage. Landers was sitting on a folding chair next to two man-sized amplifiers.

"Mr. Landers," Joshua said.

The noise was too loud.

"Mr. Landers," he yelled.

The man turned around, recognizing Joshua and Solomon. "You're interested in my photograph, I hear?" he said. The roaring had died down.

Joshua nodded. "We've got an eyewitness who says you threw the bomb under Ollie Friedkind's car."

Landers appeared stunned, then vicious. His upper lip turned up over his teeth and his eyes were suddenly wide and wild.

"You lowlife!" he spat out. "You fucking Jews and Commies are all the same. You buy somebody? How much you have to pay him to lie?"

"You're finished," Joshua said, his voice steady and hard. "You and that fat tub of pus, Maitland."

"Get the fuck out of here," Landers barked, "before I have security drag you out by your feet."

Joshua worked his way through the crowd and out of the arena, followed by Solomon and Joslin.

"Well?" Joshua asked?

Lawrence Joslin shook his head. "I don't know."

Joshua was deeply frustrated. "You sure?"

He nodded. "I think the guy had a thinner face, real bony. Maybe a couple of years older. But maybe I just didn't see him as well as I thought I did."

"Shit," Joshua muttered.

The rally was a huge success, according to the political pundits who traveled with Richard Nixon, now campaigning hard to be selected as Eisenhower's running mate at the Republican convention. Later that evening, Landers had nodded and smiled and drank his share of scotch at the reception for a few Republican high rollers at the Santa Rita Hotel. Finally, Bill Maitland had drunk enough and sated himself sufficiently on pigs-in-a-blanket hors d'oeuvres that he called it a night and made his mawkish good-byes to the party stalwarts.

Horton drove the big Cadillac north on Highway 89 toward Phoenix. The senator dozed on and off, slumped in the front seat.

"I'm not taking the rap."

Maitland looked around at Landers. "You say something?" His speech was slightly slurred.

"I'm not taking the rap."

"What the hell you talking about?"

"Ollie Friedkind."

"Who's that?"

"The U.S. marshal who got bombed."

Maitland straightened up in the seat, and his speech was clearer. "What happened?"

"The fucking eyewitnesses."

"Well, we knew that. They testified at the preliminary hearing."

"Yeah, but now Rabb must've shown them the picture they took from the *Star* the other day. They IDed *me*."

"You got to be kidding."

"No. Rabb and that Indian buck of his came to the rally with an old man, must have been one of the witnesses. Rabb told me."

"Damn! That son of a bitch is in serious need of some straightening out. I guess we just haven't impressed him enough. The guy's mule-assed stubborn. Dangerously stubborn."

Landers nodded.

"The witness say it was you?"

"That's what Rabb says."

Maitland slumped again in the seat. "You better find out where those witnesses live. I can't have none of this shit. I just can't have this."

"*I'm* not going near the witnesses."

Minutes passed. They could see the lights of the small town of Casa Grande several miles west of the highway.

Maitland was wide awake and sober. "That fucking kike. I wish he had done *him*."

More minutes of silence.

"I'm not taking the rap for this," Landers said.

Maitland stared out the side window into the desert blackness.

Bill Maitland sat before his picture window on Camelback Mountain, seeing none of the lights of Arizona's sprawling capital. He saw only the end of his career, the end of his dream of being somebody. If garbage like Dick Nixon could make it, why not he? He was better-looking than Dick, a hell of a lot wealthier, and he was one of McCarthy's closest allies. It would be the cruelest injustice if his brilliant and promising career were to end because of one scumbag lawyer in Tucson, Arizona. And it would be a loss to the country. America needed him. Rabb was injuring America.

He sat brooding for hours. He could not call so early in the morning. Joe would still be drunk from the night before, as he always was. He had to wait until three, six o'clock Washington time. Then at least he wouldn't be waking Joe up. The senator's day started early.

Three hours passed as though they were a week. He sat staring morosely out the living-room picture window.

He reached into his back pocket and pulled out his wallet. He took the small, folded piece of paper out of one of the pockets. Joe's home number. Practically nobody had his home number. A special sign of respect.

"Hello."

"Good morning, Joe. This is Bill Maitland."

"Hold on a sec, I got a mouthful of tooth powder." Pause. McCarthy hawked and spat loudly. "What's going on, Bill? It must be two, three o'clock your time. Got insomnia?"

" 'Fraid so. But I think I got the cure."

"Yeah? What?"

"I got a little trouble out here that you can help resolve."

"What?"

"There are a couple of eyewitnesses to the murder of that U.S. marshal."

Pause. "You kidding?"

"I don't kid about that."

"Jesus! What do they say?"

"They fingered Horton Landers."

Long pause. "Holy shit," McCarthy muttered. "That's real bad news."

"Horton isn't too thrilled about it either."

"What's going to happen?"

"He says he won't take the rap."

Long pause. "What do we do?"

"I don't know. But we better do something damn fast. If the county attorney down there suddenly sprouts a pair of balls, all hell's going to break loose. And you know where it leads."

"Who you talking to?" McCarthy's voice was gruff.

"Listen, Joe, help me out of this," Maitland soothed. "You can do it. I got faith in you. We've got a job to do for this country. But first we just got to root some crabgrass out of the cotton field, kill some weevils."

David Goldbergs' 1937 Packard touring limousine was parked at the curb when Joshua got home. Suddenly he was no longer thinking about Landers and Friedkind and Lawrence Joslin. Why would Mark's parents be here at nine o'clock on a weekday evening? Something had happened to Mark.

Joshua parked behind the Packard. The driveway was full, Hanna's faded yellow Chevy parked in it. That wasn't so unusual. Hanna often came back home to spend the night, do her laundry, get a good meal. But the Goldbergs?

He walked quickly up the stairs. David and Judy Goldberg were sitting on the sofa in the living room. Hanna was next to Judy. Barbara was in one of the upholstered chairs. There was sepulchral silence.

"What is it?" Joshua asked.

David handed him the flimsy single half-sheet telegram: "The President of the United States regrets to inform you that it has been notified this date by Eighth Army Headquarters, Korea, that your son, Second Lieutenant Mark Goldberg, is missing in action. The United States government shall take all possible steps to locate Lt. Goldberg and to secure his safety."

Joshua sank into the chair beside the sofa.

He sits on the edge of his bed and tears drip from his eyes. He had not let himself do this in front of the Goldbergs and Hanna. But the Goldbergs are gone now, and Hanna has gone to her room, rather than returning to Maricopa dormitory, and he can finally give in to his own grief. So much is happening. So much terrible is happening.

Is there no end to your punishment, God? Are we all Jobs, just put here for you to afflict with boils and bitter suffering?

He opens the drawer of the bedstand and takes out the Bible that had been a gift from his father so many years ago. It will keep you from harm, my son, his father had solemnly pronounced. Had Joshua believed it once? He cannot remember. It seems like three lifetimes ago in a gentler time.

He opens the Bible idly. The Psalms, the Psalms he has read so many times in the army hospital in Antwerp. He thumbs the tissuelike pages to them. "It is good for me that I have been afflicted, that I may learn thy laws, O God. Who will stand for me against the workers of iniquity? The Lord is my defense, my God is the rock of my refuge. And He shall bring upon my enemies their own iniquity and shall cut them off in their wickedness."

A perfect psalm for Maitland and McCarthy. A perfect psalm for Joshua's enemies. But was God listening?

Barbara rolls toward him on the bed and touches him gently on the shoulder. "Put the Bible away now and come to bed, honey."

"My father believes in it," he says. "Do you believe in it?"

"Yes. Come on to bed now."

"I don't know how anybody can believe it. I want to believe it. It hurts not to."

He puts the Bible in the drawer and switches off the lamp.

"I feel terrible," he whispers, "helpless. I can't help myself. I can't help my daughter. The bad guys always win."

She kisses his cheek. She touches him softly and they lie there, holding each other, trying to sleep.

*   *   *

Hanna parked the faded yellow Chevrolet convertible on the pebbly shoulder of the Nogales Highway and walked past the mesquite bosque to the line of cottonwoods and sycamores and willow trees on the west bank of the river. She sat down at the edge of the arroyo, which sloped gently at this point to the brakes where the water oozed underground. Despite the fact that it was late September, it was still a hundred degrees under a ruthless sun. She sat against the trunk of a spreading sycamore tree. It shaded her with its wide five-pointed leaves, under its smooth white bark branches like a protective mother with her arms outstretched.

The ten-mile-long *bajadas* of the Santa Rita Mountains to the east of the river sprawled in alluvial fans down from Mount Wrightson, ninety-four hundred feet high, to the Santa Cruz River bed seventy-five hundred feet below it.

The old-timers said that just seventy or eighty years ago, the Santa Cruz River had run year round in its wide channel, swift and clear, from its highest point in the Pinito Mountains of northern Sonora, Mexico, to its confluence with the Gila River about fifty miles north of Tucson. But for some reason, it had begun to meander and to cut arroyos far from its primordial channel. Then suddenly the waters began to disappear into the earth, about thirty-five or forty miles south of Tucson, forming one of the underground rivers that were unique to the Great Sonora Desert.

In the etched sides of the arroyo Hanna could see the strata of rock and sedimentary silt representing millions of years of geologic time. It was daunting, even overpowering. She had begun coming to this place three years ago, when she was sixteen and had first gotten her driver's license. She had lived next to the San Xavier Reservation then, in a tiny adobe house with a wire chicken coop attached to the side and fifty or sixty squabbling White Rock chickens that pecked at her toes when she scattered feed for them. She had been thrilled when they had moved into Tucson, six miles north of the Reservation. But Hanna still came to this place, more often now even than before. Because she and Mark used to come here together to be alone.

She listened absently to the chattering of three gray and white speckled cactus wrens vying for some treasure in the marshy brakes by the water's edge. A roadrunner had found a fallen quail's nest under a nearby cottonwood and was pecking open each of the tiny eggs.

Tears welled in her eyes and wet her cheeks. Why Mark? Why her? She had known that this would happen, and she had been helpless to do anything about it. No one could do anything about it. He was rich, he was handsome, and they had the whole world before them. But still nobody could do anything about it.

She lay back against the sycamore trunk, and ants crawled up and down, and a squirrel sat on a broad branch watching her cautiously, and a white wing dove in a nest high above her stared closely at her, watching her every move. But she did not move. She only wept.

Chapter Twenty-one

The story in the *Arizona Daily Star* was on page one, dominating almost the entire page. The first line set the tone: "The publishers of the *Arizona Daily Star* and the *Arizona Republic* wish to retract several unfortunate statements printed in the newspapers on June 26, 1951." It got better from there. They apologized for labeling Joshua Rabb a Communist and a traitor and for asserting that Hanna Rabb would be held to answer for murder at the preliminary hearing.

"It is deeply troubling to those many of us who hold journalism to be a sacred trust in the preservation of good government that from time to time our reporters are duped by unscrupulous persons who purvey lies and half-truths for the furtherance of their own scurrilous purposes. While the *Star* and the *Republic* make no judgment as to the opinions stated therein, the publishers deem it the obligation of responsible journalists to publish a press release issued four days ago by the office of Senator Margaret Chase Smith (R-Maine).

The entire press release followed.

After Senator Smith's statement, there was a short joint press release from the Phoenix offices of Senators William Maitland and Barry Goldwater:

> Extremism in the defense of liberty is not a vice. But we must be careful to investigate fully and to protect those who are innocently caught up in matters which at first blush may appear to be questionable. An injustice may have been done in the case of Joshua Rabb and his daughter Hanna. We are today asking the United States attorney for Arizona to review the matter to make certain that the Tucson office has handled it properly. This being an issue of bipartisan importance, we will also ask the attorney general of the United States to direct an independent probe of the propriety of the actions taken by the United States attorney's office in Tucson.

Joshua smiled genuinely for the first time in months. When Barbara came out of the bedroom to make breakfast for everyone, Joshua gave her the newspaper. She sat down at the kitchen table and read it, and she too smiled.

The first telephone call was from Hal Dubin at a few minutes after seven. "It's about time your husband got some good press," he said to his daughter. "Now maybe he'll get a client or two who actually have a couple bucks to spend."

The second call was from Edgar Hendly. "Harry Coyle just called me. He says as soon as he got to his office this mornin' Undersecretary Anson came in wavin' the *New York Times* and tol' him that me 'n you are off the hot seat."

"How about my indictment and the Code of Federal Regulations?"

"Seems that technical shit don't matter a whole hell of a lot at the moment. Harry says that Anson says that Secretary Kimmer says he's proud a the job we're doin' out here."

"Yeah, until McCarthy gets on his ass again."

"Now don't be so cynical, Josh boy. These are honorable politicians." Edgar cackled.

Joshua laughed. "Yeah, right."

Tim Essert sat at the kitchen table in his house. He was still in his pyjama bottoms, as was his usual routine when he read the morning newspaper. His wife and two of his children were also at the table, gabbing loudly as usual.

"Shhhhhh," he hissed at them.

His wife looked questioningly at him. Then she stared sternly at each of the two young girls and put her finger to her lips.

"What's wrong?" she asked.

"They're going to hang me out to dry."

"What?"

"They'll pin the whole fucking thing on me."

"Tim," she chided, "don't use that language in front of the children. Sister Veronica says they repeat it at school."

"Read this."

She took the newspaper and began reading. Her mouth fell open more and more. When she finished, her eyes were wide with fear.

"But Maitland said you'd be protected."

"Not when they're looking for someone to hang this whole mess on," he muttered.

He got up from the table, walked into the bedroom, and slammed the door.

Seconds later he came out again, holding an address book in his hand. "Leave me alone," he growled at his wife.

She nodded. "Come on, kids, let's go get you dressed for school."

The girls looked at their father's frightened face and they themselves became frightened. They walked into their bedroom in front of their mother, and she closed the door.

Tim Essert went to the telephone on the sink counter and dialed Big Bill Maitland's home number. Horton Landers answered.

"I need to speak to the senator," Tim said.

"He's not here, left by train for Washington last night."

"Damn."

"What's the problem?"

"I'm not happy about what I read in the paper, Mr. Landers."

"Aw, that's just politics. It'll blow over. Everybody'll forget the whole thing in a couple days."

"Yeah? Well, Judge Buchanan's not going to forget. If he thinks I fucked with Rabb, he can disbar me in federal court. Then I'm out of a job and out of a career."

"Now take it easy," Landers said. "We're going to have this thing under control before anything like that happens."

"Just remember, I'm not going down alone. You told me I was covered."

There was a long silence on the line. Landers's composure was breaking. "You've got to stay on board, Essert. We've put a lot of confidence in you."

"Just knock off the crap, Landers. I'm not getting drowned in this shit all by myself."

"Don't threaten me," Landers barked.

"Then don't let them bury me," Essert screamed into the phone and slammed it down. He stood looking out the window into his backyard, gritting his teeth so hard that his jaw muscles ached.

Landers turned to Maitland, sitting on the sofa in the living room holding the *Arizona Republic* on his lap. His face was gray and drawn.

"We got trouble with Essert," Landers said.

"You got big trouble out there, Bill. I thought you had those newspapers in your pocket."

Maitland was enraged. He held his voice steady only with great effort. "I did, Joe. I called Dick Phelps at the *Republic* just a half hour ago and asked him what the hell right he had to print these goddamn lies. He said it was orders from the publishers and their lawyers. They were afraid without the retraction, this Rabb might win the libel case against them. With these guys it's just money, Joe. Just money. They got no principles like we got."

"Well, it's all over Washington now," Joe McCarthy said. "The *Herald* and the *Sun* and the *New York Times* all picked up the story and ran it this morning.

I had the Smith thing under wraps until the shit hit the fan in your territory."

"I'm sorry, Joe. I'm really sorry. But it'll blow over, just like that bitch's 'Declaration of Conscience' last year."

In June 1950, Senator Margaret Chase Smith and several other Republican senators had published a statement decrying the deceitful, defamatory tactics of McCarthy. He had weathered the denunciation without even the smallest scar.

"Well, you've got to take care of this shit right now, Bill."

Maitland hesitated and breathed deeply. "*You* have to, Joe."

"What's that mean?"

"You sent the guy down here."

"What guy?"

"That staffer of yours from Milwaukee, Gruver."

"What about him?"

"We're not responsible for what he did."

Pause. "What the hell are you talking about?"

"Three murders."

"Now hold on just a goddamn minute. I never had anything to do with murder, and I don't know what the hell you're taking about."

"You better ask your boy Gruver. If they come looking for Horton, he'll be spilling his guts in five minutes."

"Landers isn't loyal?"

"He doesn't think loyalty goes that far."

"Kikes and Commies, goddamn it! The whole country's full of kikes and Commies."

"Well, what the hell am I supposed to do?" Maitland said, exasperated and unnerved.

"What the hell am *I* supposed to do? Don't call me talking stupid shit no more," McCarthy said, slamming down the telephone receiver.

Chapter Twenty-two

Hanna's last class on Thursdays was Southwestern Anthropology, which got out at ten minutes to five. She walked to Maricopa dorm, changed into a polo shirt, Levi's, and squaw boots, and drove home. She was still driving the old faded yellow Chevy convertible, since her father's law practice hadn't been faring too well lately. Hopefully, now that the story had appeared in the newspaper, things would get better, her father could buy the new Oldsmobile he had been looking at, and she would take over the 1948 Dodge and give the Chevy to Adam.

Dinner was much more relaxed than it had been just a day ago. Her father was actually cracking jokes and smiling for a change. There was no more constant brooding about his own criminal charges and what would happen to Hanna. You'll see, he said to her, I'll move to set aside your conviction and the other four kids, and I think that they'll have to go along with it, and then they'll have to voluntarily quash my indictment. He nodded sagely at her, and she believed him. He was right a lot of the time, and about legal stuff, he was almost always right. The only thing that kept her from feeling any joy was knowing that Mark was either dead or a prisoner of war. Every time she thought about that telegram from the Defense Department a few days ago, she became queasy, wobbly. The flood of tears had stopped, but not the grief.

It was after seven o'clock when she and Barbara went downtown to the maternity section of Goldberg's Department Store to buy some new clothes. Barbara was almost six months pregnant and rapidly outgrowing the first batch of maternity clothing that she had bought months ago. It was time to take the ultimate plunge and buy muumuus and stretch front pants and flouncy blouses.

Most of the outfits were pretty drab. Clothes companies didn't pay a lot of attention to style when it came to pregnant women, and it was hard to find anything flattering and chic, even in Tucson's finest department store. After an hour, having found only two outfits that she liked enough to buy, they walked down the block to Jacome's Department Store to see if there might be a real find just waiting for them. Surprisingly there was: a simple white muumuu with a big Van Gogh sunflower hand-painted on the front. It was so simple that it was elegant. They left when the store closed at nine o'clock.

Darkness had enveloped Tucson, and there were very few streetlamps. The sky was thickly overcast with black rain clouds. It began to sprinkle lightly. They walked quickly back to Hanna's Chevy parked in the lot behind Goldberg's. Barbara got into the passenger seat. Hanna started to get into the driver's seat. She gasped and put her hand to her mouth.

"What's wrong?" Barbara asked.

Hanna pointed to the backseat.

Barbara turned around and looked. The dim dome light was on, but it took her a moment to understand what she was looking at. She opened her door and scrambled out of the car. She vomited and fell to her knees, holding her stomach.

"Oh, my God," she groaned.

Hanna ran to her and knelt with her on the ground. Both of them were gasping and crying.

"I've got to call Daddy," Hanna said, regaining her voice.

"Where?"

"There's some pay phones on Stone in front of the Cattlemen's Hotel."

"Don't leave me here," Barbara gasped.

"Can you walk?"

"Help me up. I'll walk."

Hanna stood up and helped Barbara stand. Barbara swayed for a moment, steadied herself, and they both walked quickly toward the Cattlemen's Hotel a block away.

Joshua was there in five minutes. "Do you know who it was?"

Barbara shook her head. "I didn't look that close."

Hanna shook her head.

He drove them home and ran upstairs to telephone the sheriff's department. When he returned to the parking lot behind Goldberg's Department Store, there was a brown Chevrolet sedan with its lights on parked behind the yellow convertible. A deputy with a flashlight was leaning into the car.

"Can you see who it is?" Joshua asked.

"Who are you?" The deputy stood up and flashed the light in Joshua's face.

"Joshua Rabb. It's my car."

"How'd he get there?"

"How the hell do I know? Do you know who he is?"

The deputy nodded. "Tim Essert. The U.S. attorney."

Joshua swallowed. "Let me see," he said, disbelieving.

The deputy handed him the flashlight, and Joshua leaned into the car. He straightened up quickly.

"God," he gasped.

"How'd he get in your car?"

"I told you I don't know."

Another sheriff's car pulled into the parking lot. A deputy got out of the driver's side, and Sheriff Pat Dunphy got out of the passenger side. He casually hitched up his brown twill uniform trousers and walked over to the convertible. He was balding, short, very fat, and his stomach bulged the buttons of the short-sleeved tan cotton uniform shirt he was wearing. He sucked at a toothpick in the corner of his mouth.

"Howdy, Counselor," he said. He held out his hand for the flashlight, and Joshua handed it to him.

He leaned into the car for a moment, then handed the flashlight to the deputy.

"Got us a dead man here," he drawled.

"You're a genius," Joshua said.

"This yer old car?" Dunphy pointed. "I seem to remember you bought it with the money you got offa that killer, what was his name? Yeah, yeah, Franklin Carillo."

Joshua said nothing.

"What's ol' Timmy Essert doin' in yer backseat?"

"He isn't doing anything, far as I can tell," Joshua said.

Dunphy let out a malicious laugh. "Yer a real comedian, a real funny guy, you are."

Joshua said nothing.

"You get tired a him screwin' with you and yer daughter?"

"You think I'd have left him in the backseat of my own car?"

Dunphy raised his eyebrows and shrugged. "Who knows what you Commies'll do? Maybe you figgered the best place was your own car, throw all us rubes off lookin' for somebody who set ya up."

Joshua stared at him and frowned.

An old military ambulance pulled into the lot. Coroner Stanley Wolfe got out of the passenger side and walked up to Joshua and Dunphy.

"Got a little present fer ya, Stan," the sheriff said. He pointed to the back of the car.

The deputy handed the flashlight to the coroner, and Wolf leaned into the back of the car. He examined the body for several minutes.

"Looks like suicide," Wolfe said. "He held this .45 Colt auto up to his temple and pulled the trigger." He held up the gun. He was holding it by a pencil through the trigger housing.

"Or somebody done it to make it look like suicide," Dunphy said.

Stan Wolfe shrugged. "Possible."

"When'd it happen?" Dunphy asked.

"Can't tell yet. I'll take him to the morgue and call you later."

Dunphy nodded, then looked hard at Joshua. "Come on down to the office, Counselor. Let's have a little chat."

"Do I have a choice?"

"Sho' nuff, son, sho' nuff. Ya can choose standin' up or lyin' flat on yer back with my knuckle prints on yer jaw."

It was after midnight when the pointless inquisition ended and Joshua got back home. He walked wearily upstairs, and the lights were on in the living room. Odd. The master bedroom door was open, and Barbara wasn't there. Hanna's bedroom was empty. He ran up the stairs to the dormer, and Adam wasn't there.

He ran down to the kitchen, switched on the light, and looked on the icebox, where they left messages for each other.

"Barbara is spotting again," read the note in Hanna's handwriting. "We're going to TMC."

"Oh, God," Joshua groaned.

He ran down the stairs and drove to Tucson Medical Center. Adam and Hanna were in the waiting room. They both appeared deeply shocked.

"Barbara lost the baby," Hanna gasped.

"Go home," Joshua told them. "I'll be home in a while." He watched them leave.

Hal and Rebecca Dubin were sitting beside Barbara's bed. Rebecca wept and blew her nose into a hand-kerchief. Hal's face was twisted and ugly. Barbara was awake, staring at the ceiling.

"I'm okay, Josh," she whispered as he came to the bed. "I'm okay."

"Vay iz mir, vay iz mir," said her father. He cast bitter eyes at Joshua and jutted his chin toward her. *"Mayn aydem dortin* [My son-in-law over there]. *Ich hob an aydem, a groissen baal guyveh* [A real big shot I have for a son-in-law]."

"Stop it, Daddy. It's not Joshua's fault. It's been coming on for weeks, I've been feeling sick every morning."

Hal Dubin was unfazed. *"Moishe rabbaynu vill er zein* [He wants to be Moses our lawgiver]." He shook his finger at Joshua. "Always with the Indians and the spics and the *shvartzers.* A white man wouldn't go near your office, he might catch something and drop dead. Not ten cents in your pocket. What kind of life is this? What kind of life do you give my baby?"

"That's enough, Daddy," Barbara said. "I won't let you talk to Joshua that way."

"You won't let," he said in disgust. "You won't let. You're lying here in the hospital and your baby is dead and your husband is going to prison, and you won't let?"

He stood up and sighed and took Barbara's hand gently in both of his. "You're in pain?"

"No, I feel fine. Really." Her voice seemed to gentle him.

"Okay, I'll leave you with your mama a *bissel.* I gotta talk to this *baleboss* of yours."

"I don't want to hear loud voices, Daddy." She looked hard at him. "I'm a big girl now, and Joshua is a good man."

Hal gritted his teeth and bit back any retort. He walked out of the hospital room and Joshua followed him. They walked down the hallway into a small courtyard. It was poorly illuminated by a large yellow light on a tall pole. A small redwood picnic table sagged under a shedding mesquite tree. The table and the attached benches were littered with long green pods and furry yellow flowers. Hal either didn't notice or care. He sat down on the bench in his very expensive beige silk trousers. He was short and corpulent and wore a fire-engine red cotton dress shirt and a white silk tie. It was only about sixty-five degrees, but there were sweat stains around the collar of the shirt and under the arms, and beads of sweat rolled off his brow. He had small brown eyes and brown-dyed thinning hair cut long in an attempt to cover his almost bald head.

Joshua swept the pods and flowers off the bench and sat down.

"I can't go on seeing her live like this," Hal said.

"We've done okay till now," said Joshua, realizing how lame he sounded.

"Yeah, well now is different. Now everything is falling apart. Your Hanna is probably going to jail, and you, look at what's happening to you."

"Hanna didn't do anything so terrible, and I didn't do anything wrong at all. But some *machers* want my ass, and they're doing their best to get it. It's not my fault."

"Whose, then? The man in the moon?"

"Look, I can't live my life up to your expectations. I can't just abandon innocent people who need my help."

"Yeah, like Charlie Isaiah?"

Joshua shook his head angrily. "I do what I think is right. That's all I *can* do."

"So like the guy on the horse with the lance, you go charging windmills?"

Joshua frowned.

"This shit's gone too far," Hal said. "You ain't the messiah or a wandering *tzaddik* [righteous man]. You're just a one-armed lawyer with a wife and kids. Think of them when these assholes come to your office and beg you to take on their helpless causes. Your family is more important than these *shlimazls* [bad luck Charlies]."

"So who else is going to help these people? They go to every other lawyer in town before they come to me, and nobody wants to get involved."

"And from this you don't learn a lesson?"

Joshua shrugged.

"Whattaya got, an addiction to lost causes? You're so hooked, it don't matter what effect it has on your family, my daughter?"

"Come on, Hal, knock off the melodrama."

Hal Dubin grimaced and snorted and sat silently for a moment. "You're no longer a kid with high ideals and big notions about justice. You been a lawyer now, what, fifteen years, seventeen? You're forty-two years old, no *pisherkeh* [kid] no more. You been through plenty. Ain't you learned yet? When you gonna face real life? There ain't nothing you're gonna achieve going like you're going. You're just gonna get your ass kicked and your *betzim* [balls] ripped off by the people who really run things out there. And they ain't gonna give a shit they ruin your life. They're just gonna slap each other on the back and go play pinochle."

Joshua had nothing to say.

The citron moon peeked out from behind a black cumulus cloud that looked like oil smoke smeared over the sky.

Hal clasped his hands on top of the table and stared morosely at them. Then he walked back into the hospital.

Joshua remained seated, feeling choked with guilt and helplessness. He began to cry, sobbing loudly and gasping for breath. And then the ghosts were suddenly there again.

He closed his eyes and felt as though he were teetering on the lip of a swamp of grief, and if he made one misstep he would tumble into it, unable to breathe, unable to help anyone, stuck in an ocean of quicksand and unable to move his arms or legs or extricate himself from the enervating, debilitating miasma. Behind his eyelids lurked the incubus of the concentration camp at Medzibiez. He had thought that he had conquered it, that it was long buried; but since the evening of Mark's graduation party, it had been resuscitated, lurking in wait, ready at any moment of weakness to overwhelm him and feed like a vulture on his heart.

I set up my office in the concentration camp adminis-

tration building, which used to be SS headquarters. That same day, a woman comes hesitantly into the office. There is actually no way physically to identify her as a woman, except that she wears a filthy, ragged dress. She is tall and emaciated, perhaps only eighty or eighty-five pounds. She is bald and has lost all of her teeth. From deep hollows peer two gray-hyacinth eyes so much like Hanna's. She could be twenty or seventy. It is impossible to tell.

Her name is Tovah Knisbacher, she tells me in Yiddish. She and her husband and two children were brought here two years ago. Her daughters, two and five years old, were taken straight from the train to the showers. Ayl molay rachamim [God full of mercy], in His infinite goodness, now shelters them under his protective wings. Just two weeks ago, when news of the coming of the American army spread through the camp, the SS had panicked and begun to incinerate all of the leftover bodies that had been piled behind the barracks, waiting for burial in mass graves. But it had been a hard winter, and the ground was too frozen for digging. So twenty of the strongest inmates had been used to load the bodies on wheelbarrows to take them to the cinder-block building that contained the crematoria. And even after day after day of burning, huge piles of cadavers still remained. But the Americans had come close to the camp by then, and the SS had fled. They shot the twenty men who had been burning the bodies. Her husband was among the murdered.

He is now with their two daughters in the shelter of God's wings, she says.

I listen for the sarcasm in her voice, look for the irony in her eyes. There is none.

And now she is going to have a baby, she tells me. She is nine months pregnant, virtually full term, and her baby will come at any moment, she can feel it. Her baby must live. Whatever happens to her, live or die, her baby must live. It is the only thing important in her life. From this abattoir of suffering, from this nether-world of satanic horror, there must come this baby, to show that the Jews have survived their murderers, to prove that the chosen people of God will endure.

The chosen people of God? I say. Chosen for what, by what kind of God?

Ayl molay rachamin, she says. She looks earnestly at me with wasted eyes and says that there is no know-ing what horrible evil might have befallen the Jews if God had not intervened to protect them. I can only stare at her with a mixture of incredulity and grudging admiration that so powerful a faith could still exist in a woman like this in a place like this where evidence of God's love cannot easily be imagined, let alone discovered.

I stand up and come around the desk and take the woman's arm. She recoils from my touch.

Please come to the infirmary, I tell her. Our doctor will look after you.

She nods. We walk down the stairs of the building and across the barren yard to the tent set up as the hospital. The doctor and three medics are tending to a dozen patients on army cots. It doesn't smell like a hospital here, antiseptic, scoured. It smells like rotting eggs, like rancid meat. I signal to the doctor to come over.

Joe, this is Tovah Knisbacher, I say. Her two children were murdered here, and her husband was killed just a week ago. She's pregnant. Let's make sure that her baby is born healthy and sound.

He looks at the woman, and then he looks morosely at me and rolls his eyes. I nod encouragement to him.

I'll visit you later, I tell the woman.

I am sitting in my office eating some sort of beeflike concoction from a K-ration can when the doctor comes in and sits down wearily in the chair in front of the desk. His face is drawn and his eyes are dolorous.

The woman you brought to me, he says.

I look at him, wary.

I delivered the baby, he says, averting his eyes from mine.

I gird myself for whatever is coming.

It was a boy, he says, but it looked like a ninety-year-old man, bald, hollow-eyed, gaunt, maybe two pounds or two and a half. Just slack skin holding bones, mouth open, gaping, like a baby bird begging to be fed. Joe gasps and covers his face with both hands. He rubs his eyes, trying to blot out the memory. I went to the mess truck to get some powdered milk, he says, and when I got back, the mother had smothered it. He looks hauntedly at me. And cut her own throat with a scalpel.

I begin to tremble and cannot speak. The doctor leaves, and I begin to cry. I sit staring out the window into the bright spring sunshine of Czechoslovakia and weep uncontrollably, and I—

The door creaked open. Joshua flinched. He smelled the spearmint odor of the hyssop blossoms, ubiquitous on the San Xavier Reservation, that Magdalena crushed and used as a perfume. She knelt beside the bench.

"Hanna called me. You okay?"

He shook his head. Chuy was standing on the other side of the bench. Chuy put his arm lightly on Joshua's shoulder.

Magdalena stood up and took his head and pressed it to her bosom. She kissed his forehead and held him gently until his shoulders stopped quivering.

Chapter Twenty-three

There was no story in the *Arizona Daily Star* the next morning. The newspaper had already gone to press by the time the death had been reported. And by the day after, it was already old news because of the story in the previous evening's newspaper and the radio coverage, so it was relegated to a back page. The tragic suicide of the assistant United States attorney was unimportant to most Tucsonans. They had their jobs to worry about, their sons in Korea, the possibility of gasoline rationing because of the war.

That afternoon, Joshua called Roy Collins and asked him to meet him at Randy Stevens's office in the Pima County Courthouse at two. The three men sat glumly around Randy's desk staring at each other.

"I talked it over with Mo Udall," Randy said. "I can't do it."

Joshua was deeply frustrated. "That's ridiculous."

"The hell it is," Randy said. "When the county attorney says not enough evidence, that's the end of the story. And you haven't got any more evidence now than you had last week."

"Essert didn't commit suicide, and you know it."

"I don't know anything except what Stan Wolfe tells me."

"He didn't say it was suicide. He just said the gun was discharged while the barrel was pressed against his temple. That doesn't mean Essert pulled the trigger."

"That's not how I read Stan's report," Randy said.

"So why the hell would he commit suicide in my daughter's car? That's just crazy."

"That's what they say people are who commit suicide," said Roy.

"Come on, knock off the song and dance. Both of you guys know better. Haven't you ever had a cat?"

Randy looked at Roy and they both shrugged.

"Sure," Randy said. "Her name is Fifi and my wife thinks she's our third child."

"When a cat wants to give you a present to show how much it cares, it brings you a dead bird. Walks right up to you and lays it at your feet."

Randy nodded.

"That's what Essert was. Maitland gave him to me as a gift. Can't you see it? He's telling me everything's going to be okay, that it's time for me to lay off him."

"You been reading too many mystery novels," Roy said.

Joshua shook his head and frowned. "Essert didn't kill himself. And whoever did him did the other three."

"Who's your candidate?" Roy Collins asked.

"Horton Landers or the other guy, McCarthy's staffer, whoever he was."

"Well," Roy said, "we're never going to find out who the staffer was. Essert took the name with him to the cemetery yesterday morning, and when I called Holmes and Schlesinger at the Bureau in Washington yesterday afternoon, they developed severe amnesia. Schlesinger told me that the word around the Bureau was that it was over, hands off. I called the special agent in charge up in Phoenix, and he told me the same thing, the whole thing is off-limits, to stay away from it." Roy shrugged.

"How about you?" Joshua asked, looking at Randy.

"Listen, Joshua, I talked my head off to Mo. But there just isn't enough probable cause to go after Landers or Maitland. The ID on Landers is not tight enough. We'd never even get a judge to sign the search warrant."

"We'd turn up cordite in either Landers's or Maitland's home."

"So what? Maitland owns one of the biggest construction businesses in Arizona. His company does blasting all the time. The caliche around most of Arizona is only a foot or two below the surface. What the hell would it prove if we found twenty cases of cordite in his kitchen cabinets?"

"Nobody uses cordite for construction blasting."

"Maybe *he* does."

Joshua sighed deeply. "You mean there's four dead people, and the investigation just stops here?"

Randy looked away and squinted intently out his window at "A" Mountain. Roy Collins looked down, then bent over and carefully brushed the dust off his brown wing tips.

"Maybe I ought to save you guys some trouble and go up to Phoenix and kill Landers myself." He brandished his steel hand.

"I didn't hear that," Roy said. "And I don't want to hear any more."

It was lonely in the house. Barbara had not yet come home from the hospital, and the dead silence and emptiness of the place was oddly unnerving. Joshua sat on the living-room sofa, staring out the picture window. A vermilion flycatcher perched on the sill, chirped musically, and whooshed away. Joshua hardly noticed.

The telephone rang, and he walked slowly into the kitchen and answered it.

"Mr. Rabb?"

"Yes."

"This is Dillan Hopkins. I'm the United States attorney for Arizona."

"I know who you are."

"I'm calling about the matter on which you were indicted some time ago."

"Yes."

"I've directed Mike Brink to file a dismissal with prejudice."

Joshua was silent for a minute. With prejudice meant that the charges could never be brought again. He had expected as much, but the moment of its happening was still a huge relief.

"Thank you, Mr. Hopkins."

"Also, for your information, Senator Maitland told me that he'll be withdrawing the civil case he filed against you for abuse of process and malicious prosecution. He asked me to tell you. Now that the newspapers have retracted, your defamation action is basically moot, and the senator sees no justifiable reason to continue the suit against you."

"I've been expecting that, Mr. Hopkins. But there are two other matters that are still pending that also need your attention. The conviction of the five students for picketing and parading, and the criminal charges against Professor Livinsky."

"Well, Mr. Rabb, you yourself pled those students guilty. That's not exactly in my hands. Even if we moved to dismiss the prosecution, the judge would have to agree to it."

"I don't think that'll be a problem."

"Well, I'll think about it, Mr. Rabb."

"How about Livinsky?"

"I've reviewed it myself. The man is a card-carrying Communist who failed to register after his organization was declared a Communist front by the attorney general. Now how in the world do you expect me to overlook that?"

"That isn't why he's being prosecuted. There were seven other professors who were members of that organization and who also didn't register, and you didn't do anything to them. The only ones charged were a Jew and a Papago Indian."

Pause. His voice was harder. "I don't like what you're implying, Mr. Rabb."

"I don't give a damn what you like or don't like. This whole mess is part of Maitland's scheme to get himself known as a Communist fighter and to gain national importance. It's as plain as the nose on your face. It's about time you people up in Phoenix developed some backbone and refused to let yourselves be used by these scumbags."

"Listen, Rabb," Hopkins growled. "I've heard you're a hard case, and they weren't lying. I can understand how you feel about your daughter, but you're way out of line on this thing with Livinsky. If I don't prosecute him, they'll remove *me* from office. I have no choice."

"Knock off the bullshit! The whole damn thing is your choice. At least drop the treason charge. Failure to register fits the facts, but treason is pure bullshit. Livinsky's no traitor."

"Juries decide that, not United States attorneys." He hung up.

Joshua stood staring at the receiver, then crashed it down so hard on the wall unit that the whole thing fell to the floor, tearing loose from the wires in the wall. Joshua kicked it and sent it splintering into the wall.

Joshua dressed in his closing argument suit the next morning. The radio on the nightstand beside the bed was on, and the seven o'clock news announcer was droning on about the weather and the war and the other things of interest to Tucsonans early in the morning.

"The Washington office of Senator William Maitland announced this morning the tragic death yesterday afternoon of the senator's administrative aide in a hit-and-run automobile accident in Milwaukee, Wisconsin. The senator called his long-time aide, Horton Landers, a patriot among patriots, a man who always put country ahead of every consideration in his life. . . . The national weather service reports that . . ."

Joshua was riveted to the side of the bed, stunned, his leg in midair, putting on a shoe. He felt dizzy for a moment, then regained his equilibrium. He ran downstairs and got the morning newspaper, scanned every page for a story and found none. He turned on the radio in the kitchen and tuned to every station that had news, but they were all finished. He listened to the network that carried all-day news, but in an entire hour it didn't say anything about Landers's death.

It was two minutes after eight. He telephoned Roy Collins at his office.

"You hear about Landers?"

"Yep. Heard it on the radio this morning, and I got a teletype on it just a few minutes ago from the Bureau. There weren't any witnesses. Seems Landers got loaded, was staggering across the street last night in the dark, got hit. Pity."

"It's Maitland and McCarthy, don't you see? These bastards are crazy. Now they're covering their tracks."

"You got to be in court this morning, don't you?"

"Yeah."

"Better get on your broom." Roy hung up.

"This is the time set for the hearing of the defendants' motions to set aside their conviction," Judge Robert Buchanan said. "Please announce your appearances."

"Joshua Rabb for Hanna Rabb and Jan Diedrichs, who are present, Your Honor."

"Harry Chandler for Fred Mergen, and Diane and Deane Rustin, who are also present, Your Honor."

"Dillan Hopkins for the government, Your Honor."

The courtroom was empty. The morning newspaper had ignored the coming hearing, although it had been set for almost ten days. It seemed to Joshua that the publisher must have given orders to bury the whole picketing mess and the murders. If there were continued publicity, the public might begin to put two and two together and see a link among the killings, even a conspiracy.

Joshua looked around the courtroom, and there weren't even any reporters. J. T. Sellner was either fired, on vacation, or on assignment in Borneo.

"Your motion, Mr. Rabb." Judge Buchanan settled back in his wing chair, toying with his pocket watch in his hand.

"May it please the court, the defendants respectfully move to withdraw their pleas of guilty in this matter and to have this court dismiss the indictment of picketing and parading. It was clear at the preliminary hearing held in superior court on charges of second-degree murder that none of these defendants took part in the tragic murder of Oliver Friedkind. It has also been made clear over the preceding week that the former assistant United States attorney came under attack for what were apparently excesses and improprieties on his part in the bringing of the indictment against these five students as well as other conduct by him in his official capacity.

"I frankly admit to the court that the reason why I advised all of the defendants to enter pleas of guilty was to create a double jeopardy problem that I thought would result in the dismissal of murder charges in state court."

The judge interrupted him. "And now that your little maneuver worked, Mr. Rabb, you come in here and say you're sorry, but would I please undo what you did and make everything better."

"Well, Your Honor, I wouldn't put it exactly that way."

"Exactly how would you put it, Mr. Rabb?"

Joshua shrugged, caught off guard. "Okay, Your Honor. Perhaps that characterization is not unwarranted."

Buchanan chuckled. "Mr. Hopkins."

"It is the position of the government that the interests of justice would be best served by this court granting the defendants' motion. Therefore, we do not oppose it."

Judge Buchanan smiled. "Very well, Mr. Hopkins. On the motion of defendants, and upon stipulation of the United States attorney, this court orders that the pleas of guilty are withdrawn, that pleas of not guilty are entered on behalf of each defendant, and that the indictment is dismissed. Anything further, gentlemen?"

Joshua was speechless. He stared at Dillan Hopkins.

"Nothing, Your Honor," Hopkins said.

"No, Judge," said Harry Chandler, standing.

Judge Buchanan rapped his gavel and left the bench.

Joshua walked to Dillan Hopkins. He shook his hand firmly. "I didn't expect that," he said.

Hopkins smiled. "So I noticed. Well, it's about time I set some of the things straight that Essert fucked up down here." He shook his head and frowned. "I guess I should have kept closer tabs on the son of a bitch."

Chapter Twenty-four

Mark Goldberg woke up after less than an hour of restless sleep, groggy and disoriented, and when he tried to stand up he was disabled by the pain that radiated down his right leg. He remembered where he was and lay flat on the frozen ground, his chin on his folded arms. Overhead the wind whipped snowflakes around in eddies and slapped them onto his field jacket and steel helmet and bare neck and hands. The snow fell steadily, heavy flakes, pendulous with moisture. The frozen scabs of earth and rock that were officially Hills 894, 931, and 851, and which the marines called Heartbreak Ridge, appeared less ominous than usual under the soft white mantle.

Suddenly the artillery explosions started, as they had yesterday, as they had the day before and the day before that. He had lain here for at least a week that he could remember, and he couldn't remember how many days before that he had been wounded. The marine assault on Heartbreak had resulted in at least seventeen hundred casualties by the time that the First Battalion of the Twenty-third Regiment finally captured the highest crest, Hill 931, on September 23.

Mark had commanded C Company ever since the captain and the two first lieutenants had been killed a week earlier in the battle for Hill 894.

The First Battalion had run out of ammunition after four hours on Hill 931, and a Chinese counterattack had overrun the marines. Mark and a dozen others had been trapped in a steep ravine below the crest of the hill and had been pinned down for day after day by the American 15mm Long Toms below and the Chinese burp gunners above.

Mark pressed his body into the snow, trying to escape from the American artillery shells exploding above him. The marines must be lobbing them from somewhere at the base of Heartbreak, he thought, since he couldn't hear anything until the warheads whistled overhead and then impacted with earsplitting violence into the fortified bunkers carved into the rock on the top of the ridge.

After a half hour the shelling stopped. Mark felt for his backpack, buried in several inches of snow on the ground next to him. He rummaged inside it with a numb right hand and pulled out a small tin of K-rations. He had just two left. This one was a hockey puck-sized chunk of corned beef. He bit off a piece and chewed it without being able to feel his frozen lips, just the way it felt after leaving the dentist's office with your mouth full of Novocain.

The man beside him groaned and shuddered. He was lying on his back, his face under his steel helmet. His entire torso was covered with blood from the top of his neck to his groin, and the snow had melted from the warmth of the blood and had covered him in a soft pink cloak of mush.

"Hey, Simmons, you holding on?" Mark said with difficulty through his unmoving lips, his voice weak and hollow in the swirling snow. There was no answer. Mark called out again, but Simmons couldn't even elicit the grunts that he had been able to muster moments before.

The other eleven marines in the ravine were equally still and silent. Maybe he was the only one still alive, he thought. The others had bled to death or frozen to death. Suddenly he wanted to cry, but his face was too numb and he had no tears. He had to get warm, but he could hardly move anymore. Think about Hanna, that'll make me warm, he thought.

"Hanna," he whispered into the snow. He tried to feel the touch of her skin on his, her belly pressing against his, her breasts on his chest. But it was surreal, here in the blizzard on a rock in Korea, and he couldn't conjure up a warming image or memory that lasted more than a second. And all of the images, her face, her body, their bodies melded together, all of them cascaded into one another and shattered in fluffy white snowy explosions in his mind's eye, and he fought to remain conscious and not to become totally numb and freeze to death. He tried to stand up, but the combination of the pain and the cold paralyzed him. His mind grasped nothing. The images melted in a bright orange flame. He felt weirdly warm and cozy, and suddenly from somewhere he began to murmur the prayer that a person must say before dying: *"Sh'ma Yisroel Adonshem Elokeynu Adonshem echad*

[Hear O Isreal, the Lord is our God, the one and only God.]"

He heard sounds of firing, burp guns, M-1s, several Browning automatic rifles. They interrupted his warmth and comfort, and he closed his eyes and tried to sleep. The noise grew louder, and screams and shouts in Chinese or Korean were getting closer.

It was a huge, painful effort for him, but he managed to roll onto his side. Pains like a white-hot knife lanced through his left leg. His hands were almost completely numb, and he could hardly feel the Thompson submachine gun that was by his side. He saw several small men on the ridge above him, outlined in their quilted uniforms against the tarnished pewter sky. They were firing toward him and his men. He worked his trigger finger into the housing of the Thompson and lifted its barrel toward the ridge. With an immense effort of will that he never had before, never knew he had, he managed to flex his finger and pull the trigger. Three men on the ridge fell immediately.

There was firing behind Mark, but he was too stiff and numb to turn his head to see. The exertion of turning his body and firing the Thompson had exhausted him, and he drifted into unconsciousness.

There are nineteen army nurses here at the army hospital near Pusan, and several of them are sort of attractive. But they are all beautiful to the injured, lonely men to whom they minister, and they are as lonely as the men. Romances blossom and wilt regularly. The nurses are all officers and forbidden from fraternizing with the four hundred enlisted men, so the hospitalized officers are well attended to. At night Mark sometimes hears groans and gasps and other obvious sounds from behind the privacy curtains that can be pulled to surround the cots.

After about two weeks his leg is released from traction. He begins to take the shape of a man to the nurses. One of them in particular, a brown-haired, amber-eyed, willowy thirty-year-old captain from Alabama, lingers by his cot a little longer than her functions require. She isn't very pretty, he knows, but in here, with the war raging just a few miles to the north, she is as seductive and sumptuous as Marilyn Monroe.

The doctor has just taken Mark's catheter out, but he can't get out of bed to go to the latrine yet. So Nora puts the bedpan under the sheet, and she keeps her hand there and softly massages his swollen, sore penis and helps him adjust it to point into the pan between his legs. He is grateful for her kindness and special attention and embarrassed that he cannot pee. It takes almost an hour for his bladder and whatever muscles and sphincters and nerves have to be awakened to come to life, and finally he does. It is a monumental victory for both Nora and him, and she gives him a joyful peck on the cheek, sweeps back the privacy curtain, and carries the bedpan triumphantly to the latrine at the end of the wardroom.

The captain who stepped on a land mine and has no feet, in the bed next to Mark's, claps softly. I guess you're Nora's new friend, he says.

Mark is in pain from the exercise of peeing in the

bedpan, and he struggles onto his side away from the captain's leer.

Mark awakens in darkness, his privacy curtain drawn again, and feels a hand under the sheet reaching for him.

Feeling better now? Nora whispers. She pulls the sheet away.

Time and rest have restored him, and her gentle ministrations arouse him. He knows that he should say no, no, I have a girlfriend at home and I must not cheat on her, but no such utterances emerge from his mouth. The only sounds from him, as she wraps her lips around him and her tongue massages, emulate the groans that he has heard from behind other curtains.

Days go by, and nights, and he looks forward to the attention of Nora from Alabama, and if he feels any remorse or chagrin for cheating on Hanna, it is embalmed and interred by his excruciating loneliness and need for the female contact that Nora provides. There is nothing to do in the hospital and nowhere to go since he is bedridden from a bullet wound in his left leg. The hospital's library consists of a volume of Hemingway short stories and a Gideon Bible. He reads the stories through several times until he can read them no more, and then he starts on the Bible.

He reads it from the beginning, the creation of man and woman, to the very end, the last chapter of Revelation, where it says, "And the Spirit and the bride say, Come. And let him that heareth say, Come. And let him that is athirst, Come." He is athirst, and he does exactly as Revelation tells him to, with Nora's help. And he begins to heal quickly now.

Then one day the doctor sits down on the field chair next to his bed and tells him that what at first looked like a crippling wound that would get him out of Korea and back to the States has luckily turned out to be quite minor, and he will recover without anything but a two-inch scar. So he's not being sent home, but at least he won't be sent back to a combat outfit. Instead, he is going to light duty. He will report in two days to Koje Island as adjutant to the commander of the third logistical command, in charge of the prisoners of war being held by the United Nations on the once-picturesque island of fishermen and farmers.

Mark suddenly feels guilty. He has cheated on Hanna. Why does the shame overwhelm him only now and not weeks ago? He doesn't know. It is simply so. He writes her a letter. It is the first letter that he has written to her since coming to the hospital. He supposes that the marines have long ago notified her that he was wounded and is now recovering.

Nora comes to his bed again that night, to share herself with him, to console them both for their loneliness, and he turns his face from her and pushes her searching hands away. She creeps guiltily away. In the morning, a new nurse comes to minister to him.

Chapter Twenty-five

Mischa Livinsky's trial begins tomorrow. In the evening, Joshua goes to visit Barbara in the hospital. She still can't come home, the doctor tells him. The hemorrhaging has started again. Not serious, no, nothing to worry about. But she has to stay off her feet awhile more.

Barbara is a little dizzy and nauseated. She doesn't know why. The doctor just tells her that time will heal her. Have patience, wait. But she is impatient, her husband must go to court tomorrow, and he is always uneasy the night before. He needs to be comforted, to be with her. She wants to be with him, and she cries.

Her father and mother come to visit. Rebecca is worried about Barbara, and she knows that Joshua is also deeply worried. It is not his fault that this happened. He is a good man, this Joshua. Not so practical, maybe, not such a great provider, but a *mensch*. But Hal is still stiff toward Joshua, not the warm, joke-telling, back-slapping pal he had always been. He is gloomy, seeing his only child this way, he is depressed and bitter.

"Don Quixote," he snorts, looking at Joshua. "At windmills, you keep charging. At windmills."

"No, at bad guys," Joshua mumbles. "Otherwise who will ever do a thing about them? They ride around in limousines and make speeches about the American way and truth and justice, and people cheer and call them great patriots."

"Go home, go to sleep, honey," Barbara says. "Try to get some rest."

"They make Tim Essert the scapegoat for everything and kill him, and then they kill the guy who killed him. They're worse than the Mafia. Joe Bonanno has more honor than that."

Joshua stands up and goes to the window, staring into the pitch-black night.

"And the guy who's innocent of everything will get convicted," he murmurs. "And I can't do a damn thing about it."

He goes home a little after Barbara's parents leave. He forces himself to listen to the "Dinah Shore Show with Harry James and Johnny Mercer" and then tries to absorb himself in "Mr. and Mrs. North," "The Adventures of the Thin Man," and "Meet Corliss Archer," until the radio goes to static. He wants to lose himself in the shows, distract his attention from what will start tomorrow. But it doesn't work. There will be no sleep for him tonight, no escape from the feeling of tragedy that enshrouds him.

It is October 17, 1951.

The armistice talks in Panmunjom are stalled, as usual. The United States sends twenty-five thousand young soldiers to Korea every month, month after month, and still there is no victory over the North Koreans and the Red Chinese.

Some French guy with an unpronounceable and un-spellable name has won this year's Nobel Prize for Peace. Who he is and what he did is a general mystery to everyone in America. And with the war going on in the Far East and the Soviet Union looking like it's about to invade Europe, it doesn't seem as though this French guy has achieved much of anything. But who knows.

Senator Joseph "Tail Gunner" McCarthy and his right-hand man, Senator William "Big Bill" Maitland, are on the warpath again in Washington, D.C., but this war is against Americans. They have unearthed a despicable homosexual at the State Department whose vile unnaturalness has led him to sell government se-crets to Moscow. They have not revealed his name yet, because they don't want to scare away his co-conspirators. They are certain that there is an entire coven of these closet queers who have sold out their country to dance to Moscow's tune.

A Streetcar Named Desire is playing at the Para-mount Theater downtown. Joshua and Barbara saw it a few weeks ago, and Joshua says that it's the best movie he's ever seen. Well, *The Maltese Falcon* and *The Treasure of the Sierra Madre* were terrific, too. But they were ten years ago. *Streetcar* is the best he's seen lately. Barbara doesn't agree. She thinks that *An American in Paris* is better. I don't go to the movies to feel miserable, she says. I go for entertainment.

A writer named Herman Wouk has just published

his latest novel, *The Caine Mutiny.* Joshua thinks it portrays moral ambiguity about as clearly and brilliantly as anyone ever has.

It is October 17, 1951, and the trial of United States versus Mischa Livinsky is called by the Honorable Robert Buchanan, United States district judge for the District of Arizona.

"Announce your appearances for the record," he says.

"Michael Brink for the government, Your Honor."

"Joshua Rabb for the defendant, Your Honor."

"Thank you, gentlemen. I have assembled a panel of thirty-six prospective jurors. Is there anything to go over before I bring them in and we start the voir dire?"

"No, Your Honor," Joshua says.

Brink shakes his head.

"Bailiff will bring them in."

The courtroom is hushed. The three front rows of the spectators' section have been kept empty to seat the prospective veniremen. The rest of the courtroom is full of curious spectators. Most of them have never seen a Commie before. And this guy is the real thing, a Moscow card-carrying Jew Commie. McCarthy and Maitland have said in twenty speeches, week after week, that Livinsky fits the classic mold of the parlor pinks and parlor punks who are insidiously destroying America. Everyone with eyes has read the speeches, everyone with ears has heard them on the radio. Now they're here to see for themselves.

"Well, he don't look so bad," one of the spectators

whispers to the man next to him. "Just kinda aver-
agelike."

"That's what makes 'em so all-fired dangerous,"
says the other man. "They just blend right in, cain't
tell 'em from decent Americans till they open up
their mouths."

The first man nods.

"You hear about that lawyer Rabb?"

"You mean about his daughter, and all?"

The first man nods.

"Yeah, real strange, ain't it. Suddenly it all gets
dropped. First that Mex judge over at the county lets
her off on a murder charge, then this here judge, too."

"Yeah, it's a thinker, awright. Gotta watch these
fuckin' judges ever' minute."

Thirty-six men and women shuffle along the wooden
benches and take their seats. The judge rambles on
for fifteen minutes about the meaning of justice and
the sacred role of the jury in American democracy.
Then he questions the men and women as a group for
another twenty minutes, receiving grunted yesses and
noes in response.

"This is about the most borin' shit I ever seen,"
whispers a spectator.

"Yeah," says the elderly woman next to him, "but
this is how they always do it. I seen it on TV."

"Mr. Brink, you may voir dire," Judge Buchanan
says.

Then the prosecutor asks a bunch of questions, and
now and then he and the other lawyer huddle at the
bench with the judge hunched forward to hear them,
and slowly the panel of jurors is winnowed down to

twenty-seven. And then the judge lets the other lawyer ask a whole lot of the same questions, and there are more huddles and more folks get excused from the panel and thanked by the judge for taking the time out of their busy schedules to come to court, as if they had a choice.

And then the judge calls a recess for ten minutes and tells the lawyers to choose a jury. And the spectators file out into the hallway and wonder when the goddamn trial is really going to start, because they already wasted two hours on this shit, and they're ready to tear their hair out from boredom.

"The government calls Charles Holmes," Michael Brink said, standing at the prosecution table.

"Come forward and be sworn," Judge Buchanan said.

The handsome, strapping, blond crew-cutted Holmes walked down the aisle into the well of the courtroom and stood tall and straight before the court clerk, his hand on a Bible.

"Do you swear to tell the truth, the whole truth, and nothing but the truth, so help you God?" said the clerk.

"I do," Holmes said. He sat down in the witness chair.

The spectators were finally getting their show. They leaned forward expectantly, hanging on every word. This was the kind of wholesome American who risked his life every day for the safety of all other wholesome Americans, just like themselves.

"State your name and occupation," Brink said.

"Yes sir. Federal Bureau of Investigation Special Agent Charles Holmes. I'm a member of a special unit of the FBI attached to the attorney general's Subversive Activities Control Board. It's our duty to find the Communists who fail to register and arrest them."

"And in furtherance of your sworn duty, did you come in contact with the defendant, Mischa Livinsky?"

"I did."

"Tell the jury how that came about?"

"After Investigator Anne Marie Hauser had recommended that the Academics Against War be listed as a Communist front organization, the attorney general placed it on the subversives list. No one registered within the sixty days allotted for registration."

"So what did you do?"

"Me and my partner, Herman Schlesinger, were sent out here to meet with the assistant United States attorney for Tucson and get an indictment and an arrest warrant for Livinsky."

"Was Livinsky the only individual you intended to arrest?"

"No, we also came out for Julio Moraga. But he murdered Anne Marie Hauser and overdosed on—"

Joshua was on his feet roaring with anger. "Your Honor, I object to this outrageous testimony. I ask that it be stricken and that the court admonish the jury."

"Yes," Judge Buchanan said. He looked toward the jury. "The jury will disregard the last comment." He looked cautioningly at Michael Brink. "Don't do it again, Mr. Brink. Keep your witness under control."

"See what I tol' ya," whispered one spectator to

another. "Ya gotta watch them fuckin' judges like a hawk. He won't even let that FBI man testify about what he knows."

The other man nodded and shook his head, disgusted. "Damn judge. It ain't right."

"Did you know Anne Marie Hauser?" Brink asked.

Joshua rose once again quickly to his feet. "Objection, Your Honor. Irrelevant."

"Enlighten the court as to the relevancy, Mr. Brink," Judge Buchanan said.

"May it please the court, this is all res gestae, the background necessary to establish the basis upon which the FBI special agents came to Tucson and encountered Livinsky. Mrs. Hauser's investigation is relevant, and since she is dead, I believe that it's proper for Special Agent Holmes to introduce the significant elements."

Judge Buchanan pursed his lips, thought about it for a moment, and nodded. "All right, Mr. Brink. Proceed, but keep it tightly confined."

"Thank you, Your Honor." Turning back to the witness, "Agent Holmes, did you know Anne Marie Hauser?"

"Yes. For a year, since I was assigned to the Subversives Control Board."

"And what do you know about her?"

"She was the widow of a Marine Corps captain, killed in the Solomons in the Second World War. She worked for the House Committee on Un-American Affairs and then became a civilian investigator with the Subversives Board. She was a very good friend of Senator Joe McCarthy."

"I object, Your Honor. This is absolutely improper," Joshua said, standing up quickly.

"Mr. Brink," said the judge, fixing him with an angry glare, "I will not warn you again. One more time, and I will hold you in contempt."

The spectator nudged the other one with his elbow. "Can ya believe that Commie bastard's a *judge*?" he whispered.

"Damn shame," whispered the man.

The trial goes forward, a second day. Joshua goes to the hospital in the evening to visit Barbara. The doctor says I'm fine, she says to him. But she looks just a bit sallow, and there are lines of pain around her eyes. When he gets into his car to go home, he clutches the steering wheel and tears spring to his eyes. He is afraid for her.

It is eight o'clock in the morning, the third day of the trial. Barbara and her father are already sitting in the front row of the spectators' pews when Joshua arrives. She smiles at him, and Hal even tries an encouraging smile. Joshua kneels down in front of the wooden railing, and she leans close to him.

"Why aren't you at the hospital?" he whispers.

"I don't need to be. I need to be with you."

"But, honey, I, I—"

"I'm perfectly okay," she says. "Don't worry. Just be Joshua Rabb."

He looks into her eyes, and he suddenly wonders how he could be so lucky. He smiles at her, and she presses forward and kisses his forehead. He stands and returns to the defense table.

Mischa Livinsky takes the stand as the final witness. He is everything that everyone has waited impatiently for. He speaks English stiffly, formally, with a thick Russian accent. He actually belonged to the Communist party in Moscow. He taught political economy at a Russian university. He never denounced his party affiliation, even though he signed loyalty oaths at two American universities. He co-authored an antiwar article that was published in a national political science journal. He belonged to a group of University of Arizona professors who opposed the war. The official policy of the Soviet Union was opposition to the war. He kept notes in Yiddish about the group's meetings. He didn't register as a subversive because he is not a subversive and felt it was an unjust determination, and he was deeply insulted by it. "And," he admits, stumbling over the words, "I was defiant."

"Mr. Brink," the judge says, "you may begin your closing argument."

"Thank you, Your Honor," says the assistant United States attorney from Phoenix, standing up at the prosecution table. He is handsome, youthful, and buoyant with the rightness of his cause. It is America's cause, to take traitors like this out of the universities where they can do irreparable damage to our youth.

"I've got two kids myself," Mike Brink says. "They're just six and nine, but by the time they get to the University of Arizona, I want to make certain that there are no Commies and fellow travelers around to poison their souls."

Joshua should object to this type of argument. Brink should be arguing the evidence to the jury, not waving the flag and fatherhood. But Joshua does not object. He is hardly listening. He is having a nightmare, that is actually a daymare. It has possessed him fully now and will not free him.

Joshua believes that the jury will find that Mischa Livinsky is guilty of failure to register. They will find that Mischa Livinsky is a traitor. Judge Robert Buchanan will dismiss the jury, and with a grim and sorrowful demeanor—because he knows how unjust the verdict is—he will order the convicted man to be held without bail at the Mount Lemmon Detention Center pending sentencing in one month. There is no ambiguity about sentencing under the treason statute. Livinsky will be put to death.

But there are other things that will be done by Joshua Rabb in the interim to attempt to insure that Mischa Livinsky will not be executed, will ultimately be exonerated, at least of treason. Joshua will bring a motion for new trial, and perhaps Judge Buchanan will grant it. All of the pretrial publicity, all of the hate-filled stories and speeches that have invaded this little Southwest town and poisoned the minds of the jurors, of everyone, have created an atmosphere of hate in which the defendant was denied justice. And Joshua will bring a motion of acquittal *non obstante veredicto,* hoping that Judge Buchanan on his own will set aside the jury's verdict and spare Mischa Livinsky from the hangman's noose at Leavenworth. And failing all of that, Joshua will appeal to the Ninth Circuit Court of Appeals, and then, if need be, to the United States Supreme Court.

Somewhere in this great system of justice, justice will be done. Somewhere along the line, a grievous injustice will be avoided.

If only I believed that, Joshua thinks. If only I believed that true justice is the end of this terrible tragedy. Once I believed. Once I knew that there was God, that there was Right and Wrong, and that I knew the difference. Once I believed. Where did that faith go? Where is the certainty that once guided my life?

There is no food in the concentration camp for the former inmates. My own men are subsisting on a small supply of K-rations. An old man comes to my office. He is short and shriveled and thin like a prune on pegs. He was a history professor in Munich, he tells me. He has a fringe of white hair around a bald skull, and the skin of his face is weirdly translucent and covered with spidery capillaries. He has seen many thousands taken to the cinder-block building to join the smoke in the sky, he says in a quavering voice, but God has saved him from the ovens.

I look at him oddly and can't help wondering why God hadn't seen fit to save him from the concentration camp altogether, and why He had overlooked the hundreds of tortured and starved human beings who were being buried by my men under mounds of dirt in long mass graves at the edge of the forest.

We must have food, he says to me. My people are still dying from starvation.

Where can we get it? I ask him. My unit has only a two-day supply of K-rations for ourselves.

There are full warehouses of grain and smokehouses of beef and lamb in the village of Medzibiez, he says. He knows this because the Jewish inmates have been performing slave labor in the fields and the slaughter-house of the village for the last two years, supplying the SS and the townspeople with all of their food. He has often been on these work details and knows where the stores are.

I ask my adjutant to assemble C squad and get two deuce and a half trucks out of the motor pool. I take the old man to the motor pool, load the trucks with the eleven men, and we drive to Medzibiez. We go to a large wooden shed on the outskirts of town. I take a crowbar and pry the locked latch off the front doors. Inside are sacks of grain and potatoes. My men load one of the trucks all the way to the canvas top. I leave two of my men to guard the potatoes and grain stores.

We drive into the small town to a smaller shed with stone walls and a thatched roof. I pry the lock off the shed, and my men load smoked haunches of beef and lamb until they are three feet high in the second truck. A young man runs toward us from a butcher shop across the dirt street. He is screaming something in Czech that none of us understands. One of my squad bars his way with his M-1 and the man backs hesitantly across the street to his shop. I leave two of my men to guard the smokehouse.

The next morning I am sitting in my office when a delegation of four men from the town come to see me. They introduce themselves importantly: the mayor, the

wealthiest landowner, the principal commercial entre-
preneur, the doctor.

I don't speak Czech, I tell them.

A little German, maybe? the mayor asks.

Yes, I say.

We are happy to meet the new kommandant, he says
in fluent German. We have all prayed to the icon of
the Virgin for years to rid us of the pestilence of the
Nazis. He mock-spits on the wooden floor of my office
for emphasis. Finally our prayers have been answered,
he says.

I stare at him.

He shuffles his feet a bit, and continues. We would
like to offer you in good faith the same deal that the
SS bastards stole from us without asking: we will supply
your soldiers with all the food they need, but we need
your inmates to plant the fields and tend the herds.
Most of our young men are in the army or killed, and
we have no workers.

Which army? I ask.

He swallows and his eyes twitch and he wrings the
brim of his black felt fedora in his hands. Why, the
Red Army, of course. Your allies.

Kwatch! I mutter. This is the Sudetenland. All of
your boys are in the Wehrmacht.

What could we do? whines the landowner, an old
man with twisted hands and a bald head like a peeled
onion. The Germans came, they forced them into the
army.

None of the inmates are capable of working, I tell
them. But they do not have to. I have seized all of the

contents of the two sheds we entered yesterday so that I can feed them and my troops.

You cannot do that, sputters the mayor. Steal all of our food? And for what, for Christ killers? The Jews will cast spells on the wheat and the potatoes and you will vomit until you collapse, the meat will turn to wriggling vermin in your mouths.

I ring up my adjutant, Captain Reilly, on my field telephone. He and a squad are behind the barracks burying nineteen more of the inmates who died yesterday. Get up here with a couple of your guys, I tell him.

I sit back in my chair and stare blandly at the mayor, who looks quizzically around at the other three.

Cormac Reilly comes in with two sergeants. Yes, sir, he says.

Take these gentlemen out behind the barracks and have them dig the graves for the dead. Your men are relieved.

Reilly looks at the men and then at me. Zat legal, Major? These ain't combatants, they're Czech civilians. They ain't done nothin' wrong. I gotta clear this with division. It just ain't legal.

Fuck legal, I bark at him. If they try to run, shoot them.

Mac wrinkles his brow at me and his eyes get big. But, Major—

You got a gun, Mac. That makes it legal.

Reilly stares at me and shakes his head. You ain't the man I thought you was, Major, he says to me.

You got a fuckin' hearing disorder, Mac? I say.

No, sir. Let's go, boys, he says to the four men, and gestures for them to precede him out of the office. The two sergeants take their Colt .45 automatics out of their holsters and hold them down to their sides. Fear distorts the faces of the dignitaries, and they leave my office.

Mac lingers behind. This ain't right, Major. Them are all neutrals. We ain't got the right, Major. We can't steal all their food and then put 'em to slave labor.

I don't say anything. What is there to say? I walk out of the office and follow the men behind the barracks to the open pits that await the bodies of the dead people, my people. I look at the corpses, and each of them has my face and Hanna's and Adam's. And they have filty yellow stars stitched to their ragged sleeves or filth-stiff chest pockets, like the little gold star that my wife Rachel always wore around her neck on a thin chain.

Mac Reilly orders his men out of the pits. They climb out, staring at the Czech civilians.

Pick up the shovels and pickaxes, I tell the mayor in Yiddish, close enough to German that he fully understands.

His look of fear dissipates, and he fixes me with defiant blue eyes. I have not noticed before that he is a big man, much heavier than I am but not fat, perhaps forty or forty-five years old.

I see now the problem, he spits at me through hate-quivering lips. You are a Jew, Major. Then he looks at Sergeant Reilly behind me and says in broken English, You see? No good. No good. The priests have always tell us, no good, no good.

One of the other men, the aged, arthritic land baron, says placatingly in much better English: They were bad, the Nazis. But they knew about Jews. Not your kind, Major—he holds up his hands toward me in a halt gesture to assure me that he thinks I'm human—but these medieval Jews we had here. They were different. We had such trouble.

I step toward the mayor, and he is emboldened by the land baron's support. His lips are a thin surgical scar. He swings at me with a meaty right fist. I jerk back, letting the blow swish harmlessly in front of my face, then I step forward and kick him as hard as I can between his legs. He doubles over with a huge groan, and I smash my fist upward into his face. He topples backward into the open pit, writhing on his back, both of his hands holding his crotch. His face is covered with red as though he has suddenly been painted in Mercurochrome. I pick up a shovel and begin throwing dirt on him. Then I hurl the shovel at him like a spear. The blade crashes against his collarbone. He screams in agony, his left arm goes limp, and his right snaps upward to ward off any more blows.

Mac Reilly grabs me from behind. Jesus Christ, Major, he mutters in my ear. You outta yer mind? What the fuck you think you doin'?

I feel like shit, all hollow inside. I go back to my office. I take out a bottle of Steinhäger left behind by the SS kommandant, and I drink from it in long gulps to try to deaden my soul.

Tears press against Joshua Rabb's eyelids, and then they pour down his cheeks. *You ain't the man I thought you was, Major, Mac Reilly says.*

You're right, Mac. I'm not the man *I* thought I was.

"Mr. Rabb," Judge Buchanan says, "You may argue."

The jurors turn toward Joshua, sitting at the defense

table, tears glistening on his face. The jurors are skeptical about his tears. They know in their cynicism that he is putting on this phony show for them. It is his choreography, his lawyer's trick. A tricky lawyer with a wily Commie client. What kind of strange man is this, this one-armed, haggard-looking man, who appears and sounds like a smart and tough guy, but who sits and weeps like a chickenshit idiot while the prosecutor gives his closing argument.

Joshua stands up, not knowing exactly what he will say. And slowly words begin to come.

"I apologize to you for the tears on my face," he says, his voice hoarse. He walks up before the walnut railing of the jury box and slowly looks from one to another of them. His face is earnest. "I was not crying for Professor Livinsky, I was crying for myself." He takes a handkerchief out of his pocket and roughly dries his tears.

"I was crying because I know how deeply pressing our need can be to wreak vengeance on someone who has not wronged us, but whom we hate anyway. And I was crying because I know from my own experience that I am not exempt from that aberration of character."

The jurors stir just a bit in their seats. They stare truculently at him. What the hell is this cunning bastard trying to pull with all those big words and a confession?

"Mischa Livinsky is innocent of criminal wrongdoing, and everyone in this room knows it. The group of professors who belonged to Academics Against War, each of whom believed exactly as Professor

Livinsky did in opposing the Korean War and striving for peace, are at the university today teaching your sons and daughters. You have not demanded their ouster, you have not insisted that the president of the university be fired for his treachery in retaining them as teachers, and they are not here on trial for their lives for treason. Turn to the juror next to you and raise your eyebrows and wonder why."

"I object to this, Your Honor, it's absolutely improper," Mike Brink says angrily, standing at the prosecution table.

"No, I don't think so," Judge Buchanan says. "Go on, Mr. Rabb."

The jurors don't know whether to look at each other or to stare at Joshua. They squirm, feeling oddly threatened.

"He is on trial because he once belonged to the Communist party of Moscow, even though he fled that country twelve years ago because he feared for his life. If you had been a professor of political science at the University of Berlin in 1939, you would have had to belong to the Nazi party, but when you fled to the United States because you feared for your life, you would have been hailed as a person of courage and right judgment. What is the difference here? Why is Professor Livinsky on trial for his life? Turn to the juror next to you and raise your eyebrows and wonder why."

The jurors' faces are grim now, and they stare unhappily at Joshua, angered by the liberty he so cavalierly takes with their minds and their emotions.

"The law is an instrument of man. Not of man in

some abstract philosophical sense, but each one of us. Each of us individually is given the opportunity from time to time to help make the law, to shape it in the way that we feel is best for us, to protect us, to nurture the kind of lives we wish to live. And that is what you are doing here today. You are being asked by your own government to shape a society where evil people call someone a traitor and put him to death based on the fact that he kept notes about a pacifist organization in Yiddish. That is the only evidence of treason in this case. And you are asked to shape a society where you convict him of failing to register as a Communist when the other seven professors who also failed to register are at the university today, standing at their podiums, lecturing to your children about Aristotle and organic chemistry and Shakespeare as they did yesterday and will do tomorrow. Turn to the juror next to you and raise your eyebrows and wonder why."

Joshua looks at each of them in turn. Their eyes are riveted on him.

"I do not need to stand here any longer and lecture you about the meaning of justice. First of all, I haven't the right. And second, you know what it is just as well as I do. It is like a breeze. You cannot see it, but you feel it. It ruffles your hair, it cools your body. It comes and goes without a trace, but you know it with certainty. You know what justice is. And in this place, at this time, it is in your keeping, you are its champions, you are its sculptors, its cobblers, its carpenters."

He looks compassionately at them, and their faces are no longer hard, their eyes less opaque and flat.

"I had a very dear friend once, the former chief of the Papago tribe, Macario Antone. He is dead now, and I miss his wisdom and his gentleness. He told me a story once. He said that he grew up in a little village below the sacred Baboquivari Mountains about fifty or sixty miles from here. There was an old man who lived in a cave on the mountaintop, and he was believed by many of the villagers to be a sage, wise and unfailing in judgment. One of the young men of the village boasted that he could outsmart the sage. So he took a small bird and put it behind his back and walked up the mountain to where the man was sitting and meditating.

"And he said to him, 'Old man, what do I have behind my back?'

"And the man said, 'It is a bird.'

"Well, the young man was surprised, but he had more questions. 'Old man, in which hand am I holding it?'

" 'In your left hand,' " came the correct answer.

"The young man was astounded, but he knew that he could get him. He would ask the sage if the bird was alive or dead, and if he said alive, he would crush it.

" 'Old man, is the bird alive?' "

Joshua's arms are behind his back, as though he were holding the bird. He brings them forward, his right hand open and turned up in front of him, his stainless-steel prongs next to it.

"And the old man said, 'It is in your hands, my son.' "

He holds his hands up before them, a minute, two,

three minutes. And then he drops them slowly to his side and walks to his seat at the defense table.

Barbara is smiling at Joshua, nodding her head slowly, her mouth slightly open. Hal Dubin sits stone still, tears brimming in his eyes.

"Never seen nothin' like it," one of the spectators whispered to another. They walked out of the courtroom with the hundreds of other subdued spectators. "That one-armed som bitch had 'em in the palm of his hand."

"Sure was somethin' to see," said the second man. He shook his head. "The guy's a fuckin' alchemist, turns shit into gold."

JUSTICE, JUSTICE SHALT THOU PURSUE, read the crudely painted paper banner over Professor Livinsky's office door. It had been there since moments after the verdict, hastily prepared and tacked up by several of the professor's students.

Inside the small office on the second floor of the political science building, there was a victory celebration attended by Joshua, Barbara, Hanna, and Jan Diedrichs. Ten or twelve other students and faculty now and then stuck their heads into the small office for a few seconds, said a congratulatory word or two, and scurried quickly away to safety.

Livinsky poured Chivas Regal into several small tumblers. He passed one to each of them.

"To Joshua Rabb," he toasted, "a man of courage and ability."

They drank.

"Did either of you happen to glance at the newspaper this morning?" Barbara asked.

Joshua shook his head.

"No, I was a little distracted," Livinsky said.

"McCarthy kicked off his senatorial campaign in Milwaukee with the publication of a new book, *McCarthyism, the Fight for America.* The newspaper says that this time he accused Secretary of State Dean Acheson of being a Communist."

"Well," Livinsky said, "at least he's calling someone *else* a Commie for a change."

Barbara frowned. "When will he stop?"

Joshua shrugged. His eyes were bloodshot, and he appeared exhausted. "When God abolishes all evil from the face of the earth."

Chapter Twenty-six

Hanna came running up the stairs. Her father was sitting at the kitchen table with Barbara having lunch.

"Look!" Hanna said, brandishing an envelope at him.

Joshua took it. It was a letter from Mark Goldberg, handwritten on plain white paper stamped UNITED STATES I CORPS HOSPITAL, PUSAN. He started to read it.

"What is it honey?" Barbara asked.

"From Mark." He read it aloud:

"Dear Hanna:

"I love you, I love you, I love you. I miss you.

"I'm sure the Defense Department has notified you that I was wounded and that I'm now okay. I was in the fighting for Heartbreak Ridge, and my battalion got overrun by Chinese and NKPA (sorry, North Korean People's Army, they're the bad guys) after we captured the ridge. We ran out of ammo, and me and eleven of my men were cut off. We were all wounded and some of the guys died. There was so much of our own artillery coming down and Corsairs strafing the top of the ridge that they couldn't get to us for weeks. We just laid there until the Ninth Regiment retook the ridge.

"So anyway, I hope nobody notified you that I was KIA or anything, because I'm fine. I was wounded in the left leg during the fighting, just a pretty minor wound really, but it got infected. That's why I'm here at the hospital in Pusan. Unfortunately, it's not a million-dollar wound, so I won't be coming home. But my doctor put me down for restricted duty only. That means no combat assignment when I leave here. So I'm going to the third logistical command on Koje Island next week as an aide-de-camp to the commander, Colonel Maurice Fitzgerald. Koje is ten miles south of Pusan. It's the island where we're holding about 125,000 NKPA and Chinese Communist prisoners of war, and I Corps is building up the cadre during the armistice negotiations. It's going to be cush duty, a long way from the bullets and the mortars and the Long Toms. So anyway, when I arrive wherever I'm going in a few days, I'll write immediately and give you my address.

"I love you. I miss you more than you'll ever know. I can't wait to see you again. It won't be long."

Hanna was radiant. Barbara and Joshua both got up from the table, and all three of them threw their arms around each other, their eyes sparkling with tears.

SIGNET ONYX

SENSATIONAL LEGAL THRILLERS

☐ **AGAINST THE LAW by Michael C. Eberhardt.** When Hawaii's governor has been brutally murdered, the D.A.'s office wastes no time in arresting Peter Maikai, leader of the Hawaiian grassroots political movement. Dan Carrier, the prosecutor assigned to the case, and Peter's daughter Lily launch their own unofficial investigation. But the two find themselves trapped in a growing web of deceit and murder. (185498—$6.99)

☐ **BODY OF A CRIME by Michael C. Eberhardt.** What makes the murder charge against ex-pro athlete Chad Curtis so bizarre is that there's no evidence that anyone was killed. But his gorgeous ex-girlfriend, Robin, *has* vanished, posing one overwhelming problem for brilliant young defense attorney Sean Barrett: with no corpus delicti, and up against compelling circumstantial evidence, there's no way to prove his client *didn't* do it. (405692—$5.99)

☐ **IN SELF DEFENSE by Sarah Gregory.** Sharon Hays is a beautiful Texas lawyer on a case that can make or break her career. But she's in harm's way—as a savage sexual psychopath targets her and her little girl. She has to rip aside every veil of shame and use every trick of the lawyers' trade if she hopes to win her case. But the neatest trick of all will be staying alive long enough to address the jury. (183150—$4.99)

☐ **CRIMINAL SEDUCTION by Darian North.** A man and woman who never should have met ... a brutal murder that defies comprehension ... an eccentric life veiled in layer upon layer of secrets.... "A thriller that attacks the heart, the mind, the gut."—James Ellroy, author of *The Black Dahlia* (180224—$5.99)

*Prices slightly higher in Canada